BENEATH *the* APPLE LEAVES

Center Point
Large Print

Books are produced in the United States using U.S.-based materials

Books are printed using a revolutionary new process called THINKtech™ that lowers energy usage by 70% and increases overall quality

Books are durable and flexible because of Smyth-sewing

Paper is sourced using environmentally responsible foresting methods and the paper is acid-free

This Large Print Book carries the Seal of Approval of N.A.V.H.

BENEATH
the
APPLE LEAVES

HARMONY VERNA

CENTER POINT LARGE PRINT
THORNDIKE, MAINE

This Center Point Large Print edition
is published in the year 2018 by arrangement with
Kensington Publishing Corp.

The text of this Large Print edition is unabridged. In other aspects, this book may vary from the original edition.
Printed in the United States of America on permanent paper.
Set in 16-point Times New Roman type.

ISBN: 978-1-68324-857-6

Library of Congress Cataloging-in-Publication Data

Names: Verna, Harmony, author.
Title: Beneath the apple leaves / Harmony Verna.
Description: Center Point Large Print edition. | Thorndike, Maine : Center Point Large Print, 2018.
Identifiers: LCCN 2018015881 | ISBN 9781683248576 (hardcover : alk. paper)
Subjects: LCSH: Immigrant familiesFiction. | Immigrants—Fiction. | German Americans—Fiction. | Farm life—Fiction. | Pennsylvania—Fiction. | Large type books. | BISAC: FICTION / Coming of Age. | FICTION / Historical. | FICTION / Sagas. | GSAFD: Historical fiction. | LCGFT: Historical fiction.
Classification: LCC PS3622.E7463 B46 2018 | DDC 813/.6—dc23
LC record available at https://lccn.loc.gov/2018015881

For Eleanor,

whose love of the land pulses in my blood

Acknowledgments

Words can hardly express my deepest appreciation for the family, friends and readers who have supported and guided me during the writing of this novel. Every smile, every word of encouragement and every hug has given me the fortitude to chase this dream.

The seeds of this book came from my mother, Marilyn, who shared the stories—the sorrows and the joys—of growing up on a farm in rural Pennsylvania. A life sustained on the whims of the land is a hard one, and I am humbled and proud of the strength and sacrifice of my German ancestors. Together, they sowed a legacy of hard work and a deep respect for the land—one in which I hope to carry and pass on to my own children.

To the wholesome and beautiful people of my home city, Pittsburgh, I thank you for your unique character and rich heritage and humor. And for those brave men and women who served on the battlefield and on the home front, you will forever hold my highest esteem.

To my precious agent, Marie Lamba, of the

Jennifer De Chiara Literary Agency, you are simply the best—my fearless cheerleader to the end. And once again, sincere gratitude to my brilliant editor, John Scognamiglio, and the entire Kensington team for helping me bring this story to life.

Most of all, I want to thank my husband, Jay, and my three boys, who have supported me through deadlines and cold dinners, sleepy days and sleepless nights, all the while making me feel deeply loved and appreciated every step of the way.

Historical Note: Despite Pittsburgh's spelling with an *h* after 1911, several sources, including the *Pittsburg Press*, did not incorporate the *h* until after 1917. In order to maintain historical accuracy, I have kept the original spelling of *Pittsburg Press* throughout the novel.

PART 1

Each dawn as we rise, Lord we all know
  too well,
We face only one thing—a pit filled with
  hell.
To scratch out a living the best we can,
But deep in the heart, lies the soul of a
  man.
With black covered faces, and hard
  calloused hands,
We work the dark tunnels, unable to
  stand
To labor and toil as we harvest the coals,
We silently pray "Lord please harvest our
  souls."

—"The Coal Miner's Prayer,"
by W. Calvert

CHAPTER 1

Quiet now." The two words pounded against the walls, elongated and echoed. "Just keep your eyes closed."

Andrew obeyed the orders, held tight to his father's large hand, his own tiny fingers in the womb of the callused palm. His feet stepped blindly on the downward slope. Water dripped and tapped hollowly through the tunnel, the air cool and damp to the skin, reminiscent of the early morning fog that congealed in the valley.

His father stopped and slid from his son's grip. "Now, open your eyes."

He was still blind. He blinked again and again and again, but the darkness was whole and complete, eternal and deep as a well. Andrew rubbed his eyes, his fingers invisible and absent in front of his face. His breathing thickened and panicked in short gasps. Invisible walls pressed from above and below, from the left and the right. The black drowned, heavy as a man's boot stomping upon the lungs. Andrew reached one way for his father and then the other, his hands clawing the emptiness.

"Papa!"

"I'm right here, Son." Strong arms wrapped him instantly. "I'm right here."

Andrew clung to the rough fabric of his father's shirt, buried his head against the burly stomach, the light smell of tobacco and chopped wood bringing comfort to his senses, a familiarity to the void. He closed his eyes and fell into the scents.

His father took hold of Andrew's shoulders while he lowered to the boy's level. "I just needed you to see."

"I can't see anything!"

The man grinned, a subtle sound of lips over teeth. "Meant you just needed to see what it's like down here." A scrape and hiss came to a stone and ignited a flame. With the match, his father lit the candle on his miner's helmet, highlighting the firm streams of old wax that formed like dripping egg whites. The glow of the wick grew into a small yellow orb, just large enough to show the man's forehead, eyes and bridge of the nose.

His father squeezed the little boy's hands in urgent pulses. "I need you to know that this will not be your life." The eyes spoke, the mouth still eclipsed under the blanket of onyx. "I won't have my son picking coal. Do you hear me, Andrew?" His words were gentle in their pleading. "You work hard. Study hard. You build a life for yourself when you get older. But not here. I won't have you picking coal. Understand?"

"Yes, sir."

"Take care of your family. Always." He swallowed bitterly. "But not this way."

"Yes, sir."

The eyes watched him, moved slightly as if the missing mouth tried to form a sound. "You're better than this," his father finally said. "Don't let anyone tell you different."

Andrew listened to the words, struggled to balance the weight of them against his desire to go home, to flee into the light again. "Yes, sir."

His father stood then. "You never come down here again. Promise?"

He couldn't get out fast enough. "Yes, sir."

$\mathscr{C}$HAPTER 2

Uniontown, Pennsylvania—1916

Beneath the open and shattered hillside of the Pennsylvania coalfields, between the blurred swings of autumn and winter, Andrew Houghton bundled against the cold and put an arm around the young woman by his side. "You warm enough?" he asked.

"I'm f-f-fine." Her teeth chattered through her forced smile.

"No, you're not." Andrew stopped, shed his coat and draped it around her shoulders. "Better?"

She gave a slight sigh and nodded. "You're going to freeze without your jacket."

"Me? No! Feels like summer," he mused, and put his arm back around her, his skin shivering. "Besides, got my bruises to keep me warm."

She grimaced. "You're too handsome to be messing with those fights, Andrew." Gingerly, she touched his swollen cheek, and he stiffened. "Besides, how you going to kiss me with your lip swollen like that?"

Andrew gave a quick, uncomfortable laugh and

loosened his grip. He should have known better than to hold her so close. She stopped and pulled the large wool coat tighter around her body, her eyes beseeching. "Why haven't you ever kissed me?" she asked in earnest.

The cold cut through his thin linen shirt. "If the police captain caught me kissing his daughter, there would be a couple broken bones to go with this bruise."

"Don't tease me," she said. "You're no more afraid of my father than you are of those men in the boxing ring. So, tell me why you won't kiss me. The truth this time."

Andrew exhaled slowly, looked at the pretty young woman, her soft eyes brown as a doe's. He could kiss her. He could take her in his arms and kiss the lips that waited. After all, pleasures were few and far between in the coal patches. But that's all it would be—a quick blast of pleasure, a sweet distraction soon to sour. He didn't want to lead her on. "I can't offer you anything," he finally said.

She stuck out her chin and scoffed. "What does that mean?"

"Look," he started, and tried to think; she wasn't making this easy. "I'm just not looking for a girl right now," he said as kindly as he could. "I just don't feel that way about you. I'm sorry."

Her jaw dropped and her eyes fluttered with the rebuff. "Do you have any idea how many men would jump at the chance to be with me?"

"I don't doubt it," he consoled. "You're a beautiful—"

"Do you have any idea how many men beg to kiss me?" she shouted. "Do you?"

His skin numbed under the gooseflesh and he was tired. His face hurt in pulses. He was relieved he never kissed her. "Well, you shouldn't have any trouble finding a replacement then."

She snarled in disgust and tore off his jacket, threw it at his chest. "Should have known better than to cohort with a coal miner's son."

"Cohort," he teased, amused by her tantrum. "Is that what we were doing?"

"You think you're so smart, don't you?" She snorted white steam from her nose. "Should be kissing my feet I'd even talk to you, let alone let you walk me home."

Andrew slipped on his coat, relishing the warmth. He turned off his ears to her whiney trill and turned around.

"Never would have let you kiss me anyway, Andrew Houghton!" she hollered. "Take me a day to wipe the soot off my mouth!"

He smirked, gave a dismissive wave and kept walking.

"So proud, are you? One day you'll be picking underground and I'll be dancing over your head!" Her last ranting filtered away into the night. *Dodged a bullet with that filly,* he thought gratefully, and blew a hefty puff of white air from his mouth.

The road back home was quiet, the sky black as pitch. Lanterns were turned off in all but a few windows. A stray dog scurried nearby, licked at a fetid puddle. Andrew knelt down. "Come here, girl." He clicked his tongue.

The dog inched forward, the head bowed low, the back hunched, ready to sprint at the slightest hint of aggression. Andrew stuck out his hand, let the dog sniff his fingers, her ears pulled back protectively. He smiled and scratched the neck of the pup, who hurried forward and gave two great licks to Andrew's face. "Whoa, girl." He laughed. "What's with everybody trying to kiss me tonight?"

A garbage can tipped and crashed. A feral cat shrieked and the dog jolted into the night. Andrew stood, wiped the dog's drool from his swollen cheek with his sleeve. The silence seeped with the cold, brought a melancholy to the empty stretch ahead.

He turned from the even road of the town center toward the rutted and sloped curve that headed to the mine housing. The melancholy grew—a nostalgia for a life that didn't exist, a longing for the type of woman that didn't exist. It seemed all the women he met fell in two categories: the spoiled girls from town and the listless, broken girls from the patches. He wanted neither.

17

The lines of a poem by Atticus drifted into his thoughts, the words pantomiming each boot step forward:

Her heart was wild, but I didn't want to catch it,

I wanted to run with it, to set mine free.

CHAPTER 3

Plum, Pennsylvania—1916

L ily Morton emerged from the forest like a porcupine, the pine needles sticking stubbornly in her hair and needling through her dress. After plucking the ones deep enough to poke her scalp, she ignored the rest and plodded through the light snow toward home.

Instead of taking the shorter route through the valley, Lily climbed the slope of the old cornfield, the green pinnacles long browned and severed to splintered stalks. This was an open land, a land of even rows and endless swords of withered corn and ground straw. Her worn boots stepped with great concentration between the crisp sticks and occasional rock and tangled thorn bushes. In her imagination, she stepped like a soldier through a battlefield of bones, working hard not to desecrate as she picked her way across enemy lines. And she laughed at this. Laughed at the childish game, for she was no longer a child. The mirth left. She wasn't a child or a porcupine. This wasn't a battlefield in a brave war. She was a young woman who plodded through an old farm field that mirrored a million other farm fields in rural Pennsylvania. The cold stung her cheeks then and she veered hurriedly down to the valley.

In the open land, Lily sprouted. She changed as the seasons, expanded and contracted with the phases of the moon, shifted with the clouds and rose and rested with the tidings of the sun. She knew the soil that crunched and purred beneath her footsteps; knew the sky that hovered above her skin. She knew the songs of the birds and the secret language of the ants and bees and crickets. From the valley, Lily stretched her legs up the sharp incline of the hill and evened her stride as she reached the one-lane road—and here along the reclaimed, man-made stretch she knew her way by heart but was lost again.

Lily passed the Sullivan farm, the white farm-house quiet and sleepy in the encroaching twilight, the gentle white smoke rising from the stone chimney. A few miles more and she would pass the Mueller homestead, the smell of their hogs drowning out the natural scents of frozen earth and distant wood fires. If she walked for an eternity along this road, the pictures of those houses would repeat in a stuttering image, one after another, just like the inhabitants within the reposeful walls.

The wind cut wickedly through Lily's sweater,

the fabric silvered and shiny at the elbows. She regretted not wearing a coat and ran the last mile home. And once there, she did not refuse when her sister made her drink strong tea by the fire, did not complain as her sister plucked and pulled at the nest of pine needles in Lily's ashen hair.

The fire crackled, released the occasional spark as the flames touched upon a stick of damp wood. Lily sat cross-legged on the knotted rug, studied the lines of her palm undistracted, even as her sister tugged at her long tresses with the hairbrush, forcing her head back now and then in sudden jerks.

"Sure I'm not hurting you, Lil?" Claire asked.

"Hardly tell you're combing."

"Bet I'm squeezing tears." She grimaced. "Sorry I got to pull so hard."

"Can't feel it. That's the truth."

"How'd you get all this sap in here anyways?"

Lily shrugged. "Up in the pine tree. Got stuck in a resin patch."

"Well, you smell good. That's for sure. Fresh as the forest." Her older sister laughed softly as she worked on another tangled lump of hair. "Remember when I'd take you out to those trees when you were just a little thing? You and me? We'd sit up there for hours, nearly fell asleep up there a couple of times." Claire's voice suddenly abandoned its jovial chirp. The strokes came lighter to Lily's hair until the brush stopped moving completely.

Lily turned around. Her sister's head bowed. Lily took the brush from the woman's hand and placed it on the floor between them. Growing up, they had hid in those trees, the two of them, tangled close together for warmth and strength. Within those boughs, they had kept silent, pretended it was a game. And when his footsteps plowed through the dead leaves and his voice hollered in rage across the valley, they clung tighter to each other and endured the hours until he was gone.

These were the memories that plagued Claire Morton, that came with the wind and left the woman hollow. Lily reached her arms around the slight shoulders. "That was a long time ago, Claire," she whispered. Claire stared from the familiar abyss that made her skin chill. She was lost to the demons again.

Lily lifted her sister's chin. "We're safe, Claire. Nobody's going to hurt us ever again. I promise."

Claire blinked, then tilted her head curiously, asked nearly in despair, "Then why you still hiding up in those trees?"

CHAPTER 4

Andrew Houghton woke first. The voice of the great owl prodded from the roof, as it poked with scraping talons against the shingles, usurped the duties of the scrawny roosters that ran free from broken gates and fences. Before dawn, the silent raptors flocked to the hideous coal patches, the mine town beyond the trees where the mice were plentiful. For here the rodents scurried between the endless line of old sheds and privies, darted inside beehive ovens where burnt bread crumbs sat like anthills.

The great owl called again, chiseled the dream state until eyes opened. The hoarfrost clung to the windows and the chill shuddered through the wads of newspapers insulating the cracks and holes of the shabby wood home. Andrew sighed and placed a naked foot to the frozen floor.

The young man ran a hand through his thick dark hair, scratched above his ears to rouse. In the kitchen, he stooped over the coal box and refilled the stove, then set the water to heat. He warmed his hands above the black iron, his breath visible from his lips.

Frederick and Carolien Houghton slept soundly in the next room, Andrew's parents unburdened and secure within the wool blankets, his father's light snoring soothing in the tightness of the small house. Soon, the owl would wake them, too, and Andrew's father would head underground, pick rock from dawn until dusk.

Andrew put the tin mugs on the table, caught his tarnished reflection in the dented metal. He held a cup closer to his face, inspected his swollen lip, bruised jaw and blackened eye. Practicing a weak smile, he tried to mask the injuries with a beguiling grin, but all it did was open the cut on his lip and make him look not quite right in the head. He reached into his back pocket and took out the money he had won from the night's fight, pulled out the steel box shoved behind the crocks of lard and cured meat. The coins were deep and the box heavy, the sound of his future clinking inside. Andrew crammed the bills and clicked the clasp, then slid the bank back into place.

The movement uncovered a small piece of paper tucked under the empty sugar canister: a bill from the company store—coffee, tea, lye, oatmeal, castor oil, sugar, dried mustard, pork, cheese, beans. Black lines crossed off half the items, the edits from the store clerk of what exceeded the Houghton credit. The familiar indignation rose. Andrew folded the receipt carefully back to the original despondent creases and slid the note back under the canister, the box of coins poking out guiltily.

Feet shuffled in the bedroom. Andrew busied a cast-iron skillet to the stove. Carolien Houghton placed a waxy, gnarled hand upon his. She was a beautiful woman, young in face with blue eyes that matched his own, but her hands were shiny and warped and ancient. In the cold months, she ached from the cold, her joints tight and balled in hard, painful knots.

"Go rest, Andrew," she whispered. "No need for you to be up yet."

"Couldn't sleep." He kept his face turned. "I'll start the sausage."

"Only have scrapple," she noted while tapping his hand to release the skillet. The woman rubbed her twisted hands over the heat. Andrew brought out a few chipped plates while she poured the boiling water into the blue spotted enamel pot and stirred in the black grounds. Dawn would forever mean the scent of his mother's simmering coffee.

Andrew brought her shawl and wrapped her shoulders, partly to warm the body and partly to keep her blind to his injuries. She spooned a heap of opaque fat into the pan, the hissing loud and sputtering in the small open room.

Andrew watched his mother work over the stove as she held her shawl tight and away from the spitting grease. Carolien's life revolved around the four walls of the unpainted home, the tiny chicken coop and vegetable garden in the back, her only travel to the company store or to the pump house on washing day. In the summer, she baked, canned and pickled; in winter, she stretched the meals with buckwheat cakes, fried carrots, potatoes and meatless red sauce. And Andrew's mother did her chores as they all did, with the soundless dignity that hid the tired bones and weary limbs.

The rooster crowed from the henhouse. The shadow of the owl flickered across the window as the wings flew to the fresh forest beyond. Carolien closed her eyes, recited the short prayer she made every morning before her husband burrowed underground. Andrew, forgetting about his bruises, handed the egg basket to his mother.

The woman jolted, the wooden spoon held high and dripping above the pan. "What happened to you?"

"It's nothing." Andrew rolled his eyes and cursed himself, tried to dodge his puffy profile from her full view, but she was quick and grabbed his face.

Her mouth fell open before her lips clamped shut and formed a pursed circle. "Frederick!"

"Don't wake him—"

She stormed to the low wooden bed and shook the lump of blankets. "Get up!" Frederick buried his head under the covers, grunted and turned toward the wall, twisted the thin mattress so the burlap ticking was visible. She pulled the blanket from his body in one quick snap and dropped it to the floor.

"Eh, Frederick, enough of this now! What did I tell you about letting Andrew fight in those ham an' eggers?" She knew all about the boxing matches held every Thursday. The winner got the money; the loser got a ham sandwich. Some of the weaker miners lived on a diet of little else.

Frederick wiped the sleep from his eyes, his hair jutting in two directions at once. "Come now, Carolien, don't get yourself all in a huff—"

"A huff? Andrew's face is half-beaten!"

Andrew came up from behind, snapping his suspenders in place over his shoulders. "It doesn't hurt, Ma. I swear it."

"See." Frederick pointed. "Not so bad. And, ah, you should have seen him! Went through three rounds without a scratch until that young Pole weaved his way in. What's his name, Drew? Bobienski? Got arms like iron pistons, that one."

Andrew smiled, spurted a new line of blood on his bottom lip. "Got him square on the jaw, though."

"That you did, Son." His father winked and stretched one thick arm above his head. "That you did."

Carolien shook her head and gave up the cause, trudged to the kitchen. "Two peas in a brawny

27

pod," she mumbled, then issued sternly, "but that's the last of it. Hear me?" She sliced the scrapple and flung the mix of pork scrapings and cornmeal in the pan amid angry inner rumblings. One by one, she cracked the eggs over the skillet like mini skulls.

"He's seventeen now, not five!" Frederick bellowed from the bedroom. "Besides, he's a good fighter, good as any of those boys. Brought in more last night than I made all week." His last words came slightly drowned as he splashed water on his face. "We're getting this boy to university one way or another."

Carolien's shoulders rose to her ears as if the words were a shriek. Andrew stayed quiet, remembered the slashed bill under the canister.

Frederick took his seat at the table, the black bristles of his mustache shining with the early washing. Morning was the only time they saw the man's chiseled Dutch features uncovered from coal dust, even though the black stains of years underground still etched every crease in his face and knuckles and blackened his nails. Each breakfast Carolien fed a white, clean version of her husband, and by end of day she fed a blackened one.

Carolien picked up a small shipping box behind the stove, dropped it with disinterest on the table. "This was at the post for you."

Frederick inspected the return address and

handed the package to Andrew. "Think this is the one you wanted."

Andrew put down his fork and started opening the cardboard. Inside was a worn copy of *A System of Veterinary Medicine*, the cover half-torn and the pages stained and bloated but the ink clear. "Where'd you get this?"

"Library in Harrisburg got flooded. Got it cheap, too," chimed his father.

Carolien folded her apron and dabbed the oil spot that darkened in a circle. "Can't get enough flour to last the month and you're spending money on books."

"Hush now! Making my food taste sour," Frederick snapped. "Besides, like I said, got it for cheap. Hardly more than the post to ship it."

Carolien ignored him and picked up Andrew's creased and blackened boots, hand-me-downs from one of the boys who had died in the mine last year, decapitated by a dinky engine. She placed them near the stove to warm and swallowed. It was bad luck to argue before the sun was up. "I'm sorry," she said quietly. She kissed her son, then her husband on the cheek. "You know how the cold aches my joints."

The sun barely inched above the ridge when the men headed out. Andrew looked back at the small house, the weathered brown clapboard no different from that of the other homes lined side by side down the hill like stair steps. Next to the front door, three Sears, Roebuck shipping crates were stacked neatly. On hot evenings in the summer, they'd take dinner outside and sit upon the boxes, watch the sky as hues of pinks and orange waltzed and twirled with the gray, soot-filled air.

The coal miners appeared on the road, manifested from the mist of the pearly dawn. Those from eastern Europe strode with sleeves rolled above elbows, untouched by the cold, while the English, Dutch, Scots and Italians wore moth-eaten wool sweaters buttoned to their chins. And these men spoke little, just passed one another with a nod, their metal supper pails clanging against their thighs.

"Saw your light on late," Andrew's father noted to his son. "Not sure how you read with that eye bulging like it is."

"Still have one good one, remember?" Andrew said casually. But truth be told, his eye ached in pulses as if a tiny mallet tapped endlessly upon his brow bone.

"Figured I'd find you stumbling in near morning, especially seeing that pretty girl hooked to your arm." His father elbowed him, gave him a sly wink. "It's the Houghton charm, my boy! No one woman can resist it."

They crossed the center lane, the sides gutted

from wagon wheels and remnants of water lashes from earlier storms. The line of telegraph poles stopped. The hole in the mountain, a mouth to the earth, its lips the wooden head frame over the shaft, beckoned ahead. Activity buzzed near the entrance to the coal mine, each miner grabbing his pick and shovel, his lantern and breath, as they hooked the mules to the shuttle cars and followed them into the pit.

His father stopped and motioned to the side for Andrew to follow. Frederick's strong, fine face turned nearly impish as he dug into his pocket. "Was planning to give this to you at breakfast, but you know how your mother gets. Turns into a goose about all this talk." He handed Andrew the folded papers, his lips twisting to hold his mirth, and finally blurted, "It's an application. University of Pennsylvania."

Andrew's throat closed. He stared at the school's seal at the head, the ache to leave the coal patches throbbing. "Even if I got in, we couldn't afford it," he said quietly, feeling the burn of this life again. He tried to hand the paper back, but his father refused.

"The money will be there." Frederick showed his palms, rough and tight as stretched leather. "Long as these hands can work, we'll get you there." The man rubbed his wrist across his nostril and wiggled his shoulders against the emotion. "Just mail it, Son. Leave the rest to me." He pulled down Andrew's flat cap, slapped him on the back.

Andrew watched his father slip into line toward the shaft, adjust his carbide lamp and mining helmet. Frederick Houghton gave a wave to Andrew, glanced at the sun as if he wanted to kiss each ray before entering the pit and then walked into the darkness.

"Andrew!" Mr. Kijek hollered from the open-stalled barn, waving in frantic swats. The man's cheeks bruised purple and he cradled his right rib. "Jesus Christ, stop starin' outta space, ya idiot! Ya think I'm payin' ya to look at that damn sun? Is that what you think, ya stupid ass?"

"No, sir," Andrew answered. Kijek cursed with a mouth full of manure, but he had a good heart. He was Andrew's father's friend and the colliery barn boss. He had hired Andrew as the farrier though the old man could have done the work alone. Despite his constant abuse to humans, he was kind to the animals, never hit the mules with fist or belt.

Andrew reached for the rasps and nippers hanging on the shed wall, pointed an elbow at Kijek's injuries. "You in the ring last night?" he asked.

"Didn't see me there, did you?" he spit.

The tone was no longer light and Andrew came close. "What happened to you?"

"Mind your business," he growled. The old

32

man limped to the feed station, stuck a pitchfork in a new bale of hay. "Think these mules gonna feed 'emselves? Is that what you think?"

Even for Kijek, the man was more agitated than usual. Andrew kept quiet and helped stack the feed. A group of young miners passed the stables, heading toward the gaping portal. "Drew, you playin' ball tonight?" James McGregor, one of the redheaded Scots, called out.

"Naw," his brother Donald chimed while swinging his pick. "Don't want to get his shirt dirty for the ladies."

"Very funny." Andrew shoveled a small clump of donkey dung and catapulted it at his friend. "I'll see you on the field."

Donald jumped easily from the onslaught. "Better practice your pitch, Houghton! Yer aim stinks." He gave a sly nod in challenge, then whistled at the old man bending next to the donkey. "Nice ass, Kijek!"

Kijek turned to Andrew and snorted. "Kid says the same goddamn thing every day."

Andrew moved to the first stall and rubbed the head of one of the mules, the hair stained black from nose to tail, the original color impossible to discern. The animal stiffened under his touch, then trembled. A stream of urine landed near his boot. Andrew's gaze spread over the animal to the red sores across her back and rear end. His stomach dropped.

He found Kijek stooped over a box of rusty tools. "Who did that to her?"

Kijek didn't pivot with the question, didn't even flinch as he kept his back turned. "Let it go, Andrew," the voice warned, nearly too soft to hear.

He grabbed the old man by the shirt. "Who did it, Kijek?"

The eyes drew to his slowly, the whites cloudy and bloodshot and full of pain. His bottom lip twitched. "I said, let it go."

Andrew released the flannel sleeve, saw with new knowing the bruises and cuts along the man's face and neck. "You tried to stop them."

The old lips trembled and saliva formed in the corners. "Damn boys," he hissed. "Came here stewed on whiskey, hell-bent on hurting anything that moved. I got one of 'em, though. Got him hard in the back with that bar over there." A glimmer speckled for an instant before drowned in a stifled tear. "Till the other one took it to me. But I got one," he slobbered wretchedly. "Got one good whack in for hurtin' that beast, I did."

Andrew stared down at the feeble man, so frail and shattered it made his ribs tight and pressing against his heart. "Who was it?" he asked again.

"Please, son—" Kijek begged, the rest of the words buried.

Kijek could take a beating as well as any man, but he'd never protect someone who hurt one of

34

his animals. And then Andrew knew. "It was the Higgins boys."

"Don't start nothin', Drew." The old man grabbed his arms, the bony fingers stabbing into the skin. "You hear me?"

Andrew's fists balled as he tried to shake the grip, but Kijek clamped like a dog's jaw to a rabbit. "I know you're hot as piss, but you can't cross 'em and you know it."

"No." Andrew pulled away from the man. "They've gone too far."

"Listen, you selfish prick!" Kijek reared, blazed with a finger pointed at Andrew's nose. "You make a fuss with those boys and who you think gonna get the fallout? Eh? Your pa, that's who. Mr. Higgins send him to work the tightest veins till he's lying on his stomach picking. Then they'll go after that sweet ma of yours. Yeah, that's right. Think her credit's low now? Be lucky to get the pork fat they scrape from the floor."

Andrew glared at the man, pulled his gaze to the stalls. "When you turn so soft, Kijek?" he asked acidly.

"Ain't soft, son." He patted the young man on the shoulder. "But a dog knows when he's owned." Kijek turned back to his box of rusty tools. "Out with you now. Get to school and cool down. You can trim the hooves when you get back."

• • •

In class, Andrew was restless, still agitated from the morning. He was the only son of a coal miner who still attended school at his age and he'd graduate in the spring, top of his class. Most boys followed their fathers underground by the time they were fourteen.

Seated in the back row, he ignored the lessons and filled out the college application. He tried not to think of the beaten mule and the old man who cared for her. Instead, Andrew focused on what he planned to become. He would not pick coal. He would not work for a mine that charged a man for the tools he used or broke—for a mine that put the value of black rock above a man or animal. He'd work and study and build a place in the country for his parents—a place where his mother's flowers wouldn't wilt from bad air and where his father could sit under the sun until his skin tanned and wrinkled.

He pressed the pen harder into the paper. The mine company controlled all. They owned the houses; they owned the wood in the forest and the coal underground; they owned the bank and school and post office. They owned the miners and the food they ate. Andrew would not be owned.

A tap came to his shoulder and he looked up, startled. The classroom was empty save for Miss Kenyon, who hovered over his desk. He hadn't

36

even heard the other students leave. "Want to tell me what you've been working on for half the day?" she asked.

He handed her the college application and she smiled. "Good." She read through his answers and folded the paper neatly. "You deserve better, Andrew. You're a special young man." Miss Kenyon was only a few years older than he and a slight blush came to her cheeks with the compliment. "I'd like to write you a personal reference, if I may."

"I'd appreciate it. Thank you."

"I'll do it today, then mail it out for you." She reached for a handkerchief just as a sneeze erupted. "Sure enough, caught my first cold of the season." The coal stove in the corner had chilled and she shivered. "Would you mind refilling the coal chute for me before you go?"

Outside the school, Andrew returned the shovel to the toolshed. Two tiny shoes jutted out from behind a skinny oak tree. He inched his way over to the child, wiping his sooty hands on his trousers. "Denisa, what are you still doing here?"

The little girl shrugged her shoulders and didn't look up. Andrew knelt in the cold grass to meet her at eye level, waited for her to speak. She shrugged again and finally raised her weary face. "Jus' tired."

Andrew glanced at the thin dress and the

scratches and bruises along her stockingless legs. "You eat supper?"

She shook her head.

"Breakfast?"

The tiny shoulders shrugged again. Andrew scratched his temple. Denisa was the youngest of ten children, her mother a widow who worked a ten-hour laundry shift at the boardinghouse. Andrew opened up his food pail, pulled out the sandwich crusts he was saving for the hogs. "It's not much, but—"

Denisa grabbed the bread and stuffed the crusts into her mouth, chewed fiercely in case one tried to escape. She swallowed, licked the crumbs from her lips, shamefaced.

He tapped her on the knee. "Come to our house from now on. If you're hungry, you come over, all right?" The girl nodded, her tongue dabbing the corner of her mouth for a final morsel.

Andrew turned and curled his back. "Now, up you go, girlie." When she didn't move, he slapped his shoulders. "Come on! Giddyap time."

The tiny hands clutched his shoulders as she climbed upon his strong back. He glanced back to a full grin as she wrapped her arms around his neck and he straightened, supporting her legs with the crook of his arms as he took off with a bouncing trot.

Along the road, his worn boots crushed the pebbly ground toward the first houses of the patch. He breathed heavily against the steely air and hoped the child was warm enough. The air promised snow and he glanced into the gray sky expecting to see flakes.

A whistle cut the air in two.

The shrill tone pierced the eardrum. Denisa's nails dug into his shoulders. Movement stopped. Breathing halted. Eyes turned automatically toward the blank distance of the mine center.

The whistle wailed again.

Denisa started to weep; four of her brothers were down there. Andrew put her to the ground, his heart thundering in his chest. He clutched her by the shoulders. "Go home, Denisa. Do you understand?" She nodded stiffly, her chin wrinkled. "Only home."

He let go of her shoulders and then he ran. The sound of his boots running thumped in his head, chased him. There were no thoughts. Just running forward. The pounding of his feet below, the brown houses blurring. Running. Running.

Andrew did not go home. There was no need. Everyone would be at the mine. The whistle blew again and his insides fell. Gray smoke billowed into the sky. Andrew rounded the corner where the next line of houses lay sunk in the valley, one by one, like wooden dominoes. The crowds rushed—waves of mothers, children, men. The mine police—the yellow dogs, they were called—were shouting, barking, pushing people aside for the ambulance wagons.

Andrew weaved through the bodies, looked for his mother when the first surge of miners crawled out of the black hole. Smoke rose and curled feebly, the choking fumes wafting through the air and stinging the eyes. A woman screamed. Crying, waffling in and around the gray clouds, seeped into the air and shuddered the earth. Through crowding bodies and pushing elbows and hips, Andrew rushed the mine entrance. A policeman grabbed him by the backs of his arms. "You can't go in there!"

"My father's down there!" He struggled against the thick arms that held him tight. He thought of Kijek; he'd be down the shaft with the mules. "I work here!" he shouted.

An explosion. The ground rattled under their feet. The policeman let go, whistled frantically, waved more officers forward.

"Andrew!" Carolien Houghton floundered from the crowd, grabbed him by the collar and pulled him to her, her body shaking in spasms. "He's not out yet." Her voice fluttered high, then dropped. "Okay. It's okay. He's just behind. He's coming, Andrew. He's coming out. I know it."

Blackened men trickled out, coughed and choked and stumbled to find oxygen. The crowd loosened. The stream of miners emerging dwindled. The ambulance wagons sat idle, the horses stiff and immobile with waiting. The dark, moving figures slowed like the last drips from a well pump.

Until they stopped.

Carolien Houghton's hands dropped from her son, her eyes fixed upon the mine's mouth that would announce her husband's fate as if with words. Only smoke pillowed now. Nothing more. Nothing.

Carolien Houghton collapsed to her knees.

CHAPTER 5

L ily Morton carried in the firewood, the splinters scraping against her forearms. She loaded the logs into the already-stacked fireplace. The flames jolted up the chimney flue, her face burning with the rush of searing heat. Claire and her husband, Frank, were in town and Lily didn't have much time.

The cardboard boxes were already disintegrating, layered in dust and taped at the corners. She picked out the old photos first, tossed them in the fire, the sepia edges browning and curling, the faces cremating. A cry erupted from her throat and her hands trembled with urgency. *Get out!*

She lifted the box and shook the contents out into the flames: letters, ancient promissory notes, old deeds, scraps of scribbled paper. *Get out!* The tears choked as she banished the ghosts. They haunted her, lingered in the old house and clawed at her while she slept. Her skin itched with the curses and she wanted to throw her dress into the sparks, to run naked to the forest, without memories, without thorns.

The papers—her family's slim, ugly history—turned to ash and blew near the rug. Lily was born a Hanson, forced to become a Morton after her sister married. Branded by both, the names seared into her skin and scarred her flesh. *Get out!* Hanson. Morton. Ugly men and ugly lies now melting in the fires they started.

Lily picked up the iron poker and stabbed at the logs, shoveled the charcoaled reminders beneath the burning wood. Her tears stopped. The smoke filled her nostrils and tasted like burnt cedar in the back of her throat.

She sat in front of the fire. She didn't blink and her eyes grew dry and she was glad for it. She was tired of the tears. People grieved all the time; this she knew. They mourned the loss of family, of lovers. But the wounds healed over time. But for Lily, the grief was reversed. She did not ache for what was taken away but for what was never given. And for this, she did not know how to heal.

The old Ford pulled into the lane, the engine parts shouting and grunting like an old married couple. Lily tucked the loose hairs behind her ears, put another log in the fireplace and went to the kitchen to start dinner.

CHAPTER 6

Ninety-eight miners were killed that day. The fire started from the kerosene torches placed along the mine walls. Kijek had dropped the bales of hay down the hoist to feed the animals stationed underground. A daily habit, except a torch slipped from its bearing and ignited the hay. The miners had their escape route blocked. The dynamite exploded. The workers were suffocated or blown to bits, their bodies disintegrated. Kijek died trying to save his mules. James and Donald McGregor and half the young men from the baseball team were killed. And Frederick Houghton's remains could only be identified by his brass miner tags.

The same day as the accident, the call for new miners was sent out across the state. Widows and mothers of the deceased were given thirty days to vacate the housing unless another male in the home was old enough to take a spot underground. And so, a week after his father's funeral, Andrew Houghton placed his new brass tag around his neck, overlapping the black and warped one of his father, and followed Frederick Houghton's footsteps into the mine.

"I won't have you picking coal. Understand?"

"Yes, sir."

"You never come down here again. Promise?"

"Yes, sir."

The memory of those words snapped like brittle sticks as Andrew broke the vow he had made to his father so long ago. And Andrew knew with each sickening step he took into the pit Frederick Houghton writhed in despair.

Weeks and months passed in unfiltered darkness. There was not enough air in the caves and Andrew's lungs starved to expand, the weight of the ground above making him claustrophobic, nearly driving him insane. He worked next to the new miners, dark men who kept to themselves and picked at the endless black walls that glistened like oil in the lamplight. And Andrew shoveled the shiny black rocks into the cars, rocks that stunk like poison and crumbled to a fine dust that choked the throat. But it was the lack of air that plagued him. When he opened his mouth to bring in more the coal dust gagged, and when he kept his mouth closed he thought he might pass out. So, he buried his mouth in his shirt and concentrated on each inhale, one after the other, until his ten-hour shift was completed for the day.

He would not pick coal. He would not be owned

by the mine—the words he had recited since childhood. And here he was, underground. But he would not stay in this pit. Andrew shoveled harder, wheezed against the coal dust in defiance. He was better than this. He would not allow a future that stretched plain and dark; a future that would swell with little more than black rock, shoveling and loading, of hunched and broken spine, of cherished and waning sunlight amid a world of darkness. And it was this knowing that kept him from dying every time his body drowned and sank beneath the earth.

Aboveground, full winter swept into Fayette County subtly as if called forth through the grief of tragedy. The air was cold without snow, a gravel-colored sky with hard wind. Andrew finished his shift and came home, dropped his boots and coat on the narrow porch before entering the house. His mother spoke rarely now, only insignificant details about food or bills, topics that dropped from the tongue mechanically. She wasn't confined to work underground, but Carolien suffocated just the same.

In the kitchen, the zinc washbasin waited, the steam from the water rising and glistening the ceiling. Andrew stripped to his waist and knelt. Carolien bent over the strong back and scrubbed the shoulders and the neck with the hard soap and brush. She had done the same ritual to his father for as long as Andrew could remember and now she repeated the service for her son.

He cringed knowing his mother's back tweaked with the scrubbing and her hands stung from the soap. He turned his head and tried uselessly again, "You don't need—" but she gently placed her hand on his crown and turned him forward again until she had finished. Then she stood and handed him the soap and stretched the square sheet that acted as the only wall for privacy.

Andrew shed the rest of his clothes, stepped naked into the tub, his knees bending against his chest as his six-foot frame contorted to fit. The clear water gleamed black within moments, highlighting the pale skin that hid beneath the soot.

In the hot water, his muscles relaxed, gave rise to the pain between his shoulder blades and lower vertebrae from constant stooping under the shallow tunnels. He ran his hands along the ripples of the water; the skin along the palms hardened. His fingers were still slender—the fingers of a surgeon, his father had always said. Now the nails were rough, the cuticles black, the object of Andrew's surgery the endless walls of bituminous coal.

Andrew rubbed the soap into his neck and his face, plunged his face into the dark water and cleaned his hair. The muscles in his arms and stomach were defined now but left him feeling weak and unhealthy. They were the hard muscles of work that stressed the body instead of strengthening it. He rubbed his arms. He ran a hand through his dark hair. His blue eyes stared back in reflection. The smell of his mother's cooking brought his stomach rumbling, though the fight to sleep was stronger than that to eat.

He climbed from the tub and dried off, his skin instantly tight from the harsh soap, and changed for dinner, unclipped the sheet and emptied the black wash water, bucket by bucket, out the front door.

A plate of roasted rabbit and glazed carrots centered the table. He looked up in surprise at the delicacy and saw his mother had been crying, her face pale with long pink streaks against her cheeks. The woman drifted in a grief-gutted dream and yet this was the first time he had seen her cry.

She sniffled and shook her head, stared at the browned, dead rabbit, its flesh shiny and taut as the skin over her knuckles. Between them, the night swelled in the house, the cold winter air permeating between termite-ravished boards. Carolien's eyes lifted to his, held him in a memory. "I've made arrangements for us, Andrew."

He waited. Under the table, he gripped his knee just to know it was still there.

"I've written my sister, Eveline. In Pittsburgh."

She looked as if she had said enough, as if he understood what she had left out. Her blue irises set in red-rimmed eyes scanned the room as if she were seeing it for the last time. "We can't stay here." Her voice deadened. "I can't live like this anymore."

The wind wheezed through the slats. The smell of the food disappeared. His mother folded her hands on the table. "Eveline's husband, Wilhelm Kiser, has a good job with the railroad. He's agreed to give you an apprenticeship."

The room spun and stood still all at once. "College." The word simply dribbled out. "I—I have my application in."

Her face twisted in near disgust. "College?" Disbelief brought a short laugh to her throat. "Are you a fool, Andrew?

"Are you?" his mother asked again, sincerely perplexed. "You're not going to college." Her tone unrecognizable, foreign and harsh. "You never were."

"We were saving." Andrew's ears burned. "We have—"

"We," she shouted, "have nothing!" Carolien grabbed the open empty metal box and shook it upside down violently. "You were never going to college, Andrew! Your father was cruel to put those thoughts in your head."

His mother's lost, weary eyes looked as ancient as her twisted fingers. "You can spend the rest

49

of your life picking coal underground or you can take this apprenticeship on the railroad. You have no other options."

The college application, the old, worn veterinary books, fanned on his bed caught fire in his mind, burned behind his eyes, the smoke stinging and hot. "I don't know anything about the railroad." It was all he could think of to say, his own voice dead.

"It doesn't matter. You're smart and will learn. A job on the railroad pays well." Her vision grazed the empty chair sitting at the table. "It's safe." His mother stretched out her neck as if she were trying to swallow something that did not taste right. "My sister and I aren't close, Andrew. We haven't spoken in over a decade. But she's a good woman and has promised to take care of you in my absence."

"Your absence?"

She broke, sobbed in a short burst. Her head rested upon the heel of her palm and she smacked her forehead ruefully. Her lips stretched over her teeth as she tried to speak. "I can't . . . I can't stay here." Her palm rubbed hard against one bloodshot eye and then the next. "I'm going back to Holland. Your father had enough saved to pay for one ticket."

The fire rose up Andrew's neck again. "He saved that for my schooling."

"That's enough!" She pounded her hand on the

table. "I won't hear of it again, Andrew." She scanned the tiny kitchen. "I can't live here without your father. I can't. I can't even be in this country anymore. I just want to go home. I hurt all the time." Her face begged. "I just need to go home."

Her crying slowly subsided and she was resolute, the decision made and now accepted. She carved into the rabbit. "My sister sent money for your train ticket. Once I have enough saved, I'll send for you." She put the pale meat on his plate, the knife trembling between her fingers. "Will only be for a few years."

His throat tightened. His father had kept him abreast on all the happenings in Europe since the war started overseas, the rabid fighting and bloodshed.

"There's war," he reminded her softly, wondering if his mother had forgotten in the midst of her grief. "It's too dangerous."

"The Netherlands has stayed neutral. It'll be safe."

"Belgium was neutral, too," he argued. "Until Germany invaded. Now the Belgian refugees are flooding Holland. It's too dangerous," he repeated. He wanted to sound strong and forceful, but his voice fell. He was nearly a man, but she was still his mother.

"I need to go home, Andrew. I can find work there. The Dutch are supplying food and goods to Belgium and as far as Britain. They don't have enough workers as it is."

"Then let me come with you," he pleaded. "Take the money from your sister and I'll come with you. We can work twice as hard."

She shook her head, wide and low. "You'd be drafted."

"Netherlands is neutral, remember?"

"Damn it, Andrew!" She hit her fist on the table. "They've plucked the strongest boys and put them on the borders. If Germany invades, they'll be the first ones killed."

"Then it's not safe."

"It *is* safe." The quiver in her voice belied the words and they both heard the tone. "But for me. Not for you."

Andrew pushed his food away, the meat a rotting carcass. The metal tags scraped against his chest, scalded. His father was dead. His mother was leaving. He was moving to Pittsburgh to work on the railroad. He was never going to college. His life—his future—was dissolving before his very eyes and there wasn't a thing he could do to stop it.

CHAPTER 7

Lily Morton parked the buggy on the outskirts of the maple grove, far enough from the church to be hidden. She pressed her curled fingers into her stomach to calm the twisting inside. The thin yellow dress belonged to one of Mrs. Sullivan's daughters, fell too long for the fashion, the heel to one black shoe broken and slabbed with tar to keep it in place. Lily thought about turning home, wasn't even sure why she was here. All she knew was that Claire had lost another baby. This one was only a clot of bulbous growth, but the loss filled the house and seeped into the woods that would normally give Lily comfort.

She didn't expect the church to bring her peace or to anoint with words of consolation. A hope for distraction, perhaps. Any hope. For now, the church would be the only place open, the only place she could block out the grief of her sister. And so here Lily was, walking crookedly over wobbly heels, holding the hanging dress hem above her toes, toward the small white chapel.

The oak doors whined mercilessly as she

entered and every neck turned in response. The priest nodded once from the pulpit, the gravity of the expression indicating a clear dissatisfaction with her presence. Faces turned forward again while eyes followed the intruder peripherally as she searched for an open pew. Little Thomas, the youngest of the Forrester clan, scooted over and patted his seat. His mother's chin jutted forward in silent reprimand but turned away when Lily sat. Lily smiled at the child gratefully, the poor boy's neck red and pinched from the starched white collar.

Lily glanced at the congregation, the Catholics she recognized from town and the farmers from the high country. Mr. Campbell, the owner of the general store, was stationed near the front, his wife's strong shoulders and refined posture a deep contrast to her husband's bored slouch, his balding head reflecting the candlelight. The three Campbell girls, the oldest a young woman of her own age, shimmered respectively in their crisp dresses and shiny shoes. Each carried a different-colored satin ribbon in her hair, the dark curls reflecting the light of the stained-glass window in rainbows. Lily glanced down at her own broken shoe and the faded dress tucked around her knees.

Deep in her thoughts, she did not notice the shuffling until the boy next to her tapped her knee and motioned for her to kneel like the rest of them. She bent her forehead to her prayer-pointed fingers and observed those around her from beneath nearly closed eyelids. The priest's voice droned in a steady monotone, the words blurred and pointless above her cramming insecurity.

Thomas's mother rubbed his shoulder. Across the aisle, Gerda Mueller held a handkerchief to her daughter's nose. Mr. and Mrs. Johnson held wizened hands until their hunched frames seemed one body. The space between Lily and the parishioners widened with grim duality.

The organ blasted and young Thomas nudged her again. As dutiful as a lamb, she entered the queue of people headed for the priest. Then she was before him, his hand held out, then pulled back, his brows scrunching incredulously. "You can't take communion, Lilith." The eyes watched her from all sides; the feet tapped behind her.

"I—"

His eyebrows now rose high and mighty. "You aren't a Christian."

You don't belong here, Lilith. The words came louder than if they had been uttered. *You don't belong anywhere.*

She broke from the line. The Campbell girls snickered. Mrs. Johnson whispered gravely to her husband's old and hairy ear. Lily hurried to the exit, the open length between the pews elongating cruelly. Her ankle twisted and the glued heel cracked from the sole. She pushed through the aching front door and threw the broken shoe into the teasing sun, pulled the other off and twisted it in her hands to maim and break its spine.

Barefoot, she fled over the icy ground to the grove of cedars, the red bark peeling and splintered and dense enough to curl beneath. She ripped the pearl barrette from her hair and let the long strands drape around her shoulders, rubbed the hair clip sternly under her thumb. The iron bell in the chapel rocked, tolled above the chatter and emerging bodies now leaving the church. Families trickled out. Homes would be warming for supper and smelling of baked bread. Fathers would sit in wide armchairs, smoking pipes and basking in a day without chopping wood or hunting. At night, mothers would tuck sons and daughters in tight and kiss their foreheads.

Lily Morton hugged her knees, watched the families enviously from her spot below the boughs.

You don't belong here, Lilith, they would say. *Too wild to be human . . .*

A cardinal wrestled in the decomposing leaves, picked at a pinecone. Lily leaned to the bird, opened her palm and bent her fingertips in a call to friendship. She inched closer, reached out slowly to stroke the feathers before the scarlet wings spread and burst into the air. Lily sank back against the rough tree.

Too human to be wild.

CHAPTER 8

In early spring, Andrew's scant possessions were shipped to Pittsburgh: a few clean shirts and trousers, a wool overcoat, his books and notebooks, a football and baseball. The furniture was sold. A new Bohemian family who smelled of garlic and old mushrooms stepped into the empty brown patch house as the Houghtons stepped out.

Along the railway line, Andrew hugged his mother for the last time. Or so it felt, or didn't feel. All he knew was that everything hurt and was numb at once. He only recognized life in the coal patches of southwestern Pennsylvania, had never ventured farther. To go to Pittsburgh seemed as foreign as the moon; to think of his mother moving to the Netherlands seemed like it was a different planet altogether.

The metal tracks shone silver and endless, pulled his heart forward and then back. He could not stay here. There was no going back. But Frederick Houghton still lived in the mine, forever buried under the stone heaps that had crushed his dead body.

"Your uncle will be waiting for you in Pittsburgh," Andrew's mother broke into the memory. "As soon as I get to Holland, I'll wire you."

Carolien Houghton placed her palm against his cheek, gazed over his face as if she were memorizing each pore. Her eyes filled and his chest burned. He wanted the train to come now before he crumbled.

The mournful wail of the steam locomotive rose from across the valley. The first puff of smoke billowed distantly above his mother's bent head. People who had been sitting on benches now rose, picked up their baggage. Movement quickened and voices chatted with the high notes of good-byes. The whistle cried again, louder now, shuddered through Andrew's nerves, jolted him. He was leaving the coal patches. Sudden liberation vibrated through his muscles, flexed his biceps and stomach with confirmation. He was *leaving*. For the first time since his father's death, lucidity entered—he wasn't abandoning his father; he was renewing his promise.

Andrew took his mother's tortured hands and massaged the knuckles gently. The gift she had given finally revealed itself, the diamond formed from coal—a new life. Opportunity outside the gritty patches. Hope. "I'll build a better life for us," he said, determined. He could still save for college. He could still get there. Along the rails of this endless track, he could still get there.

The black smoke thickened as the giant black steam engine chugged into view. The brakes screeched, assaulted the deep inner core of the ear. "I promise." The resolution aged his voice, gave it the firmness of his father's and made Carolien blink with recognition. He kissed her on the cheek.

Sparks hopped from the wheels, metal ground against metal, until the steel beast stopped, the engine panting heavily after its long run. Andrew faced the giant locomotive as if in challenge. The thrust of open rails and possibilities gleamed within the steel monolith.

Andrew wasn't leaving his father in the mine shaft; he was pulling him out.

PART 2

Pittsburgh. Hell with the lid off.

—James Parton

$\mathscr{C}$HAPTER 9

Pittsburgh, Pennsylvania—March 1917

The train eased into Union Station, the gateway to Pittsburgh, the gateway to the West. Andrew stepped from the passenger car and followed the crowds into the massive rotunda, a grand circular skylight rounding the ceiling like a great lens, supported by four arched corners, each heralding the four mighty destinations of Pittsburgh, New York, Philadelphia and Chicago. With neck craned to the light flooding the grand ceiling, he stumbled into the main waiting room at the bottom of the atrium. Three-story arches framed the perimeter openings that led to men's and women's lounges, a dining room, the ticket office and baggage office.

Andrew waited at the center concourse under the giant clock for over an hour, his bag crumpled at his feet, his hands resting in the front of his pant pockets. Passengers weaved in an endless web. Men traveled with fine silk top hats and three-piece suits while others donned creased trousers with turned-up cuffs, their shoes filled with short gaiters. A group of boys wearing Norfolk jackets and knickerbockers smoked hand-rolled cigarettes, posed as miniature men in the corner. Women clicked upon the white marble floors with high heels, fox stoles wrapped around necks. There were middle-class men in dark broadcloth and workingmen in homespun cloth, encumbered with shipping trunks and luggage. But no coal miners darted between the travelers; no men in soot left footprints across the clean, smooth floor. Absently, Andrew pressed his father's miner tags for comfort. He saw the station from his father's vision, could feel the thudding of his heart along with his own. This would be a new world for them both.

A nun led a pyramid of girls in ascending levels of age pointedly through the concourse. The oldest girls in the last row of crisp pinafores glanced at him, whispered coyly before the prettiest gave a short wave. "Constance!" called the Sister. The girl quickly hid her hand but continued to stare as she walked dutifully ahead. And for the first time, Andrew thought of the other benefits Pittsburgh might offer a young man.

"You Andrew?" asked a gruff voice.

He turned and picked up his bag. "Yes, sir." The man was formidable in figure. Andrew was six-foot, but this man was a near match. His denim overalls and cap were worn and soft but his white shirt clean and unwrinkled.

"Wilhelm Kiser," he greeted Andrew. "Been waiting long?"

"No, sir."

"All right, let's get you settled. Train leaves in thirty. Ever been in a caboose?"

"No, sir."

"Well." He laughed. "You're in for a treat. Hope you're steady on your feet."

The days upon the railroad blended in a landscape of brackish rivers, squat brick towns, and smoking factories and mills. Andrew rose from the bottom bunk in the dark, held on to the wooden walls of the caboose with both hands to keep from falling. The last car rattled and rocked endlessly, felt as if the couplings were trying to disjoint from the rest of the train. In the rear of the space, he tried to keep steady while using the toilet—the straight-dump kind that sent everything over the rails. He was glad his uncle slept; otherwise there was no privacy at all.

Andrew shoveled coal into the stove just as he had done for his mother not long ago. The car was frigid away from the stove and excruciatingly hot near it. The caboose always smelled of smoke. When he ate his oatmeal, the cereal tasted like ashes. The burning coal from the stove and the firebox between the engine and the tender made his eyes water and tear black. The caboose, insufferably loud, played with the brain, held it between two palms that shook vigorously.

Wilhelm Kiser creaked down the ladder from the top bunk, nodded to his nephew as he headed to relieve himself. The cast-iron stove was bolted to the floor and Andrew made the coffee and boiled oats upon the top surface, the metal lip secured to keep the pots from falling off with the train movement. When breakfast was ready, they sat across from each other on splintered dynamite boxes, their bodies swaying in tandem to the rolling train. The tracks followed the Monongahela River, the churning water foaming yellow and sordid with chunks of debris.

"We'll be coming upon Braddock in a bit." Wilhelm stirred his coffee and licked the spoon. "You can check the couplings like I showed, make sure they're properly set." He sipped the scalding drink between nearly closed lips. He was a lean and muscular man, his dark brown hair neatly trimmed under his cap.

"Need to look out for signs of hotbox, too. Our last load heated up the axle bearings something rough. Remember that smell? If it overheats, be twice that. Smells so bad it burns the nose hairs outta your nostrils."

Andrew and his uncle settled in with each other. The first few days had been tense, lags of silence as they found their rhythm and space within the tight quarters.

"My wife's looking forward to having you. You got her eyes. She'll like that." Wilhelm said the words plainly and without flattery. "Eveline and your ma didn't get along, she tell you that?"

Andrew nodded. "Because my mother eloped." He wondered how far along the Atlantic his mother had traveled by now, hoped her body was warm within the ship.

"She don't hold any grudge against you, though," Wilhelm explained. "Be good for her to have you around. Got two sons and twins on the way. She'll be happy to have someone over the age of six in the house."

The man chuckled then, low and gruff. "Should probably warn you, though. My Eve hates the city. Here she is with one of the finest houses in Troy Hill and all she does is complain. Nags me about moving to the country. Got an indoor toilet, you know that?" He took a large scoop of oatmeal and chewed it carefully. "Only telling you this because that'll be the first and last thing you hear every day—Eveline asking for a damn farm."

Between his sentences, the monotony of the pistons and the clang of the ties grew bold. The drum of noise lulled the thoughts. Usually Wilhelm was not a man for idle chatter, but today he was animated and there was a comfort to the conversation.

"I grew up on a farm and I'll never go back." Wilhelm folded his arms loosely at his chest and leaned back. "Watched my father turn weak and sour against the land. Saw it drain every ounce of strength from him and my mother and I vowed never to follow the same fate. As soon as I was sixteen, I ran off with a circus train and never looked back."

Wilhelm drank his coffee, finished his oats and placed the dishes on the side shelf to be washed at the next stop. His voice dropped low. "Sorry about you losing your father. Should have told you that straightaway."

Andrew paused, swallowed the cereal lodged in his throat. "He was a good man." A memory of his father sweetened the air, made the coffee less bitter. "He used to play the violin. How he wooed my mother, he said. Stood under her window and played until she agreed to marry him."

Wilhelm lowered his chin and thought about this. "A romantic, eh?"

"Except he was the worst violinist you ever heard." Andrew chuckled and raised his eyebrows. "He was awful. God-awful. Pretty sure my mother married him just to make him stop."

Andrew was no longer in the caboose; he was sitting in their tiny patch house watching his father on the fiddle, his foot stomping in uneven rhythm. "He played at home in the evenings sometimes, screeching on that thing. Could hear dogs howling for miles." He laughed. "Then my mother would start singing to the music and she was just as awful. Guess they were made for each other. Love is blind, guess it's deaf, too."

Wilhelm grinned. "What about you? Got a girl waiting for you back there?"

"No," he answered without regret, rubbed the rim of his mug with his thumb. "Courted a few for sure, but"—he paused to run the pretty faces through his mind—"never felt anything close to what my parents had. Didn't want to settle. Still have some girls there cursing my name because of it."

"Heartbreaker, eh?"

"To be honest, I'm glad I didn't have the distraction. Just wanted to get out of Uniontown." Andrew dropped his spoon in the empty bowl, met Wilhelm's eyes square. "My parents sacrificed everything so I wouldn't have to pick coal like my father. Every day I watched as the mine crushed my family, my friends." He stood, placed the dish next to Wilhelm's on the shelf. "Through spirit or body or both."

Wilhelm's stance softened. "Guess we're both running then," he said. "Me from tilling the land above and you from picking it below."

His uncle cocked his head, smiled affably. "Want to take a look at the roof? Old girl's dancing on slippers today. Rails as smooth as you could want."

"Really?"

"Yeah, feels good. Free as a bird up there. Once walked across the full length of the train with my arms out like a tightrope walker. Makes you feel alive. Besides, it's a rite of passage."

Andrew smiled, felt the rush before he even stepped outside. He opened the side door, looked down at the ground rushing past his feet in a continuous blur. From the rain, the landscape appeared a charcoal sketch that had been erased and smeared with speed. The wind ripped at his shirt, puffed the fabric, tried to drag him into its pull. With effort, Andrew held his breath and grabbed the ladder rung. He flung his body against the caboose siding, his forehead pressing against the wood.

"Just hold on tight and take it one step at a time!" Wilhelm ordered above the clattering cacophony of the rails. "You'll be fine."

Andrew began his ascent, one rung and then another. On the top of the train, he pulled at the handrail, pushed his belly against the roof. Slowly, he bent his legs and sat upright. The curve of the train snaked along the contours of the rails, the puffing steam engine leading the charge.

The rush of cold air washed over his face and body, enlivened every cell. The pulsating caboose below seeped into his muscles, made them tight and strong. His heart raced, but his breathing slowed, each inhale a conscious movement that filled his lungs and expanded his rib cage. He was free. Any fear melted away. He lifted his hands from the roof and settled his arms on his bent knees, his body flowing with the train as if welded. He was free. He tilted his head back, his eyes following the trail of smoke that stretched and morphed against the endless sky. Andrew never wanted to look down again. All his life he had waited to move forward and here he was—moving forward—faster than any other man on earth.

Andrew closed his eyes. The rain pelted his face in stinging droplets that tingled the skin. His father was with him now. The dark memories faded behind the curtain of happier times. He would bring the light back, erase the darkness once and for all.

A short blast shot through the steam whistle at the locomotive. Andrew opened his eyes, the sound shuddering. He snapped out of reverie, his ears alert. The train whistle shrieked again, long and desperate. Something wasn't right.

Steadily, Andrew pulled himself upright, reached his arms out for balance. From the curve in the tracks, the conductor in the front engine was visible for a moment, waving madly before the tracks straightened and he was out of sight. The whistle screamed. Instinct took over. Andrew lunged for the handgrip. The train

71

jolted. From below in the caboose, the rear brake ground, crashing Andrew to his knees. He slid on his stomach, his hip spinning without traction on the wet iron. He rolled to the edge, his legs flaying over the side of the caboose while his knuckles and fingertips squeezed the weather-beaten seams.

The wind tossed him, dragged his legs outward. He grunted and gritted his teeth, worked to pull himself up, his shoulder nearly disjointing from the socket. His muscles turned to cement, his limbs threatening to shatter as he braced against the wood with all his strength. The train jerked again. The wheels ground in anguish. Sparks jumped from the rails, rose high as his body. Andrew clawed at the paint, his nails useless against the pull of the wind. His muscles twisted and yanked his limbs from the roof. He reached for the ladder. His fingers grasped empty air.

In one eternal instant, Andrew Houghton faced the clouds, the rain soft and listless across his eyelids, before his body crashed to the moving earth below.

$\mathscr{C}$HAPTER 10

E veline Kiser draped the bedsheet over the pine ironing board before lifting the flatiron from the stove. She rubbed the heavy tool over the creases, the thick bottom making a *thump, thump, thump* over the fabric. Young Edgar darted under the board, under the fabric, then back again, letting the sheet drape across his face before going back under.

"That's enough," Eveline scolded. "I've already flattened this sheet twice; I won't do it a third time." But the five-year-old only giggled and continued his game.

Her other son shot into the kitchen with purpose. "Toilet's overflowing again," announced Will.

"All right." Eveline sighed and put the iron in the sink, the steam swooshing and fogging the window. She wiped her face with the dish towel, placed her hand at the small of her back routinely, the growing twins pressing against her nerves, sending a dull pain down the back of her thigh. *That damn toilet,* she thought. Wilhelm was so proud of that magical wonder of innovation, Eveline had no doubt that if that toilet could have been shrunk and set in gold her husband would have made it her wedding ring.

Eveline huffed upstairs, the two boys close to her heels in order to witness any job involving tools and spilling sewage. The pain in her back made her grit her teeth with each step. She had been short-tempered with the boys all morning, hadn't slept well, as she never did when Wilhelm was out on one of his hundred-mile runs.

Eveline jiggled and pulled the toilet chain before giving up and mopping up the floor. Edgar and Will hopped into the inching puddle and jumped out again, their socks soaked to the ankles. "Boys! Can't you—" A hefty knock came to the front door.

"Will, go on and get that for me." She called back to the retreating child, "And take off those wet socks!"

Eveline met her son at the bottom of the stairs just as the front door slammed shut. "Telegram," Will said helpfully as he stuck out the square card.

She pulled out a chair at the table and rested her elbows on the oilcloth as she opened the note. Her gaze bounced from one word to the next, then back again. Her quivering fingertips met her bottom lip. Edgar stole a blueberry muffin from a plate on the counter, but she was blind to his movements, to anything but the typed paper in her hand.

"Ma!" Will's call echoed distantly from upstairs. "Toilet's leaking again!"

Someone took my arm. Andrew Houghton writhed in the trenches. Gunfire and bombs spotted his vision. The gas stung his eyes and burned his body. Skin on fire. His mother was there, her face and dress filthy. She ducked the bullets as she tried to sew him back together with needle and thread.

My arm. The lanterns were out in the mine shaft. He tripped and floundered and spun to find the light. Air was leaving, compressing his lungs. His father called for him under the coal. A candle met his touch. He lit the wick, the stick igniting into a sparkling hiss. The dynamite exploded in his hand.

My arm! The screaming reverberated in his skull. He heard it, but his mouth was gone. His own shouting bounced between the walls of the room. Flashing lights. Blackness, then open eyes. A nurse held Andrew's cheeks and mouthed soundlessly—a fish without water, without resonance. She didn't see. His mother leaned against his bed and cried. He reached for her, grabbed her skirt. *Tell them!* The woman raised her head and he pulled back. He didn't know who she was. Her face morphed with his mother's until he couldn't see one or the other, just a blur of shifting features.

75

A jab to the arm, a quick prick. Then another. *No! Not that one.* He tried to scream. He floated above the bed and under it. The room darkened and lit. He was going to throw up. He tried to run, pushed against the mattress. He tried to talk. His lips fused and words gurgled in his throat. His eyes were closing with weights from a scale, one on each lid. *No!* He had to make them. . . .

Slowly, over days of burning heat and frigid chills, Andrew awakened, and still nothing was real. The woman who had been crying, who had been next to his bed at every moment, was not his mother. There was no need for introductions, the fine cheekbones and nose as discernable as his own, the eyes the same deep blue.

Andrew tried to speak, but his throat was dry and raw. His aunt touched his mouth lightly and then shook her finger for silence. She gave him water. He lifted the tiny glass, the effort making his arm stutter. He placed the rim to his lips, could see his body magnified through the water, saw the emptiness on his left side—only pressed sheets where his arm should have rested. He didn't scream now. He didn't know how.

Eveline Kiser waited until her nephew slept again before letting her tears flow. The inhumanity of a young life stalled and severed nearly cracked her to the bone. Bandages stretched and wrapped around the young man's chest and covered the amputation at his left shoulder. She rubbed the dark hair and wiped the cold sweat from his pale forehead. He was as handsome as any man she had ever seen. And yet here he was, broken and on the edge of life. For one mournful moment, she wondered if God should let him die.

Outside the hospital, the noise from the street continued to rise. Eveline went to the window and lifted one edge of the curtain. Confetti rained down upon the crowds. Men stood upon automobiles whistling and waving newspapers. The thick walls of the room muffled the sounds slightly but only enough to distort the honking and cheering and shouting to a hideous war hum.

Before this day, the war had been confined to a battered and ravaged Europe—a war far across the sea, a war in which Woodrow Wilson promised America would stay neutral and out of conflict. But even waves that begin so far away eventually ebb and flow onto every shore, lap into every life. And until this day of April 6, 1917—the day America declared war on Germany—Eveline had cared little about the great battle. War was a topic that Wilhelm and other men spoke of and read about and debated their views on, no different to her from talk of strikes, women voting or prohibition.

But the war was upon her now, upon them all—stark and bold and flooding the streets of their city. The twins stirred within her depths and a deadness ached her legs, made her stomach plummet. She thought of her husband and their sons—of Andrew. She thought of the future that would be ahead of them all. She closed the curtain, let the roar of the crowds seep into a longing for a life that would never be the same again.

After Andrew's stitches healed and the subsequent fever dissipated, the doctors allowed him to be transported to the Kiser home. In his new room, converted hastily from the nursery, Eveline sat at the edge of his bed. Her nephew leaned straight-backed against the propped pillows. The scar at his shoulder was jagged and bright red, but she was used to it now. She could see the tortured flesh without crumbling.

Despite the fever and loss of weight, lines of muscle definition were still visible upon the young man's body, belying a strength that did not atrophy. Andrew's face had thinned, making the fine cheekbones more prominent; his dark hair provided a bold contrast to the pale skin and nearly indigo eyes.

The handsome face stared stonily out the window, his profile hard and immobile against the sunlight filtering through the lace curtains. Eveline picked up one of the shirts draped over the iron bed frame and folded the material on her lap. "I'll have your shirts mended, sealed at the shoulder," she said quietly. "Better than the sleeve hanging loose."

She saw his jaw clench. "You have every right to be angry."

"I'm not angry," he answered hollowly, his face still turned.

Eveline touched the buttons of the shirt she held in her hands. "I haven't heard back from your mother, but I'll wire her again. It's hard to know what gets through with the war. We'll pay whatever it costs to bring her home."

"I don't want her here." He snapped his gaze from the window. "I don't want her to see me like this." His chest rose and fell rapidly, expanding across his ribs.

Eveline patted the blanket covering his legs. "Well, for what it's worth, I'm grateful you're here, Andrew. A bit of my family came back to me in you. We lose things and we gain things, son. What you lost in body will take shape in other ways." She shook her head. "I know these sound like simple words, but I hope they bring you some comfort."

Eveline stood and picked up the rest of his shirts from the dresser for stitching, remembered the letter in her pocket. "Almost forgot, this came for you. Must be a friend from back home." She held out the letter, but he didn't take it, turned back to the window.

"Take as long as you need," she said softly. "You grieve. Get angry if that calls to you." She placed the envelope on the bed near his covered thigh. "And then when you're ready, you'll stand again. You'll find your way again."

The door closed. The silence left in his aunt's wake drummed in his ears. His insides were sick, his mind numb. He grimaced against the endless pain in his shoulder. Waves of sharp fire mingled with the settling agony. He closed his eyes. Each time he opened them, he thought the arm would return, appear like a forgotten joke. But the nightmare continued—asleep or awake— the constant truth of what had been taken away. He didn't want to live; he didn't want to die. He simply wanted to close his eyes and disappear.

He picked up the envelope, the return address scrawled in the corner from C. Kenyon of Uniontown. His left hand went to hold the paper, but the arm wasn't there, and again he had to drill into his skull that the limb was gone. He shimmied his thumb nail under the seal, then used his teeth to rip the top and pulled out the letter. A note on simple pink stationery was clipped to the top.

Dear Andrew,
    I hope this letter finds you well. The classroom isn't the same without you.

The students miss you a great deal, as do I. The attached letter came to the post for you under my attention. I hope it brings you as much joy as it brought me. Be proud, dear Andrew, and congratulations.
Sincerely,
Miss Kenyon

He removed the note to read the letter below. It was from the University of Pennsylvania—congratulating him on getting accepted into the veterinary program.

Andrew stared at the typed words. *Congratulations.* The sentiment replayed, mocked cruelly. He was never going to college. He didn't have a cent to his name. He was never going to be a veterinarian. He was now the charity case of a family he hardly knew. He couldn't even open a simple envelope without using his teeth.

The burn in his shoulder ignited again, made him nauseous with pain. He grimaced and clamped his eyelids shut. Blindly, he balled the paper and threw it against the wall, the simple action leaving him weak and limp.

CHAPTER 11

L ily Morton crossed her arms high upon her chest, an abrasive pose against the battered screen door. "What do you want, Dan?" she hissed.

"What's wrong, little Lily? Ain't you happy to see me?"

"No, I *ain't*," she said, imitating his loose slang.

He stepped forward to enter the house and she blocked his way, the top of her head only reaching to his thick, sunburnt neck. He laughed. "Know I can come if I want. Don't weigh more than a feather, little Lily. I sneeze and you'll be floating to the roof."

His hand reached for her hip and she slapped it away. "Don't touch me," she growled.

"Hello, Dan." Claire emerged from the black raspberry bushes edging the lane. "Didn't hear you come up." She balanced a bowl filled with berries in one hand, her fingers stained purple.

"Morning." Dan Simpson took off his hat, gave a quick nod. "Makin' jam?"

Claire nodded shyly. "And maybe a pie or two.

Never had such a good crop." She handed the bowl to Lily, who cradled it against her stomach. "You looking for Frank?"

"Yeah. American Protective League is meeting. Looks like Frank's gonna head it up for Plum. Gotta keep an eye on those Germans, you know."

Lily rolled her eyes. That was all the men talked about these days. War. Germans. Now the APL, giving out cheap badges to the likes of Dan Simpson and Frank Morton so they had permission to spew their hate.

"Think Frank's around the back," Claire noted. "I'll go grab him. Give my best to your dad at the bank."

"Will do." He tipped his hat and waited until she scurried behind the house. His eyes remained in that distant gaze as he asked, "See, why can't you be friendly like Claire?" He turned coldly back to Lily. "Got some nerve treatin' me the way you do."

Lily stepped back and tried to push the screen closed, but Dan stuck a boot in the opening, leaned in. "You'll change your tune one day, little Lily," he warned. "Won't be getting any offers as good as mine and you know it."

She kicked his boot hard and slammed the screen shut, pressed her back against the door and waited until his chuckling faded away.

CHAPTER 12

Pittsburgh—the arsenal of the allies, the arsenal of the world. With World War I, the already-factory-bloated city grew to 250 war plants and employed over five hundred thousand men and women, produced half the steel used by the war. Eighty percent of army ammunitions were born from this city of endless smoke and fire. And the metal burned eternally, the foundries pumping morning and night. Accidents buried. More men brought in. Stop the strikes. Spy on the German workers. Bring up blacks from the South. Draw in the immigrants. Sweat the life from them. Burn the eyes and lungs with noxious fumes. Dig the coal. Build the bullets. Send the guns. Burden the trains harder, faster, longer. And so the city moved in a manic and maddening and sickening frenzy to satisfy the appetite of a world at war.

After Andrew's accident, Wilhelm returned to work on the railroad, but he was nervous and edgy, short-tempered. In bed, his dreams were horrid and left him screaming and soaked in his own fear. His hands shook when he left for work.

He would not speak of the accident or enter Andrew's room.

The hours on the rails were unrelenting, an urgency chugging the locomotives without rest, the heaving coal cars and flatbeds and boxcars following in an infinite line. The Red Cross plastered posters across the station platforms showing a young injured soldier in agony upon a stretcher. *"If I fail, he dies,"* the signs promised. And the prophecy hung on the shoulders of the men whose sons were overseas and rung in the ears of any worker who slacked.

Howitzer shells, tin cans for army rations, rifle grenades, millions of bullets, gas masks, steel tank plates, electric motors, machine guns marched from Pittsburgh factories to the waiting and weary arms of the men overseas. Railroad lines clogged and jammed, made the men of the rails bang fists upon the steel beast as they waited for movement. Delays meant death, a doughboy without a gas mask or a round of bullets or a working gun. *"If I fail, he dies."*

Wilhelm would not speak of the war. For hours in the evening, he would read the headlines in the pages of the *Pittsburg Press* and then sit in stillness, his eyes unmoving, his focus on the white space between the words. And when Eveline found a crumpled and ripped poster in his bag that promoted *Death to Germans*, she did not question him.

Then, one day in late afternoon, Wilhelm returned home without warning, sent his children upstairs and met his pregnant wife at the table. For a long while, he simply slouched against the backing of the cane chair, head bowed.

Eveline remained quiet, placed an unsteady touch against her babies. "What is it?"

He sat immobilized, his eyes blank. "I was fired."

"I don't understand." She blinked hurriedly. The sound of her children upstairs thumped in Andrew's room and an explanation entered. "The accident." She halted. "What happened on that train wasn't your fault."

A quick spasm twitched his face. "He shouldn't have been up there," he seethed. "I shouldn't have let him up there."

"But to fire you—"

"I froze!" His upper lip rose in disgust. "Yesterday, I nearly derailed the train!"

His head dropped into his hands and he pulled at the roots of his chestnut hair. "I froze, Eve. The tracks were wet; everything was damp." His pupils dilated with the image. "It was just like that day. Except we were coming up to a stalled train and I couldn't brake. Couldn't touch it. The whistle kept blowing, over and over again. But I couldn't move. Kept seeing his body falling from the roof, the shadow going by the window." He fell into the trance of his words. "I froze."

Eveline reached for his hand, but he pulled back ferociously as if she were trying to bite him. "I told you I didn't want that boy working with me. Didn't I? Didn't I tell you we had no business helping him?"

The twins kicked against her ribs and she breathed through her nose with effort. "He lost his father, Wilhelm. They barely had enough money to live."

"Well," he snarled. "He's ours now, isn't he? Another mouth to feed, a crippled one at that."

"How can you say such a thing?" His words made her sick. "You can go to the Baltimore and Ohio," she reassured hotly. "Even the New York Central. They'd jump at the chance to hire you."

Wilhelm leaned back and crossed his arms. He laughed then, long and cynical. "Don't get it, do you? They've been waiting to let me go. Think they want a German—a German with the name Kiser no less—working the rails? Think they trust a German transporting all the raw materials for their artillery and machines?"

"You've been reading too many stories." She removed the newspaper from the table and folded it, threw the pages in the trash before returning to the table. "The enemy is overseas, not a humble brakeman living in Troy Hill."

The scowl expanded to the lines of his face. "Want to know what was waiting for me in the bunk of my caboose?" His voice sank low and deep and his eyes stretched in horror. "Want to know what I found wrapped in a bloody blanket on my bed? A German shepherd with its throat sliced."

Chills crept up her spine and itched her scalp.

"And tied to its mouth was a sign that said: 'To Hell with the Huns.'"

"My God." She hushed. Eveline hid her face in her hands, but Wilhelm pulled her fingers away.

"You don't know what's going on out there," he snarled. "Don't have a clue!"

"What will we do?" She said the words out loud and regretted it. Eveline tried to realign her thoughts, unable to remove the vision of the slain dog from her mind. "Move to another city?" She never hid her hatred of Pittsburgh, but the thought of moving to Philadelphia or even New York made her ill.

He laughed then. Long and slow. "Got good news for you, Eve. Traded this house for a place in the country."

"What?"

"Never have to live in this city again. Never have to live in *any* city again."

Her temples throbbed and she rubbed one with her finger. "When did you—"

"What, no smile? No hug? Come on, doll!" he crooned sarcastically. "Like a dream come true!"

"You're not well, Wilhelm," she said evenly

and with concern. Eveline rose then, pushed away from the table. "You don't even know what you're saying."

He stood as well, the fake levity gone. "I know exactly what I'm saying." And with a hostility that was quite unlike her husband, he grabbed her wrist and shoved a deed in her hand and made her fingers clutch it, made them crunch the paper in her forced fist.

"You got your farm, Eve," he proclaimed. Wilhelm smiled then in an unkind, ugly way. "Just what you always wanted."

The book rested on Andrew's knee, the pages fanned out from under the center binding. The warm air from the open window brought in the scent of Eveline's climbing rose and the words from the conversation below. When the exchange had finished and the front door slammed, Andrew closed his eyes. The words echoed and pounded like steady stab wounds. Dully, he opened his lids, let his vision draw to the endless sea of slate roofs that twisted along the city street. A group of pigeons settled upon the nearest eave, bobbing heads until taking flight in tandem.

The young Kiser boys suspended their marble game on his rug after hearing the shouting from downstairs. They waited for Andrew to turn to them, address them in some way with reassurance, but he couldn't face them and just fell away to the emptiness found in the roofs and chimneys and cooing pigeons.

Seven-year-old Will approached the bed and perched upon the mattress, bending one knee so it shelved his chin. "What's a German shepherd?" the boy asked.

"It's a dog," Andrew finally answered, the words soft and apologetic.

The child's face drained, stricken to the core. A marble rolled in the tiny, soft fingers. He turned back to Andrew, his doleful gaze drifting to his cousin's severed arm. "Does it hurt?"

Andrew nodded. "Yeah," he said wearily. "It hurts."

The child had meant the arm, but the answer summed up an existence. Andrew dropped his eyelids again, wrestled with the anger, the bitterness, the burn. The doctor had said the pain would stop once the nerve endings healed, but the searing heat was with Andrew always—an ache in a body part that didn't exist, like the memory of a broken heart, like the memory of his parents and his muzzled ambitions.

Will inched closer to his cousin and squinted at the remnants of the amputation, studied the ragged scar. "Looks like the smokestack at the Heinz factory."

Edgar climbed up from the floor and scooted past his brother. "Let me see." Andrew cringed as the little boys inspected the cuts. "Oh, I see it!" In the air, Edgar traced the line of the incision. "Looks just like it, got lines like smoke an' everything."

Andrew watched the curious faces that held no pity. Consciously, he released the tension that hunched his shoulders and stiffened his neck, his body loosening like a deflating balloon. In spite of himself, he cracked a smile, the strange curve foreign, nearly forgotten. He allowed the boys to stare at the ravaged flesh, their inquisitive gaze softening the sting, a slight salve to the harsh words spoken down in the kitchen.

Wilhelm Kiser might see him as a cripple, but—Andrew thought gratefully—these boys only saw a Pittsburgh landmark.

PART 3

All good things are wild and free.

—Henry David Thoreau

CHAPTER 13

Plum, Pennsylvania—1917

Lilith Morton stretched her arms wide, ran down the slope of the bristled farmland, the gusts pushing her to the valley, then uplifting her to the highest mounds. And she ran with the air, then ran against the thrusts so it pressed against her cheeks and whipped her wild hair in knotted wisps. She was a hawk—a kestrel. She was free and as she surged with the wind she held her breath for the moment when her feet would rise from the earth and her body would reach the sky.

In her flight, the bread wagon rattled on the main road. She knew this without looking, had heard the familiar chains and squeaky wheels for as long as she could remember. She knew that perched on top were old man Stevens and his Negro wife, Bernice. Lilith knew they couldn't see her from the road, but she was suddenly self-conscious, her wings clipped. She was not a hawk. She was a lanky girl of seventeen with tangled hair and muddy dress who wanted to live in the trees and sprout wings.

She plopped onto the ground and plucked the sticky burrs and thorns off her sleeves and hem. The August heat seeped into her skin. It was a heavy heat that slowed the world, made the body want to rest and bask in thick warmth. Grasshoppers jumped around her hips, their dull green bodies clicking as wings stretched and then retreated. The honey- and bumblebees buzzed from long dandelions to nearly hidden violets. When she was a child, she would hold the bees in her palm, convinced that they would see that she was good and would not sting her. She was stung every time.

Lily twisted a goldenrod stem around her finger and gazed at the deserted farm. She remembered a time when the old clapboard house had sparkled white. Now it was gray and peeling, with only spots of dull cream, like snow melting over a road of gravel.

She rose from the patch of weeds and bugs, traced the line of the broken slate walkway to the ancient apple tree that leaned precariously over half the yard. Her old boots were long accustomed to finding the knots and bevels in the ridged bark and she climbed easily. Her knees scraped but had long ago grown numb against the rough grain. She stood upon the thickest, lowest branch and reached above to hoist up and continued that way until she sat in the crook of the highest limbs. Her back rested against the trunk as if in a man's lap, the strong arms protecting on either side.

The leaves speckled shadows across her light dress and across her skin. The sparrows and finches flew back to their perches, now fully used to her visits and handfuls of sunflower seeds. She reached for one of the apples, just starting to ripen under the sun, and plucked it off, leaned into the wooden arms and chewed the crisp, tart apple slowly, shielding her eyes against the spears of sun that peeked through the limbs and tickled her eyelids and forehead.

A barn cat slunk along the perimeter of the lifeless house and stretched front paws forward and arched her back, the tummy low and flaccid from birthing litters. The calico flopped on her side and licked a front paw, then squinted at Lily in the tree and meowed. Lily threw the shreds of baked chicken from her pocket, the cat instantly upon them, chewing with back teeth. Lily sighed. This place was her home. She shared it with the birds and the bugs, with the wild cats and the weeds, and the sun and the moss and the old trees. But this was the last day. This farm was hers only for today and no more after.

A bell rang far above the valley, shuddered in its clanging way across the hills. The chime hollered her name as clearly as if it had been a voice: *Lily! Lilith,* it called, *time to come home!*

She closed her ears and her eyes, felt the warmth of this place leaving quickly. She took another bite of the apple, glanced down at the dilapidated farmhouse below. From up high she could see the moss on the far end of the roof and the spotted siding, holes where woodpeckers had started and then robins had built stick homes and wasps hung their paper nests the size of slop buckets.

The bell rang again and the apple tasted sour. She threw the core to the ground, where it bounced. Her sister would be worried, but for once, she didn't care. This was her space, her own corner of the earth. The farmhouse she imagined was hers and hers alone, her own garden, her own everything, to be made new and fresh and beautiful again.

But it wasn't her place or her tree. The new owners were coming in a day and wouldn't take too kindly to a skinny bird girl perched in their tree. She rolled her eyes. Her arms would never be wings, just scrawny limbs that hung without vigor.

Hope they got kids, she thought. *Not enough little ones so close.* The land along this stretch had aged along with the bodies that tilled it. Hearing kids laughing would be nice, almost as nice as sitting in this tree forever. Almost.

The bell rang a third time. She could feel her sister's panic as if it were her own. She sighed and looked up, took in the bright red apples like stars in twilight. Lily Morton swiveled and kissed the wooden heart between the limbs before inching down slowly and making her way back home.

CHAPTER 14

The Tin Lizzie cramped with a family on the move. While farmers were leaving the fields for work in the steel mills and factories of Pittsburgh—an exodus from rural to urban—the Kisers wormed backwards, heading to a life in reverse. So, the Ford drove from the soot-squeezed city over paved and even roads and crossed the divide from town to country—barreled onwards over narrow lanes and rocky, brickless paths to their future.

The August morning seeped hot and hazy, so humid that the fabric of even the most diaphanous material clung to the skin and squeezed beads of sweat over foreheads, under arms and down the back. Wilhelm drove, his face hard. Eveline held her stomach with each bump, tried to keep the twins from being birthed en route. Andrew scrunched in the back, his long legs bent, while Edgar slept on his lap. Will sat next to him, his head bobbing against Andrew's arm, the cotton shirt spotted wet with the boy's drool.

The hot car crossed deeper into the land. Towns grew farther apart. Vegetation replaced humans.

Black-and-white cows dotted the hills and the air grew thick with the smell of manure and animal hair and fur. Over the miles, the sky filtered out the gray and the blue expanded. Clouds, white as down, floated in bloated puffs. The body felt clean, perspired salted water instead of toxins. Even Wilhelm breathed in the air deeply through his nostrils. The poison of the city was leaving.

The Kisers passed farm after farm—white clapboard beauties with new, glimmering silos; red barns with chocolate brown mares milling about split-rail fences. There were older farms, too, built with limestone blocks and pure white mortar. Old plows scattered like rusty tombstones attesting to years of hard labor. But beyond the homes it was the land that called forth and welcomed in open expanse. The golden hay and wheat that rippled and waved. The green spears of corn that saluted the sky above. The waves of alfalfa and clover that blanketed the hills in undulating emerald silk.

By afternoon, they passed into Plum Township. They passed a covered bridge over Pucketa Creek, whose water would eventually join hands with the Allegheny River and from there merge with the Monongahela and Ohio Rivers, the outlines to the iconic Pittsburgh triangle. All seemed to flow to that great Pittsburgh—except for Wilhelm and his family, the man who flowed backwards with his family, against the current.

From the tiny Plum town, the roads narrowed, veined off from the main street and cut through a line of corn higher than the car on each side, forming an unroofed green tunnel. As they emerged from the maize, a white farmhouse stood to the left, neat and perfect among the zinnias that bordered the picket fence. Two spotted horses galloped in a ring behind the house. And so they drove on, passed a wooded grove of oaks and maples and ragged cedars leaning toward the road, tipping roots forward as if attempting to cross.

Wilhelm adjusted in the seat, his bottom sticking to the leather. He pulled out a map and glanced intermittently back at the winding road. "Should be the next one." He folded the paper and pushed it aside, his knuckles gripping the wheel tight as his eyes danced between each side of the road.

"I see it!" Will pointed from the back open window. "Through the trees. I saw it!"

"Looks like we're home." Wilhelm's voice mixed in equal parts of expectation and terror. They rose over another mound and the entrance to the lane came into view. A ragged, metal mailbox leaned forward as a head nods in slumber. They turned into the lane and as the front wheel landed in a deep hole the car jerked fiercely and stalled.

Wilhelm stepped out of the car and inspected the front wheel, the tire ripped with the jagged edge of the crevice. "Guess we're walking from here."

One by one, they stepped out of the car, stretched stooped muscles and inert legs. The lane was a disaster. One side deep and nearly washed out from years of hard rain and lack of use. To the right, a long creek sliced through the land—a jagged cut, twisting and rough, with sides of clumped weeds threatening to fall into the shallow stream.

"How could they have delivered our furniture?" Eveline asked.

Wilhelm pointed at the dip below and the wood slats covering the crevice. "Must have brought the wood along, laid it out inch by inch."

They passed the makeshift bridge, then a line of trees before the homestead stretched ahead. But there were no squeals of delight, no sounds at all.

The wood-sided farmhouse tilted, the white paint long chipped away. The wrought-iron yard fence was covered in rust and large lines lay flat on the ground sinking into the soil. One shutter clung to the siding for dear life, a pathetic black rectangle hanging on the bottom window. The roof grew black and green with moss and mildew, the edge eaten away from hard weather and vegetation. A huge, unpruned apple tree stalked the yard, so majestic the expanse nearly eclipsed the house.

But as they looked at the old house—at the

broken fence and cracked slate walkway, the worn brown barn and sheds, rusted old plows and scattered and unnamable mechanical pieces—one revelation stood out more than any other: There wasn't a blade of grass in sight.

Wilhelm stared at the farm for a very long time, his legs spread and hands at his hips. He stared so long that the boys grew restless.

"Maybe it ain't the right place," Edgar ventured.

"Isn't," corrected Eveline softly, her manner as stunned as her husband's stance. "Isn't the right place."

Edgar and Will exchanged worried glances, then looked up to Andrew, but his face was void of any expression. All figures waited for Wilhelm, the statue that didn't move or seem to exhale or inhale.

Unable to keep quiet any longer, Edgar hopped, held his pants. "I gotta go."

Andrew pointed his elbow at the decrepit outhouse. The boy looked aghast. "Isn't there a toilet in the house?"

At this Wilhelm smiled wryly and rubbed the dampness glistening the back of his neck. "Not likely."

Edgar galloped to the wooden closet, let the door bang behind him. In two seconds, the child flew out, his nose buried in his shirt. "I'm going in the woods!"

Wilhelm settled his gaze on his wife. "Home sweet home," he said coldly.

She turned away from the iced words and headed to the privy, the twins sitting on her bladder. Eveline closed the door to the outhouse, setting off an eruption of flies from the black hole cut in the wooden bench. An ancient Sears catalog rotted next to the round pit, half the pages ripped out for wiping by the last inhabitant.

The stink wrapped around Eveline's body instantly and she buried her mouth and nose in the dress collar. In the dim light, the ceiling thickened with cobwebs, sagging and heavy with flies and curled mosquitos. She hoisted her skirt around her hips and sat on the wooden bench, leaned her elbows on her knees, her hands clasped in prayer.

Light shone through the crescent moon carved into the door, the shape lying distorted across her shoe. With her stillness, the flies flew to the corners of the structure, beating their wings and buzzing against the walls. Eveline watched their ugliness, watched as they made this place of filth their home. Her fingers touched her lips, felt them stretch and frown as she cried. She brought her palms to her eyes and wiped them roughly, willed the tears to stop. She would not leave this space with wet eyes. After all, this was what she had nagged Wilhelm for since the beginning of their marriage.

The crescent moon of light lay broken at her foot and the weight of the shadows clutched her heart. The twins kicked, the hard limbs distorting the shape of her round belly. This was the home where she would birth them. This was the land where Will and Edgar would be raised. This would be their life. *My God, what have we done?*

CHAPTER 15

One by one, each window in the house was pried open, the wood splintering and cracking with the thrusts, the harder ones needing a crowbar to shimmy them upward. With the onslaught of fresh air to the closed home, the spiderwebs swayed, dropped dead flies and silk-wrapped insects to the floor, the hollow bodies crisp and crunching underfoot. Hornet nests peppered and buzzed in two of the upstairs bedrooms and small bats darkened nearly every corner. Even with the windows open, the house reeked of mouse droppings and moth wings, each scent exacerbated and succulent within the late summer mugginess.

Eveline tackled the kitchen, had Edgar and Will clean out the iron stove of ancient ashes. Despite the mess, she was pleased with the space. Two ranges buffered the wall across from the brick fireplace. The stoves had cooking space for eight pots and ovens that could cook bread, a rack of lamb and a cake at the same time. The icebox seemed new. The pantry had shelves enough to feed a small town and revealed a hidden door that led down to the cold fruit cellar below.

Eveline turned the faucet over the sink. The water spluttered and retched, the copper pipes convulsing so loudly that she twisted the knob off before the plumbing hopped out of the wall. She sent Will to the well to lug in water one bucket at a time.

Eveline wiped her brow against her shoulder as she scrubbed the shelving, her large belly pressing against the counter space. Her abdomen had been tight for days and the twins quiet with the stress of the move. *Not today,* she beseeched. *Not yet.*

Upstairs, Wilhelm and Andrew cleaned out the largest of the bedrooms. Wilhelm swept the wide plank oak floors and cleaned out the fireplace while Andrew steadied the dustpan and ash pail and tossed the years of filth out the window. They scraped the disintegrating wallpaper and washed away the hardened glue left behind.

When the room was ready, Wilhelm stopped, breathed heavily. "Need to get the furniture in," he said, contemplating, his brows furrowed. His eyes flickered to Andrew.

"I can help," Andrew answered the question on his uncle's mind.

"You sure?" Wilhelm bit his lip in debate. "It's heavy."

"Yeah." Andrew went to the hall and carried in a side rail for the brass bed. Wilhelm followed and together they carried in the pieces, then assembled the bed. They pushed the Victorian walnut dresser to the clean wall, the weight of it slamming into Andrew's shoulder as he gripped and pushed with all his might. He dug through the pain, dug for strength at his very core. He wasn't a cripple and come hell or high water, he'd prove it, even if it meant breaking his body in the process.

Wilhelm's face dotted with dust and the sweat slicked the hair around his forehead. He wiped a cloth around his neck. "I'll grab some drinks." He glanced at his nephew wearily. "You all right?" The look was softer now and Andrew nodded.

"Good." Wilhelm blew an exhausted breath of air. "Christ, it's hot." Taking the broom in one hand and the dustpan in the other, he stepped out to the hall. "Going to start on the boys' room next. Finish up in here and we'll get Eveline settled. Woman's been on her feet since we got here."

The heavy footsteps thumped down the narrow stairwell and Andrew slunk into the corner, dropped his head back against the wall with fatigue. His right arm pulsed, the biceps twitching. He raised his hand and the fingers shook uncontrollably with the strain of carrying, lugging, pushing, cleaning. Andrew swallowed, his mouth so parched it left him dizzy. With forced will, he stood again and headed to the next bedroom.

• • •

On that summer evening, darkness settled languidly over the quiet fields and surrounded the broken farmhouse with the first shade of the endless day. Cool air did not transcend but blocked out the mightiest of the degrees so that pores felt free to dry again.

The family ate outside, lined like stepping-stones upon the granite slab at the porch. They ate cold bologna sandwiches, the warm bread soft and chewy. Jaws moved mechanically while bodies hunched and ached for bed. Crickets chirped, the song rising upon the heated earth as steam between bittersweet vines. A barn owl hooted. Another called in return and so they danced, back and forth, in a melody that welcomed the night.

A calico cat inched from the weeds, slunk low as she sniffed the air. Andrew tossed a small bit of bologna in her direction and the cat crawled upon her belly and gobbled it up, licking her lips. Andrew tore another morsel from his sandwich, held it out. The cat came closer, led by her wet nose.

"It'll bite you," Wilhelm warned.

Andrew fed the cat anyway and a purr emerged. The cat rubbed against his thigh and he scratched her under the chin. "Somebody's been feeding her. She trusts us."

"How you know it's a girl?" Will asked.

"Calicos are always female," he told him.

Little Edgar tossed the rest of his meat to the cat, touched the fur with delight as she chewed. "Looks like you got your first pet," Andrew noted.

Edgar smiled and before he knew it the cat climbed upon his lap and started to lick his lips. The little boy erupted in giggles, his futile shoves against the cat only making her lick harder.

"Great," Wilhelm chided, a grin forming. "Now the cat's giving him worms."

"I'll name her Wormy," Edgar announced. He put his chubby arms around the cat. "Come here, little Wormy."

Eveline covered her mouth, stifled her laugh. Andrew chuckled easily, met his aunt's face. She reached over, squeezed his knee. "Nice to see you smile," she whispered.

After dinner, with only one bedroom suitable for inhabitants, Eveline and Wilhelm headed upstairs and Andrew and the boys headed to the barn's hayloft with a pile of blankets and pillows. As they had never known a home outside of their manicured Pittsburgh house, Will's and Edgar's eyes were wide with the expanse of the open barn and the adventure of sleeping so high off the ground.

Above in the loft, Andrew spread out the blankets and stuffed the rotting hay under for padding. Will scrunched up his nose. "We're gonna smell like cows."

"I like it," said Edgar as he curled up next to Andrew's long body. "I don't ever want to go home."

"We are home, you dingbat." Will lay down on the other side of Andrew, stared up at the rafters. "But I like it, too."

Andrew grinned in the dim light. "Why's that?"

"I don't know." Will thought about this, the soft features of the young boy taking on a seriousness well beyond his years. "Hard to say. Kinda feels like I'm a chipmunk that just got let out of a shoe box."

"Yeah," agreed Edgar, his voice fading. "Me too."

In the next moment, both boys were sound asleep, their gentle breathing keeping pace note to note with the hum of insects outside the barn wood.

Andrew's body sank into the coarse blanket, every nerve slinking toward slumber except for the ones occupying his mind. He lay on his back, his one hand resting behind his head. In the shadows, he stared at the beams of the roof. A few holes in the shingles left gaps to see the stars. One was large enough to show the tip of the half-moon. He couldn't remember ever seeing the sky clear enough to see the stars so bold.

The hayloft was comfortable, cooler than the house. Will snuggled and inched closer to his side, the young boy's brow crinkled with deep dreaming. A raccoon or a skunk slunk around the floor below, the wet nose sniffing in the corners, the claws scraping against the wood. Shadows flapped along the roof as bats darted, bringing a slight breeze across the skin.

Andrew tried to sleep, tried to force his thoughts to rest as his body desired, but to no avail. Gently, he scooted Will's body from his side. He crouched under the low beams and silently moved through the loft and climbed down the ladder and went outside. The sky was wide as it was deep in midnight blue and the constellations scattered in an order they had arranged since the beginning of creation. In the warm night, the crickets hummed from all sides, made the earth vibrate below his feet. Lightning bugs flashed around the trees and low bushes, lit the night like pinpoints of sulphur-tipped matches.

Andrew sat under the enormous, ancient tree that hovered over the yard. The canopy of leaves hung low with apples at every branch. Something rubbed against his leg, meowed. "Hello, Wormy." He scratched the warm fur and smiled. "Sorry about the name. Had nothing to do with it." The cat jumped on his lap, put a paw on his chest. He curled the cat into the crook of his arm, the purr vibrating through his chest.

Five months had passed since the train accident. In a year, he had lost his father, his mother, his home, his friends, his arm, his future. He didn't recognize this new life, couldn't find his place in it, like he was walking in circles through a fog-filled maze.

The cat rubbed against Andrew's maimed side. Over the months, the burn had lessened, the pain now nearly gone. Numbness had replaced the pain but made it feel dead instead. The pain held a form of life and now even that was gone.

He remembered the thick volume of poems Miss Kenyon had given him once—Dante's *Divine Comedy*, a story outlining a journey through Hell, Purgatory and Paradise. Andrew knew Hell now—fire in all its forms. He peered at the old farmhouse, listened to the gentle purr of the cat and hum of the soft land. And this was Purgatory.

Paradise. If the story were true, Paradise would follow. Andrew laughed then, elicited a surprised chirp from the feline. *Not likely.* He raised his eyes to the sky above the tree limbs, awed by the stars again, bright as diamonds without the smog. And he wondered, *Maybe things have to fall apart in order for the stars to shine?*

He was tired of feeling sorry for himself. He had one arm. He hated it, cursed it, but he had one good one left and he would focus there, try to find his way again.

"Paradise." He said the word jeeringly as he gave the cat a long rub. "What do you think, Wormy? Anything out there for me?" The calico climbed to his shoulder and jumped to the tree behind him. He turned to see where she landed and noticed a roughly scraped spot in the bark, a circle shaved to its smooth, pale underside. He squinted to examine the solitary word carved into the wood: "Lily."

CHAPTER 16

L ily Morton bent over the washtub, scrubbed
the last bits of hay and dirt and grease from
the work clothes. Her long hair hung in a plait
between her shoulder blades, but the top of her
light brown head was full of loose hairs, straying
in every direction. She rubbed her itchy nose
against her shoulder, then heaved the soaking
clothes up, fed them through the wringer and
hung them on the clothesline to dry. Her brother-
in-law's pants dripped heavily next to her and
her sister's dresses. With a scowl, Lily pulled up
the male undergarments from the soapy water
and wrung them in her bare hands like a neck
and sloppily hung them in a queue, sticking her
tongue out in disgust.

Leaves crunched behind the house from the
barn. Her sister stumbled forward, bent over
as she struggled with the two full pails of fresh
milk, the precious contents sloshing over the rim.
Lily ran to her side and took the pails from her
hands, the metal handles leaving a red mark on
each palm.

"Claire, it's too much. You know that," she

scolded. "See, you spilled half the milk. Don't have to carry so much at one time."

The woman rubbed her sore hands, rubbed them more than necessary, over and over as if she were balling dough. "I thought I had them. Didn't want to leave them in the field case they got sp-sp-spilt," she stuttered.

Lily touched her sister's arm consolingly, instantly sorry she had scolded Claire. She was thirteen years Lily's senior but was childlike more times than not. The doctor had said it was from the mule kick she suffered as a girl. *Shame,* the neighbors had said. *Such a beautiful girl. Shame that damn mule made her stutter and soft as a turtle egg.* But Lily knew the truth. The only damn mule that ever kicked Claire was her father.

"You didn't do anything wrong." Lily placed her hands atop Claire's rolling ones. "Just let me get the milk from now on, all right?" She squeezed until the toiling fingers stopped and her sister nodded.

"All right, Lily." The woman's mouth twitched. "I'm sorry I made you mad."

"I'm not mad. Not at you anyway." She looked over at the drying long johns and stuck out her tongue again. "Can't you at least get Frank to wipe his bum for once in his life? Looks like his underclothes been run over by wagon wheels that got stuck in the mud!"

Claire broke out in giggles, laughed so hard she

117

had to cover her mouth. Lily laughed, too, loved to see her sister happy and smiling. "Can't you slip a diaper on him when he's sleeping? Pin it on good and tight?"

Claire doubled over. "Stop!" Tears of laughter squeezed from her eyes. "You better hush. He'll hear you," she warned between giggles.

"He's not hearing a thing." Lily put her arm around her sister's slight shoulders and mocked seriousness. "Except his own noises echoing in the outhouse." The women erupted with giggles again, their heads locked together in devilish mirth.

Claire had raised Lily, even if it was like being reared by an infant. Lily's father took no part in her upbringing. His eyes were dead. Seemed he wanted to make everything else dead, too. Seemed he wanted to beat the life out of anything that had life running through it.

He always smelled of drink. When she was a child, she didn't know the smell of whiskey, just thought it was the smell of men, that all fathers smelled like that in mouth and skin. Only later, when she ran into men coming from the saloons, did she recognize the scent and it made her feel frail and sad at the same time. But she always had Claire. It was Claire who fed her and changed her, rocked her and slept with her at night. It was Claire who took the force of their father's blows when he was missing his dead wife and cursing his life, blows that left Lily's sister simple and scared of anything that moved.

Lily glanced at the ditch not too far off from where the laundry was hung—the last place she ever saw her father, shot in the back and bleeding to death in the mud. She turned her view and concentrated on the milk in the buckets, turned the memories of red blood to white. She picked the pails up and brought them to the house carefully, setting them near the door so she could strain the cream after supper.

Frank Morton shoveled the last of the eggs into his mouth and wiped his lips against the napkin. He wore his new silver-tipped boots and his favorite beige Stetson atop his head. He looked a fool, thought Lily. Frank deemed himself a cowboy. Thought himself handsome in his polished boots and spurs, though she was pretty sure he'd never been on top of a horse in his life. Women found him attractive—this she knew—but for what reason she hadn't a clue. But she saw the way the ladies glanced at him in the general store and the way the wives of his clients hung upon his stupid words and his awkward swagger.

Claire pulled out another pie from the oven and placed the pan on the window ledge with the others, the syrups bubbling from the fork holes.

"How many pies you making?" he asked.

"Seven." She took down one of the cooled ones

and began to slice. "Figured you could bring a few down to the new neighbors."

"I'll do that," Frank decided.

Lily picked up his plate and fork and dropped them in the wash bucket roughly. "Why they want that beat-up Anderson place anyway?" she asked, her tone sour.

"Beats me." Frank leaned back and rubbed his belly. He was midway through his thirties and his torso was starting to show it. "Traded that house in Troy Hill without even seeing the place."

Lily poured the hot water over the dishes. "Traded it even?"

"Just about. The rest paid for the movers and the livestock coming."

Claire sliced through a fresh pie and placed it on a small plate, handed it to her husband. "You told them about the farm?" she asked tentatively. "I mean, you let them know what kind of shape it's in, right?"

"I can't believe it." Frank whistled loudly. "My own wife thinking I'm trying to swindle folks."

Claire blushed hotly. "I'm sorry. I-I-I didn't mean that."

"Course I told them!" Frank cut into the warm pie, blew the steam rising from the cooked cherries. "Could have said I was selling him a snake pit and don't think it would have mattered. Never saw a man looking to leave the city so fast."

He chewed carefully, opening his mouth wider than normal to cool the fruit. "Heard something happened on the man's job with the railroad. What I heard in town, anyway. People saying it had to do with him being a Kiser and all."

"What's his name got to do with anything?" Claire asked.

"He's German, Claire." Frank rolled his eyes. "Spies comin' in all the time. Last thing you need is some German infiltrating the rails, wrecking them to pieces like in France. You heard about the Black Tom explosion in New Jersey. Those German agents destroyed all the munitions headed to the Allies. Could do the same to the railroads in Pittsburgh. End up crippling our side of the war."

Frank chewed the pie, stuck out his tongue with the heat. "Can't believe we're getting another goddamn German in this town. A Kiser no less." He shook his head. "How come we got so many Germans on this street?"

"Only the Muellers," Claire interjected.

"Air gonna smell like sauerkraut."

"I like sauerkraut," said Claire.

Frank growled under his breath. "Don't always have to take things so literal." He stood and adjusted his belt buckle. Then, spitting on the tips of his fingers, he wiped the dirt off the silver of his boots and admired one and then the other. "All right. Off to meet the new neighbors. Claire, hand me one of those pies."

CHAPTER 17

E veline cleaned up breakfast, relieved the
eggs they had brought from Pittsburgh only
suffered minor casualties. A distant rooster from
a distant farm called through the open window.
Eveline stretched to the sound, let the long
screech settle upon her ears. And in its pause
there was quiet and she strained her ears as if
the void were a tease. No trams. No clanging
cars along the brick city streets. No pigeons
defecating on the dirty windows. Silence. She
breathed deeply, had slept with the window open,
and this morning her sheets were not lined in soot
and her lungs were clear. She wiped her eyes and
no black smudges dyed her fingers. The heaviness from their arrival lifted. She had been tired;
the trip, long. Today was a new beginning.

Eveline turned her eyes to the cracked plaster
along the ceiling, heard her husband's footsteps
as he moved furniture and hammered wood along
the baseboards. Wilhelm had become a different
man since the accident and she knew that moving
to the country and leaving his job, his house and
his comfort felt like applying leeches to bleed

him. But he would see the life the land would bring and he would rise from the earth just as the great oaks did. One day he would thank her; his eyes would shine again; his skin would darken from the sun instead of from choking soot. And he would know himself as a man not by the steel beast that he could brake, but by the land he could tame and nurture.

Eveline left the kitchen and stepped into the parlor to the large windows that winged the formal fireplace. She'd hang the curtains today, she decided. Clean the windows and then hang the rose-colored valance and the long lace curtains below. She'd pick wild phlox and put them in a vase on the table. There was much work to be done, but today she would make the house feel like a home.

Out the window, a figure moved down their ragged lane. Eveline squinted at her reflection in the wavy window glass and cringed at her appearance. "Wilhelm!" She scurried up the stairs before the visitor arrived. "A man's coming this way to see you."

CHAPTER 18

"Too late in the season to plant," Frank Morton noted as the men crunched the gravel toward the top field. He nodded to Andrew as he joined them, eyed the missing limb suspiciously. "Come to think of it," Frank continued. "Too late to do much of anything. Gonna have to stock it all. Cost you a fair piece."

Wilhelm's head bent as they climbed the narrow path from the edge of the lane. He remained silent.

"Like I told you back in Pittsburgh, the sheep did a number on the place. Old Anderson just let them flocks run wild and they ate every last blade. Can see that line of dead birch along the creek. His sheep shredded everything to a man's waist. Whole flock had mites like you never seen before, their fleece all patchy."

Wilhelm slapped a mosquito at his neck, inspected the bloody insect in the palm of his hand before wiping the blob off on his jeans. His brows were set low; Frank's voice was starting to bite with the bugs.

"Barn's in good shape," Frank continued.

"Needs to be cleaned. Couple patches to the roof, but the animals will do fine. Should be coming in a few days. How many you got coming again?"

"Seven cows. A horse. Couple pigs and a load of chickens." Wilhelm eyed Frank as if in challenge. "Guess we aren't as farm poor as you think."

Frank's lip rose above his teeth as he gave a short laugh. "Still have to feed those animals. Remember that."

The exchange between the men drifted back to Andrew. A mutual distrust sprung from their figures that squared their shoulders, made their gaits heavier than necessary.

"Used to work the railroad?" Frank asked the question he already knew the answer to, and the knowing made the inquiry taunting.

"Yep. Brakeman."

Frank stuck out his bottom lip and pondered this. "Good living working the rails."

The sun heated from the ground up, squashed the pleasantries and made the muscles tight and in need of shade. Wilhelm Kiser stopped then, turned to Frank and folded his arms against his chest. "You finished implying?"

Frank scoffed, crossing his arms in mirrored response. "Implying?"

"Implying I don't got no sense in managing a farm. Implying I'm stupid for giving up a job in the city for this shit piece of land. Implying I'm gonna let my family starve and freeze out here because I got no sense for farming."

Andrew stepped forward. "Don't think that's what Mr. Morton was saying."

Wilhelm's ears were red as he turned on his nephew. "Wasn't talking to you, was I?" His eyes turned back to Frank and then his face followed. "I grew up farming. My father before me in Germany and every father in line before him worked the land. This isn't new to me, Mr. Morton. I know what I got into the day I signed that deed with you. So, I'll ask you not to question me with implying."

Frank put his hands up and smiled, the glint in his eye hard and black. "My mistake. No disrespect intended. Sounds like a rich history. Makes a man proud from where he came. Loyal, no?" The innuendo clear.

Wilhelm scratched the spot from the mosquito bite absently, the welt inflamed and rising. "A man's loyalty sits where his family sleeps."

Andrew had fallen away from the men, kept his hearing tuned to the rise and pitch of the words. Upon the last sentence, he took his place between the men, buffered the tension with his body. "When's the tractor coming?" he asked Wilhelm.

"Tractor?" Frank inquired. "You're not using Anderson's relic?"

Wilhelm shook his head, and with it an air of pride relaxed his shoulder blades. "Have a new Fordson coming."

Frank whistled. "Pricey piece of farm machinery."

The pride grew in Wilhelm and he leaned into the new topic as a man floats upon a lazy river. "Had some investments in Westinghouse and Carnegie Steel. Did all right over the years." Then added humbly, "Not as well as some but did all right."

Andrew fell back again. Let the men find their way on new ground. A welcome breeze rose across the naked earth and steadied stances. The sweat cooled just enough to unclench the jaw. With the slight wind, their neighbor turned his face to the sky, dismissed the previous hard conversation like puffs of milkweed cotton upon the zephyrs. He seemed to be reading the galaxy, searching for stars in the daylight.

"Saying it'll be an early winter," Frank prophesized. "Hard winter. What they're saying, anyway." Frank rubbed his heel in the dirt. "Be wise to set up credit at the general store in town. Campbell's. Whatever they don't got in stock they can get."

"I'll do that." The horns unlocked and Wilhelm scratched harder at the bug bite. "Look. Sorry about snapping at you the way I did. Still tired from the move. Got more wasp stings than I can count."

"Oh, they're fierce, all right. Put up a hell of a fight, once that nest is set." Frank turned his back to the field and took a step toward the farmhouse. "I'll tell you what: How about you all head into town with me tomorrow. I'll grab the wagon from Mrs. Sullivan down the way. Get you set up with Campbell and show you around."

Wilhelm rubbed the whiskers along his cheek. "That'll be good. Need to grab some paint and supplies for the house. Order the feed for the animals."

"Good." Frank gave one hearty nod and adjusted his belt buckle. "I'll be over first thing. Now," he said, rubbing his hands together. "How about we cut into that pie I brought. My wife makes the best damn pies in all of Pennsylvania."

Eveline unpacked the wooden boxes in the kitchen when the men came in. Edgar and Will crawled on their knees along the floor throwing packing straw in confetti strands.

"You boys making a heap of a mess for your mother," Wilhelm accused.

Eveline wiped off a line of glasses set upside down on the counter. "Straw and paper the least we got to clean up in this place." She shot a look at her husband, then took a double take at the man by his side.

Frank stepped forward and held out a hand. "You must be Eveline."

She took the strong, smooth hand, no roughness or calluses across the palm. She shook the hand limply as if her wrist held no bones. Suddenly self-conscious of her pregnancy, she positioned her arms in front of her girth.

"Wilhelm tells me you were born in Holland."

She nodded and tucked a stray hair behind her ear. He was a tall man, wide with strength but not heavyset. His face had been shaved that morning. She could tell right away. Wilhelm only shaved on Sundays now and she recognized the smooth glow at the man's cheeks and jawbone.

"What part?"

"Excuse me?"

He chuckled. "Just curious what part of the Netherlands?"

She hadn't been asked that question in so long that she had to think. Hadn't been asked a question in so long it felt strange and left her unsure of her own speech. "Rotterdam."

"Ah."

"You know it?"

"I do. Passed through there to Amsterdam once. Beautiful country."

"Yes, it is." She hung on the memory and thought she saw the scenery of her hometown reflected in his pupils. Most people didn't know where Holland was on the map and this man knew her town of Rotterdam.

Wilhelm pulled out a chair. "Frank's wife made us a pie."

"Saw it on the porch. That was very kind. Hope

she'll call on us when we get settled in a bit more." Eveline set out the plates and divided the slices between the men and her sons. "Where's Andrew?"

Wilhelm peered behind his shoulder and shrugged. "Beats me."

As the men talked over moving forks, Eveline dug into the next crate. She let out a disappointed sigh and pulled out large shards of glass.

"What's wrong?" Wilhelm asked.

"It's the Waterford pitcher. Must have cracked during the move."

Wilhelm shoveled in his food. "One less thing to put away and dust, I reckon."

She glared at him and he looked up dumbly. "All I'm saying is that stuff is fine for the city, but we got to be practical here. A fancy crystal pitcher is about as useful as a house without a roof."

Eveline looked up at the cracked ceiling. "Guess that makes two things we haven't got," she mumbled.

Frank put down his fork and came up to the counter. "Mind if I take a look?" Gently, his fine hands took the thick crystal from her fingers. "Good-looking piece. Was a good-looking piece," he joked sympathetically. "You have glasses with this?"

Eveline took out the tumblers from the box. "Still intact."

"Well, that's something," he reassured, winking at her.

The heat rose up her neck and she stretched out her collar, feeling suddenly warm and stifled in the new kitchen.

CHAPTER 19

Frank Morton arrived the next morning wrangling two horses and a wide wagon. Wilhelm climbed upon the front seat and the boys piled into the back. "Sure you don't want to come?" Wilhelm asked his nephew.

"Better I stay," Andrew answered. "Try to get Aunt Eveline to stay off her feet." He saw the way Frank's gaze always fell to his crippled side. He wasn't ready to face the same reaction from the people in town.

Andrew ruffled the hair on the little heads of his cousins. "When you get back, we'll catch tadpoles in the creek like I promised."

"Don't start till we get back," Will ordered as if Andrew would be wading in the shallow water before the horses were on the main road. "Promise?"

He put his hand on his heart. "Not a fish or a tadpole until you get back. Promise." Relieved, the boys settled into the creaking wagon and waved as they headed out.

Back in the house, Andrew found Eveline resting upon the davenport in the parlor, her eyes closed but not in sleep. Her face wrinkled in a strained, tight expression. "Aunt Eveline?"

With the voice, her eyes popped open and her pupils searched the room. "I didn't hear you come in, Andrew. Startled me." She gave a short laugh and tried to sit up but leaned back into the pillow instead. "Feeling a bit dizzy this morning. Would you mind bringing me a bit of lemon?"

He returned a moment later with the slices wrapped in an embroidered napkin. Eveline sucked on the pulp and shuddered with the sourness. "Not feeling so well today. Must be the heat."

The enormous belly appeared perfectly round and taut beneath the fabric of her dress. He met her eyes with questioning.

"No," she said. "I don't think it's time."

"If you need me to get Wilhelm, I can try to catch them before they get to town."

"No need." She chuckled with effort. "He'd think I'm a nervous woman." A thin coating of sweat beaded her forehead. "It's just the heat. I should know better than to overdo it. Just going to rest while there's a breeze."

The fine lace curtains, slightly yellowed from the sun, drifted back and forth, billowing into the room and then sucking back against the window frame. "I'm glad you're here, Andrew," she said deeply. "I know this can't be easy for you. You've had a lot of change in a very short time. Wilhelm's not pushing you too hard, is he?"

"No." He stretched out his hand, then curled it. "Feels good to work. Keeps me from feeling sorry for myself," he said wryly.

"Well, the boys adore you. In case you haven't noticed."

"Feeling's mutual." And he meant it, their cheery friendship a light in the dark.

She watched him carefully. "Been worrying about your mother, haven't you?"

He nodded. "Should have heard from her by now."

Eveline propped her pillow, straightened her back. "You'll hear soon. War was slowing everything in Pittsburgh. Who knows how long we got to wait for news here."

Andrew smiled at the woman, her belly huge and dominant over her slight figure. "You're a lot like my mother, you know that? Except happier."

"Carolien had a hard life. You both have." She frowned with a memory. "I was so angry after she ran off with your father. Seems like such a silly grudge now." Her face twisted in regret before grinning. "She and Frederick couldn't have raised a better son."

He let the compliment settle warmly. Then inspected the slices of fruit in her lap and winked. "That's very sweet coming from someone who sucks on lemons."

"Very funny." She smacked him on the knee

134

and laughed. "Out with you, now. Leave me in peace with my lemons."

Outside, Andrew let the profound and saturated heat grab his clothing and roast his crown. He bent his head back and closed his eyes against the brilliancy of sun. When he opened his eyes again, the sky spotted and morphed turquoise against the green leaves of the trees. He took in the full expanse of the property. The rounded hills and gentle valleys of the inert fields; the creek that snaked between clumps of stringy cattails; the rust-colored barn that bowed slightly at the base as if sitting on its haunches.

From the side of the house, the old garden reposed in rotting splendor, the tangled weeds and ancient vegetables overgrown, but the patch was big enough to feed two families. Come spring, they'd fix the beds and plant and till. They'd edge and discipline the pricker bushes and have enough fresh berries for jam in every flavor.

A branch cracked from high in the great apple tree. Several apples dropped and bounced against the hard ground. Andrew walked over to the tree and peered into the dense branches, caught sight of a dress and a woman's legs as they climbed down.

Seeing more than was proper, he turned away quickly, his face reddening before the shock of the trespasser took hold. Andrew turned back to the tree, stuffed his hand into his front pocket and waited.

The sound of torn fabric came from the leaves. "Ouch!" The boughs jostled as if a bear wrestled the trunk. Angry cursing muffled between the cracking sticks.

Andrew raised one eyebrow. "Need some help?" he called out.

The apple tree turned as still and silent as stone.

He inched closer and grinned. "Know you're up there, by the way."

Still the great tree did not waver.

Andrew scratched his head, thoroughly perplexed and amused. "I guess I'm going to have to come up there then."

Suddenly, an apple whizzed past his head. "Hey!" he shouted as he ducked another and then another. In the midst of the onslaught, a young woman jumped to the ground, her arms full of apples, her hand readied in the air with her round, red weapon.

"Who are you?" she shouted.

Andrew's mouth fell open. "Who am *I*?"

She squeezed the apple, pulled back her arm in preparation. "I said who are you?"

He took a bold step forward and she launched the apple, which he caught easily in his right hand, taking her off guard. "Considering this is my property," he said sternly, "how about you tell me who you are?"

"You live here?" she spluttered before pouting and flustering. "Thought you all went to town. Didn't think anyone would be here." The young woman emptied the apples into a pile at the base of the tree. Her long hair fell over her collarbone and reached past her elbow. She wore a pair of men's work boots and a pale green dress that was ripped at the shoulder. "I'll just be on my way," she said quickly as she ran atop the broken slate.

"Wait." He hurried to catch up. "Your sleeve is ripped. Is your arm hurt?"

She turned her head, investigated the torn fabric and the red gash. "Just a scratch."

"Think it's worse than that." Andrew stepped in front of her and her body tightened as if she might flee at any second. Gingerly, he touched the fabric, felt her tense as it stuck to the line of blood below.

She pulled away fiercely. "It's just a scratch, I said!"

"Okay. Okay." He put his hand up in innocence. The light filtered in an abrupt ray from behind a moving cloud and held to the hazel irises that stared in defiance at him. He swallowed and her eyebrows furrowed at the strange look that inched across his face.

The emerald eyes scanned him accusingly. "What?"

"Nothing," he said softly, his own voice odd and unnatural. The heat was getting to him and he felt dizzy, wished he had some of Eveline's lemon slices to wake him up. He met the eyes again. "What's your name?" he asked gently.

"Lily." She lowered her gaze. "Lily Morton."

The name smacked him hard in the back. "You're Frank Morton's wife?"

"No!" Her face contorted in revulsion. "Ugh! How could you think that?"

"I just thought—" Andrew laughed then. Laughed at the absurdity of the conversation, at the fact that a woman was hiding in his tree and throwing apples at him, laughed that he wasn't even sure what his name was anymore.

Lily twisted her chin and stuck a tongue in her cheek. "What's so funny?" she asked hotly.

He couldn't think of a reply, stood there dumb and smirking. Her eyes flickered to his, and her brows lowered. She crossed her arms over her middle. "Why are you staring at me like that?" she asked, livid. "You're laughing at my dress, aren't you? My big, dirty boots?" she seethed. "Well, take a good look and have your laugh. It's all I got and I like them just fine even if they aren't pretty to look at."

Andrew stopped laughing, shook his head to clear it.

Her face distorted with shame. "I know we're not rich like you, but that don't give you a right to laugh at me," she vented.

He was mortified, sorry to his bones. "I wasn't

looking at your clothes. I swear." He floundered for an apology. "I'm sorry . . . that wasn't it at all. I think your dress is fine. I really do."

"My dress isn't fine and you know it."

"Honestly." He stepped closer and leaned down so she would raise her eyes to look at him. "I wasn't looking at your dress or your boots." He smiled amiably. "I was just thinking about you throwing those apples. Nearly beaned me in the head. Got a good arm." He clicked his tongue. "For a girl anyway."

She studied him with reserve, squinted her eyes to see if he was teasing or being mean. Then her whole demeanor relaxed and she yielded. "Sorry I threw apples at you."

"Tell you what, let's start over." He stuck out his hand. "Andrew."

A cry broke from the house. A long, pained scream followed.

Andrew ran to the porch and into the parlor and found his aunt bent over in front of the rocking chair, her hands gripping the curved arms as if she rocked a ghost in the empty chair. The woman's hair hung loose around her face and her features twisted in agony. Andrew put an arm around her waist. "Come to the sofa," he ordered.

"No," she panted. Short, quick breaths blew from her pursed lips. "They're coming."

"I'll find a horse and get to town, get the

doctor." He let go, but she grabbed his wrist, her grip strong as a bear trap.

"There's no time." Then her lips rose about her teeth and she curled inward, wailed low and deep, the sound raw and primal. She breathed hard again, winced with terror and pain. "They're coming now." Her body writhed. "They're coming now!" she cried. "Oh, God."

"Mrs. Kiser?" The young woman in the torn green dress appeared in the room beside him. "We need to get you walking," she urged with pointed control. With that, she took one of the woman's limp arms and put it around her shoulder. She motioned with her head for Andrew to do the same and together they etched a circle in the room while Eveline hobbled between them.

"Who are you?" Eveline panted as the next contraction began building.

"Lily Morton. Live across the way." She gave a slight curtsy under the weight of the woman. "Good to meet you."

Eveline gave a short laugh at that before crumpling into the next wave of pain. "Oh, God!" she cried again. "Not now."

"Bring her to the couch," Lily ordered, and led the way. Eveline lay down and arched her back, clutched her stomach.

"Andrew," Lily called to him, her voice calm and steady, rigid with authority. "You need to boil a whole pot of water, do you understand? I need a pile of clean sheets and some towels." She swallowed and lowered her voice. "Need you to boil a kitchen knife, too. Just in case."

Andrew blanched but went to the kitchen. He picked up the pot but was so nervous that it slipped from his fingers and crashed loudly against the floor. *Stay calm.* He lit the stove and stared at the pot for a long moment before he realized there was no water within the base. He ran to the well pump and filled a bucket, brought it back into the house, his speed sloshing half the water across the floor and making him slip.

He ran up the stairs, taking the steps three at a time. From the parlor, Eveline screamed. He shivered to his bones, grabbed the clean sheets, brought them downstairs. Eveline's dress was up past her knees while Lily inspected the state of the birth.

Lily lowered the skirt quickly and took the sheets from Andrew, placed one under Eveline along with several towels. "I need to wash my hands, Mrs. Kiser. Andrew'll stay with you for a minute." She patted the woman's knee. "It's going to be all right, you hear me? Just keep breathing like that. In and out when the pain comes." Lily imitated the technique, her eyes wide with instruction. "Won't be much longer now."

Andrew sat next to his aunt and held her hand, her clutched fingers so tight that his knuckles turned white. Her nostrils flared; her eyes stretched in horror. "I'm scared."

He didn't know what to say. Every time he opened his mouth, nothing came out, so he just sat there with an unwilling vow of silence and let her squeeze his hand. When the screaming began again, he closed his eyes against the strain, to witness such pain and do nothing nearly unbearable.

Lily returned, her sleeves rolled up past her elbows. "You better go now," she told him. "But stay close."

Andrew backed out of the room, headed to the porch and leaned against the wall. The shouting came quicker, lasted longer, stopped and started, over and over again endlessly until the house radiated with one excruciating howl. He slid to the floor and bent his knees to his chest, buried his head and prayed for the woman's pain to end.

Lily cut the cords with the knife and laid one baby boy to Eveline's chest and then another. Eveline gazed at each child, her features pulled in disbelief. Lily wadded up the bloodied sheets and towels and replaced them with fresh ones. The red and wrinkled babies were tiny, premature by months, but breathing and intact. Lily's body finally relaxed, though her muscles were shaky and weak from the stress of the last hours.

Warmly, Lily watched the mother with her newborn sons. Mrs. Kiser was entranced with the children in the crook of her arms and Lily ached with the look. "What are you going to name them?" she asked.

"I don't know." Eveline smiled. She was a beautiful woman, the love shining straight from her skin. "Sure I was having girls. Didn't even think of any boy names."

"It'll come to you." Lily stood then and took the crumpled sheets with her. She stopped in the doorway to the porch and watched the young man pacing back and forth, from one end all the way to the other end. "They're boys," she announced quietly.

His jaw dropped and he wiped his face as if he had just washed it. "Are they okay? Is she okay?"

Lily nodded and curved a finger for him to follow. In the parlor, Eveline glowed with the infants. "Come meet your new cousins."

Andrew didn't move, stunned by the tiny infants who hadn't been here this morning, seemed to have appeared out of thin air. Lily nudged him and he wiped his hand upon his pants. He stepped as if his footsteps might shatter the babies, looking lost. Lily touched her throat as she watched the tall, proud figure kneel next to the couch.

Eveline tilted one side of her body to her nephew. "Go ahead and hold him."

Andrew rose. "I better not."

"He won't break," Eveline coaxed. "They're sturdier than you think."

Andrew's chin lowered and he shook his head only once, the glance resting on his missing arm. "Just better if I don't."

"Sit," she ordered, the tone still peaceful.

Andrew obeyed and knelt again, let Eveline place one of the babies into the curve of his arm. The terror left. His lips parted, his features melting in sweet wonderment. "I've never held a baby before," he admitted, his voice daunted. "How did you—" He couldn't put words to the emotions. "It's like a miracle."

Lily removed herself from the room, the young man's sensitivity touching the sore places within her. In the kitchen, she threw away the soiled sheets and towels, washed and scrubbed her bloodstained hands. For a moment, she did not recognize the kitchen she had so often investigated during those years of dormancy. The curtains and flowers and clean counters and working stove sprouted in the space like the first signs of life on a desert plain. The Kisers had only been here for a few days and yet the old, rotted smell was already replaced with the scents of coffee, summer air and burning wood. She dried her hands with the clean towel, a longing relaxing deeply into her belly. There was life here now. New life and growing life.

She touched the small vase of wild white roses, smelled the deep aroma within their folds.

"For the record," came the deep voice behind her, "you can throw apples at me anytime you want."

She folded the towel and smiled at the young man, suddenly taller and larger than he appeared before. He came toward her and for the first time she noticed the radiant blue eyes. A thump, nearly a knock, jolted her heart and she tapped on her chest to quell the sensation.

"How did you know what to do?" he asked, the eyes highlighted sapphire by the bright light streaming through the windows, the pupils stranded in awe.

The ache seized again. She wouldn't tell him that she was seven years old the first time she helped her sister deliver a stillborn. "Just something you pick up, I guess. Being a woman and all."

For a long moment, the man's gentle face turned and stared unfocused across the room, forlorn and intense. "I don't know what I would have done if you weren't here." He faced her then, the awe and qualm growing. He stared so long that she needed to shift under his gaze.

The intensity of the day rose in waves and hung upon her shoulders, oppressive as the still heat within the house. Raw memories battled with raw hope and she felt unsteady with the emotions mounting. She pushed the sensations down, but they crawled through the skin and made her knees shake. "I need to go home now." The statement was sudden and panicked and she knew this. Hated the weakness that her voice hinted at.

She poured a glass of water from the pitcher and went to the parlor, set it on the table. "I need to be going now, Mrs. Kiser."

"Won't you stay?" Eveline asked. "My husband should be back from town soon."

"I wish I could." She busied her mind for an excuse. "My sister will be worried. She gets nervous with me gone." The thought of meeting the other Kisers, the joys and shock of seeing the new babies while she stood in the wings and watched a family grow and celebrate, would remind her of all the ways her life was not that.

"May I come by tomorrow to visit?" Her throat started to clog with tears, could find no reason for them. She blushed at her body's betrayal, wished she could be normal for once in her life. Fit in just once. "I could bring my sister, Claire. Would that be all right?" She inched slowly from the couch.

The weariness of the birth settled upon Eveline and her eyes drooped heavily, gave no sign or notice to Lily's unbridled nerves. "That would be lovely."

Lily turned, but Eveline called out to her.

"Lily," she said as she adjusted under the weight of the babies. "I don't know how I can ever thank you."

The compliment was too much and her voice faltered. "I—they're beautiful babies, Mrs. Kiser." She sniffled and wanted to run, held her body inert for a pained moment. "Don't think I've ever seen such beautiful babies."

She brushed past Andrew, floundered with her torn sleeve as she tried to tuck the fabric back in place instead of letting it flap over her shoulder. She cursed herself as she headed outside, her footsteps thick with restrained flight.

"Hey." Andrew caught up at a trot. "Are you all right?"

She tried not to acknowledge him, hoped he would disappear along the stones or she would disappear altogether. But he stopped her, studied her profile unabashedly and without apology.

"I just don't feel well." And she didn't. She placed her hand against her forehead.

He touched her back kindly, just for a moment. "Sit for a bit. There's no rush."

She pulled her body away savagely. "Don't touch me!"

As if slapped, he stepped back. His stricken face pale. "I'm sorry. I . . ."

She dissolved into her palms, her face completely hidden behind her hands. She didn't know what was happening. She wanted to scream and punch him, wanted to beg for forgiveness, wanted to run for the forest even as she wanted to stay on this land forever. "I'm sorry," she cried.

One strong arm, hard as marble and soft as goose down, wrapped around her shoulder, turned her to his chest. He did not stroke her back, did not touch her more than necessary, simply held her as if she were about to slide into the sea.

She tried to stop crying, but everything cracked inside. She tried to breathe and stop the tears, but they broke and shattered. And still he held her without a word.

Her skin shuddered. Her sobbing finally slowed until the tears ceased. Andrew's unbleached cotton shirt cushioned wetly against her cheek. The arm around her stayed steady. The sound of a blue jay cackled from the trees. The trickle of the stream nearby went on uninterrupted. And yet here she was, her face buried into the shirt of a stranger—a stranger she had thrown apples at, screamed at, cried on.

She pulled back and he let go. "I'm sorry," she said again. "Don't know what came over me."

The young man with the blue eyes of the sky held her face in the tenderness of his expression. She could not name her grief with words, but in the gaze of this man she saw that he understood it more than she did.

"I'd like to walk you home," he said firmly.

She wiped her eyes with her torn sleeve, saw the gash at her shoulder. She smiled wearily, any fight gone. "I'm a mess, aren't I?"

"Yes." He smiled good-naturedly. "More of a disaster, actually."

She snorted. "I like to make a good first impression."

"Oh, you made an impression, all right. Doubt I'll ever walk by that tree again without cringing in fear for my life."

She rolled her eyes and shielded her brows in embarrassment.

"Ever think of enlisting?" he teased. "Send you overseas and the Germans would surrender in one day."

She crossed her arms and laughed. "Are you enjoying this?"

"Very much so." He grinned playfully and he held her eyes until the smile softened. "Come on, Honus Wagner, let's get you home."

"Who is Honus Wagner?"

"Who is Honus Wagner?" Andrew repeated loudly. "Plays for the Pittsburgh Pirates?" He grunted as if in pain. "The Flying Dutchman?"

"Who cares about football," she said slyly.

"Baseball!" He rolled his eyes in exasperation, frowned and shook his head long and low. "Oh, Lily girl, what are we going to do with you?"

She cocked her head at this.

"What?"

"You called me Lily girl."

"Hmmm." He thought of this for a moment. "So I did."

They crested the hill and walked side by side toward the sun that sparkled the weeds and the mica in the stones. The old work boots, ancient hand-me-downs from her father, grazed her knees with each step. They were too big, but the blisters had healed years ago and so they slid against her heels without a wince.

She stepped off the side flats of low grass and entered the road, walked right in the middle without any fear of meeting another soul or vehicle. Lily pointed to the right, her arm grazing his chest. "Those are the Muellers down that way. Hog farmers."

Andrew crinkled his nose. "No surprise there."

"Sure they'll pay you a visit soon. Heard they were upstate with family. Pieter Mueller's your age. You two'll probably get along fine." She turned to him curiously. "If you don't mind me saying, you don't seem like a farmer."

"No?" He shoved his hand into his pocket self-consciously, wondered if she was referring to his injury. He peeked at her, saw the eyes open and without pity, and he felt reassured. "Well, guess it doesn't matter if I seem like one or not, just what I am now." He couldn't shake her eyes peering into him.

"I always wanted to take care of animals." His

voice fell slightly. "I know that seems silly, but just what I always wanted to do. Help them, you know?"

Her eyes widened as if she was just seeing him for the first time and he realized she didn't think it was silly at all. He smiled. "They talk to me sometimes." Then corrected himself with a laugh. "Well, not really talk to me with words, but I feel like I can understand them. We're not any different if you think about it. Animals and people. We still feel. Still get scared and mad. We're not different at all, when you think about it."

She bit her lip. "I draw animals. Sometimes."

"Yeah?"

She nodded. "They're not very good. Just like to draw them, makes me feel closer to them, like you were saying. Like I don't have to hide or pretend with them." She clamped her mouth as if she had said too much.

Andrew smiled widely at her, liked her so much right then that he didn't feel the road beneath his feet or the sky above his head.

"I think it's nice you care about the animals," she said. "I think there's a special place saved in Heaven for people who care for all the creatures."

"They're probably sitting with those people who know how to deliver babies." He gave her a quick wink.

They were quiet for a while when she glanced

at him, glanced back quickly to her old work boots. "Can I ask you something? Mrs. Kiser isn't your ma, is she?"

"No. My aunt." He kicked at a pebble along the road.

"Where are your parents?" She tried to soften her voice. "I mean, if you don't mind me asking."

"My mother's in Holland. My father passed away." He grew quiet and this time she watched him, waited for an answer. When none came, she strode on quietly.

He didn't want to think about death. He wanted to keep talking to this girl with the soft smile and tender eyes. He felt playful for the first time since his accident. He brushed her arm lightly with his elbow to get her attention. "My last name isn't Kiser, by the way. It's Houghton."

From the corner of his eye, he could see her watching his profile, her expression intense. "My father was a coal miner down in Fayette County," he confided. "Died in a mining accident."

Lily walked absently, her eyes wide and staring. "Is that how you lost your arm?" she asked. "In the coal mine?"

He turned away, tightened his jaw. "No. I was working on the railroad with my uncle. I was on the roof of the train when . . . I fell." He didn't need to say more.

He turned to her and was instantly taken aback by the full, open look of her face, a look that seemed to wrap around him in an embrace. "You're lucky to be alive." The words nearly a gasp.

He had never thought of it like that. "I guess so. I nearly didn't make it. Fever almost did me in."

She brushed her elbow against his accidentally. "I'm glad it didn't."

They were silent for a few more moments before she asked, "Do you miss them? Your parents?"

"I do." He smiled at her searching face, the purity of its questioning. "I miss my father a lot. He was a good man. I miss them both."

A breeze picked up, blew Lily's golden hair around her neck. "I don't have many memories of my father," she added. "And the ones I have aren't worth remembering."

The heaviness of her words settled in his chest. "I'm sorry."

She shrugged. "My sister's all the family I have."

"And your brother-in-law."

She shot him a spark of fire before relenting. "He's not family. He's my sister's husband. I had no say in it. Didn't even have a choice about taking on his last name."

Andrew and Lily walked the miles to the Morton home in comfortable strides with small talk of the weather mingled with stories of neighbors' crops, innocuous, casual bantering that came from the throat, but between them was a steady warmth of the skin that could not have found conversation to match. And as they neared the long and rutted gravel drive through the woods, Andrew wished the walk had been much longer.

The house was not what he had expected and left him sullen. The siding was worn, the paint chipped and curling like Mary Pickford's hair. The stone walkway broken so badly that one had to walk on the parallel dirt path instead of on the stepping-stones. Lily's mood instantly turned inward and the smile seemed long forgotten as they approached the warped screen door.

"Claire?" Lily called out. She peered into the kitchen. "Claire, you in there? Want to introduce you to our neighbor."

The room was quiet until a croaked sobbing filtered over the creaking floorboards. Lily hurried into the kitchen. A woman about Eveline's age huddled in the corner, a wire basket overturned by her side. Yolks and egg whites and shells spread in a gooey mass across the splintered floor. Lily knelt next to her sister, stroked the woman's blond hair. "Claire, what's wrong?"

The woman trembled, watched the broken eggs in horror as if they were some moving assailants. "B-b-broke them, Lil. I broke them all. All of them. I b-b-br . . ."

Andrew began scooping the mess into his hand, threw it in the compost bucket. The ooze dripped through his fingers as he corralled the shells and broken bits.

"It was an accident, Claire," Lily whispered to her sister, petted the hair in long strokes. "No need to get so upset. No need." She cradled her older sister as she would a child. "It's all right, Claire. I promise."

Andrew washed his hand, picked up the wire basket and washed it off, set it next to the sink and then wet a towel, set to wiping up the last remnants of egg along the floor.

But despite her sister's comfort, Claire became more agitated and shouted, "All of them, Lil! All of them!"

Lily held her sister tight even as Claire's limbs quivered. Andrew sat down next to Claire and Lily shook her head fiercely at him in silent pleading. *Just go,* she mouthed.

He ignored her and lifted the woman's hand, held it tight in his palm. "Look at me, Claire," he ordered kindly.

"No! I b-b-broke them!"

He squeezed her hand. "Look at the floor, Claire. Just look." He let go of her fingers and forced the bobbing pupils to look where he directed. "It's all gone. It's all better. You see?"

She blinked at the space as if finally emerging from a nightmare. "It's all better," he repeated.

"We have eggs at our place. Lily will bring you a whole basket of eggs. More than you can eat. It's all better now, you see?"

A sparkle entered the wet eyes; the irises stopped their spastic movements. "Yes." She nodded. The lucidity, the clarity, cutting through the anxiety. "I'll make the cake tomorrow." She squeezed Lily's hand. "You'll bring me the eggs?"

Lily nodded, her chin set as granite, and Andrew knew if she spoke her voice would not mirror that strength.

Claire stood then, wiped down the folds of her skirt. She smiled widely, the childish smile of a toddler who fell and scraped her knee and then was off running again. She turned to Andrew, the hysterics forgotten, and she beamed. "I'll make a cake for you, too. All right?"

Andrew nodded, attempted to smile, but his insides were too sad.

"Good." Without another word, she walked to the sink, picked up the compost bucket and took it outside. The screen door banged loudly behind her.

Andrew still stared at the wake left by the woman when the warmth of Lily drifted to his skin, her expression wide and open, full and soft. He blushed without warning, the look of gratitude too deep.

"Thank you."

He drifted into the face that peered up at him. "I only cleaned up the eggs," he answered.

Lily's brow wrinkled. "Not many people are nice to her. You were nice without even trying. Didn't make her feel like there was something wrong with her."

There weren't any other words to speak in the presence of such heart. And so Andrew turned and watched his feet as they headed back to the farm, the way back as forgotten as his own name.

CHAPTER 20

Edgar and Will returned from town with pockets stuffed with white and red peppermints. Wilhelm came back with sacks of flour and sugar, salt, cartons of eggs, milk, cheese, racks of beef and lamb. He had burdened the wagon with paint cans, new saws, chisels, hammers, steel sheathing and roof tar. He carried an ice block wrapped in newspaper and set in sawdust for the icebox. He clutched in his fist a list three pages long of supplies ordered for the farm. Ice and bread would be delivered twice a week, milk and eggs every two weeks until the farm could produce its own. But no purchase or prize in town could compare with the introduction to the newly arrived Otto and Harold Kiser.

Eveline could not stay idle and was washed, dressed and presentable. Her hips and pelvis ached, but the discomfort was still less than when the twins had pummeled inside her womb. When Wilhelm returned, found her sitting in the rocking chair cradling his new sons, he was no longer a man fired from the railroad or displaced into a corroding farmhouse; he was a man who had sired four sons.

"I'll drive back to town tomorrow and bring up the doctor," Wilhelm promised as he held the tiny boys bundled in Edgar's old baby blankets.

"No need." Eveline stretched and stood, placed her hand at her lower back out of habit, pleased the shooting nerve pain was gone. "Thank goodness for that Lily Morton."

"Shouldn't have left you," Wilhelm said curtly.

"Left me?" Eveline touched one of the tiny hands that opened and closed in a feeble fist. "The poor girl delivered our babies! Should have seen the look on her face when she left. Think the labor was harder on her than it was on me."

"It's not the girl." Wilhelm's lips were tight. "I shouldn't have left you." His eyes flowed across her face and then down to the babies. "What if she hadn't been here?"

"Then Andrew would have a good story to tell his grandchildren." She rubbed her deflating belly. "He would have taken care of it. He's delivered enough animals in his life to know what to do."

"Doubt that."

She stopped then, recognized the bitter, drawn look. "Did something happen in town?"

"Know they're renaming all the German foods? Thought it was just in the city. Took the boys to supper and the menu listed hamburgers as

159

liberty sandwiches, changed sauerkraut to liberty cabbage." He chuckled wryly and without humor. "They'll be making us change our name before we know it."

"It's just food, Wilhelm."

He didn't hear her, nearly spoke on top of her last words. "But figured out why Frank Morton was so pleased to give me a ride." One of his arms squeezed Otto too tightly and the baby let out a cry. Wilhelm handed the child to his wife and she rocked him until he hushed.

"Man made me look the fool, Eve." He tensed again but made sure the pressure did not reach the sleeping Harold. She rocked Otto back and forth, kept her ears alert to Wilhelm's speech.

"Morton showed us around, all right. Paraded us to the post office, the butcher, the brewery, to Campbell's store. Talked up about the new tractor, my investments." She watched her husband carefully, not sure where he was going.

"Then started the talk."

"What talk?"

"The war talk, Eve! What do you think?"

"Don't get terse with me," she warned. She had just birthed two babies with the sheer strength of her will and body and she would not take that tone.

"Sorry." The corners of Wilhelm's mouth drooped regretfully. "It's just that before I knew it, I had half the town asking me how many

160

Liberty Bonds I'm planning on buying. How many Postal Savings Stamps. How much I'm giving to the Red Cross. Giving me a look like I'm feeding the Germans instead of the Allies." He handed the other baby to Eveline. "Frank set me up."

Men. Eveline blustered, "Frank Morton helped you, Wilhelm Kiser! He was kind enough to give you and the boys a ride to town and put in a good word for you. You should be thanking him instead of cursing him."

"No." He looked coldly ahead. "I've seen men like that before, Eve. Always trying to work an angle." He laughed then. "But he didn't get the reaction he thought. Should have seen their faces when I didn't need credit from the store. Put them in their place quick, I did." His pupils flickered as he muttered, "Liberty sandwiches. I'll be damned."

CHAPTER 21

L ily started the two-mile journey before the sun awoke. She was so grateful the Kisers had moved in. Liked them right away. Hearing those babies, holding their little hands and feet in her fingers, made her want to bury her face in their skin and nibble on their toes.

She hurried down the Kiser lane and hoped the family hadn't started breakfast yet. A light was on in an upstairs window and she entered the unlocked back door to the porch. The house was quiet and she went straight to the kitchen, loaded wood into the large stove and lit the logs with a match. She found the food supplies in the pantry and started the coffee in the black pot. She brought down two cast-iron skillets from the hook and unsheathed the bacon for frying while she mixed the batter for buttermilk pancakes.

"My word, child, what are you doing?"

Eveline's sudden voice in the kitchen startled her. "Oh, I hope you don't mind, Mrs. Kiser. I wanted to surprise you with a nice breakfast and a clean kitchen." She pushed a stray hair from her eye. "I felt terrible leaving you the way I did yesterday," she said mournfully. "Had no right walking out on you after you had those babies."

Eveline looked at the fire, stunned, her house-coat wrapped tightly around her waist. "What time did you leave your house?"

"Four thirty. I milk early. Cows get so full. Like to relieve them as soon as I can. Gets painful for them otherwise."

Eveline sat down, stared at the kitchen in confusion. Lily stirred the batter slower and slower. She had thought she was doing a nice thing for the woman, but now she realized she might have acted improperly. She didn't know. The air bubbles popped in the yellow mixture. Seemed she never knew what was right and what was wrong; she wished she'd had a mother who could have taught her manners and etiquette.

"Suppose I should have checked with you first before barging into your house," Lily said. The shame lowered her voice. She felt the fool. She had no right intruding into the Kiser home and the realization hit hard.

The woman laughed, laughed so heartily that she rocked in her chair. She finally stopped and smiled at the young woman. "Lily, I think this is about the nicest thing anyone's ever done for me."

"I'm glad." Lily let out a sigh of relief, took to ladling the griddlecakes into the hot pan with renewed vigor. "How are you feeling?"

"Better than when I was pregnant."

"And the babies?"

Eveline leaned back, the fatigue settling in dark circles under her eyes. "Can't say any of us slept. Twins cried most of the night."

"I was thinking that maybe . . ." Lily paused, kept the spatula hovering over the pan. "Well, it's just that if you need some help, I'd be happy to watch the little ones for you. Now and then, if you want."

As if on cue, a small cry wafted from upstairs followed by a second, the cries accelerating and feeding off one another. "Dear Lily," Eveline said as she pulled herself up from the chair. "I think you might have been sent straight from Heaven."

With breakfast over and the family well fed, Lily scraped the pans and washed the dishes in the boiled water, then took over with the twins while Eveline unpacked the rest of the house, still piled high with boxes from the move. Lily took the twins outside, bundling them up tightly and carrying them like two brown grocery bags against her shoulders. And their little bodies warmed her just as she warmed them, and together they explored the farm in a cozy embrace.

She turned near the barn and saw Mr. Kiser and Andrew repairing a corncrib, tightening the bolts that would keep the metal frame compact for the day when it would be bloated with corn shucks and cobs. The older boys, Will and Edgar, scattered in the yard, picking up sticks and drying them in the sun for kindling.

Lily parked on a rock under the great apple tree and peered up through the canopy of reddening apples. She had sat in those limbs whining for weeks about the Kisers coming and now she could have sung with the bluebirds. As she cradled the babies, she turned her attention back to the men at the barn—to Andrew—and tried not to look like she was staring. The young man must have been her age, probably a bit older. She watched the way he worked with the one arm, saw the set features harden when he struggled to gain a grip or was pushed aside from his uncle. She looked at her own arm, pondered what it would feel like to only have one.

Baby Otto scrunched against her breast and let out a loud wail. Both men looked up. Andrew laid his wrench on the ground and walked toward her. Suddenly shy, she wanted to run away, whispered to the baby to hush even as she angered at her own hammering pulse. She scurried off the rock and turned to head back to the house.

"Nice to see you armed with babies instead of apples," Andrew quipped from behind her.

She turned and her body stiffened, nearly calcified with the strong voice. She wanted to flee. She didn't know why, grew anxious and nervous as her sister.

Andrew came so close that his shadow climbed upon her own. "I never got to thank you for breakfast. Best meal I've had in a year." He smiled softly, beautifully, his teeth white and straight below the gentle curve of his lip. She blushed and she didn't know what was happening. She hoisted the twins up higher, thought the heat from the little bodies made her sweat. She didn't want to look at him.

"It was nothing." She started to turn back to the house, just needed some air, needed to feel normal again.

"Here." He inched closer. "Let me take one of them for you."

"No." She pulled away, felt a fierce heat fire up her neck.

"Oh." His mouth evened with the rebuff.

"It's just—" She inched back. "It's just they need to feed now. Why they're so fussy is all."

He nodded and turned around, walked slowly back to the corncrib. Lily pressed her forehead against Harold's. She felt dizzy. Scared and dizzy and she didn't know why.

Lily didn't want to stare at the young man with one arm, but she found her eyes glued upon his figure whenever he came into view, her will little against the pull. She watched him work. His tall, muscular body already tanning with the outdoor labor, his face always strong and intent with focus. But it was the light of him that seized her. A light that warmed the veins, brought color to her cheeks and made her stomach churn with anxiety when his body neared.

On this night, after working at the Kisers' all day, Lily returned home in the same dull darkness that dawn had brought that morning. Her thoughts were heavy, not with work but with an indescribable weight. There was warmth back at the Kiser homestead. Despite the crumbling, mildew-stained house, the warmth of babies and smiles and family erased all that was unlovely.

Andrew flashed before her again and the heat came back, made her swallow. He was always being so nice to her and she didn't know why. She couldn't even speak to him without wanting to run away. Maybe inside he mocked her. This made her insides sour. After all, she was just a dumb country girl. She had been to town enough times to know what pretty girls looked like, and she wasn't one of them. The young women in town had clean, store-bought dresses and satin ribbons tied in their hair. They wore shiny shoes and stockings that made their legs appear longer and more defined. She'd never been jealous of those girls before, more curious than anything. Lily was of the same gender but a different breed altogether.

Andrew's blue eyes followed her home, so clear and deep that they pierced into her skin.

Yes, that was it. They saw right through her, and nobody wanted to see what was in there. When he looked at her, there was nowhere to hide and she wanted to hide. It was always safer to hide.

Lily entered the worn Morton house distracted and feeling low. She had probably overstayed her welcome at the Kisers', but she didn't want to leave, would have gladly slept in the limbs of the apple tree if given the chance. But she had happily helped Eveline get the twins down and the older boys to bed. Made her feel good. Feel useful.

All the lights were off except for the oil lamp that Claire had left on in the kitchen. Lily turned off the flame and headed upstairs to her room. Frank's snoring labored from behind the wall. Lily lit the Rochester wick on her old lamp and turned the knob to the lowest brightness. From beneath her mattress she pulled out a sketchbook and a pencil worn down to half its original length. She flipped the pages, nearly all the spaces filled with drawings. She cherished the book as her only true belonging. One day, the pages would be filled, with no more space to sketch, and her fingers would lie idle.

This night she drew a rabbit, small and fragile beneath an expanse of trees, the round eyes black and glistening. They peered up to the boughs and leaves, wanted to be them instead of a small creature hiding amid the blades of grass.

The light flickered at her nightstand, seemed to glisten the matte lead and make the rabbit's eyes truly bright. She closed the book and hid it and the pencil back under the mattress.

Lily inspected her hand, the right side of the palm gray from rubbing on the graphite. She stared at the ceiling, the warped and sagging plaster, and the heaviness came and wet her eyes. *Don't let my light go out,* she begged silently, her prayer since childhood. She closed her eyes and tears squeezed from the corners. The darkness pulsed around her covers, slinking and waiting for her to be weak and let it in. *But I won't.* She gritted her teeth stubbornly, defiantly. *I won't let you take me.* She cried now, kept the tears locked in her thumping chest so no one would hear. *Please, God.* She prayed to everything and nothing. *Please don't let my light go out.*

CHAPTER 22

A ndrew took the smallest bedroom in the house. After Will and Edgar worked by his side repainting the walls, they displayed his few belongings and books along the top of the bureau. Will picked up Andrew's football, the threadbare leather patched at the tips. "You play football?" he asked.

"Used to." Andrew pressed the top of the paint can loosely, then hammered down the rim. "You can have it if you want."

The little boy rubbed the ball. "Could you play with me? With me and Edgar?" he asked, the question tentative.

"It's too late. Maybe tomorrow." He was distracted and half-listened, had been irritable all day. "Why don't you and Edgar run off to bed now. I'll finish up in here."

Will stepped closer. "I could help you."

I don't need any help, he wanted to shout but kept his mouth shut, ignored the child's offer.

Will gave a slight toss to the football, but when he tried to catch it the ball landed on one of the paintbrushes and knocked it to the floor, splattering cream paint across the hardwood.

"I'm sorry—" Will chased the wayward ball, but Andrew caught it first.

"Just go," Andrew snapped. His temper rose without warning. "Both of you. Just give me some peace, all right?"

Edgar and Will dropped their heads. "Just wanted to help," Will sniffled.

Andrew turned away without a response, began wiping up the spilled paint with an old rag. Two small arms came from behind and hugged his waist. "I'm sorry," came the little voice before the two boys left the room and closed the door.

Andrew threw the rag to the floor and plopped down on his bottom, rubbed his forehead. He stared at the newly painted walls, his cousins' artistry that left patches of white between uneven and sloppy paint strokes. He shouldn't have been harsh with the boys. He saw Will's face, the crushed expression, and the guilt poked. After all, on most days the little boys were the only ones who helped him forget the pain, the loss and homesickness that waited in the shadows.

But even the boys couldn't offer relief today. For the telegram came this morning from his mother overseas. Only an address, nothing more. No words of her travel. No words of the fighting or her health. No warm memories of his father or mention of his severed limb. Only her address. And the absence of sentiment spoke louder than any commissioned typing—after the loss of her husband, the pain of her son's deformity was more than she could bear.

The contrast between his mother's rebuff and his cousins' affinity stood out bold and blunt. He'd make it up to them tomorrow, play ball until it was too dark to see. But he knew it wasn't just his mother's telegram that set him off. He was getting too close to this family. Growing up in the coal mines, one learns quickly not to give away the heart so freely; in the mines, every greeting is laced with a farewell. He had been well taught and the lesson learned—life has a way of taking away what you love the most.

Andrew finished cleaning up the paint cans, the brushes and the floor. With hand at his hip, he viewed the room. Home. And yet he never felt more lost.

The window in his room yawned widely, the temperate night air full with the infused scents of honeysuckle and lilac. Andrew took off his shirt to cool his skin and sat cross-legged on the quilt, swinging his father's miner tags in front of him like a pendulum. He thought about the work of the day, the inability to do any task quickly or efficiently. He had tried to carry rocks for the new stone wall but couldn't grip the round edges with his one hand. He settled for smaller stones and filled the wheelbarrow. He lifted the handgrip and thought he could balance, only to have the wheelbarrow fall to the side and the rocks roll out. He couldn't patch the roof because he couldn't work and hold on at the same time. He was the first one up and the last one to bed and still his efforts were only a quarter of his former production.

Andrew stopped swinging the miner tags and peered into the warped metal for answers. "I don't know how to do this," he whispered to his father. His nostrils flared. "I don't know what to do."

His chest was bare and he forced his eyes to his torn left shoulder. He wanted nothing more than to turn away, but he kept his focus on the curled and unnatural flesh, the raw ugliness of it. The very sight of the amputation site nauseated to the core and yet this body was all he had—an ugliness he would own for the rest of his life.

Finally, he pulled his eyes away and dropped the tags on the patchwork quilt. A coyote howled plaintively far away in the woods. Another followed and then a series of devilish yaps crowded the previously calm night. He peered out the window, couldn't see another light or house. He wondered if he was the only one awake, wondered if the woman with green eyes and golden hair was asleep in her bed.

He pushed the density of the day away, ripped the telegram in his mind and focused on the young woman up the road. Andrew grinned then, his mood levitating with the breeze. There was a wildness to Lily Morton but a grace as well, the way a meadow can be wild and overgrown with flowers—a simple, natural beauty that fills the heart with hope that such a land will never be tamed and will always bloom freely.

Thank God she delivered those babies, he thought to himself for the hundredth time. Andrew flopped back to his pillow, ran his fingers through his hair so the strands stood up by the roots. He smiled in reverence. He knew she had been scared delivering those twins, but no one else would have seen it. He wasn't sure why he could, but he knew she had been as terrified as he had been.

He waited for exhaustion to take over as his thoughts drifted off to a woman in a torn green dress and old work boots with a smile that blinded everything around its edges. Yes, Lily was the meadow. He rolled over and the nerves pinched painfully around the missing limb. And, he reflected contritely, he was the severed stump on the outskirts.

The cows arrived from the dairy farm in Cumberland County, filled the stalls of the barn. The new hogs grunted in the pen behind. The horse and chickens would arrive in a few days. And the Kiser clan left the grind and the hardness of the city behind and eased into farm life one animal and chore at a time. The transition left them cringing at first, until they sighed into the new routines, the way one pulls thick socks off blistered feet.

Andrew and Wilhelm patched the holes and cracks in the barn with new wood. They lined rocks and mortar along the foundation. Wilhelm covered the holes in the old roof with new shingles Andrew handed up to him. Hay stocks, fresh and dusty, filled the lofts and stacked the sides of the barn. The lane, still impassable, necessitated the use of pitchforks and bale hooks to transport the hay squares from wagon to hand-pushed wheelbarrows, the work long and prickly.

The privy was long bloated and honey dippers were called to dig a new one, bury the old and move the ratty wooden closet atop the new hole. Edgar and Will delighted in calling down the clean pit while their voices ricocheted against the black sides.

After supper, Andrew worked in the chicken coop, scooping out the years of compact feces and seed husks from the floor, nearly a foot high. The stink had long been removed, but the feathers and history of warm chickens itched his skin. He took a thick shovelful of muck out and was leaning the wooden handle hard against his shoulder for leverage when Will came running up the hill.

"Andrew!" Will hollered from the lane. Little

Edgar ran close to his heels. Andrew propped the shovel against the coop.

"Somebody's out there!" Edgar cried. The boys screeched to a halt, their eyes wide and nervous. "He's throwing rocks at us!"

"Big rocks and sticks and stuff," Will huffed between breaths, showing a small scratch on his cheek. They pointed down the lane in unison.

"All right," Andrew said. "I'll check it out."

Will grabbed his arm. "He's a big man. Like a monster."

Edgar nodded. "Like a big, hairy monster."

"All right." Andrew patted Edgar's head. "Stay here and I'll be back in a minute."

But the boys looked all around in a panic. "We can't stay here. What if he finds us?" Will whined. "He'll lock us in the coop and eat our brains or something."

Andrew grinned. "Okay, come with me then. Show me where you saw this monster."

Andrew walked steadily down the lane while Will and Edgar hid behind his back, weaving unnaturally like a Chinese lion parade.

"Ouch!" Edgar rubbed his arm.

"What's wrong—ouch!" The small rock bounced against Andrew's chest before another one knocked him on the forehead. Will cried, retreated to the house.

Andrew grabbed Edgar by the collar and pulled him to safety in the barn. More rocks pelted the sky, the source of the assault stemming from a large arm throwing in a steady pitch. Andrew put Edgar in one of the stalls. "Stay here. Got it?"

Stealthy as a fox, Andrew shimmied around the back of the barn, saw the back of a mammoth of a man crouching around the corner. Andrew picked up a slender metal pipe and tiptoed closer to the form. Without a sound, he jabbed the pipe between the man's enormous shoulder blades. "Stand up."

The man stiffened and began to shake, started to turn around.

"Look straight ahead!" Andrew ordered. "Put your hands up."

The man stretched to his full height and Andrew gulped; he'd never seen a man so tall. The hands in the air quaked violently.

"Who are you?"

The arms shook more, rattled down the wide back.

"I said, who are you?" Andrew pushed the pipe harder into the back.

A whimper radiated from the enormous body. "Don't shoot me!" he wailed. Deep sobs winded the man. "I'm sorry!"

Andrew pulled the pipe away. "Turn around."

Slowly, the man faced Andrew, his face red and slimy from tears. But it was not the face of a man, the features puffy and nearly childlike, a young boy's head transplanted on a statue of a lumberjack. "I'm sorry," he whimpered. "Didn't mean to hurt nobody. I'm sorry."

"For Christ's sake, Fritz!" Another voice gained momentum as a figure jogged down the lane.

The blubbering man ran and grabbed on to the stranger. He bent and cried into his shoulder. "I'm sorry, Pieter! I'm sorry!"

"Goddammit, Fritz, what you go and do now?" Pieter's anger waned as he patted the big man-child on the back. "Settle down now. Okay? Just settle yourself." He met Andrew's eyes square and then rolled them. "I'm sorry about this. My brother doesn't know what he's doing sometimes. He didn't hurt anyone, did he?" Fritz looked up at Andrew, his eyes pleading.

Andrew dropped the pipe and kicked it away. "He was throwing some rocks is all. Kids got spooked."

Edgar snuck out of the barn and pointed. "He threw rocks at me and Will. Hit me square in the head!"

Pieter shook his head. "What the hell you doing throwing rocks at kids, Fritz?" he scolded, exasperated. "Know better than that! What the hell you doing that for?"

Fritz crumpled onto his bottom and held his knees to his chest, rocked against the reprimand.

Edgar glanced at Andrew and approached the crying form. "I'm okay," he consoled tentatively.

"Didn't really hurt." He fished through his pocket and pulled out a piece of hard candy, unwrapped and stuck with pocket lint. "Here." He handed the sweet to the man-boy. "It's butterscotch."

Fritz blinked at the outstretched hand and smiled so widely through his tears that the sun nearly came from his skin. He took the dirty butterscotch and put it in his mouth, stared at the little boy as if he loved him.

"What you say to these people now?" prodded Pieter.

The man sucked on the butterscotch, content and lively. "I'm sorry I threw rocks at you. I ain't gonna ever do it again." His enormous jaw bit into the candy. "Fritz ain't never gonna cause trouble again."

Edgar, suddenly enlivened by his new friend, the rock pummeling now erased from his mind, grabbed Fritz's hand. "Come on. You can help me clean the coop."

Pieter watched the two disappear around the corner. He rubbed the back of his neck, struggling between humor and embarrassment. "Sorry about my brother. He's not a bad kid, just doesn't know any better." He carved the toe of his boot into the ground. "Wouldn't know it by looking at him, but he's as gentle as a mouse. Just thought he was playing a game. He just doesn't know better." He stuck out a hand of goodwill. "Pieter Mueller."

"Andrew Houghton."

"Houghton? Heard the name was Kiser."

"My uncle. Wilhelm Kiser."

The young man pumped the hand heartily. "Well, you already met my brother, Fritz. Would have come by sooner but been visiting my sister upstate. Just had her fifth kid. Was on my way over to invite you all up for dinner when Fritz barreled ahead. Ma didn't want to bother you yet case your aunt didn't have the house ready for guests. Women get all funny with that stuff, don't they? Give me a rock to sit on and I'm happy as a goat."

Pieter mirrored his age, maybe a bit older, mid-height and slim, night and day from his brother. He had blond hair and freckles from the sun that carried down his forehead and across the bridge of his nose. He pointed to the new pigpen behind the barn. "How many pigs you got?"

"Two."

"Mind if I take a look? Know a thing or two about hogs. Got more than we can count up our way. Heard of Mueller sausage? Best damn German sausage in the state. Pa grew up in Nuremberg making the stuff." He raised one eyebrow confidentially. "Secret family recipe."

Andrew led the way to the sty where two enormous sows rolled in the mud and sunned scaly pink skin. "Look fine," Pieter acknowledged, impressed. "Never can tell what you're getting when you bring them in. Even at auction, can't hardly tell if they're switching out stock right before they load them up."

A deep draw of air left Pieter's mouth. "One of our gilts birthed early. Not able to feed the lot of them. Only enough milk to feed about two. Big birth, too. Nearly twelve in the litter. Two full ones, the rest runts."

Andrew splashed freshwater from the rain barrel into the trough. "What are you going to do with them?"

"Nothing to do. Little ones won't last more than a few days."

"You bottle-feeding?"

"Piglets won't make it. No use."

Andrew thought of this, looked over at the two large pigs. "Would you be open to me taking the runts?"

"What for?" Pieter scrunched his face as if Andrew had made a sick joke, like he worried Andrew might do something cruel.

"Might be able to save a few."

Relief flooded the man's face. "Be pleased to. Nobody likes to see the runts die slow like that; don't want to drown them, either. Squealing too much for the heart."

Andrew threw the empty bucket next to the barrel. "Nursed calves before, can't imagine piglets are too different."

"Bit flat chested, I think," Pieter crooned, and smacked him in the ribs. "Tell you what, come over and grab the runts and if they live they're yours. Course, your nips might never be the same again."

"Very funny." Andrew laughed. Pieter reminded him of his friends at the mine, good-natured and quick, easygoing.

"Between you and me, we've been mighty relieved knowing Germans moving into this place." Pieter looked around. "War making people itch like they got fleas. Looking for someone to blame for all that itching. Guess it's us getting the brunt."

Pieter scanned the fields. "Jesus Christ, you don't got more than a heap of weeds and crabgrass trying to grow out there. Frank Morton swindle you into this place?"

"Far as I can see, my uncle went in with eyes wide open."

"He needs glasses then," cackled Pieter. He slapped Andrew on the back. "You come for dinner tomorrow night, all right? Ma make you the best goddamn sausage you ever ate. I'll get those piglets ready, too." He suddenly dropped his tone and pointed his chin at Andrew. "How'd you lose your arm?" The question fell out as easily as if he inquired about the rain.

"Fell off a train."

"Ouch!" Pieter gritted his teeth. "Well, we all got something to live with, don't we?" His eyes took on a hint of remorse as he looked at his brother playing hide-and-seek near the chicken coop. "Let Fritz clean out the coop for you. Take that ox an hour with those muscles. Teach him a lesson to not throw rocks at little kids." He started to walk backwards. "Just send him home when he's done."

Pieter walked forward and then swiveled, hollered back, "Kiser, huh?" He gave a robust laugh. "Thought we had it bad. One hell of a name, my friend. One hell of a name for sure!"

CHAPTER 23

The residents of the Kiser farm made the long walk to the Muellers' and each ached at the sight of the newly painted farmhouse with wide porch and perfect fence. Edgar jumped from the road into the wide front lawn. "They have grass!" And in those simple three words, the young child summed up the vast lack of their own homestead.

With the sound of guests walking the even lane, two men appeared from the high red barn. One a reflection of the other, a future aged imprint. Pieter Mueller approached from the gate and Wilhelm stuck out his hand. "Pieter and Heinrich Mueller, I'm guessing."

The older shook hands greedily. "*Ja*! Good t'meet you. Velcome!"

Andrew and Pieter nodded to each other in the casual way of young men.

"Come, come!" The man hurried and waved them to the house where they were greeted by an enormous Gerda Mueller, who hugged them with arms as large as thighs. She had yellow-and-white-streaked hair piled high into a bun on the back of her head and a spirit and voice to match the body. The difference between the figures of the married Muellers could not have been more extreme.

Gerda grabbed the twins from Eveline and rocked them gently, whispered German words into their ears. A pounding on the stairs above gave way to Fritz and soon, behind him, a little girl. Gerda explained that their older children were spread out in Indiana and Jefferson Counties, while Pieter, his younger brother, Fritz, and eight-year-old Anna still remained at home.

Minutes after arriving, the groups branched off into tributaries of commonality. The younger children and Fritz ran off to the outdoors, sharing that secret laughter of searching for an adventure that an adult would never understand. Pieter took Andrew to the barns to show him the piglets and the other animals. Eveline took back the twins and followed Gerda into a kitchen that smelled of hot bread, potatoes and peppercorns.

Gerda Mueller placed a spread of cheeses and hard sausage, pickled cucumbers and onions at the table. Then added loaves of brown bread with a bowl of butter. She brought steins, three in each enormous hand, each nearly big enough for a quart, and set them next to the worn cask on the side table. Heinrich poured the liquid, dark as molasses, into two steins and handed one to Wilhelm. "I brew myself," he said proudly. "Grow the grains. Everyt'ing by hand. Made here by me."

The beer was rich and strong and cold. With that first taste Wilhelm relaxed, couldn't remember the last time he had a real drink, hadn't realized how stiff he had been. His muscles melted like warm butter under the sun.

Mr. Mueller watched him expectantly. "You like?"

Wilhelm smiled and wiped the froth from his lips. "I like."

Heinrich Mueller wrestled a hand to Wilhelm's shoulder. "Course you like!" He opened his arms wide and then thumped his chest. "Everyt'ing I make here. Beer. Sausage. I don't need not'in' from out there no more. Got twelve children an' six grandchildren." He thumped his chest again. "More Muellers in Pennsylvania than veevils!" He guffawed richly and it took a minute for Wilhelm to understand the accent. *Weevils. More Muellers than weevils.* Wilhelm laughed hard, a good, deep laugh of a man, and it felt good. He took another deep gulp of beer. It was good to be a man, feel like a man again.

Heinrich turned serious eyes on his neighbor. "Vhy you come this time, Vilhelm? To the land, I mean. Spring much better, no?"

Wilhelm didn't answer at first. Chewed the question along with the blue-veined cheese.

"You find trouble in Pittsburgh?" Heinrich asked. "Vith the German var?"

The man's thick accent was getting easier to understand or maybe the stout helped translate. "No, had nothing to do with the war." He didn't want to share the details and glanced at the kitchen. "My wife. Been wanting to move from the city since we married. But you're right about poor timing. Spending a small fortune bringing in supplies."

"*Ja, ja,*" he agreed. "Land is poor, too. But few years of thick manure in the fields, the soil be good again. Plant corn in the high fields and hay where ground is clay. Will break it up over time. Plus, hay sells. Good hay, poor hay. It sells." He nodded knowingly. "Sweet potatoes, too. Can grow through rocks."

Wilhelm didn't want to talk about the land that mocked him, told him he was a fool. He wanted to drink beer and eat smoked sausage. He didn't want to think about the outpouring of money that had outpaced even his most inflated planning. Didn't want to think about the animals and the human mouths that had to be fed or the house that he should have inspected before buying but was too ill in spirit to do so.

Heinrich observed him, read his thoughts. "Hard times, no?" The man smacked him on the knee.

Wilhelm stared at the dark liquid and nodded.

"I know this. I know this vell, my friend." He winked like a wise sage. "Vhen Gerda and I come here, ve don't have nothin'. Less than nothin'." His hands opened widely with an empty expanse. "Then the babies come. I vas like a lost man. I did any job to find work. Plowing, seeding, thrashing, milking. It vas a very hard time for me. For us. But ve vorked hard. I vork very, very hard." He waved out his hand and displayed the comfort of the sitting room proudly. "I vork hard to provide fer my family, and I did." He winked again and drank a large swig of beer. "You'll get there, too. Long as you can vork, you can get there."

The alcohol and sentiment warmed, thickened his bones and muscles again, pushed the gray out. The farm would be there tomorrow. Today, he would drink and listen to an old German's stories; he'd debate about the state of the war and listen to the hooting and yelling of children playing outside. He would not think of the winter that loomed or the emaciated figures of his accounts. Wilhelm found the dry bottom of the stein and held it out. "May I?" Heinrich laughed happily and refilled each of their mugs.

Next to the kitchen stove, Gerda checked on the roast, ladled the juices over the giant slab of meat. Eveline's mouth watered with the smell. Gerda peeked at the men in the other room and made a light-sounding click with her tongue. "Your husband a drinker?"

The question surprised her. "No. Hardly at all."

Gerda chuckled and raised her eyebrows. "Vell, he might be sleepin' late tomorrow. Heinrich's beer stronger than it looks." She fluttered suddenly and went to the cupboard and took out a tall glass bottle without a label, the syrupy liquid holding a tint of yellow. She poured two small glasses and handed one to Eveline.

"Oh, I don't drink," she said, and pushed the glass away.

"No, you'll like this one," Gerda insisted, and pushed it back toward her. "Pear schnapps. Ever try?"

"No."

Gerda watched her with widening eyes as she gave the daintiest taste to the liquid. It smelled like a dream and tasted like sweet sugar fire. She touched her lips, giggled. "It's quite good."

"*Ja!*" Gerda put the glass rim to her lips and drank it clean, poured another. "Men don't need to have all the fun, no?" She smiled, sisterly, and Eveline saw the beauty of the woman beyond the large features. There was a strength to her, a beauty that came from confidence and sureness of something akin to power and she was envious.

Gerda sipped this one slowly, tilted her head to the other room again. "Men talkin' about vork and var. Men always think the world rests on their shoulders, that they run it. But ve vomen know, don't ve, Eveline? Ve know that vithout the vomen, there are no men. Vithout the vomen, the men be sittin' in the outhouse sucking their thumbs and cryin' into their dirty undershirts."

A sudden burst of laughter escaped from Eveline and she covered her mouth.

"The men be sitting on that privy sucking thumbs and starving," Gerda managed between bouts of laughter. "Eating raw onions from the fields and shitting themselves because they don't know how to butter their own bread."

Eveline rocked and held her belly, giggled until tears sprung to her eyes.

"Vhat you hens cackling about?" Heinrich called with amusement from the next room.

Gerda put her finger to her lips secretly and calmed her tittering. "Lady stuff. Talkin' babies and hairpins, my sveet."

Two loud humphs echoed in response and the women held their mouths.

"Speakin' of babies. Let's have a good look at these two." Gerda reached to the basket on the floor and pulled each baby to her lap expertly, supporting the heads in the corners of her arms.

Eveline turned away and drank her schnapps. She had a hard time looking at her own babies. Couldn't even enjoy their little faces for fear the mouths would open in howling and begging.

Gerda turned to Eveline, her eyes no longer

jovial. "They're light." She shook her head gravely. "Like air, these two."

Eveline held the empty glass between her hands, felt the heat of shame knowing she couldn't feed her own babies. "They're colicky." It was all she knew how to say.

"No," the woman said grimly. "No, not colicky. Hungry." She tried to get Eveline to look at her. "Are you dry?"

"Yes." She pressed against the glass, thought it might break between her fingers. "Wasn't at first. Had more milk than I could manage. But they wouldn't drink, and when they did they threw it up. I've been nervous. I don't know."

Gerda's eyes filled with concern as she propped one baby and then the other.

"The doctor came out. He—"

"Dr. Neeb?" Gerda interrupted.

"Yes."

"Ack." She rolled her eyes. "Man shouldn't touch a baby. He vorks vith the dead more than the living." She raised her eyebrows wisely. "Trust me. He digs up dead bodies and studies them. Keeps them in his basement. Fishes out frogs from the creeks and opens 'em up, stores the innards in jars." She shuddered.

Eveline remembered the smell of formaldehyde on the little man and cringed. "Well, he told me to stop nursing and only feed them cow's milk. We give them the milk from the healthiest cow we got. None of us touch it for butter or cream or for ourselves. Just for the babies and they cough it all up." The words tasted bitter. She reached for the schnapps to wipe the taste away.

"These babies are sick, Eveline," the woman said gently but firmly. "There's something in the milk that no good for them."

"What am I supposed to do, stop giving them milk?" She said the words as if they were crazed speech.

"That's exactly vhat I'm saying. Something not right vith the milk for them. Try goat milk. If still comes up, mash up oatmeal or rice vith vater."

"I tried that, but they choke on it." Her hand reached for her throat as if something held it.

Gerda leaned forward and patted her knee. "This is no fault of yours, Eveline. Take no shame."

Her chin wrinkled. She did take shame in it. "I can't feed my own children," she whispered, despondent.

"God gives vomen the greatest gift, to be able to create and carry and birth a new life. God gives vomen—only vomen!—that miracle." The woman held her eyes and would not let her look away. "But God also gives a curse in the same gift. For ve love these little ones that grow inside of us so much that ve forget that ve are only humans and our bodies can do only vhat they can do."

Gerda leaned back then and smiled at the drowsy babies. "I had twelve children. Twelve miracles. But there has been suffering, too. And I felt this shame that you feel, dear Eveline. That I did something wrong. That I was not a goot enough woman and so my children had to suffer."

Her gaze wandered to the window. "You saw my Fritz. Saw that his mind no good. Doesn't work right." Sadness drifted over the large features, aged them. "My Fritz a good boy. As good a boy as you could get but slow, you see. Nearly a man but vith the mind of a little boy. His birth vas hard, Eveline. Very hard." She shuddered with the remembrance. "Ten children before came out like vith a sneeze, but not this one. Feet first and the cord wrapped around his neck. Blue he vas. Blue like a sky ripe vith storm. But he lived but vas never right. But it's okay. He a good boy. Works hard. Like an ox." She patted Eveline on the sleeve. "You need a strong back, call on my Fritz."

The woman's hands went idle in her large lap. "Then, there's my youngest, my sweet Anna."

Eveline was surprised. The girl seemed perfect in every way.

Gerda nodded at this, read her mind. "Yes, seems perfect. But look closely and you'll see." She painted a line at the edge of her forehead at the hairline. "She vears a vig. My Anna hasn't a hair on her head. Got scarlet fever when she was four. Almost lost her, but by some miracle she lived, but she'll be bald her whole life."

Eveline's chest hollowed. "I'm so sorry, Gerda."

But the woman's eyes sparkled. "It's just hair, you see. And my Fritz, it's just his mind. They're still here vith me."

She turned back to the babies and her eyes grew sad. And Eveline knew Gerda did not see the same life in her children as she saw in Anna and Fritz.

Andrew and Pieter stepped through one of five pigpens at the far north of the property. The earth was hard and packed, as the rains had been lean that August. Only the areas near the long troughs were wet and slick, thick with mud laced with withering lettuce leaves and carrot tops. Pieter took him over to a low, wooden covered stall and peeked in the door. "Piglets are in there. Lost another one overnight, so doubt they'll make it through the week. But give it a try. I'll wrap them in a basket before you leave."

The men entered the wide door of the three-story bank barn, the air warm and husky, sweetened with fresh hay and the smell of steaming farm animals. The barn was huge and Pieter examined the girth with hands on his hips, nodded with approval as if he had built it. "It's a good barn. Strong. Some of those beams over a foot thick." He walked to the right to the cow stalls. "These are our new ones, Holsteins. Can't get better milkers than the Holsteins. Even the farmers that hate the Germans know that." He nodded proudly. "This bunch only been here a couple weeks, but been milking as good as our others."

Pieter patted the nose of a large black-and-white cow, her nose wet and wide. "She's our lead cow. Make sure you have one, too. If they get out, haul the lead cow in first and the others will follow."

Andrew noticed all the fresh feed stacked in the corners. "That's a lot of hay."

"Yeah, but you're gonna need a hell of a lot more, my friend. Got no grass, remember?"

"How could I forget? We've been letting the cows feed in the woods until the cold sets in. Trying to conserve the hay."

Pieter stuck out his tongue. "Need to watch that. Milk starts to taste like pine needles. If you got a pregnant cow, the needles will make her abort. Happened to us a few times before we fenced the woods off."

The young man smacked the cow's backside affectionately before walking the length of the barn to check out the goats and the pigs. A barn cat and her kittens watched from a dark corner, the mama kitty oblivious to the strangers while her kittens pressed the milk from her underside.

Andrew inspected the other animals, robust in good health. Pieter watched him. "If you don't mind me saying, you don't strike me as the farming type."

Andrew chuckled at that. "You're the second person to tell me that. I have a book engraved on my forehead or something?"

"Not sure what it is. Farmers got a certain look to them, you know? Like they couldn't talk fast if they wanted to. You got that look like you're ready to sprint."

"Well, you're right about not knowing farming, but I know animals." He rubbed the hair of the spotted horse that sidled up to the paddock. "Used to help with the animals growing up and know how to till a garden, but farming a property I don't have a clue."

Pieter made a face like he was going to whistle. "Well, you getting off to a great start, my friend. A hundred acres without a blade of grass or chicken for soup."

Andrew nodded. "Well, we got apples. Saw that first thing," he said lightly. "And the chickens are coming."

Pieter slapped him on the back. "Yeah, you got apples, my friend. About the only thing you guys got up there. But don't worry. We Muellers haven't got sense for anything but farming. We'll help you if you need it."

The young men left the animals behind.

Fritz passed them, took turns carrying the little children upon his broad shoulders as they lanced imaginary knights on imaginary steeds. Will and Edgar, two foals who finally found strength within their spindly legs, hiccupped with laughter that sang upon the air no different than the chirps of sparrows.

Pieter and Andrew headed off to a trail in the woods, through the layer of pines and into the rows of oaks and maples and tulip trees. The young men shuffled a pinecone between them, back and forth over the sticks and raised roots. The air was cooler under the trees and they were comfortable, only stopping when a stealth spider-web clung on a low limb to drape upon a face.

Andrew kicked the cone to Pieter's shin. "We met the Mortons. Lily's been working at the house, helping my aunt with the babies," he shared.

A slight chuckle left Pieter's mouth. He nodded but did not add anything, his smile in a thin, amused line. He kicked the cone back.

Andrew added, "Seem nice."

With that, Pieter smiled unabashedly and kicked his pinecone deep into the woods. "She's pretty, isn't she? Lily, I mean."

"Yeah," Andrew agreed, and suddenly realized that Lily and Pieter might be more than neighbors.

"Pretty as poison."

Andrew stopped. "What does that mean?"

Pieter smiled, but warning tainted his expression. "If you're smart, you'll stay away from that one."

"If she's your girl, just say so."

"Ha!" Pieter smacked at a fly hovering around his nose. "Don't have to worry about that. Poison, remember?" Pieter rubbed his elbow, contrite. "Better keep your distance. That's all. Morton house carries more skeletons than the cemetery."

Andrew's pace slackened when they started moving again. He kicked at the stones along the path, missed having the pinecone as a distraction.

Pieter jumped to reach an old bird's nest, averting the twigs by inches. His face grew serious. "The Morton house used to belong to Claire and Lily's father—Mr. Hanson." He pointed up the drive to an unseen spot above the road.

"Before Mr. Hanson moved up this way, word is he traveled around the mills, targeting the immigrants, scamming them. A grifter. Guess word started getting round about him, so he left the city and moved to the house where the Mortons are now. But they never farmed that land. Had some cows and chickens but not even a vegetable patch as far as I can remember. Anyway, folks say he took the money he made from all those scams and started lending to rural immigrants. Before you knew it, he was giving loans to half the farmers up this way. Not my pa, though. Pa said he'd feed us hay and oats before he'd take a nickel from that son of a bitch— '*Sohn von einem Weibchen,*' he'd scream out." Pieter laughed at his imitation of his father.

Pieter rubbed the back of his neck then, looked like a man with heavy accounts resting on his shoulders. "We've had tough times here. Tough years for sure. Pa could have gone running to Hanson more times than I could count. Pa always said that a man who got to pick at the carcass of a man falling on hard times is no better than a cockroach.

"After Hanson's wife died, something happened to that man. Like all the bad things he done to people came outta his skin, like he was going crazy with rage. I was young at the time, but my sisters said they'd see Claire heading to school bleeding most days, bruised nearly all the time. Then she stopped coming altogether. Ma went up there a couple times, but no one answered the door. She'd leave food on their front steps on Sundays, but never knew if or who ate it."

Pieter gave a clean spit to the ground. "Then about ten years ago, Hanson was found shot in the back, lying in the puddle near the house. No one ever figured out who did it. The man made so many enemies could have been anyone."

Pieter's face shifted again face tightened with

anger. "Frank Morton stepped up soon after and married Claire straightaway. Took over Hanson's loans and property before the dust settled on the grave. Turned out to be as ruthless as Hanson."

Pieter's sudden vehemence shocked him. A rush of heat simmered down his nerves and he pulled Pieter to a stop by the arm. "Is he hitting those women?"

"No, nothing like that," Pieter scoffed. "Not that I know of, anyway. Doubt Lilith would let him put a hand on her or her sister. She's a tough cookie, that one." He winked. "Once I saw some boys throwing rocks at a cat they had cornered and she came charging at them with a stick half her size. She came screaming like a banshee, swinging that stick at their backs till they ran crying. And these weren't little boys, either, near men."

Pieter laughed at that before turning serious again. "There was a farm about ten miles north from here. Norwegian family named Paulsen. Nice family. There was a girl there, Mary." He fell into thought for a moment, a long, pained moment. "She and Lily were friends. Lily usually kept to herself, but she and Mary got on. We were all friends, playing in the woods like kids do. But Mary was my girl. Pa always made a fuss about her not being German, but inside he liked her as much as everybody else."

His voice dropped. "Paulsens got in debt with

Frank and lost the farm. Lost everything and had to move back to Minnesota. Still remember seeing Mary, couldn't even look at me as they drove away in that wagon, kids and pots and chairs piled high. And at the auction—when they were rattling off all their farm stuff—who you think was sitting front and center picking at the bones?"

"Frank?"

"No." He stepped forward and glowered. "Lily. Raising her number for everything Mary used to own. Dresses. Jewelry. Even the tea set she played with as a girl.

"Look, I'm not trying to tell you what to do or who to like." He pointed up the lane. "But there's a lot of demons up that way. Better to stay clear of them all." Pieter twisted his mouth. "Said you got apples at your place, about all you got, right? Well, you know what they say about apples . . . don't fall far from the tree."

The two men inched down a deep slope, the boot soles sliding in the underbrush. "You play baseball?" Pieter asked suddenly.

"Used to."

"What position?"

"Pitcher."

"Yeah? We got a game coming up against the Hornets, team on the other side of town. Play every week. You in?"

He hadn't touched a baseball since the accident,

probably couldn't throw straight if he wanted. "There's a lot of work to do. Doubt it."

Pieter studied him. "All right. Think about it. We got the only Germans on our side and the other boys act like they're going to war against us at every bat. Feel good to teach them a lesson now and then."

"Maybe I'll come and watch." He smirked and challenged, "Maybe I'll bring Lily with me."

Pieter grew quiet. "You'll see Lily's not welcomed too many places, Andrew." Any chiding faded away and he was quite serious. "Might want to align yourself with a different girl."

"Skeletons or not," Andrew defended, "she seems fine to me."

"Still haven't figured it out yet, have you." It wasn't a question but an accusation. "The truth about Claire?"

"Truth?"

"About who she is."

"She's Lily's sister." Andrew put his hand to his hip, tiring of the riddles. "And a sweet one at that."

"Yeah. She's Lily's sister," Pieter agreed, then lowered his voice. "She's also her mother."

Dinner with the Muellers ran late into the night with laughter and stomachs nearly breaking at the sides from food. They kept eating and drinking stout and telling stories and the Kisers did not want to leave. But when they did, the family held on to the memories of the evening as they traversed the quiet miles back to the homestead. Pieter had whittled toy trains for Edgar and Will, and when they blew through the center holes a perfect train whistle sounded.

Three awake, four asleep—Eveline carried the twins, Wilhelm had Will and Andrew carried little Edgar, the boy clutching the toy train in his tiny fist. Andrew would come back for the piglets tomorrow.

The evening air danced between summer and autumn and when they returned home, the house was cool and each curled into light blankets to warm tired bodies. And Wilhelm, still thick with drink, and Eveline, still high from schnapps, touched each other under the covers until Eveline opened her body to her husband and they made love upon the creaking springs like they had when they were young.

CHAPTER 24

White old man Stevens and his black wife, Bernice, parked their bread wagon on the road and waited for Eveline. "Hallo, purdy lady!" Bob Stevens shouted, and waved, his bottom dancing off the wagon seat. Bernice gave a shy, gentle twist of her hand in greeting.

Eveline stepped up to the wagon and wiped her brow. "You gonna get that bridge fixed soon?" the old man asked. "Shame you got to walk all this way just to meet us."

"I don't mind. Have Lily Morton helping me with the babies. Nice to get out and walk a bit."

"That Lily's a sweet one, ain't she?" He reached back and grabbed the fresh loaves wrapped in brown paper. "How many boys you got, Mrs. Kiser?" he asked. One wide eye watched her as the other squeezed tight against the sun's glare.

"Four." She thought about this with a grin. "Six if you count the men."

"Christ almighty! And here you is with the hips of a teeny girl! Birthin' all those boys an' lookin' as fresh an' pretty as a daisy." He elbowed his wife. "Ain't that right, Bernie? Ain't she a fine-lookin' woman?"

"She is." Bernice nodded seriously and then shook her head to stave off any chance of an argument. "You is a fine-lookin' woman, Mrs. Kiser. Bob an' me be talkin' 'bout that all the way up here."

Eveline put her hand on her heart, smiled until her face hurt with the sincere compliment. Bob Stevens was a remnant of the Civil War, met Bernice near the battlefields of Vicksburg. Fell in love and smuggled her up to Pennsylvania. The man told the story to anyone with ears, even if they had heard it a thousand times before.

Together, Bob and Bernice shared one tooth between them. They weren't legally married, but all knew them as husband and wife. And by any definition, they were ugly individuals. But together, when their toothless, gummy grins were wide and their eyes sparkled as if they were still teenagers, there glowed a beauty that made the couple all that could be opposite of ugly. They were cracked and ancient like the musket balls from that very war, walking souvenirs that clung to each other like the smell of yeast against their skin. And it was worth the price of bread just to witness their bond.

"Hey, where's that nephew a yours?" Bob asked.

"Andrew? Believe he's working in the barn. You need him?"

"Naw! Jus' my Bernie thinks he's a looker. Has a thing fer 'em blue eyes."

"Shush!" Bernice swatted his arm. "I ain't never said such a thing. Why ya gotta go sayin' stuff like that? Mrs. Kiser think I'm a dirty ole woman starin' at her boy."

Bob laughed and hugged his wife close. "Ya can't fool me, Bernie! I see ya lookin' fer the boy as soon we come drivin' up." Daintily, he imitated his wife fixing her collar and straightening out her dress.

Bernice laughed then, pinched him on the knee. "Now, that ain't so an' ya know it!" Then she leaned over and whispered to Eveline, "Well, he is a fine-lookin' young man. My ears don't work so good no more, but my eyes see jus' fine!"

"Told ya!" Bob shouted merrily. "An' here she is pinchin' me jus' fer speakin' the truth. Told ya!"

With a click of his tongue, old man Bob had his lone, old horse moving again and gave a high wave to Eveline as they headed down to Widow Sullivan's house. The cackling of the couple rode above the wheels and made the roses open a little wider.

Back at the house, Eveline placed the bread on the counter next to Lily as she finished up the breakfast dishes and then went back outside to the clothesline and hung up the full line of Kiser clothing. When the last dress was hung, the rope unwound from its square knot and dropped to the ground, jumbling the clothes in a soiled bundle.

Eveline sighed and picked up the rope, wobbled unsteadily upon a footstool as she tried to reattach the clothesline to the old post, the wet clothes now spotted. Her fingers reached to hook the rope but were just shy of the height, the step stool leaning unstably to the right when two large hands grabbed her waist to keep her from falling.

Frank lowered her to the ground and took the rope from her hand, easily latched it into place.

Eveline patted her chest, the adrenaline pumping from nearly toppling over and by the surprise of the man at her side. "Thank you, Mr. Morton."

"Frank." He tipped his hat.

The soiled underclothes draped and swayed in the wind. Eveline frantically pulled each off the line. "They'll all need washing again," she said absently, making an excuse.

"Women work too hard," he commiserated as he reached up and added a second knot to the line. "Hope your husband appreciates all you do for him."

She laughed at this. "My husband works hard himself."

He watched her in a calm, easy way. "Sure, he does. Wasn't saying he didn't. Just that men get the recognition, so to speak. Women get treated like their work's expected without the appreciation."

She gave him an incredulous look, had never heard a man speak like that before. "Well," she said stoically. "We all do what we must, whether we're appreciated or not, don't we?"

"Guess so." He put his leather boot on the stool, showing the silver tip and the stylish stitching.

Eveline gathered the last of the clothes and hustled them tight against her abdomen. Lily came outside and huffed when she saw her brother-in-law. She pushed past Frank. "I can take those for you," she offered. Lily shimmied in front of Eveline as she handed off the clothes.

"Frank, don't you need to get going?" Lily suggested roughly. "Thought you were heading out."

"No, I got time." He pointed to the load in her hands. "Better get those rinsed before the mud sets." Grudgingly, Lily turned back to the kitchen, peeking back several times before losing them in view.

"Gorgeous day, eh?" Frank said simply. "Enjoy it while you can. Feeling the cold inching from the north already."

She could still feel the heat against her waist where his strong hands had touched. "Are you looking for Wilhelm?" she asked as the guilt plucked.

"No. Heading to Pittsburgh today. Wanted to see if you needed anything."

"That's very kind of you. I'm sorry Wilhelm's not here for you to ask."

"No disrespect to your husband, but the question was for you. Can't find too many pretty lady things in the country."

The phrase was completely innocent, yet her mind spontaneously tied "lady things" to under-garments and she blushed. "Thank you, but no. I don't believe I need anything."

Frank looped a finger through a belt ring, seemed to smell the air. "How's Lily doing? She helping you?"

"Lily's been a godsend. Not sure how I ever managed without her."

He nodded in approval. "Good. Glad to hear it." His face turned soft. "It's been hard taking care of her and Claire all these years. Not com-plaining, mind you, just been hard trying to do what's best for them."

With the confiding tone, Eveline relaxed. Frank's large face was open and vulnerable. His forehead wrinkled right in the center as if a pea pressed against the skin.

Frank twisted his thin wedding ring around his finger, his hands large and fine. "Have to apologize for my wife not paying a visit. She's a very shy woman. Gets nervous leaving the house. But I'll have Lily bring her over one day so you can meet." He smirked apologetically. "She's a lovely woman, but anxious. But you'll see what

I'm talking about. Takes a lot of work keeping her calm. Mind you, I'm not complaining, just makes it hard always trying to keep things smooth so she doesn't have to worry."

"I'm sure she's lovely." Eveline moved closer and their shadows overlapped. She wondered how such a fine man could be married to a woman so fragile. "Looking forward to meeting her."

He read her mind. "Guess I got a bit of the rescuer in me. Claire and Lily came from a bad home. Their father was a brute. Treated them real bad. Once he died, I came in, felt like I had to take care of them." Frank bowed his head mournfully. "Let's just say a whipping post had an easier life than my wife did."

Eveline listened with her whole body. "I had no idea."

He met her eyes. His were so tender, so soft, and she felt like she knew him as she would an old friend. A terrible thought entered. "What about Lily? Please tell me, he didn't harm that girl?"

Frank shook his head. "No. Claire always protected her. Till the day her father died, Claire wouldn't let him touch her. Paid for it dearly, too." He looked at her almost pleadingly. "See why I had to step in? Poor woman had it rough enough without having to run that house by herself." He laughed then and smiled wryly. "Course, bit of a change from my bachelor days, suddenly with a wife and a child to support. And Lily can be difficult at times. I'm not her father, so she don't like to listen much."

Eveline placed a hand on his shoulder, felt the strong muscle that connected to the tan neck. "You're a good man."

He took the compliment lightly. "We do what we can to make things right, don't we, Eveline?"

She squeezed the shoulder, realized she touched him. She pulled her hand away, didn't want to let go of the fabric. "Stay right here, Mr. Morton. I'm going to bring you out some lemonade."

"It's Frank, remember!" he hollered back amicably.

When she came back, he was raking out an old tangled mess near a fallen fence. "Know you have grapevines out here?"

"Really?" Eveline put the tray on the stool and looked at the spot he tilled.

"Concord, far as I can see. Bet this whole stretch is lined with them. You build some new rods and pull up the vines with string, you'll have yourself a lovely vineyard."

If he had produced a rainbow with his words, she couldn't have been happier. She already envisioned the vines vibrant and clustered with purple grapes by autumn.

"Well, I can promise you one thing, Mr.—I mean Frank—the first batch of jam is coming your way."

She picked up a glass of lemonade and offered it to him, the action reminding him of something. He held up a finger for her to wait while he picked up a brown box and handed it to her.

"What's this?" Her eyes widened.

"Open it."

She knew she was blushing, the heat creeping all the way to her hairline. She opened the cardboard flaps and pulled out the Waterford pitcher. "I don't believe it," she said. She stared at the crystal, rotated it in her hands. "It's the same one that I had. The one that broke."

He turned bashful. "Felt terrible that day when I saw you open that crate to find it broken. Know a guy in town who can get anything. Shipped it to me the next day."

Her mouth fell open and she couldn't speak. "I can't accept this." She handed it back, but he stepped away.

"No refunds, I'm afraid. You got to take it. Hurt my heart something bad if you don't." His face mollified to that of a puppy, looked at her with complete seriousness. "A woman needs pretty things, Eveline. Especially, a lady as pretty as you."

Her heart fluttered. "I simply don't know what to say." But then she cradled the pitcher against her chest. "Thank you, Frank."

He sat down, picked up the lemonade, sipped slowly. "Can I be honest with you?"

She couldn't remember talking to a man like this, ever. "What is it?"

"I'm not going to lie. This gift is a bit of a bribe."

She laughed. "A bribe? For what?"

"For your trust." He turned his gaze to his hands. "You're going to hear things about me. Things that aren't true." He gave a half-smile, his smooth cheeks strong and firm. "All I ask is you make your own opinion instead of following gossip."

"My word, what kinds of things do you think I'll hear?"

"It's given the business that I am in. I loan out money to the people who can't get credit from the banks. Sure, I got to charge a bit more in interest, but I'm also putting my neck out. But sometimes these people don't pay back and they lose their property. Doesn't happen often, but it happens. Had one man took out a loan for a new harvester and spent it all on drink. Had to come in and take the harvester right from under him. Nearly got myself shot in the process.

"But you see, I got these girls to care for. I don't want to see a man losing his property. Breaks my heart. But hell, I got to make a living, too. It's a contract, you see? You make an agreement. I keep my end of the bargain. Just ask they do the same."

"Sounds reasonable. Like any other business."

"Exactly. But people don't see it like that. They make up stories like I'm a monster. Make me sound like I evict babies onto the street. Nearly everybody pays back, but sometimes you got the ones that can't. Breaks my heart. It does. But what am I supposed to do? Sit back while they take my money and then spend it on drink?"

Eveline sighed. "Well, I haven't heard any rumors. But thanks for setting the story straight just in case."

"Oh, you'll hear. Mark my words." He turned silent, swirled the lemonade in the glass, the sugar crystals at the bottom capering. "I'm not a bad guy." He met her eyes square and her breath caught. "I just didn't want you to think I was."

He smiled and looked down again. "I like you, Eveline. You've got eyes that make a man feel warm. Makes a man feel like he doesn't have to be different than what he is. Saw that the first day I came over here." He drank his drink in one gulp and wiped his mouth with his sleeve. "About the prettiest eyes I ever laid eyes on."

The conversation was inappropriate and she knew this, felt the panic and the rush of the words. And she loved it at the same time, to feel the blood in her veins in a way that she hadn't felt in a very, very long time. She stood and felt faint, felt a young woman without children or raw hands from washing.

"I should be heading back," he said. "Glad we could chat a bit."

She nodded too quickly and too long. "Yes."

"You and the family need anything—anything at all—let me know. All right?"

"Thank you."

He gave a short wave and ambled back through the gate, her eyes drawn to the curve of his back pockets and the wide shoulders.

"You want me to hang these back up, Mrs. Kiser?"

Eveline nearly jumped out of her skin, instantly ashamed. Hoped Lily hadn't seen her staring at her brother-in-law . . . her sister's husband.

"Frank bring you that?" Lily reproached, pointing to the pitcher in her hands.

"Yes." Eveline wanted to dip her head in the well bucket to cool off, clear her mind. "Was very kind of him." She calmed and smiled at Lily. "He's a very sweet man."

A hard glint shone in the girl's eye. "He's not sweet, Mrs. Kiser."

She was taken aback. Lily seemed ungrateful, even selfish. "Well, seems he's given a roof over your head. Takes good care of you and your sister," she huffed.

Lily sighed and turned away. "I better get these hung before the clouds set in."

CHAPTER 25

W ill, you have the line and hooks?" asked Andrew. The child nodded, held up a tangled mess of threads, hooks and sticks.

"I got the sandwiches," Edgar declared helpfully as he raised the picnic basket with unbending arms.

"Good. Let's go."

"Mind if I join you?" Lily stood next to the barn, her thin sweater cradling a small pile of apples. "Unless you think I might scare away the fish," she added.

"Sure, Lily!" Edgar welcomed. "Here, you can put the apples in my basket." The little boy hoisted the wicker handle and brought it to her side.

"Got enough sandwiches in here to feed an army!" Lily exclaimed.

"Men work up an appetite when they fish. Don't we?" Andrew winked at the boys, who puffed with pride.

"Ma says we're growing outta our shoes faster than she can buy 'em," shared Will. "Says we'll be eating the bark off the trees if she don't keep us fed."

"Well, certainly don't want that," agreed Lily. "Sheep already nibbled this place raw." She laughed and picked up the picnic basket weighted with food. "I'll make sure I bring a batch of cookies next time I come over."

"Oatmeal raisin?"

"If you like."

Together, Lily, Andrew and the boys followed the curve of the creek as it meandered through the property and spilled out to a large pond surrounded by weeping willows. Andrew stopped then and put a finger to his lips for quiet, bent down on one knee and tilted his head in the direction of the reeds. A blue heron, majestic and slender, stepped lightly upon the shallow marsh, the long neck straightening and then curving nearly to an S. In a blink of an eye, the yellow beak seized the water and gripped a shiner, swallowed the body whole.

"Whoa!" shouted the boys. "Did you see that?"

Andrew chuckled, glanced at Lily, who was resting on her haunches, holding her knees. The light brown hair spun to gold under the sun, framed her face in silk. The collar of the pale pink dress reflected the hue to her cheeks and brightened the smiling lips. And the figure blended into the grass, competed with the beauty of the day and won without a fight. Her eyes met his and they held the light in one saturated moment.

"I caught one!" Will cried. "I got—"

The giant bullfrog hopped out of his slimy hands and plopped near Edgar's foot. "I got him!" Edgar shouted. "I got him!" The frog bounced from the boy's staggered chasing until leaping into the stream just as Edgar slipped, belly first, in the mud.

Andrew plucked his cousin up by the waistband, the boy wet and dripping in pond sludge. "Yuck!" Edgar shook his hair and hands, splaying dirt and scum into the air.

"We're supposed to be catching fish, not the other way around," Andrew joked.

Under the willow, Lily helped pull the hooks from the wad of fishing line and salvage which pieces were long enough to use. Andrew and the boys collected worms from under the soft moss.

Andrew picked a leaf from the cluster of jewelweed growing on the bank. "Will. Edgar. I want to show you something." He took the leaf to the water's edge, submerged it and tilted the green that morphed to silver no different from metal. "Magic, see?"

The boys' jaws dropped; they pulled up the leaf that turned green again before submerging it again and turning it silver for themselves. "It's the only leaf that does that. Far as I know any-way," Andrew said.

While the boys marveled at the plant's alchemy, Andrew picked up a round, flat stone and flicked it across the water, sending it skipping four times before sinking.

"How'd you do that?" Edgar asked, dropping the jewelweed into the current.

"Have to find the thinnest ones you can." Andrew took a stone and placed it in Edgar's fingers, stood behind him and showed him the back-and-forth motion for launch. Edgar released and the stone skipped once and sank. "Like that?" The little boy's eyes grew wide and brown as a cow's.

"Just like that." Andrew stacked a small pyramid of stones. "Keep practicing and you'll get it six times across, I bet."

A heat shimmered from below the willow, vibrated down his skin, and he knew Lily watched him. He plopped down beside her and brushed the dust off his thigh. "You hungry?" he asked.

She shook her head, smiled as Edgar squatted and readied his stone, his nose scrunching in concentration. "You're really good with them," she said.

"They're good boys." Andrew unwrapped one of the ham sandwiches. "After the accident, they practically lived in my room playing marbles and Old Maid. Always with a million questions, those two," he said affectionately. Andrew rested his elbow on his knee and stared at the bread in his hand. "But it was good having them there. Kept me distracted. Kept me from thinking about the pain." He took a small bite of the sandwich and chewed easily.

"Does it still hurt?"

"Yeah. Sometimes."

The light reflected off the water in ripples, lazy white lines that sparkled at the tips. Edgar flung his stone and it bounced three times.

"Nice one!" Andrew hollered, and the boy beamed. Will followed suit and picked up a stone, watched his little brother's technique carefully before attempting his own.

"You're very lucky." Lily's voice hummed wistful and longing. "I'd give anything to have a family like this."

Andrew swallowed his food, watched his cousins, scanned the meandering creek and followed it to its source at the Kiser homestead. Family. Until then he hadn't thought of the Kisers in that way, and the realization prickled his skin with gratitude.

Lily leaned on one arm, tucked a section of hair behind her ear. "All I ever wanted was to have a family. Piles of kids. My own house. My own animals. A garden so big that I would get winded going from one end to the other." She picked up a small stick and traced a shape in the dirt. "Want to know something? Before you moved here, I used to come up to your farm every day. Pretended it was mine." Her head turned to scan the view. "Even when I was little, I'd see the Andersons out here with their sheep, thinking this land belonged to me and not them. Silly, isn't it?"

"Is that why you carved your name in the apple tree?"

"Oh, you saw that?" She smiled and shrugged. "I love that tree. Couldn't even tell you how many apples I ate from that one tree. You'd think I'd have cider running through my veins instead of blood."

"Eveline loves that tree, too. See her out there every day picking up the fruit and polishing them like diamonds before she puts them in the apple chute."

Andrew finished his sandwich just as Will and Edgar trotted up with their long fishing sticks. Will handed his to Andrew. "Can you tie the line for me?"

"Me too," Edgar said, accidentally jabbing the tip of his rod against Andrew's leg.

"Sure." Taking the fishing line, he measured it up to the top of the first stick and then paused. His fingers played with the line, rolled the thread despondently between them, unable to make a simple knot one handed. The boys waited, shuffled feet in impatience. Andrew pushed the fishing rods away. "I can't tie it," he said scornfully.

Lily scooted next to his side and quickly tied a

line and hook to each stick, handing them back to Will and Edgar. "Thanks, Lily!" they called, and ran off to the edge of the water.

Andrew relapsed into an insulted silence. Lily held her hands in the skirt of her dress as they watched the little boys splash in the water, scaring away any fish they hoped to hook.

"Claire and I used to fish down here, too," said Lily, her face fallen, her voice siphoned. "Sometimes we didn't have anything to eat except for the fish and turtles we caught down this way."

The reeds tapped against the hollow sticks, now starting to brown and become brittle. Lily's face turned somber, softened with the faraway thoughts. "Claire used to hunt as good as any man. Could pluck a rabbit or squirrel without missing a shot."

Will pulled hard at his line, pulled up a clump of old branches, searched the black leaves for his worm. "But after our father died, she couldn't hunt anymore. Couldn't stand the sight of blood." The cool wind blew Lily's collar so the fabric fluttered under her chin. "Couldn't even kill a chicken after that. She tried, once. Left her screaming for days. Sometimes we had nothing to eat except for your apples and a couple of potatoes. Ate them raw out of the bin a few times." She licked her bottom lip as if she could taste the baseness of them. "Guess that's why she married Frank. To keep me from starving." Lily picked up a small rock and hurled it to the water. "Guess that's why she'll never leave him."

The words from Andrew's conversation with Pieter trickled between the notes of Lily's speech. *She's Lily's sister. She's also her mother.* "Have you and Claire always been close?" Andrew ventured.

She nodded and then shook her head as if the two sides of her mind argued. "Claire's the only one who's ever been there for me. Ever." Her features scrunched in a pained moment. "She raised me from the day I was born, but . . ."

"What?"

"It's hard to explain. It's like standing in a crowd of people and feeling more alone than if you were the only one there." She swallowed. "How it felt growing up, I guess. Claire was always there but gone at the same time. Like a ghost who was seen but fading away." Her voice trailed and she bit her lip. "Part of me was always afraid that if I got too close or if I didn't try to make everything right or if I said the wrong thing she'd disappear straight from my fingertips."

Andrew watched her. *Take care of your family. Always.* His father's voice came from the willow leaves above. Andrew wished he could have been there for Lily, wished he could have brought her warm stews and bread melted over with butter. Wished he could have made fires for her when she had been cold, held her to him when she was scared. Wished he could have taken away the scars of her birth and the wounds of her raising. The severed arm stung then in pulses. He couldn't even tie a knot, let alone build a life for this woman.

Lily pulled the picnic basket over and stationed the wicker between them. "Want another sand-wich?"

"No." Andrew bent his fingers around the ball of fishing line left by the boys, tossed it under the tree.

Lily kept her arms locked around her knees, stared off at the frogs that hopped onto the warm stones and then off again, making small ripples with their back legs. "The boys don't care that you can't tie a knot." She turned to him. "I don't, either."

"You wouldn't understand." Andrew sighed. His jaw clicked once below the smooth skin. "Don't know what it feels like not to be able to do something so simple. Something everyone else in the world can do."

"Actually, I do."

Andrew turned to her, the lovely face twisted in humiliation even as she tried to smile through it. "I don't know how to read."

The feed stockpiled in the hayloft of the barn looked enough to sustain a herd, but Wilhelm and Andrew knew they'd be lucky to get two months out of it. To conserve, they sent the cows to graze in the farthest patches of the property, let them cross old property barriers outlined with crooked stone walls and enter into the woods to forage. Then, each evening, Andrew, Edgar and Will would hunt down the wayward cows, turning it into a game of finding the black-and-white-spotted spies hiding in foreign territory. They'd find Maggie, the lead cow, and walk her back to the barn; then out of the recesses the other cows would follow like children trailing their parents into church on Sunday.

Andrew kept the six surviving runts from Pieter Mueller in the closed porch. With the cooling nights, the piglets were confined to that one room, bedded in straw-lined wooden crates. The animals had come to him listless, but under his care their bellies swelled and they squirmed and tumbled over one another as they found strength in their legs.

After the day of fishing and tadpole catching with his cousins, a day squeezing some fun between feeding the chickens, hogs and cows, the night came fast and hard and it was nearly dark before dinner.

Lily was pulling her sweater on when Andrew plopped down next to his charges, the box of pigs lighting up with squeals. It was no small effort to feed one piglet while the others fought against the bottle for their turn. Without his other arm to tame the mob, he had to use his knee as an inadequate buffer against the mass of hungry pink bodies.

"Need some help before I go?" asked Lily.

He nodded, the small action taking his focus off the feeding and sending the offended animal into a rage of grunts. Andrew slid to the side to make room for Lily.

"My gosh, they're loud!" Lily leaned over and picked up a piglet from the pile. Andrew could smell the handmade soap on Lily's skin and a warmth flooded down his stomach and heated his thighs.

The young woman nestled the pig into her arm, fed it from one of the warm bottles with the cork nipple while she watched Andrew drip milk with precision and concentration. "You were good to save them," she noted. "Don't think they would have lived more than a few days."

"Not out of the woods yet." He put the sated and drowsy piglet into the straw and picked up the next. "This nursemaid business is harder than it looks. But I guess you know all about that. Twins have been fussing nonstop. Surprised you're not deaf yet."

Lily didn't laugh and her forehead furrowed. "Can I tell you something?"

He faced her completely. "Of course."

"Those babies—" She stopped for a moment. "They don't look well."

"I know."

She glanced at the door to make sure no one was listening. "Mrs. Kiser's been giving them cow's milk, but . . ." She concentrated on the piglet in her arm. "They're crying just like these runts."

"Did you talk to her?"

"She knows it, so I didn't want to make it worse." Lily bit her lip. "Women take that stuff hard. Becomes personal, you know?" She used a free finger to rub the top of the animal's wrinkled forehead.

"Dr. Neeb came a few weeks back."

"I know, but he's no good. About the weakest man I ever laid eyes on. Sooner have these pigs healing me than Dr. Neeb.

"Your aunt's scared, Andrew." Lily pleaded with her whole face. "She's scared for her babies and she doesn't know what to do. Making her angry."

Andrew's gaze melted into the gentle profile, the perfect slope of her nose and curve of the lips. "Well, if it makes you feel better, you've been a big help to her. She likes having you around."

"I don't know about that. Feel like I get in the way more often than not. Hurts me something awful to hear those babies crying like that."

She leaned closer to him, reached over and put the piglet down. So close a few soft hairs from her head touched his cheek. She retreated then and leaned against the wall, folding her legs up under her. "Saw Pieter in the barn with you today. You get on well, don't you?" she asked uneasily, the color draining from her cheeks.

"Yeah. He's a good man."

"Did . . ." She waited, swallowed quickly. "Did he tell you anything about my family?" She flustered. "About me?"

"Yeah." Andrew nodded. He didn't want to lie to her. "He shared some things."

"He tell you about Mary Paulsen?"

Andrew nodded again.

"I hated Frank for that." Lily's mouth trembled for just a moment. "Hated him for what he did to the Paulsens. Seeing Mary and her family kicked off their land like that." Her eyes glistened. "Mary wouldn't talk to me, wouldn't even look at me. Not that I blame her. Pieter still hates me because of it."

Lily pulled her knees to her chest and hugged them, rocked slightly. "I took all the money I had and went to the auction. Bought as much of Mary's possessions as I could afford. She had the prettiest dresses, Andrew. Her mother made them all by hand. You've never seen such lovely clothes. I was lucky to get them."

He turned away from her now, didn't understand how the woman who made his heart jump could have acted so greedily.

"Should of seen Claire and me at the post office." She grinned then. "I got so upset because I didn't have enough money to mail the box to Minnesota. Poor clerk finally took pity on me and paid the rest." She sighed. "Never heard back from Mary. Don't even know if she got all her things I sent. But I hope so. Helps me rest at night thinking that she was still wearing those dresses."

The relief was sudden and nearly left him giddy. "You bought her things so you could send them to her?"

"Of course. What did you think?" She looked wounded.

"Nothing." Andrew smiled widely. "You should tell Pieter, though."

"Wouldn't matter. Frank's done enough to the people around here that we're all tainted." Lily's eyelids lowered and she became very still. "Did Pieter tell you anything else?" Resignation tinged the question, spiked with a scar that threatened to reopen.

Andrew knew what she was asking and he would not open her wound. "No." He tucked the last sleeping piglet into the straw. "That was all he said."

She exhaled gratefully and stood to go, wrapping the worn sweater tight at her waist. Andrew rose as well. "I'll walk you home."

She shook her head. "If you don't mind, I'd

like to go alone." Her words softened without any trace of insult. "Been a long day is all."

"You sure?" He watched her carefully until she grinned under his gaze and turned away bashfully.

"Besides," she scolded, "you got dark circles under your eyes. Should treat yourself to a good nap before Mrs. Kiser calls you to dinner." She pushed him lightly in the chest, the touch tingling down to his pelvis. "Give you a chance to dream about digging holes or pretty girls or whatever you men think about."

"Think I'm too tired to dream." He walked her to the door and held it open, then closed it gently again right before she was about to walk through. He blocked her way with his body but met her humbly in the space. "I could teach you how to read, Lily," he offered gently. "If you want me to."

Her hand fumbled with the top button of her sweater. "I don't—" Her voice cracked feebly. "I don't want you to think I'm stupid."

"You're not stupid, Lily." He said it so firmly that she listened.

"I would like that." She smiled then, haltingly at first before her lips bloomed. "I'd like that very much."

Without knowing he was going to do it, Andrew leaned down and kissed her on the forehead. "Good night, Lily girl."

• • •

Andrew awoke from his nap on the sofa to babies screaming and Wilhelm shouting from the next room. The sky pitched black through the windows. He could smell dinner cooking.

Andrew walked into the kitchen. The babies screamed in the corner. Screamed. The high shrill pierced the eardrum, one in each ear. Eveline plopped the mashed potatoes on the plates. On Wilhelm's the starch stuck stubbornly to the spoon, and she pounded on the dish until the food came off in a giant white blob. The boys tried to eat but gave up to hold their ears. The weight of the noise sat like bricks upon the rib cage, pressured the head and temples, reverberated in the walls of the room.

Wilhelm threw down his fork. "For Christ's sake, can't you do something?"

"Do something?" Eveline smacked the pot on the counter. "What would you have me do?"

"Feed them. Walk them. I don't know." He rubbed his eyebrows. "Just do something!"

Eveline wanted to throw the pot at him. *Do something, he says. Feed them, he says. Feed them!* Her head was going to explode. The crying made her want to hurt them. She could see herself doing it, throwing them right out the window. She could feel the sensation of tossing them, one baby right after the other, into the dirt and then locking the window. She gripped the counter.

Wilhelm simply poked at his stew and she wanted to throw the pot at him. *Do something.* His words screamed between her ears; the twins screamed within them and all she wanted to do was to scream louder than them all.

Eveline grabbed Wilhelm's wool coat and flung it over her shoulder. She grabbed the babies and shoved them together in one arm, stepped into her boots.

"What are you doing?" Wilhelm asked.

"Taking care of it!" she shouted, and stormed out of the house, the waning cries of the twins slowly fading away.

Everyone's ears stung with the sudden and forced silence. Edgar glanced at Andrew, then to his father. "What's she doing with them?" he asked nervously.

"Nothing you need to worry about." Wilhelm turned to his food. Stabbed the overcooked beef. "Eat your dinner."

Before the meal had finished, Eveline returned, coatless. Her face was red with exertion, the hem of her dress stuck with old leaves. No one asked where the babies were. No one asked anything.

She sat at her chair, her plate of food long cold. Her hair strayed from the bun. The divide between husband and wife a jagged fissure, a torn space that everyone sensed and no one would acknowledge. Eveline finally pushed her plate away, left the table and went upstairs, slamming the bedroom door.

Wilhelm stood up. "Clean up the table for your mother," he directed. The boys picked up their plates and headed to the sink.

Andrew rose from the table and faced his uncle, obstructed his passage. "You can't leave them out there."

"Yes, I can."

The boys turned from the sink, their eyes worried and pleading. With one last scalding look, Andrew grabbed his coat and stormed out of the house. The sky was dark and the newly fallen leaves crunched under his feet. He stomped up the yard, past the apple tree in the direction of the distant cries. The temperature was low, and when the wind blew it forced his neck down into his collar for warmth. He took long, swift strides up the ridge toward the cornfields, the moon only now inching above the curve of the horizon. There was little light, trees and boulders in various shades of gray and black and dark brown—a world in decay.

A faraway cry carried upon the wind and his legs hurried, crested the ridge, followed the growing volume. Upon flat ground, he ran, found the babies between rows of dead corn, bundled together tightly in Wilhelm's large coat, their limbs struggling to free themselves. Andrew sat on the hard earth and gathered them against his chest, their wet faces soaking his shirt, the cries raspy and sore and painful. He held them, rocked them, kissed the tiny heads.

His heart thumped in dull beats. There were no thoughts, only a mournful solidity that seemed to drill him into the dirt amid the dead stalks. "I'm sorry," he whispered. He rocked them gently against his warm body until the crying waned, their snoring wheezy from clogged nostrils. It was difficult carrying the two in one arm and he had to stop often to lift their sliding bodies with his hip. But they were peaceful now, warm, as he brought them back to the house and laid them into the crib in the heated kitchen.

Andrew removed his hat and coat, hung them on the hook behind the door. The lamp glowed from the parlor. Wilhelm sat in his chair reading the paper by the dim light, his glasses near the bottom of his nose.

"The twins are sleeping," Andrew announced coldly.

Wilhelm didn't look up. "Good."

Andrew pulled back his shoulders and straightened his spine, stared down at the man. "They could have died out there."

His uncle turned the page of the paper. "Well, they didn't, did they?"

Andrew watched him from that angle, studied him. He hardly recognized the man he had ridden in the caboose with. That man had been full of muscle and brawn, hard humor and wit. This man was as grayed as the walls, in tones lighter or darker but always gray. They were both men but as different as two genders.

Andrew rose well before the sun, his sleep restless. He woke often to rock the twins when their crying started up again. Wilhelm usually milked the cows, but he'd do it this morning. He lit the lantern and went to the back of the barn to the youngest cow, set down the three-legged stool and milking pail beside her. The hay that had been left out the night before still remained untouched. The cow stared at it listlessly, drops of drool dripping in long strands to the straw along the ground. He touched the cow's neck, bent down to listen near her mouth, her breathing labored. "What's going on with you, girl?" he asked softly.

The cow stared straight as if she didn't know he was there. He sat down on the stool and reached for the udder, but it shook. The back legs vibrated. He kicked the stool out of the way and touched the hind leg, felt the thigh tremble uncontrollably under his hands. Words flashed from the recesses of his mind, long ago in his medical books. He touched the lower back of the cow, the shaking fierce, and then he went numb. *No.* Pieces joined, collected and clicked into place. *Oh, God. No.*

Andrew grabbed the lantern and sprinted from the barn through the fields to the beginning edge of the dark woods. *Please don't be here.* He fanned the lantern over the dark, moist ground, the leaves thick, and he pushed them away with his foot to uncover the underbrush. *Please, no.* He stooped along the edge, kicking up damp leaves and crunching sticks. And then he saw it. The round, white flowers, most dead but a few still vibrant atop long green leaves. He dropped the lantern to the ground and covered his face with his hand, the biliousness stirring his insides. Fiercely, he pulled at the plant, jerking up the roots from the soil and then grinding them dead with his boot heel.

By the time he made it back to the house, the light in Eveline's room shone and he didn't pause to think, ran up the stairs and bolted through the door. Wilhelm was buttoning his shirt. "What the hell you think—"

Andrew grabbed the bottle from Eveline's hands. Before she could say a word or close her mouth, he panted, "It's the milk."

The babies roared in her arms. "What are you talking about?" she yelled over the cries.

"The milk." He tried to catch his breath. "It's poisoned. The cow's been eating white snakeroot. You need to get the doctor here. Now."

CHAPTER 26

Otto died first, cradled in Eveline's arm. The declining cry faded until the baby slept and then the breathing stopped. Eveline held the dead infant as if the child simply rested, as if the unmoving chest were just pausing and would start up again in moments. And she spent the night in this way, cradling one dead child in one arm and one living one in the other. And she watched them in the dark, too tired to sleep, too numb to move. Wilhelm slept soundly next to her, his broad back hunched over the pillow that lay crunched at his stomach instead of under his head.

A light flutter floated from Harold. And with it, the air of life glided away and did not return. Still Eveline sat, her ears ringing from the quiet, perhaps the loudest quiet she had ever heard, the kind that made the blood throb in the ears.

Eveline closed her eyes and a tear squeezed and dripped down her cheek, but it was not of sadness but of disgrace. She wasn't sad. She looked at her babies in horror with her own stoicism. *I'm not sad.* Tears of infamy slid down her face. *I'm*

holding my dead babies and I don't feel anything.
Dear God.

God. Dr. Neeb had scratched his head, said it was up to God. The same doctor who told her to stop nursing and give the twins only cow's milk; the same doctor who suddenly remembered that the previous owner had lost a quarter of his sheep to the same snakeroot plant. *It's up to God now,* the doctor had said. And so it was.

The rooster hollered mournfully before the promise of light turned the black sky to slate. Wilhelm turned on his back, grabbed the pillow and shoved it under his skull.

"They're dead, Wilhelm," she revealed quietly.

Her husband pulled up on one elbow. Blurry-eyed and disheveled, he looked at one baby and then the next. A sound Eveline had never heard cracked from his throat as he reached for the babies, took his sons from her stiff arms and held them to his chest. She had never seen him cry. Ever. And the sight sent a fury through her veins.

"Stop it!" she snapped. The contrast between his despair and her own callousness frightened her, made her feel inhuman, and she wanted to hit him, wanted to punch him in the jaw for his sensitivity and her lack.

"They were sick from the start," she told him. "Better they went now instead of suffering on." Her voice leveled with effort. "God did us a charitable grace by taking them without further pain."

Wilhelm's tears flowed unending upon the pale heads. "That's enough!" she commanded, her hands shaking. She pulled the babies and wrapped them in the crocheted blanket. "You need to tell the pastor."

Wilhelm turned as if in a dream, his skin still stained with drying tears as he pulled on his pants and snapped the suspenders over his bent shoulders and slunk downstairs.

Eveline moved the babies to the crib and did not look at them again. She made the bed and set off to the kitchen to start breakfast.

The small funeral service only highlighted their isolation. A few parishioners from the Protestant church attended, those who felt their presence mandatory at any event hosted by a pastor, as if their absence would be instantly recognized by God and in his anger he would strike down a herd of locusts to wipe out every crop.

Widow Sullivan came and drove her small buggy by herself, holding the reins with her aged and gnarled hands. The Muellers attended with their brood of children and grandchildren. So many Muellers joined the Kisers at the church that a stranger would mistakenly think them quite fortunate in friends. Old man Stevens and Bernice were there, childless and holding each other's cracked hands. The Mortons were there as well, Frank's customary cowboy hat left at home and his thick hair combed neatly behind his ears. Between the Mortons and the Muellers the Kisers formed a wedge, and the eyes of one family did not meet those of the other. And when the tiny babies were finally blessed with humble words, they were brought back to the Kiser farm to be buried beneath the apple tree.

The mourners gathered in the Kisers' dining room, ate the food brought by the neighbors and spoke idly about the cold and lamented about the harsh winter expected.

But Eveline couldn't feel. As the chatter rose and fell, words exchanged, she couldn't feel any of it. Her fingers held the silver serving spoon as she scooped corn onto a plate and yet the silver did not seem to exist against her skin.

Frank Morton approached, put his hand lightly against her forearm, and *this* she felt. In fact, the heat was such a contrast from the numbness that she withdrew her arm quickly, as if she had been burned. She rubbed the spot absently.

"I didn't mean to startle you," he said. "Lily would still be happy to help you out with the house. Don't need to pay her. She'd be happy to do it."

Eveline folded her arms at her waist and acknowledged Frank's offer. "I'd like that very much. Lily is welcome anytime." At that moment, she wanted him to wrap his arms around her, press her head against his broad chest and stroke her back. She wanted him to tell her about the time he visited Holland, wanted him to paint a picture that would bring happier memories, wanted his touch to spread fire to the parts that had grown dead.

Instead, Frank turned to the woman who approached meekly from behind. "I know this isn't the best time for introductions, but I want you to meet my wife, Claire." He put his hand on the woman's slight back and nudged her forward.

The woman rattled slightly with nerves. "I-I-I'm sorry for your loss, Mrs. Kiser."

The words fell hollow and empty upon her ears and Eveline hated her. Claire was weak and shy and didn't deserve the man at her side, Eveline thought. "That's very kind of you, Mrs. Morton," she answered coldly. "We're glad to have you."

That evening, the neighbors left one by one save for Lily and Claire. Lily tucked in Will and Edgar upstairs. Wilhelm talked to Heinrich Mueller outside. Andrew was nowhere to be found.

Claire worked in the kitchen cleaning off plates and wrapping up the leftover meats and casseroles, her movements quieter than a mouse.

Eveline was exhausted, stuck in sludge, wanted the woman to leave. "No need for you to stay, Mrs. Morton." Her skin prickled just being near her. "Wilhelm will drive you home."

"No, I'll stay," she stated plainly. "And please, call me Claire."

The woman invaded Eveline's space, *her* kitchen, irritated like ants on the skin.

Claire bustled for activity, twisted her hands. "I'll make us some tea," Claire offered, her voice high and nervous. She filled the teakettle and set it upon the iron stove, her movements jittery.

Eveline followed the woman's figure as she went through her cupboards and found the tea, sugar and cups. Eveline's back twitched, her shoulders hunching around her ears. *Just leave.* The woman placed the hot tea in front of her.

Claire pulled up a chair and stirred her own cup, her eyes hypnotized by the circling spoon.

Drink your damn tea and leave me in peace. A gnawing grated inside, the animosity making her sweat. The kitchen and Frank's wife trapped and stoked her.

Claire took a reserved sip of her hot drink, then rested the cup on her lap. "Seeing y-y-young ones—" She stopped, pursed her lips as she tried to tame her tongue. She began again, slowly this time. "Seeing young ones dying just isn't right." Her eyes flitted back and forth in their sockets as if she were reading a sad story in the newspaper.

The heat pulsed through Eveline's neck. *How dare you.* She balled her fists, thought she might overturn the table just to get away from the woman and her empty words of condolence.

"Thank you for your sentiments, but I don't especially feel like talking, Claire. Been a long day, as you can imagine. Besides, mothers lose their babies every day. It's God's will." There was a jab in the tone, a stab at a God who had done nothing to protect her children. She put the hot tea to her lips gently even as her fingers squeezed the handle so hard, the cup nearly broke into shattered chunks.

Gently, Claire removed the tea from Eveline's hands and put it down on the table. "You haven't buried those babies yet." The voice was nearly mute, but Eveline heard every word.

She wanted to spit at the face, at the eyes that hung with pity. "I *just* buried them," she hissed. She wanted her tea back to hold, to keep her hands busy. "You were there."

"They're not buried." Claire winced, shook her head long and low. "Not yet. Not until you've grieved for them."

Things were rising from inside and it made her mad. So mad she wanted to kick over the chair, so mad she wanted to push Claire off her chair. So mad she wanted to bite someone, put her teeth into skin and pull like a rabid dog. The fury burned her face and she wanted to scream loud enough to break the windows. "I don't need to cry or grieve for those babies," she sneered. "You know why?" Her body shook in convulsions and she couldn't think straight, let the words tumble out unconfined. "Because I was glad when they were gone! So, don't preach to me about grieving over babies I never felt love for from the start." The sobs broke and she snorted hot air from her nose.

Eveline stormed up, wanted to rip the woman's hair out by the roots, call her a simpleminded idiot. "I did everything I could to make them drink and be healthy and they wouldn't do it. They cried all the time. They were so weak and I knew I was losing them! I knew it!" She cried so hard she couldn't breathe and she gasped for air. "Do you know what it's like to hold your infants in your arms every waking minute knowing they are fading away? Do you have any idea what that feels like?" she accused roughly.

"Yes." Claire's eyes were wide with compassion, glistened with tears. "I do."

Eveline's crying slowed and her body dulled. She wrinkled the folds of her dress in her hands. She looked up at the woman's face and saw it for the first time. And in Claire Morton she saw the mirror of her own grief, and it nearly knocked the wind from her lungs.

"I miss them," Eveline gasped. Claire nodded, a lone tear dripping down her cheek and under her jaw. "Miss them so much it feels like I don't have skin, that everything's just open and raw."

"I know."

And the women sat at the table in the tired, creaking house. The tea grew cold in their silence even as a warmth, thick as an embrace, joined them as one.

Andrew didn't turn his lamp on, just sat blanketed in the dark of his room. The house was noiseless, but he could still hear the distant, echoed cries of the babies, as if they lay embedded within the grains of the old clapboard.

He should have known better than to let the cows graze in the forest. The sickness could have killed them all. He thought of Edgar and Will, thought of what would have happened if all the cows had been poisoned; thought of the sure fate of his cousins had they been allowed to drink the same milk as their baby brothers. He pressed his stomach, thought of the little boys who galloped like horses and laughed to tears with his tickles, imagined them buried next to the twins, and he was cold and numb to his feet.

Andrew remembered carrying the twins back to the house the night Eveline had left them in the fields. They had nearly slipped from his arm and yet they did slip. And here he sat, in the dark, a body broken, unable to help anyone, unable to save a life. His father. The twins. In the end, they all slipped away.

A knock tapped softly on his door but didn't

register between the tortured thoughts. Andrew heard the sound as one hears the wind shudder through the panes of a window or a bat flap in the attic crevices.

The door creaked and Lily entered, closed it behind her. His back was turned, but he knew it was she, felt the woman's presence as water feels the ripples of a dropped stone.

She stepped across the floorboards toward him and the currents grew as if his senses only tuned to that soundless movement. The bed creaked and lowered as Lily sat next to him. Her body was the only substance alive. This woman. Everything else was dead and black and dismal. Yet her form, her form alone, pulsed while every other stagnated—a green leaf in a lifeless and burned forest.

Andrew heard her swallow, but she didn't speak. But she breathed, and the life was enough—enough to know that one bit of the world was still alive. She turned to him, only a vibration of change. And then her head leaned on his shoulder. He closed his eyes.

He loved her then. Beneath the grief, he loved her—the softness of the hair at his neck and under his jaw, the scent of her skin, a scent of the mingling of nature and flesh, of wind and air and life. Lily seeped into his bones, flowed into his blood. And he loved her. The warmth of her skin did not stop at his neck but spread across his flesh and deep into his marrow.

But Andrew did not want to love this woman. It was not a love from Cupid's most tender arrow, but a thrusting spear. Lily would be another cut, another scar, another part of him that would not last—another piece that would slip from his floundering grip. She would enter his life, make him love her, and then she would disappear and the pain would be worse. He could not grieve again.

Andrew turned, let her hair tickle over his cheek. He opened his mouth to tell her to leave, but instead his lips grazed her temple, warm skin against the thin line between his lips. Her face rose and his closed kiss slid across her forehead to her sealed eyes and down her nose. In the quiet, her neck leaned back and her lips met his, traced the shape of each other, as the blind run fingers over Braille, until their lips parted and fell into the pattern of their kiss. And Andrew pulled from this kiss even as he fell into its depth; he loved her even as he cursed the longing and desire. He ran from her even as his hand slid up her back and etched the angles of her shoulder blades.

He didn't want to love her.

Their lips were slow and tender, wrapped into the silence, and filled the cold room with warmth that tingled across each nerve. Lily slowly broke the kiss, pressed her forehead against his.

He didn't want to love her.

She met his downcast eyes and slowly, tenderly, pulled his head to her neck and hugged him tightly until he wept.

CHAPTER 27

The mighty black steam engines of the Pennsylvania Railroad strained unnaturally when placed in reverse. Pistons worked on overdrive, the wheels grinding like gritted teeth as the beast forced backwards for shunting, coupling or switching tracks. And the men of the train would watch from the window as a world dripped by in withdrawal, listen to the engine moan and struggle. All the while, the smooth rails in front stretched endlessly, beaconed for full steam and speed.

Since the day of Andrew's accident, Wilhelm's life had skulked in retreat and he had swallowed it all. For a man must swallow many things. In fact, it is not the strength of his muscle or the reserve of his power but his ability to swallow that which is distasteful to him without making a face that truly makes him a man.

So much in a man's world must be swallowed and endured. An overcooked and gristly piece of stew meat must be chewed to keep the wife from throwing a skillet at his head. Tears of grief over dying sons must be gulped and accepted as fate. And through life, a man gets quite good at swallowing until the throat stops moving and he chokes to death.

The rancid sighs of the old house unsettled Wilhelm, and when he couldn't fight his way back to sleep he rose and dressed in the shadows. On the small nightstand next to the bed was the toy train that Pieter Mueller had crafted for Edgar. The former brakeman of the Pennsylvania Railroad smelled the pine, still fresh and the color of cream. He inspected the train, a relic that would be played with and then set upon a table to be forgotten. The railroad had been him—Wilhelm Kiser. The hefty brake housed in the caboose, his arm—an extension of his body and all he had worked for. Now he was as wooden and lifeless as this toy.

Wilhelm Kiser was born and raised a farmer—a few years in Germany, the rest in America. But the land had not been kind to the Kisers. To his father and mother, the land was no haven of bounty. And from his first memories, Wilhelm hated farming life—the digging, planting, the smell of animals, and the flies and the waking up before dawn. The land had been a curse and he had watched his parents disintegrate under the sun. He watched them wither behind the plow as a slave bends to the whip, and he grew to hate this land as a heartless master and couldn't wait until he could flee to start fresh. And he did.

Wilhelm worked himself up the railroad chain from loader to fireman assistant to fireman to brakeman. And he took comfort in that wooden chamber, for it was strong and moved fast and was all things masculine. If females were flowers and puffy clouds, a man was steel and smoke, and Wilhelm guzzled in the soot as if it were iron for the blood.

Wilhelm placed the toy train back upon the tiny table. The day neared dawn and the first curves of frost lined the windows, promising a frigid fall morning. The black of this hour always seemed unnatural when the beds still held warmth. Nothing was right to this time of day; a body had no right to be out of blankets and out of slumber. Even the birds and the mammals knew this period existed for rest, perhaps more important than the minutes of midnight. But here he walked, taking the pail to the goddamn barn to sit on a cold goddamn stool to squeeze at a cow's goddamn teats. And he felt the hand choking his neck, made it hard to swallow, made all that was digested want to come back up.

Wilhelm headed out to the barn, past the enormous apple tree that seemed to judder as he passed. He looked up into the bare boughs, a few old apples still clinging to the limbs, and he gazed at the tree, the strength of its girth. And emotion bubbled—emotion akin to reverence and jealousy as this creature of bark and leaves

251

cradled his dead sons amid its mighty roots.

Wilhelm entered the dark barn and lit the lantern, sat down on the icy stool and bent his back. He took the warm teat in his grip, the cow flinching from his ice-cold hands. But he didn't care. *Just a goddamn cow.* And he pulled and squirted, pulled and squirted, the metallic splatter of milk rhythmic in the pail. And here he sat—in reverse.

He squeezed harder and faster. The years of the railroad a lost dream that had broken up the fabric of his existence in rural Pennsylvania—a small reprieve—a gap of freedom that was quickly sewn shut again in the quilting of the farm life that seemed to be his destiny. And as he sat on the cold goddamn three-legged stool he felt worn as the old rotted wood.

Wilhelm caught his stretched reflection in the silver milk pail, saw his father's eyes staring back, quivered with the debilitating pull of a life gone backwards, of repeating a history so hard fought to erase. But here Wilhelm sat. His father was back, his son his living ghost, and Wilhelm swallowed the image even as the truth lodged solid in his throat.

His mind drifted to his father again—a stubborn, stoic German, blood born from a whole line of other stubborn, stoic Germans. He had been nothing but practical. When the house or a table or a wall needed painting, Wilhelm's old man took all the paint cans from the shed and mixed the paint together, leaving everything they owned in a dull painted gray. Wilhelm always remembered that. Remembered how the gray seeped into his mother until she wasn't pretty anymore, just dull and muted without color.

When Wilhelm moved to Pittsburgh, he vowed not to turn his wife gray. He went against his grain and allowed Eveline the finer possessions, the thick rugs and feather comforters, the bone china and scented oils from France. But money hadn't been an issue then. It was now and he suffered the weight of his accounts also going in reverse, of a family to feed and a land to tame.

He glanced at the new Fordson tractor parked behind the cows. For this much land, rocky and clay-packed land, he couldn't take a chance with a used model. But now the purchase draped with frivolity. From savings Wilhelm had budgeted enough money to last a year and a half. Now he'd be lucky if it lasted through winter. And this, like so much else, he would ingest, keep to himself. He would not share the financial concerns with Eveline. Women didn't understand money, didn't understand what it took to care for a family, he thought. Their life centered around children and food and cleaning. And yet they complained. A life of simplicity and comfort and they still complained.

Well, his wife had her precious farm now. And

yes, the corn and hay would grow. The hens would lay. The cows would bring milk. The pigs would breed and be sold to the butcher. The garden would feed the family. But Wilhelm had grown up a farmer and he knew these things took time and conditions must be right. Wilhelm Kiser knew the toll and work involved for every kernel of growth.

When the cow was dry, Wilhelm moved the stool to the next bovine, began again and tried not to let this life choke him.

Eveline flipped the potato pancakes with the spatula, the cakes browning quickly in the oil until they contracted and rounded like smashed, rotting zinnias. Wilhelm slammed the door of the porch and set the pails of milk near the pantry.

"Can't you close that door without slamming it every time," she snapped.

"Case you couldn't tell, my hands were full," he snapped back.

Eveline huffed, lifted each pancake, let the oil drip back onto the cast iron and piled them on the plate. Her husband would be whining about not having side meat with breakfast and she waited, itched for a fight. Eveline wiped her brow with the back of her hand. She was tired, irritated. It was all she could do to grate the potatoes and onions.

At the table, young Will wrapped one hand

around his fist and cracked his knuckles. The noise brought her shoulders to her jaws. He switched hands and cracked the other.

"Will!" Eveline's shout jumped everyone at the table. "How many times have I told you to stop cracking those fingers?" she scolded.

Will folded his arms and tucked his hands away sullenly, embarrassed by the direction and strength of her wrath.

"Leave him be, Eve," Wilhelm ordered. "Boy didn't do anything wrong. Christ, you're testy today."

Eveline beat a mash of potato and egg in her hand and tossed it in the hot oil. The burning grease jumped and bit her arm. She pinched her lips while the heat extinguished. *Leave him be! he says. Not listen to your mother. No, simply leave him be! Testy today.*

She poked at the spluttering cakes. She was testy, couldn't help it. Everything about Wilhelm bothered her: his voice, his gait, the way a few hairs sprung from his ears. She'd been testy since she woke. Some dream or another interrupted by her husband's snoring and she spent the last hour of night staring at the ceiling trying to remember what she had dreamed, what had made her want to smile in her pillow and sleep forever.

"Aunt Eveline's right," offered Andrew to his young cousin. "Shouldn't crack your knuckles. Makes a man's hand ugly."

Eveline stirred the cakes slowly now, listened with both ears to his words.

"Huh?" Will questioned.

"Yep. Makes the joints all gnarled and sore when you get old."

"No, it don't," argued the boy.

"Yes, it does." Andrew got up from the table and went to the counter for the applesauce, poked his aunt playfully. "Knew a man back in the mines who cracked his knuckles since he was a kid. His hands ended up looking like bear claws." He stretched out his hand like a grizzly to demonstrate. "Even when he dropped his shovel at the end of the day, his hands were so twisted it looked like he was still holding the handle."

"Just from cracking his knuckles?"

"Yep." Andrew dropped a spoonful of sauce on Will's plate, watched as the boy inspected his fingers under the table, stretching them out and then balling them into a fist, analyzing whether there could be truth in the statement.

Eveline brought the plate of potato pancakes to the table, served Andrew before Wilhelm. She smiled at the young man. He was good through and through. There weren't many men built like Andrew, strong in form and sensitive in heart.

"Where's the meat?" Wilhelm asked.

"Didn't make any."

"Why not?"

She held the plate in one hand and put the other

256

at her hip. "Because I didn't feel like making any, that's why."

Wilhelm rolled his eyes. "Must be that woman time," he murmured.

Eveline took the empty plate to the sink. No, she thought, Wilhelm would never be one of those men, rare as they were. Andrew was one. Frank was one, too. A clear image and thrust of feeling entered. And suddenly she remembered what and whom her dream had been about. She blushed to her hairline, caught sight of Wilhelm forlorn and eating his bland cakes, and she shook with guilt. She brought out the sliced ham and started cooking the side meat.

Once Lily arrived, Eveline headed down the creaking steps to the fruit cellar with the lantern hanging from her fist, only inches from her face. At the bottom, she put the other two lanterns she had carried on the earthen ground, lit one and then the other, the three forming a triangle of light with her in the center. The cobwebs hung thick with dust blanketing every corner and hung in strings across every shelf. The temperature was temperate, not too cold, heavy to the nose with the mustiness of dust and dead rodents. The space did little to lighten her mood. For a moment, the task appeared too much to tackle and she just stood within the light unable to decide where to start.

Lily followed down the steps, her boots echoing dull and hollow against the stone walls. "Biggest fruit cellar I ever saw!" she exclaimed. "Hasn't been touched in forever, I think."

A line of jars, some cracked, some with indistinguishable green or yellow blobs, crowded two of the shelves, the metal tops swollen and humped.

"Food's no good." Lily, oblivious to the cobwebs, inspected some of the glass containers. "Would poison a goat. Not a good one in the lot." She brushed another cobweb out of the way and wiped the sticky webbing across her skirt. She pulled out some empty jars from the back. "These ones are good, Mrs. Kiser. Come see. Not a crack in them."

Eveline inspected and, sure enough, they were solid and would be good for pickling after a hot soak and cleaning.

"I'll run up and get some boxes so we can sort," said Lily. Her eyes sparkled with the project and Eveline smiled, the enthusiasm contagious. She liked the girl very much, reminded her of herself when she was young. Though the young woman held something behind the eyes, a haunting to every smile.

When Lily returned, the women worked sweeping and wiping down the shelves. The old cloths blackened with dead flies and dust with every swipe. Eveline stopped for a moment and watched Lily work. She was small boned and tiny but not weak. And her face so soft and pretty, it could have belonged to an angel. "You're a hard worker, Miss Morton."

"Been working my whole life, Mrs. Kiser. Cleaning up cobwebs as long as I can remember." Her voice dropped then and fell away. She turned to Eveline and looked about to say more but stopped.

"What is it?"

"Just wondering why you moved out this way. Seems like you had a nice life in Pittsburgh. Frank's been there a lot. Says where you lived was beautiful."

Eveline remembered their brick house. The comforts, the warmth in winter from the fireplaces that made January no different from summer. She remembered the cook and the cleaner who came every day at noon. She remembered the proximity to town and the women who would come for tea. The memories brought a weariness to her chore, for she remembered Wilhelm's face during that time, the pride that nearly blasted out of his skin, the way children and men stared in reverence as if he were a star from vaudeville. And she compared that image to the face she knew now and her chest hurt with the contrast.

"I guess it's in my blood," Eveline shared. "Working and living on the land, I mean. Wanted my boys to grow up out of the city, where the air was clean. Learn to work and respect the land."

Eveline stood up quickly and took the broom to the corner, a sudden urge to move the demons out. Lily took the cue that the subject was dropped and took her broom handle to the ceiling and twirled the cobwebs like cotton candy.

Eveline dry brushed the dirt floor, pulling piles of dried wasps, leaves and other disintegrating objects from the corners. Abruptly, Lily dropped her broom, stared at Eveline as if she had seen a phantom.

"What is it?" Eveline asked.

Lily slowly bent down for the broom, her sight holding tight to Eveline's shoulder. She moved slowly toward her and whispered, "Don't move." With a blurred motion, she knocked something large and black from the woman's shoulder.

Eveline saw the stunned glossy black spider by her shoe, the red hourglass on its back, and jammed her boot heel into the spider. The long limbs rose and twitched until she ground it immobile.

Eveline held her heart, the pounding thumping in her ears. The room darkened and their eyes drifted to the one window flush with the outside ground. The leaves piled thick and deep and the natural light strained to enter. She looked back at the dead, smashed spider, stepped back with disgust and horror. But it was not proximity to a creature so noxious that made her whimper; it was the one fact she knew about the black widow—the females mate with the males and then eat them alive.

And Eveline Kiser shivered to the core.

CHAPTER 28

The air bulked with the scent of the turning season. Nearly overnight, the remnants of a dying summer's breath expired, leaving in its wake the crisp chill of autumn. The vibrant hues of dying leaves darkened and browned, and the leaves fell from gray limbs and gathered in mounds that crackled beneath boots. On days of sun, the sky held an iron light, bright without warmth; and on days of clouds, the air rubbed like steel wool against the chin and cheeks.

Through the night, the rains lashed against the old farmhouse, revealing the roof spots that still needed repair. Metal pots and kettles dotted the floor of the room where the water dripped from the heavens, worming through the shingles, and splashed upon the dishes. The endless dripping continued to morning even after the sun replaced the rain.

Wilhelm sent Will and Edgar to the chicken coop to collect eggs and clean out the feed basins. Come spring the boys would be in charge of raising all the new chicks, and so they got to work cleaning out the highest shelves where the heat could rise and warm the hatchlings. And the boys didn't complain, happy to spend the day in the warm confines of the coop until Fritz could come over to play.

In the barn, Andrew screwed nails shallowly into the wood planks and then hammered the heads firmly to hang the chains and harnesses. Outside, Wilhelm fiddled with the crank of the car. "Ford's not working," he accused, hollering into the barn.

Andrew put down his hammer and peeked in the right side of the raised hood. "What's the problem?"

"How the hell should I know," Wilhelm cursed. "I look like a damn mechanic?"

Andrew ignored the tone. "I could ask Frank to take a look at it."

The man grunted. "I'll figure it out." Wilhelm slammed the hood closed. "Help me get this wagon mended."

The old wagon had been left by Mr. Anderson, the iron bolts and center spoke rings caked with rust. Andrew sanded down the gritty red steel, squirted oil on all the moving parts. They tested it with the horse. Wilhelm held up the shafts while Andrew backed in the horse and buckled the holdbacks. When they were satisfied, the men unhooked the horse and backed her off. Then one of the axles heaved and the front of the wagon landed against Wilhelm's thigh and pinned him, sending him shouting in pain. Andrew did his best to shimmy his shoulder under the wood and lift so his uncle could crawl out. The man's pants were torn and a large red gash swelled his thigh.

Wilhelm limped in a circle, stopped and fiercely kicked the wagon with his boot. He pointed at Andrew. "Told you not to leave the car outside! Now the whole goddamn engine's waterlogged."

"I didn't leave the car outside," Andrew said flatly.

"The hell you didn't! I told you we were getting rain. Stood right here and told you to put the damn car away!"

Andrew waited inertly in the cold barn and faced his uncle, the air coming from Wilhelm's nostrils white. "I put the car away," Andrew insisted, his voice clear. "You moved it back out when you fixed the cobbler bench."

Wilhelm had opened his mouth to retort when the words settled and took effect. He kicked the wagon again with a dull thud and this time he motioned to the house. "I want those damn pigs off the porch. You hear me?"

Andrew nodded. "Yes, sir."

"Sick and tired of tripping over them, hearing them squealing all hours." He rubbed his cut leg and grimaced. "It's a house, not a goddamn pigpen."

Andrew let his uncle vent. Having never heard

him so upset made Andrew watch the man carefully—a ball of twine unraveling.

Wilhelm's face steadily contorted in anger, his teeth bared. "Got to do all the damn work around this place myself." He made a gesture at Andrew's missing arm and spit into the ground. "But nobody pitying me, are they? Nobody expects anything outta you. Nobody's going to expect the cripple to turn this piece of shit property into something, but they expect it of me, don't they?"

Andrew's insides turned. The reproach burned hot in his cheeks. He walked past his uncle to the wide doors.

Wilhelm suddenly turned mournful, clutched his hair with two hands. "I didn't mean that." He rubbed his eyes hard as if he'd been asleep. "I'm sorry, Andrew. I didn't mean a word of that."

But Andrew forged ahead, went to the house to move the pigs.

Pieter Mueller placed a pitchfork in the pigs' slop trough and mixed the old potatoes, apples and parsnips Andrew dumped in. "I can't believe you saved those hogs," Pieter confessed. "Thought they were goners."

Andrew scooped the pig waste with the shovel, tossed each scoop into the manure pile behind the sty. The sting from his uncle's insult still fresh and biting.

"Quadrupled your stock, just like that," Pieter continued in disbelief. "Word gets around, you'll be called to every farm in a hundred miles."

Andrew stabbed his shovel into the ground and twisted his jaw. "You done?"

Pieter balked. "Excuse me?"

"Trying to pump me up." Andrew pried the shovel back up and stepped forward in challenge. "Don't stroke me, Pieter," he warned. "I don't need your pity."

Pieter scratched his head. "Pity?" he faulted in disgust. "You hit yourself in the head with that shovel?"

Andrew glared at his neighbor. "Just drop it."

"Sure," Pieter agreed, but the man stiffened, his features hard and instigating. He filled one of the pails from the water pump and stepped past Andrew, bumping him roughly and splashing his pants with frigid water. "Sorry about that," he said curtly.

Andrew grimaced at his sopping pants. "Watch it!"

Pouring the water into the pigs' pool, Pieter gave a quick look to his friend. "So, you give any more thought to joining the team?" he asked lazily. "Pitcher just enlisted. Players dropping like flies."

"No." A hog plowed to the trough to eat, nearly knocking Andrew from his feet, the mud wet and thick from the overnight rain. "Christ, these pigs." He turned back to the question. "Got too much to do here."

Pieter chuckled, began whistling as he checked the ears of one of his former runts.

"What's so funny?" The smell of the hogs stuck to Andrew's skin and he couldn't wait to get in a hot tub and scrub off.

"You're a sissy," Pieter announced loudly. "Anyone ever tell you that?"

Andrew stepped forward, the muscles in his stomach contracting under his shirt. "What did you say?"

"Said you're a sissy." Pieter stepped forward in equal stride.

The space between the men simmered. The hogs grunted, moved together in one lump to the other side of the pen. "Better watch your mouth, Pieter."

The German spit to the ground, the saliva splashing a spot near Andrew's mud-soaked boot. "Make me, Dutch boy."

Andrew tossed the shovel, put his face square in front of Pieter's. "Get off my property."

"Your property?" The young man laughed at this before his lip curled. "Don't give yourself so much credit, Houghton."

Pieter challenged him nose to nose, pushed him hard in the shoulder.

"So help me." Andrew readied a fist. "I don't want to hit you, Pieter."

"Hit me?" Pieter threw his head back and laughed. "My little sister could hit harder than you."

Andrew's bones grew rigid with restraint. Pieter Mueller poked him hard in the chest. "Your property? Face it. You're just a hand-me-down, Houghton. Nothing but a crippled son of a poor coal miner."

Andrew's fist smashed into the side of Pieter's face, knocked him stumbling into the mud. Pieter shimmied up, charged at him, ramming him in the chest with his shoulder and sending them both upon the filthy ground. The two men rolled and punched, their fists slipping futilely against their slippery, grimy skin.

Edgar and Will ran to the fence, stared at the battling men, climbed upon the rail for a better view. "Get him, Andrew!" yelled Edgar joyfully. Inspired by the fight and not wanting it to end, Will hollered over his brother, "Get him, Pieter!"

Andrew's and Pieter's muscles sagged and rebelled even as their balled hands still fought to connect with a rib or a jaw or a nose. Beneath his muck-plastered face, Pieter began to howl, laughed so hard that he let go of Andrew's shirt and held his sides.

Andrew spit the filth from his mouth, shook his head, his friend's jabs finally clear with original intent. Pieter rolled over and pulled himself up, extended a hand.

Andrew squinted at the sun above Pieter Mueller's head. "You're a son of a bitch, you know that?" He grinned and grabbed the hand, his bottom sucking against the fluid ground.

Pieter blindly patted his friend on the arm and calmed his hysterics. "Finally done feeling sorry for yourself?"

Andrew rotated his shoulder, sore after the thrust of useless punches. Every inch of his clothing caked and tightened stiff with drying sludge. "Yeah, I'm done."

Pieter threw a muddy arm around Andrew's neck. "You'll join the team then, you big sissy?"

"Yeah," he surrendered. Even covered in muck, he felt cleaner and lighter. "I'll be there."

Pieter gave a hearty wave to Edgar and Will before bowing gracefully before the crowd. "Enjoy the show, boys?"

They clapped and hooted while Pieter rubbed his bruised jaw, shifted the bone left and right to make sure it wasn't broken. "I'll tell you what," he said to Andrew. "You pitch anything like you hit and we might win a game yet."

CHAPTER 29

At breakfast, Andrew handed the letter to Wilhelm. "Could you mail this when you go to Pittsburgh today? Get there faster coming from the city." He had written his mother. The letter bland, a quick outline of life on the farm. He made no mention of his missing arm or the accident. If he didn't acknowledge it, maybe she would forget.

"You can mail it yourself," Wilhelm said. He drank his coffee black, finishing in nearly one gulp, and pushed the empty mug onto the table. "I'm taking you to Pittsburgh with me."

Andrew stopped mid-chew. "Me?"

"Yeah, you." Wilhelm grinned affably and Andrew had to look over his shoulder to see if he were talking to someone else in the room. "Finish up and we'll head out. Take us most of the day as it is."

"What about the Ford?"

Wilhelm headed out of the room and called back without turning, "All fixed."

During the journey, silence hovered between the men, alleviated only by the constant grind of the engine and clattering fan belt below the hood. "I shouldn't have said what I did to you the other day. Wasn't right and I didn't mean it. Not a word of it," Wilhelm finally confessed. "I'm sorry."

Andrew faced the window, cracked at the top, the wind whipping at his hair and leaving him chilled. "Don't have to apologize."

"Yes, I do. Had no right speaking to you the way I did." Wilhelm gripped the steering wheel, bit the inside of his cheek. "You're working just as hard as the rest of us. Probably harder. Saved my family by finding that snakeroot when you did."

But not in time to save the twins. Andrew pressed his feet into the floor of the car.

"That's why I'm bringing you to the city." Wilhelm glanced at his nephew sheepishly. "Call it a thank-you."

Wilhelm and Andrew headed into the streets of Pittsburgh, the roads crowded with cars, the city thick with gray soot—a world shifting from color to black-and-white. His uncle turned into a side street lined with stone houses and topped with slate roofs. Large sycamores hovered on both sides, their leaves nearly eclipsing the iron street-lights planted between them. He parked the car in front of a tall house with a wide porch. Climbing roses, the flowers now browning, dotted the stiff, thorny stems.

Wilhelm got out of the car and Andrew followed, climbed up the flat steps, avoiding the ones with the broken and peeling slate. The door opened before they needed to knock and a woman in a green and yellow dress stepped out to the porch.

"Willy!" Her hands found her hips and she looked him over in dismay. "My word, it's been too long!"

"Hey, Francine." Wilhelm smiled, bashful. "Looking lovely as always."

The woman squeezed his shoulder with affection. "Heard you moved out to the country with that pretty wife of yours. How's farm life treating you?"

"Not as good as the railroad." He shrugged, immediately sullen with the mention. "But Eveline's happy. I think, anyway." He seemed confused by his own thoughts, awkward with the description.

Just then, both faces turned to Andrew. The woman pressed her hands together. "My word! Is this Andrew?"

Wilhelm nodded and she smacked him coyly. "Could have at least told me what a handsome man he is! My word, boy, about the best-looking fella I ever laid eyes on."

Andrew blushed, not sure how to respond to the compliment or the open sentiment. The woman wasn't unattractive, must have been pretty at one time, but her face wrinkled with tired lines. She wore too much makeup, which gave her a caked, powdery look. She was older than he, maybe in the mid-twenties, but carried a whole life in the circles under her eyes. Her dress appeared a size too small and her bosom and hips bulged from the fabric in mounds.

Wilhelm put his hat back on and turned to go. "Take good care of him, all right?"

She rested her hand on Andrew's shoulder, the touch light and gentle and too friendly. "Don't have to worry about that, Willy. Leave it to me."

He winked at Andrew. "You can thank me later." And went to the car.

Andrew's heart raced, felt part of a story with a hidden plot. The woman put her arm around him and her voice softened, cooed in his ear. "My name's Francine, but you can call me Frannie. Hell, you can call me anything you like, Blue Eyes."

They walked into the house. She moved to the edge of the steps. The top buttons of her dress were undone and the crease of her bosom curved like a black moon. The low hall light tinged her blond hair green. "Come on in, son," she said gently. "You don't need to be afraid. I'll take good care of you."

She took his hand and led him through the door and he did not protest as she drew him up the carpeted stairs, threadbare in the center from traffic. Different scents of heavy toilet water—lilac, rose, jasmine—mingled and grew and his head dizzied in their garden. She brought him into a room that had little more than a giant bed covered in dark green velvet. She closed the door and came up from behind, her warm breath against his neck before her arms wrapped around his waist and reached to undo his belt.

Clarity broke and he jumped from her touch. He put up his hand. "Hold on," he called out. His hand flew to his hair, grated through the strands as he tried to compose his thoughts. "I think there's been some sort of mistake."

She covered her mouth and looked at him like a charming puppy. "Wilhelm didn't tell you then?"

"Tell me what?"

She stopped laughing and approached seductively, nearly crawling toward him. "He didn't tell you why you are here or what I *do?*"

Andrew stepped back, but she followed, etched the shape of his chin in her soft fingers. "I take care of a man's needs, Andrew." Her fingers touched his neck, played with the collar of his shirt. "I touch a man where he likes it best," she whispered, playing with the top button of his shirt. She leaned to his ear and touched her tongue to his lobe. "I'm going to take you between my legs, Andrew." She reached down to his pants and cupped his groin.

Everything caught fire, ignited all at once. He hardened in her hand and couldn't think. Only one working organ pulsed in his whole body. She kissed his neck, her dry curly hair rubbing against his cheek, and lucidity entered again. He stepped back, but she followed. "Just stop for a minute," he ordered. "Just stop. All right." His voice waffled, shifted disorientedly. She pouted a bottom lip with the scolding.

"All right," she consented haughtily. The woman brushed past and sat at the edge of the bed, one leg crossed high on the thigh of the other, her garter belt visible above her stockings.

Andrew paced. He was sweating. "It's nothing personal, miss."

"Francine," she interjected.

"Francine." He walked back and forth, turned in short circles. "Look, it's not that I'm not flattered or appreciative of what you . . . *do*. But I'm not going to do this. Not this way. Just doesn't feel right." A hurt look flashed in her eyes. "Nothing against you. I'm not judging you, miss—I mean, Francine. It's just, I'd rather do this with my own girl, in my own time."

Francine studied him and her demeanor changed, turned from sultry and forced to warm. When she smiled this time, the tiredness left her eyes as if she was relieved of some duty or expectation. She became pretty then, in a worn way. And he saw the effects of what the profession had taken from what must have been a very sweet and beautiful girl.

Andrew sat next to her on the bed, the anxiety, the threat, now subdued. "I'm not sure why my uncle brought me here. It doesn't seem like him."

"He feels bad." Her eyes softened, rounded in kindness. "He blames himself for what happened to you. This is his way of making amends."

Andrew glanced at his missing arm, the fabric sewn shut at the shoulder. "You mean he feels sorry for me." The wind knocked out of his chest left him hollow and angry. "Didn't think any girl would be with me. So he paid for one." The clearness of the pity, the hanging thought, stung more than the amputation.

She touched his knee for a moment. "It's his own guilt that's shaming him, Andrew. In his mind, this was a gift to you, an atonement maybe."

He squeezed his fist, the hurt raw and deep. His uncle's insult worse than the one delivered in the barn.

Francine tilted her head as she watched him. "You're a handsome man, Andrew. Nearly took my breath away when I saw you, and trust me, I see a lot of men walk through these doors. But you're different. The guys come in here looking to feel like a man and here you are, already being one, not needing anyone to show you how.

"That arm being gone ain't nothing. Any girl

be blessed and honored to spend a night or a life with you. Can see that without hardly knowing you at all. You got kind eyes, honest eyes. Any girl be lucky to be with you."

She smiled but then looked mischievous, glanced over his shoulder at the clock next to the bed. "Listen, we still got over an hour and it's all paid for. I think I can still do something for you, young man. If you're open to it."

He blushed again and shook his head. "I told you, I wouldn't feel right being with you. Hardly knowing you at all as it is."

She laughed. "I know. That's not what I'm talking about, love. I'm talking more about a"— she searched the ceiling for the right word— "a lesson."

Francine stood before him. "Think of me as a teacher," she said as she began to undo the buttons on her dress. "One day you're going to meet the girl of your dreams and it'll be a good idea if you know how to please her." She stripped the dress off her shoulders, remained there half-naked in her corset. Andrew grew hard again, stared in wonder at the body, fascinated by the pale skin and the feminine curves. She unsnapped the corset methodically, dropped it to the floor. He gulped.

"Most men don't know how to touch a woman, Andrew. Come to think of it, most don't care, either. But you do what I say and you'll have your woman screaming out your name to the rooftops."

Francine jumped on the bed and leaned back on the pillows. She spread her thighs, the hair between her legs opening to reveal the pink flesh between. He stared, couldn't have stopped staring if he had a gun pointed to his head.

She squirmed comfortably, slid her fingers to her crotch. "Now, watch carefully. . . ."

When her paid hour finished, Francine walked Andrew to the door, whispered instructions as if he were taking notes. "Now remember what I showed you. You can do that just as well with the tongue, too. Lick like a cat drinks water, not the way a hound dog does." She grimaced for emphasis. "And remember to take your time with a woman, make her want it and make her wait. Kiss her softly with not too much tongue; keep it dry, you know? Not too wet. Kiss the neck, too."

Wilhelm waited for them on the porch, did not meet Andrew's face and only acknowledged Francine, his manner much more self-conscious than before. She wiped her brow dramatically. "Sugar wore me out!"

Awkwardly, Wilhelm pulled bills from his wallet and handed them to Francine. "Thanks, Frannie."

"Was my pleasure." She winked at Andrew. "My pleasure indeed."

The men rode in the car, the endless churn of the engine rattling along the map of roads. Andrew glanced at his uncle's face, the absent and distant focus, as he drove before saying, "I need to ask you something."

Wilhelm stiffened with the tone. "What is it?"

"Have you been there before?" He tapped his foot on the floor of the Ford. The thought of a betrayal to Aunt Eveline flattened his frame against the seat—the woman had become a second mother to him. "Have you been with those women?" he accused.

Wilhelm Kiser veered off the side of the road, the wheels bouncing dangerously across the rocks before he set the brake. "You listen here and listen good. I've never laid a hand on one of those women!" His voice rose fiercely. "Never once!"

Andrew wasn't afraid, met the man's fierceness with his own hard gaze.

His uncle pulled away first, eased the car back onto the main road. "Though I guess I could see why you'd think that," he admitted, and leaned back into the seat. "Look, a lot of the rail men visited places like that. Lost more men on the line from syphilis than accidents. A man gets lonely being en route for weeks at a time."

He turned suddenly to Andrew. "But I swear on my life, on my boys, I've never been with one of those ladies. Never cheated on Eveline and never would. You got it?"

Andrew nodded, the relief expanding his chest. From there, they fell into their own reverie as they passed the morbid, stinking factories and fetid skyline of the city's heart. As they paralleled the railroad lines, a Pennsylvania steamer barreled past. Wilhelm followed the train through the glass, stared at its trail in the rearview mirror until the caboose disappeared under a tail of black smoke, his face forlorn and sagging.

"The accident wasn't your fault," Andrew said softly.

The man's grip tightened on the steering wheel and his knuckles whitened. His Adam's apple rose and dropped in his throat.

"I don't blame you," Andrew said. "Never have."

Wilhelm turned his head to the window, bit his bottom lip. "Not a day goes by I don't blame myself for what happened." His voice sounded as an echo that bounced upon the recesses of his mind, a long-buried regret birthed into words.

CHAPTER 30

Lily tasted blood in her mouth. She wiped the corner with her finger and the red tip confirmed it. Frank had hit her before, but it had been when she was still a child, when she had cried from the slap and run hiding into the woods.

Her cheek stung and throbbed, but she would not cradle it for comfort. She was no longer a child. She tasted the blood again, the iron of her own blood, and was not afraid. She turned her head back in line and stared stonily at her brother-in-law until he budged.

"Why you got to push me, Lilith?" Frank scratched his forehead. "Why you got to be so goddamn stubborn?" He lifted a hand again and feigned restraint. "If I tell you to do something, by God you better listen to me!"

"Hit me again, Frank," she ordered. "I'm never going to listen to you, so you better hit me again!"

He stepped forward now, his face high above her own. She breathed heavily through her nose to keep up her confidence. She leaned back as to not break focus with her intent, to not waver from his look.

Frank Morton smiled. He reached out and smoothed down her hair tenderly. She recoiled, the touch making her skin crawl. She'd gladly endure a thousand smacks to those fingers dancing on her cheek.

"I won't ever hit you again, Lilith," he clucked. "Never again."

Now she felt a child. Now she wanted to cry and run hiding into the woods. He sensed her fear and inched closer, rubbed his finger down her neck. "You've always been prettier than your sister. Smarter, too."

Her chin quivered, her body frozen in fear and disgust.

"I could take you if I wanted." He drew a line under her neck to her collarbone. "Know I could." He chuckled. "And you wouldn't be able to do a damn thing about it."

"I'd scream," she hissed, her voice barely audible.

"No, you wouldn't." He rubbed her arms knowingly. "You'd scare Claire. I could do anything I wanted to you and you wouldn't make a peep, would you?"

Tears began to flow over her rigid face, her mind blank, curled in terror. Her legs begged to run. *Run. Run.*

Suddenly, he let go and stepped back. "But I'm

not going to lie with you, little Lily." He winked and started to walk away. "A moonshiner knows enough not to get drunk on his own stock."

Despite his most noble attempts, Andrew could not shake the experience in Pittsburgh with that woman. His blood flowed hotter. The nerve endings under his skin vibrated and the urges pulsed and left him too restless at night to sleep and too agitated during the day to think straight. And when the desires ached to a near pain, he would chop wood until his hand blistered and the ax shuddered. Then he would look at the thick forest and wonder if there would be enough wood to get him through another day of longing.

But it was not the wanting of the prostitute within the stone house. The ache called for a woman whose name sat carved beneath the apple leaves. Lily hadn't come in over a week and he missed her, missed the smile and the fresh scent of her skin. And before he knew it, he found himself picking up the ax again.

"Oh, didn't I tell you?" Eveline asked to his inquiry. "Frank stopped by and said Lily needed to help Mrs. Sullivan for a while." She folded a sheet in her hands. "Woman hasn't been well, apparently."

That evening after chores, Andrew headed down to the widow's house. He pulled down his cloth cap and kept his hand warm in his pocket.

He rounded the lane to the old woman's charming homestead and rapped on the door. "I'll get it," Lily's voice echoed from inside. She looked startled when she saw Andrew. As a shield, she put her hand to her cheek.

"Hi," he said.

She looked behind her and then at the floor. "Now's not a good time. Mrs. Sullivan can't talk right now."

"Didn't come to see Mrs. Sullivan."

Lily kept her hand to her face. "I can't talk now, either."

"Who's there, Lilith?" Mrs. Sullivan hobbled to the door, her hunched back nearly humped. "For goodness' sake, child, why didn't you invite the boy in?" The widow didn't wait for an answer and opened the door, pulled Andrew in by his elbow.

"It's freezing out there," she harped. "Come warm yourself by the fire, son."

Andrew allowed the woman to lead him, saw Lily shrink into the shadows. "How's your aunt doing?" she inquired. "Haven't seen her since the funeral."

"Better." He smiled at the old woman, his muscles thawing in the cozy room.

"So hard for me to get around these days," she lamented. "Can't even use the buggy—" She wiped a pearly eye with a handkerchief. "Oh, never mind. You'd think me a silly ole fool."

"You're not silly, Mrs. Sullivan." Lily picked at the crocheted blanket draped over the sofa. "Nothing silly about caring for your horse."

The woman's wrinkled lips quivered and she dabbed her eye again. "Got herself all sick," she told Andrew. "Stomach's swelled up like a water tank. Can't hardly walk."

"May I take a look?"

"Andrew was planning to be a veterinarian," Lily added.

The old woman lit up. "Would you? Was going to send for Mr. Thompson in town. Course, he knows more about butchering than nurturing, but thought he might help." She cocked her head at Andrew and studied his face. "My word, son. Look at those eyes! My sight isn't what it used to be, but on my word, I can see those!" She looked for Lily one way and then another before she found her tucked next to the sofa. "Lilith, have you seen this boy's eyes?"

"No." Lily reddened and moved against the wall.

"Ha!" The woman cackled mischievously and gave Andrew a lively pat on the knee. "Oh, she's seen them. Yes sir, she can't fool an old woman."

Lily sighed and folded her arms. "Didn't you want to show him the horse?"

"Oh yes. Yes!"

Together, the three bundled into coats and headed out to the barn. Sure enough, the roan

285

leaned against the stall, head hanging, her belly round and painfully swollen. The widow took her own shawl and wrapped the knitting around the poor beast.

"Can't lose this one. Not this one," Mrs. Sullivan whispered. "Belongs to my oldest daughter. If something happened to this horse, I don't think she'd ever visit me again." She tried to make the sound light, but the loneliness and worry were clear.

Andrew touched the horse caringly, inspected the feedbag that hadn't been touched. He went out of the stall and inspected the rest of the barn, found a burlap bag that was ripped. Green oats spilled from the hole and lay in a mound on the dirt floor.

He asked, "Have you been feeding the horse these oats?"

She came close and squinted at the pile of grains in his hand. "No." She shook her head. "Was planning to return that one. Too green." She twisted her mouth. "Rodents must have ripped the bag. Campbell never take it back now."

"It's not the rodents, Mrs. Sullivan. It's your horse." Andrew emptied the grains back into the sack. "That's why she's all bloated."

The woman's mouth fell open. "Well, my word!"

"If you have an empty syringe, I can fix her

back up quick. Just need some strong coffee and a little whiskey, if you have it."

"Little young to be drinking that hard stuff, don't you think?" She laughed heartily at that and hugged him. "Just fooling with you, son."

"I'll bring it from the house," Lily offered before ducking out the barn door.

A little after an hour had passed since administering the laxative, a rush of gas expired from the horse and her girth visibly diminished. Widow Stevens smiled all the way back to the warm house and wouldn't let go of Andrew's arm in gratitude.

In the parlor, she took out her purse and handed him several bills. "Thank you."

"That's not necessary." Andrew stepped back. "I can't take your money."

"Yes, you can and yes, you will." She grabbed his hand forcibly and stuffed the bills in his palm. "You just saved that horse's life and you'll take this money whether you want to or not." She pointed at him sternly and with great affection. "I got money, son. Not a lot, but enough to pay for a service when it's given. So, you take this money and make an old woman happy. Got it?"

He nodded reluctantly and reached for his coat. He gave the old woman a sweet peck on the cheek and she giggled like a schoolgirl. "And walk Lily home, would you?"

Lily's brows inched together. "I'm spending the night, remember?"

Mrs. Sullivan turned off the lamp and smiled slyly. "Not anymore. You're going to let this nice young man walk you home."

Lily walked briskly up the incline of the road, nearly at a trot, a battered notebook pressed against her chest. Her breath rose in wooly puffs against the chilled air as her boots crunched along the road's gravel. A month had passed since the funeral, since their first kiss, and they had hardly spoken since, the affection mired with the grief they had both felt that night.

The sky rested dark with the new moon, the constellations popping without lunar competition. Andrew leaned back to look at the stars. "Missed having you around lately. Was hoping you'd stop by for a reading lesson." *Lesson.* He remembered what Francine had taught him in Pittsburgh and he turned red, thankful for the lack of light.

"Been busy. Helping Mrs. Sullivan and all." She met his gaze quickly.

For the first time, he saw the bruise to the right of her mouth. A dark draft scuttled across his skin. He stopped her. "Lily, what happened to your face?"

Her hand flew to her cheek and she turned, began walking again. "Nothing."

He took her sleeve and pulled her close. "Did somebody . . ."

"No," she said. "Nobody did anything. All right? Just clumsy is all. Banged my face in the barn. Didn't have my lantern lit and couldn't see a thing."

She pulled her arm away and her voice rose angrily. "I don't need you looking out for me, Andrew Houghton. All right? I don't need you asking me about a stupid bruise. And I don't need you walking me home, either. I've been doing just fine in this life all by myself." Her voice rose sharply and trembled with the pitch.

"What's this all about, Lily?"

"Nothing." A long tear flowed from each eye and she wiped them roughly away. "Just better if you leave me be."

He kissed her then, felt the salty tears upon her lips and the new ones that splashed against his cheeks. She tried to pull away even as her body and lips melded against his. He held her face with his hand, combed it through her hair, leaned her neck back and kissed her throat. She curled into his neck. "Please," she begged uselessly. "Just leave me be."

He shook his head. "No." Andrew wrapped his arm around her shoulders, felt the way she crumpled against him. "I'm not going to do that, Lily girl."

She reached for him and the notebook she had

been clutching dropped to the ground with spread pages, revealing the pencil drawings. "You drew these?"

"They're not very good." Lily went to grab the notebook, but he got to it first.

"Can I at least look at them?"

Lily grunted and snatched the notebook, securing it easily from his loose grip. "Told you they're not very good." She fanned the drawings in front of him, one animal after another, before slamming the pages closed. "Happy now?"

"Yes. And for the record, they're very good."

She scoffed, then abated. "You think?"

"Yeah. They're very good, Lily." Then, he motioned to the remnants of an old stone wall. "Come sit with me for a sec."

They rested on the cold stones. "Do you have a pencil?" he asked. Lily pulled out her drawing tool from her pocket, handed it over. "Mind if I add something?"

Her eyebrows scrunched inquisitively as she opened her notebook and held it on her lap. On the first page, he wrote the word "Deer," on the second, "Rabbit," on the third, "Hawk." Page by page, he titled each of the animals. He handed the pencil back. "There. Your first reading lesson."

The corners of her mouth rose. The bruise on her cheek pinched, leaving him empty and wanting to put a light kiss against the injury. She touched the letters he had sketched on each page, moved her lips soundlessly as she formed each word.

Lily's innocence, the purity and beauty of her, washed over his flesh and left him flushed. "We better get you home before you freeze to death," he said with effort. Andrew took her hand until she stood and did not release the fingers entwined in his own.

They climbed the rest of the miles as one body, clung tightly against each other in the frozen air, and yet they were warm. Lily turned to him. "You never said why you came to Widow Sullivan's?"

"Wanted to ask you something." He gripped her hand, the nerves taking him by surprise. "I'm playing baseball this Saturday and thought you might like to come. Thought maybe after, I could take you to town." He grinned bashfully. "We could see a show at the nickelodeon or do whatever you'd like."

Her lips pressed together happily and her cheeks glowed. "Are you asking me out on a date?"

"Suppose I am."

Lily grew a full inch and her posture straightened. "I would like that very much."

With sheer relief, he kissed her on the top of her silky hair, wanted to drown in the softness. At the Morton door, Andrew kissed her again on the lips, careful not to graze the bruise near her mouth. She sighed languidly as he pulled away. "Good night, Lily girl. See you Saturday."

"Good night, Dr. Houghton," she said fondly.

"Dr.?"

She tilted her head and watched him with reverence. "Tonight, you became a paid veterinarian, remember?" She blew a kiss at him. "Good night, Dr. Houghton."

The ache for the career renewed in that moment. He wasn't a vet, but perhaps he had a service to offer after all. "Good night," he said again, the hope and pride sudden and gleaming in the cold night air.

CHAPTER 31

A ndrew climbed onto the bench of the Muellers' wagon. Fritz sat behind in a pile of straw, his back leaning against the men's seat. Pieter threw a red cap and shirt at Andrew.

"Creekers?" Andrew laughed as he read the shirt. "I'm playing for a team called the Creekers?"

"Yeah," Pieter agreed with a shiver. He plucked a piece of straw from the back and chewed on the tip. "On account we live closest to Pucketa Creek."

"No wonder you haven't won a game."

"Hey," Pieter defended. "Won one this season. Don't take that away from us. Besides, we were almost called the Plums." Pieter laughed. " 'Creekers' don't seem so bad compared to that."

Fritz hummed disjointedly from behind, the singsong mixing with the clomping of the horse's shoes and the rattling wood wheels. "Never said why you were in Pittsburgh the other day," mentioned Pieter.

Andrew blew a long stream of air out of his mouth and took off the stiff baseball cap. "Wouldn't believe me if I told you."

Pieter narrowed his eyes. "Try me."

"Wilhelm brought me to a prostitute."

The horse pulled back with the sudden jerk from Pieter's reins. "A whore?" Pieter gasped. The young man leaned on his knees, disbelief peaking his eyebrows. Once composed, he gave a quick *click, click* to the horse, got her back moving again. "A whore?" he repeated.

Andrew gave a quick look to Fritz. Pieter followed his gaze. "Don't worry about him. Fritz don't know the difference between a whore and a crow." He stared at Andrew, his eyes wide for news. "He really take you to a prostitute?"

Andrew nodded, punched the inside of the cap to break in the seams.

"Was she pretty?"

"Yes."

"Well?" Pieter squirmed in his seat, waved his hands in prodding. "So, out with it. How was it?"

Andrew raised a boot to the sideboard. "Wouldn't know."

Pieter grimaced. "Stop toying with me, Houghton."

"Seriously." Andrew raised his hand in the air in oath. "I couldn't do it."

"Oh, man." Pieter's mouth fell and he grew remorseful. " 'Cause of the accident?" he asked hesitantly. "Parts aren't working down there?"

"No!" Andrew hit him with the baseball cap. "Parts are working just fine." He shivered. "For

Pete's sake, man! Be a fate worse than death."

"Amen." Pieter prompted again with his open face. "So, what happened?"

"She was pretty and all. Nice lady, too. But it didn't feel right. Kept thinking what my ma would think."

"You're standing next to a woman ready to have sex with you and you're thinking about your ma?"

"Well," he conceded, "I did until she took off her clothes. Couldn't think much about anything after that."

Pieter's legs twitched. "She was naked?"

"Naked as a jaybird."

"Oh, God." Pieter wiped his forehead.

"You okay?"

"Yeah, but you better start talking," he ordered. "Better not leave anything out, either."

"Nothing to tell," Andrew said. "Told her I couldn't do it. Just didn't feel right."

"That's it?" Pieter's whole face contorted in revulsion. "Telling me you just sat there with a naked woman? What, you two just play a nice game of checkers and sip tea the whole time?"

"Gave me a lesson." Andrew shoved the cap on his head and pulled down the visor. "Explained the proper way to please a woman."

"Explained?" Pieter's eyes grew wide and intense.

"Showed me, actually."

"Said you didn't touch her," he accused.

"I didn't."

"Then how she show . . ." Pieter paused, his mouth suspended with the image materializing in his mind. "Oh."

Andrew gave a slight tug to the forgotten reins in Pieter's palm. "We're here."

"Go on ahead." Pieter put his baseball mitt on top of his crotch. "I'm going to need a minute."

Lily took her best dress off the line, pressed the fabric quickly under the hot iron, the lace around the sleeves and collar mended this morning. She bathed and brushed her hair, tied back the front sections in a pearl barrette. She didn't have any rosewater so rubbed rosemary leaves across her skin and pinched her cheeks for rouge.

"Don't you look pretty," Claire said. "You meeting Andrew at the game?"

Lily nodded. She hadn't seen Andrew since their last kiss and couldn't think of anything else since she had felt his lips, the tenderness and eagerness of them, the softness that had melted the bones under her muscles. Her heart raced all night and all this morning and her hands still felt jittery as she climbed upon the buggy and headed to the ball field.

On the edge of Pucketa Creek, it seemed every young person in town had attended to watch the game. Lily climbed down from the buggy, evened out her dress. She rarely left home and the sight of the crowd intimidated her, nearly enough to make her turn back. But she thought of Andrew. A date. An actual date. As she walked toward the wooden rows of benches, she walked in a dream. For once she wasn't an outcast; she was a young woman, dressed neat and proper, watching her beau play baseball. She was normal for once in her life.

Emily Campbell sat with a group of girls in the front row, their giggling and close conversation bringing the nerves to Lily's reserve again. She took a seat a row over from the group, tried to ignore their stares and snickers. Lily focused on the men milling on the far edge of the field. On one side, men in red shirts; on the other, those in green. She had no idea which team Andrew was on. Then the men broke and headed into the brown open dirt to take their positions and line up.

"Is that him?" Emily asked her friend. "The pitcher?"

"That's him," the young woman confirmed. "Andrew. Kiser, I think."

The chatter floated and Lily strained for every word.

"Your father have a fit if he found you courting a German," another girl warned.

"Well, Daddy won't find out, will he?" Emily Campbell stretched out her neck to see better.

"Besides, not courting him. Just looking." She played with the satin ribbons in her pretty hair and turned around, saw Lily looking at her.

"Mind your business, Morton!" she hollered.

For once, Lily met the woman's beady eyes and didn't flinch. From the field, a handsome young man called to Lily, waved his red cap in the air. She stretched her arm out high and waved back, her breath catching at the sight of Andrew.

Emily glowered and pointed to Fritz Mueller sitting alone on the next bench. "Shouldn't you be sitting with the other freaks?"

Lily stood, faced Emily unwaveringly. "Actually, I think I will. Smells like horse over here." *She* was courting Andrew and the pride made her bold, made her walk calmly past the gossiping lips.

"Watch out, Lilith," called Emily cruelly. "Your horns might start to show. Inbreeding does that to a girl."

The slap came hard and swift, cracked open the mortification and shame that always threatened to seep and drown her no matter how hard she tried to bury the truth. Shovelful after shovelful, hands and body dirty—nothing more than covering broken shells with sand only to have them washed up again.

So long ago, Claire had been the first target of the harsh words, those rare days of heading to town to buy what little food they could afford, her hand clasped in Claire's, the taunting fresh and blinding to Lily's innocence. And her sister's hand would sweat under the teasing, squeeze her fingers with the ridicule. She would look up to Claire's white face and lips, witness the trembling of her chin, and Lily knew that she was the cause, knew it to her core. And so they shared this condemnation, the scars, and held securely to each other as they fought to stay upright. Lily had felt Claire's terror, her stigma, since birth— she had inhaled it with her first breath of life.

The sound of a bat against a ball brought her back. The heat burned, but Lily gritted her teeth and crushed the memories to pulp. She headed for the other bleachers, pushed the evil words and chortling of the girls away. "Fritz," she asked softly, her voice tormented, "may I sit with you?"

"Sure, Lily." The giant man-boy moved his bottom over to the right. "Sure thing!"

Breathe. Breathe. Fritz probably did not know her past, and if he did it was as incomprehensible to him as it had been for her—as it still was for her. She had always known Claire was her mother, the same way she knew that fact should never be mentioned or acknowledged. One does not speak or analyze depravity; one runs from it as if it were a plague.

A man in a green jersey stepped up to the plate and readied his bat. Andrew pulled back his right arm, lifted his knee and blasted a ball past home plate. "Good one, Andrew!" Fritz screamed. He clapped his hands clumsily, tried to whistle through his fingers but only made a wet wheezing sound instead.

Breathe. The wind fluttered her skirt; her hands sat smooth and feminine on the folds. *Today, she thought, I will not be soiled. Today, I can be pretty. Normal.* She turned to the young man by her side, grateful beyond words for his simple, beautiful ignorance. "You like him very much, don't you?" she asked with affection.

"Uh-ha."

Her body weakened at the sight of Andrew. Here she could watch him openly. Here she was allowed to stare and smile while she thought of his strong body next to hers. Another ball whizzed past the plate. "Strike two!"

Fritz pounded the wood with his fist. "There you go!"

"We're lucky they moved from Pittsburgh, aren't we?" she said, relaxing. It was nice to talk to someone in public, even if he didn't respond. If Fritz weren't here, she'd still be stuck a row over from Emily Campbell.

"Andrew goes to Pittsburgh," Fritz said as he watched the players.

"Strike three! You're out!"

"No," Lily corrected kindly. "He's *from* Pittsburgh."

"No, Andrew go to Pittsburgh." He clapped his

300

hands heartily as the next batter took his stance. "To see the whore."

Something deep inside of her curled and died. "What did you say?"

Fritz smiled, drooled slightly. "To see the whore. Pretty lady, too."

Lily's hand found her stomach. There was no way. She looked at Fritz's profile to see if there was truth in the words, but he just stared out to the ball field. Fritz was slow minded, she reminded herself. He didn't know what he was saying.

"Fritz," she asked softly, "do you know what that is?"

"A whore?" he asked loudly. "Yeah, Fritz knows!" He laughed mischievously. "Naked lady. Wants to have sex. Sex with Andrew." He giggled impishly. "Pretty lady, too. Taught him good."

A tied dog barked near the wagons, strained to chase a wayward baseball. Emily and her friends laughed loudly from beyond the way, clicked and chatted like beetles. Men smoked in a small ring behind the dugout. "Out!" yelled the umpire.

The noise drummed around her ears, made her want to shove her hands against the inner canals. Lily folded her arms into her stomach, her insides swaying and queasy.

"Fritz knows about the whore." He slapped his knee, then rubbed it ferociously. "She showed him how to please her. How to touch a woman, he said. She was pretty." He whispered to Lily secretly, "Pieter want one, too. Can tell he wants one just like Andrew had. A whore. Pieter want one bad."

Lily covered her mouth. The hope, the dream, fractured—the sharp points stabbing ruthlessly. *Watch out, Lilith. Your horns might start to show. Inbreeding does that to a girl.* Andrew had seen the horns. He saw the malady she was, the curse she brought to this world. And he would rather run to the arms of a whore than touch her.

She fled to her buggy, the tears forming in rivulets over her cheeks, stinging and constricting her throat. Fritz cheered from his seat. The crowd clapped and rose.

"You're out!"

While the brown dust from the field rose and coiled around Andrew's ankles, the mood of the opposing team sank and stirred into the dirt. The men in green brooded as they chewed tobacco. With each passing inning, the rust-colored spit flung with more vigor and less-focused aim.

Andrew rolled the ball in his fingers, the stitching comfortable and familiar against the tender spots. He waited patiently as the next batter went through his ritual of kicking the plate, rubbing his hands upon his pants, kicking the plate again, spitting tobacco and adjusting the bat in his large hands.

"Cripple's gettin' tired, Sam!" a man hollered. "See that arm shaking from here!"

Andrew readied his stance, his body tight and expectant.

"Kaiser's biggest fan!" another shouted. "Spawned straight from the devil himself!" another quipped.

He pulled back and hurled the ball across home plate.

"Strike one!"

The batter narrowed his eyes, his back bracing and hunched. He practiced three hard swings that could have smashed a tree. Andrew rubbed the worn leather of the ball, tan from use.

"Coal miner piece of shit!"

Andrew turned his head, raised his knee, pulled back his shoulder.

"Least his pa's dead. One less German we gotta deal with!"

Andrew launched the ball, aiming it at the heckler, the ball crunching him in the skull. The batter dropped his bat, charged the pitcher mound. The men from the Creekers flooded forward with punching fists as Andrew walked away, the insults beating him harder than fists. But the fight broke quickly and the teams separated, the fissure widening with disgruntled force.

Pieter wiped a bloody nose and jogged to Andrew. "Bastard had it coming."

The adrenaline fired through Andrew's body, his chest heaving. Pieter took the corner of his shirt and dabbed his nose, inspected the growing stain. "It's getting bad," Pieter warned. "Like everyone's all twisted up."

Andrew wasn't listening. He looked out into the crowd, scanned the benches for the woman with the green eyes, the woman whose light would numb the black words and make his heart pump with desire instead of anger. But Lily was gone. Andrew took off the baseball shirt and hat and shoved them in Pieter's arms. "I'm done."

CHAPTER 32

Lily went back to doing laundry and mending for Frank's clients—dry basting clothes, starching and ironing until her face flushed with moisture and steam. Hidden in the back of her dresser drawer, in an old sock of her father's, the coins from her egg money jingled pathetically. The money tugged, now more than ever. *Just leave. Go away, Lily. There's nothing here for you.* But the coins mocked her with their words, for the meager total wouldn't even get her past Pittsburgh.

On this evening, Frank had gone to town to play cards with the sheriff, the town clerk and the other townmen. They would talk about the war and she was glad they were in town and not here at the house. Always war, war, war. She was tired of the talk. Lily did not like to think of the battles across the sea. Always about the Germans. She thought of the ones she knew, and they did not match the pictures painted by the men in town. There was Mrs. Mueller who used to drop off food to Claire when she was too sore from beatings to cook. There was Mr. Cossman down at the brewery who always brought extra grains to Mrs. Sullivan for her horses. And the Kisers. Lily fanned these Germans in her mind and didn't believe that the men against the Allies could be so different. Hearing Frank talk, they were a pack of savages, no hearts, just guns and a thirst for killing babies and raping women and taking over the world. But somewhere those men had mothers and sisters; they were somebody's sons and brothers and lovers.

Andrew floated into her mind and the rosiness in her cheeks grew even as the steam lessened. She tried to push him from her thoughts, to rid herself of the memory of his fake kisses and vacant words. She was worthless and he knew it, the reality numb and harsh. She was drained of tears and dead to hope. Lily had just been a temporary fix between the women who could satisfy his needs.

Lily placed the flatirons back on the stove to heat again. Claire sat next to the table lamp and mended buttons on the shirts. The coins tugged again; a draft blew from the old windows, tapped her across the shoulder blades, and she bit her lip. Lily watched her sister carefully before beginning, "Winter's going to be a hard one, don't you think?"

Claire shuddered. "Sounds like the hardest one yet."

She picked up an iron and spit to test the heat, let it rest a bit more.

"I get to feeling it in my bones, you know?" Claire rubbed her fingertips together. "Get all numb by the nails now." She grinned. "When we were kids, we'd run around in the snow with only our dresses and boots. Remember that? Don't even remember feeling the cold. Funny how that is."

Lily agreed, picked up the iron and let the humid, wet air trickle to her face and gush her pores. "Be nice to head south, don't you think?" She glanced furtively at Claire for any sign of unrest. "Florida's nice all year. Heard people got lemon and orange trees growing in their backyards. Be nice making fresh juice, wouldn't it?"

"Ah, that'd be nice." Her sister smiled into her needle and thread.

Lily draped the shirt over the chair and picked another from the pile. "We could do it. You and me." Her heart beat slowly, cautiously. "Just for a visit maybe."

She shook her head. "Frank can't leave; you know that. Got too much with the business."

"I know. But was thinking just the two of us could go. Wouldn't be gone long."

Claire glanced up and knowledge hinted behind the slow eyes, recognition. But then the child returned and nearly stomped. "No, no. Frank wouldn't like that. Me going away like that. You know how he gets, Lil. He wouldn't like that at all." She pulled the moth-eaten sweater tighter around her middle.

A knock came to the front door and Claire stood, craned her neck to see the outline of the porch. "It's Andrew," Claire said merrily. "And he's got flowers."

"I don't want to see him." Lily threw the shirt on the chair, retreated to the corner.

"But he looks so handsome, Lil—"

"Just tell him I'm not here."

The door knocked again. "You sure?" Claire asked.

"Please, just make him go away." Lily curled farther into the wall, her lashes wet.

Claire stepped out of the room and the door to the porch opened, creaked loudly. "Lily can't see you now, I'm afraid," mumbled Claire.

Lily couldn't hear Andrew, but his presence filled the house, made the pain of what he did that much harder.

"J-j-just better if you go," her sister flustered. "I don't know. All right. I will. Thanks, Andrew. Best to your family."

The door creaked again. Claire found Lily and handed her the bouquet of white and purple mums, the woody scent filling her nose and weighting her chest with missing.

Claire's expression mixed with remorse and

confusion. "Why would you slight him like that, Lily? He do something mean to you?" Claire waited for an answer, but none came. "Should have seen him. Looked like he lost his best friend in the whole world."

Lily pushed the flowers at Claire. "You keep them. I don't want them." She picked up the hot iron again and the steam stung her eyes, made tears form when she was using every reserve to keep them down. Her stomach ached and twisted.

Claire put the flowers in a vase, set them on the side table. "Pretty, aren't they?"

Lily's fingers covered her mouth and her lips opened. "Keep an eye on the iron, Claire." Her voice doleful, weak. "I need some air." She hurried outside, passed the remnants of her tiny vegetable garden, the old lettuce leaves translucent and lacey from morning frosts. The tiny barn tilted menacingly to the right, the low splintered roof a poor shelter to their two cows. Lily entered the stall, rubbed the nose of the black beast.

She remembered when Frank bought the cow and how she gave birth soon after. Frank sold the calf a few days later and the mama brayed endlessly in grief for nearly a month. Lily had hid her head under the pillow and cried with the low mourning, vowed to never let a calf be separated again.

She placed her forehead to the cow's. "I'm sorry." She wept into the soft fur, the wet nose thick with breathing under her chin. "I'm sorry what we do to you." And she wept for the cow and she wept for the calf and she wept for not what was taken away from her life, but for what was never given.

The cow snorted and backed up. Lily dried her eyes on her shoulder.

"Lily?"

She spun around. Andrew stood in the open door, tall and handsome, and her soul burned to run into his arms. But she knew what he had done and so she stepped back. His presence, the very sight of him, deveined her.

He inched forward. "You've been crying," he said. She shook and Andrew didn't understand. Didn't understand the look of hatred upon her face.

"I don't want to see you anymore," she hissed. The vicious words shocked him, left him cold.

"Why?" he challenged, his figure unyielding. "If you don't want to see me, I won't bother you again. But I want to know why."

"I heard things at the game, Andrew," she huffed, and wouldn't look at him. "About you."

He remembered the slurs of the baseball players, didn't realize Lily had heard them as well. And instead of staying there for him, supporting him, she had left. The disloyalty made him fierce. "You heard what they said and you're blaming me?"

"You're not even going to deny it?"

"Deny what?" He rubbed his hand through his hair gruffly. He wasn't going to apologize for defending himself or Pieter. "That I enjoyed doing what I did? That I acted like a man?"

Her face twisted in disgust and new tears threatened to spill over her eyes. "How could you?" she spluttered. "A man doesn't do that. You should be ashamed of yourself."

Andrew seethed, put his hand on his hip and stared at the broken slats of the barn. She didn't have a clue. "I'll tell you what," he stated harshly. "If tempted, I'll do it again. Not a man who wouldn't." He turned to leave. "And if you can't understand that, Lily, then I don't want to see you either."

CHAPTER 33

Winter barreled upon Pennsylvania, the easygoing fall finally pushed out the door no different from unwanted guests. And as fall pushed out, all was pushed in. The cows and sheep and pigs were locked in the barn, the annoyed grunts echoing through the beams as their boredom and tight quarters crowded their sensitivities. The chickens were locked in the coop, the windows so dirty that even in full sun the coop stayed in semidarkness and the chickens responded with rebellion against egg production. And the Kisers shoved within the confines of the old farmhouse, without the grace of transition, without that grace of insulating the house or chopping enough firewood or cleaning the nests and old leaves from the clogged chimneys.

Everything had to be bought, every ounce of food had to be brought in or delivered and Wilhelm watched the numbers of the bank account lessen like the backward twist of a clock.

The first major snowfall landed and did not stop. It paused and napped briefly but then started up more sternly than before. The snowdrifts blew to white pyramids scattered against the high points of the property and the farmhouse sat in a palm of snow, the fingers reaching to the bottoms of the windows.

Wilhelm hoped to put off his final run to town for supplies, but when the snow showed no signs of waning for the season he realized he couldn't wait another day or they'd all be eating pinecones. So, he bundled himself in a wool coat and hat, layered his long johns under his trousers and stuffed the bottoms into his socks and walked to the only friend he had, Heinrich Mueller.

Wilhelm stomped through the snow that met his knees, the air panting loud and labored as he huffed down the valley, over the frozen stream and up to the main road. He already was heated beneath the wool layers even as his nostrils, chin and cheeks numbed. He looked up at the steel gray sky, at the white flakes drifting toward the earth. And they landed on his eyebrows and the whiskers of his jaw. As a boy he would have stuck out his tongue to catch the snow, but he wasn't a boy and so the thought never crossed his mind.

A few miles to go and he stepped methodically, one foot over the other, faster until he felt chased. The old farmhouse, barely in view, faded behind the large white flakes, the distance bringing more relief than anything in his life. For a moment, he thought, *I'll just keep walking*. He would walk to the train tracks, hop on a car and go as far away as the engine would travel. He would have no money, but he could start over. He could run away and ride the trains and leave that dreary farmhouse and the dead cries of the twins that still hung in his ears and Eveline's scolding and Andrew's arm behind like a bad smell. And for a moment there was hope. His footsteps livened. The farther he moved away from the farm, the fresher the air, and he breathed it in, let it scald his lungs with ice. And he wanted to run. Panic for freedom shrieked in his cells: *Run, run, run!*

Wilhelm stopped then, stared—a solitary figure amid the falling snow and the abandoned street. He observed the wide expanse where he was not trapped, where there was a future and possibilities. But then he saw his footsteps etched in the snow. Realized that he'd have to retrace the steps back. The gray of the sky permeated then, the ash sledging through his veins no different from sewage through a clogged pipe. And he did not want to run any longer, did not want to watch the flakes fall from an endless sky. The gray took over and dragged him like a lamb to the Muellers' front steps.

"Mr. Kiser, vhat are you doing out dere!" Mrs. Mueller took to the man as if he were a naked infant left out in the cold. "Come! My vord! Come in from dat snow, Mr. Kiser!" She pulled him in with the hands and arms of a man, took off his hat and patted the piles of snow off his coat. "Heinrich! Mr. Kiser's come in from the farm nearly froze to death! Anna, bring hot broth for our guest!" she yelled through the house.

Wilhelm was touched by the instant generosity, the instant warmth of the house, tried not to think of the direct opposite of his own living situation. "Thank you, Mrs. Mueller. It's all right. Worked up a sweat on the walk over."

"*Nein, nein,*" she harped. "Your face like a frozen tomato." Her hot, plump hands pressed into his cheeks. "Take orf your boots and sit by the fire, now. You go now." She pointed animatedly as if he didn't know where the fire was.

Heinrich came in buttoning a wool sweater over his flannel. "Vilhelm!"

Little Anna came in with a steaming mug of broth and Wilhelm took it by the fire but did not sit, knowing his pants were quite wet from the snow. Heinrich hit him on the back. "Vhat brings you here, my friend?"

He went quiet. The exertion from the walk left him shaky. The warmth of the house, the quaintness and finished aspects, made him think of his own home with horror. Heinrich lost his smile and nodded, read his neighbor's demeanor as one remembers a dream or his own story. Without taking his eyes off Wilhelm, he called out to his wife, "Gerda, bring up the new stout. A man needs a bit more fire than broth."

Gerda laughed. "Ha. Fire is right. Dat stout burn the chest hair right orf ya. Pieter," she called. "Bring up the stout."

Heinrich pointed to the chair and waved off the wet pants with a nod that said, *Will dry.* A few minutes later, Pieter carried the familiar worn cask, set it on the table between them. "Hello, Mr. Kiser," he greeted merrily, his cheeks pink with health.

"Hello, Pieter," he answered. "Good to see you."

"Andrew come with you?"

"No, trek was enough for one man."

"Yeah. Tell him I'll come down once the snow stops and we'll go hunting."

Heinrich poured the beer and waited for Wilhelm to speak.

"Didn't expect the cold to set in so quick," he finally said. "Can't get the car or wagon up the lane. Why I came to see you. To ask a favor." He weakened with the words. Never remembered asking a favor from anyone.

Heinrich perked, waited to be of assistance.

"I need a ride to town. Need to load up on food for the winter."

Heinrich laughed, waved him off. "That's all you come to ask? But of course." He waved it off as silliness again. "We'll go tomorrow in the vagon. Car too much trouble in the snow. We'll load you up and the boys will help carry. Fritz is all muscle and can carry the whole load on his shoulders, I t'ink!"

Heinrich pulled a cigarette from a dented case and offered one to Wilhelm, who declined. The man smoked easily, his worn and wrinkled face still young despite years of hard labor. Wilhelm glanced at the house, at the comfortable furnishings. Heinrich followed his gaze slowly. "Need more than just a ride, *ja*?" he asked.

Wilhelm rubbed the back of his neck. "I'm short for spring. Winter's going to drain us." The words constricted his throat, his voice low and deep. "Was thinking about going to Morton for a bridge loan. Just enough to cover the seed and new hay."

His neighbor took out his cigarette, stuck out his tongue like the tobacco had leaked out and soured it. He shook his head roughly. "No, Vilhelm. You don't do business vith dat man. No."

"I know. Heard people talking. But it's a short loan. Six months at most until the sows are ready to be sold and chicks can lay." The bank wasn't an option. The manager knew there was nothing left in the account, would never loan to a German, regardless. Campbell had cut off credit at the store. Between the bank and the general store, they had him in a choke hold and knew it, enjoyed watching him squirm.

"Frank Morton." Mr. Mueller said the name

317

as a conviction, leaned forward and bore with the intensity of a giant. "Dat man no good. No heart." He thumped his chest.

"Don't see I have much choice. Besides, he's been kind to Eveline." The words brought a heat to his hands that he didn't expect. "His wife and sister-in-law have been good to us," he corrected.

Heinrich stared at the carpeting between their feet. "I have some seed, Vilhelm. It not much but could give you an acre. From that, you vould have enough seed next year. It would be a hard year vithout, but a man goes through many hard years. Take the seed and make do. Work in town if you have to, but don't go to Frank."

"I won't take your seed, Heinrich." The man started to insist and Wilhelm held up a hand. "I won't take it." His chest puffed with decision. "I'll think about what you said."

Heinrich patted his shoulder sadly and stood. He cleared the air with a clap of his hands. "Now, you come and eat vith us, get warm and drunk, before your walk."

Wilhelm ate with the family. He drank so much beer that the faces blurred and the voices slurred into one. He ate homemade blood sausage and spaetzle and roasted chicken and he ate until his pants cut into his waist. And he laughed. Forgot that he knew how to laugh. Laughed at the stories and the German songs that spewed out of Heinrich like soap from a washtub.

When Wilhelm left, the full moon, brightened as a lighthouse lamp, dyed the snow blue and sparkled. He was drunk and did not feel the cold, his footsteps uneven and curved from side to side so it looked like several men left footprints instead of one. And he walked with unbuttoned coat, sang at the top of his lungs the German songs that he didn't even know the words to, and he felt alive with food and drink and didn't care how long it would take to get home, didn't even care if there was a home to get back to.

But he did get home and Eveline waited at the door in her night coat, her limbs stuttering in cold and anger. But Wilhelm, still happy with stout, stumbled toward his wife, who seemed so beautiful, and he puckered to kiss her sweet lips.

She slapped him hard and square across the cheek. "Do you know what time it is?" she screamed. "Been scared to death that you froze out there and here you come staggering in drunk and smelling of beer and gravy!"

He sobered now, the cold blasting, the songs and the waiting lips and the warmth of a cozy fire and friendly stories slapped away by her cold fingers. The dead twins screeched in his ears.

The next morning, Eveline shoveled pancakes onto her husband's plate. They were pale and broken. Hardly an egg had been laid this week and she mixed the batter with only one.

Wilhelm's eyes were bloodshot and she knew his head throbbed with the hangover from the Muellers' hospitality. While she poured his coffee, she subtly inspected his cheek to see if a mark showed from where she had slapped him.

She regretted her temper. She had never acted out violently and she didn't understand how she could have hit her husband. The guilt, hot and terrible, nearly too fierce to utter an apology. She didn't know why she had been so angry. All she knew was that she was left in this cold home eating stale bread and listening to Will and Edgar whine while Wilhelm perched warm and fed at the Muellers'.

And then she realized why she had struck him. Because this was the life she had chosen for them. This was the life she had begged for, a life that at times seemed to slowly squeeze the life out of them all. And she panicked that her husband wouldn't come back, either by choice or by accident, and she would be left in this freezer on her own. It was her fear that had hit him and the regret stung sharply.

"Do you want Andrew to go with you?" she asked timidly. "To town?"

Wilhelm shook his head, finished the last of his bland breakfast and pushed the plate away. She wanted to hold him, tell him she was sorry— sorry for everything. But she took his plate and turned away without another word, didn't even say good-bye as he picked up his coat and headed out to meet the Muellers' wagon on the main road.

Lily shimmied into the creases of the old sofa, the cushions long bleached from sun and wear, frayed and bald along the rounded arms. Claire made bread in the kitchen, the punching of the dough in a steady beat, a slight pitter-patter like a child's feet playing hopscotch. Frank stayed in his office all morning.

The hour had been late when Wilhelm Kiser knocked on the door, swaying and loud and asking to see Frank. The men had met briefly, just long enough to sign papers. And Lily's heart sank then, fell in sympathy for Will and Edgar, for Mrs. Kiser—for no one came to Frank unless in desperate straits.

Andrew. The pain fluttered to the pit of her stomach, the missing sticking to the walls of the closed house, the absence of him leaving her lost in each listless day. She pushed his smooth, strong features from her thoughts and dug through the tangled yarn basket next to the sofa.

Lily pulled a clump of rose-tinted wool, dyed long ago with beet juice, and found her knitting needles in the bottom. In quick, harsh loops, she started the scarf, the tools *clicking, clicking, clicking.*

Frank's footsteps clomped upstairs on the floorboards, pacing. The oven in the kitchen clattered metallically as Claire rearranged pots and bread pans above the fires. The snow carried softly outside the window, hung upon the skeletons of the bushes in lines of new white. And through it all, Lily's fingers found the knots and fell into the design of her knitting absently and without observation. Until she paused. She looked at the yarn, the tiny baby sock that had taken shape between the pointed x of the needles.

She rubbed the little sock, the smooth bumps along the heel. For a moment, the dream flowed again, trickled to the man of blue eyes and gentle tones, to the farmhouse that she could clean and cook in and to the great apple tree that she had once climbed and where she had found the man she loved.

Frank's boots stomped down the stairs and Lily buried the small bootie under the mounds of hand-spun wool.

Winter in the Kiser farmhouse morphed into a world unto its own that lasted years or centuries between the slow seconds. They spent Christmas with the Muellers. But for that day, life outside the frozen home did not exist, as they pulled themselves within the walls and hibernated.

In the evenings, Wilhelm read the *Pittsburg Press*, the news drafted in black-and-white English clarity—Americans were good; Germans were evil. Andrew and Eveline didn't read the newspaper. The headlines were enough to add to the weariness, the photos of tanks and cartoons of sabers through the Kaiser and his Huns. They all saw the listed lines of the deceased—the doughboys hot to enlist only to return to American soil in burnt and shattered pieces. But the adults did not speak of these notices, of the stories of feral bloodshed, and when Will and Edgar were present the paper was turned over or folded to reveal innocuous advertisements for Maytag washers and Hawthorne bicycles. The young boys did not need to know of this war. Not yet.

Andrew strained under the confines of the house and the strength in his shoulders and thighs weakened. They ached, as only the muscles of the young do, for action and movement, for physical labor and exertion. When the body lay idle, the thoughts grew strong, as if all the physical movements dwarfed into mental movements and pounded within his skull. The missing of many things clung to him as the black ashes clung to the bricks of the fireplaces.

His right arm scolded his former left one, lamented on the imbalance and the inadequacy of being able to do half of what it used to. And the missing left one argued back. Said that the right had no right to complain, that it was useful and alive—that it did not sting and burn and throb in an infinite display of mockery. And then Andrew would curse himself, ignore the rival sides. But upon their quieting, the missing and longing would set in. The missing of his parents, of the laughter around an old, worn table at breakfast and dinner, of a tiny house whose timber and warmth proclaimed a safety that had eclipsed the poverty. There were thoughts of a young woman also, and these thoughts made him heat from the hips and made him want to climb the walls and dunk his head in a bucket of snow. But then he remembered that she had stood by and defended men who made slurs, who took their side over his own, and so he squashed the wanting and shoveled snow and carried firewood and cleaned the frozen cow stalls until he was too tired to think or feel.

At night, Andrew turned his focus to old passions—reading veterinary texts and plotting a better future, the words of his father replaying, reminding him to take care of his family. But he had two families now, the attachment to this home growing stronger in equal measure with the burdens to help them. And so he studied; he wrote letters to his mother full of promises for a better life. And he tried not to believe that the tasks were as useless as a bird without wings.

Over the frigid months, the house sighed with waiting, with the cold that shuddered from the wind and the sour moods under its rooflines.

Outside, under the weight of blowing wind and thick flakes, the great apple tree drooped, the old bark moaning as its branches divided and hung as a canopy over the hidden roots. Tips of wizened limbs jutted closer to the house, picked like fingers at the peeling paint, the nails *tapping, tapping, tapping* like a bored child at a school desk.

And so winter carried into 1918 with a steady and unrelenting weariness—a heavy, dull cold that settles into the limbs and numbs the appendages and wonders if warmth will ever be known again.

PART 4

The military masters of Germany . . .
filled our unsuspecting communities
with vicious spies and conspirators.

—President Woodrow Wilson

CHAPTER 34

In April 1918, the thaw came quickly and without notice, started in the night and raised temperatures so robustly that by morning the earth heated from the inside out.

Steam rose across the hills, thickened into fog along the valleys and pulled high on the sun's strings to the heavens. The robins and bluebirds appeared from the smoking landscape, chatted loud enough to make up for their winter absence. Mourning doves darted in chase between the whitening birch trees. Red-winged blackbirds clung to the old reeds and cattails along the thawing creek, their weight bouncing the spindly stalks up and down like a greased well pump.

Between the brambles, the black raspberry prickers glowed purple and the grapevines twisted brown with barky texture. Forsythia budded green with a promise of yellow and the pussy willows grew furry pods soft as rabbit paws. Striped crocus erupted in sunspots between clusters of daffodils. The land bloomed; the land sang and spread its aroma of birth and renewal.

Andrew Houghton emerged from the house,

smelled the nimble scents of warm snow melting into musty loam. He leaned his neck back, his skin soaking in the natural warmth, the first heat uninspired by a coal stove or a burning log in more months than he could count. And within the balminess, the cells of his body ignited and the rush of energy made weary limbs suddenly alive and young and drunk on spirit. Coatless, he stepped off the footpath and sank six inches into the ground. "What the . . ." Using his left leg as a brace against the stone, he sucked his buried foot from the soupy mud and squinted at the melting, oozing, grassless landscape.

Andrew rubbed his forehead and chuckled incredulously. The screen door slammed and Wilhelm mirrored Andrew's entrance with a full grin to the bright sky until his nephew placed a hand of warning to the man's chest and pointed to the flowing ground. Wilhelm scratched the stubble at his chin, the light shining it silver, and he shook his head, a resigned laugh coming from the throat. "Ah, Christ." He shook his head again and shrugged his shoulders. "I'll be damned."

But mud or no mud, the hard, deep, black winter was over and with each inch of rising sun the lips curved upward and the nostrils widened and they paused in their work just to relish the glory of the turned season.

The apple tree shook off the last ridges of

snow, and with a sigh and flicker the limbs out-stretched and unbent, took woody claws off the house and quieted the unending tapping. Eveline tied the clothesline to the heavy trunk and patted the bark, noticed for the first time the word "Lily" etched into the side. And she peeked at Andrew heading to the lane and wondered with a tickle if he had carved the word.

Wilhelm and Andrew stepped discriminatingly from exposed rock to old wood just to keep from sinking into the black, sliding land. The snow melted in pools, overflowed into the grassless dirt, cut eddies and lines like plow marks through chocolate. The dip in the drive filled with rushing black water, the sludge piling into dams forcing the water to cut into the gravel, widening the gap to an impassable river.

Andrew pushed back his cloth cap and put his hand to his bent knee in assessment. "We could rebuild the lane a hundred times over, but the water's going to come through. No stopping Mother Nature."

Wilhelm nodded. "We'll build a bridge. The only way. Think the Muellers would give us a hand?"

"I'll speak to Pieter."

The sun warmed their backs as they stood shoulder to shoulder overlooking the expanse of weather-beaten land, but there was hope and the mud did not appear a curse but a symbol of movement, a sliding away of all that was old and rotting and cold.

Lily did not mind the walk. The spring sudden and light, making her want to live under the sun and put the dreary days of gray and frost behind forever. Small gnats and a few new flies buzzed around her neck, but she paid them no mind, let them tickle her skin until they moved on to find the cows, horses and pigs newly released from the barns.

She swung the empty basket back and forth near her hip, her arms now unstrained from carrying the food she had dropped off with Mrs. Sullivan. *Nice old woman,* Lily thought. With her daughter away so much, Lily was happy bringing the woman food now and then. She liked being near the widow, the way the house always smelled of cinnamon and seemed to be filled with sunshine even on cloudy days. She was a woman who when she hugged you she hugged you. Squeezed you so tight that her warm nature and kind spirit soaked into the skin and you didn't want her to let go. Lily wondered what it must have been like for the Sullivan children to grow up in that kind of home. Wondered what it would feel like to be hugged like that since birth, made to feel that you were the very thing that kept the Earth aligned in the universe. If she ever had children, she'd hug them every day, just like that.

Lily smiled then. *Every day,* she thought. They'd know they were the sprouting angel wings in her eyes.

Lily passed the lane to the Kisers', kept her eyes focused on the line of thin maples skirting the other side of the road. A few miles more and she passed the Mueller farm, the smoke rising from the kitchen chimney, the small outcroppings of red buildings bright, nearly crimson in the sunbeams. Her heart grew heavy. Seemed like every farm held a family, told stories around the hearth, kept one another warm even on the coldest days. She had Claire, a woman too trapped in her past and anxiety to expel any comfort.

In the quiet of the road, the horse coming from the south could be heard well before it crested the hill. She moved to the right. When the brown horse came into view, she recognized the man perched on top and grimaced. Dan Simpson.

Dan did more and more odd jobs for Frank. Mr. Simpson, Dan's father, was a clerk at the bank, had connections with everyone in town and played cards with Frank each week. The three of them made her mouth dry, tasteless and craving to spit.

With the heightening pitch of approaching hooves, Lily's body constricted protectively, her elbows locking to her sides. She wanted to turn around, beat a pace back to the Sullivan house, but it was too late. Dan had seen her and stopped the horse, dismounted and walked toward her with that smug look upon his face.

"Lily Morton," he chirped. "Didn't expect to see such a pretty sight this mornin'."

"Hello, Dan," she greeted with reserve. She stood straight, held the basket in front of her as a poor shield.

"Got anything good in there for me?" He nodded at the basket, but his eyes glued to her blouse.

Her fingers gripped the woven handle tighter. Dan was always making advances, not in a way that flattered but in a way that made you feel like dirty hands were playing with your hair. He even did it in front of Frank, who would just laugh. But there was an anger laced to Dan's flirtations, a sharpness to his eye that didn't make a woman laugh, made her want to run.

"Just dropping off soup to Mrs. Sullivan." Her voice unsteadied and she cursed herself. Dan could smell insecurity a mile away and moved closer. The quiet road suddenly seemed deserted for miles in every direction. She was halfway between home and the Muellers'. If she had to run, she wasn't sure which way to go.

Lily brought forth her strongest posture and strained not to flinch from his wandering eyes. "What are you doing here? A bit out of your territory, aren't you?"

"Yep." He stuck out his bottom lip and squinted

at the sun. "Makin' the rounds, you could say."

His words slurred, didn't sound right, as if he spoke from an injured throat. He stepped closer and brushed the hair off her shoulder, the sensation raising the nerves along her neck. Her legs tightened for flight.

"Miss Lily," he announced, "you're looking at Private Dan Simpson." The smell of sour whiskey trailed his breath and she scowled.

His eyes turned black. "I just got done tellin' you I signed up an' you're giving me a look like that?"

She had to watch herself now. She had to think. She swallowed. "You just surprised me is all."

The blackness stayed, but he chuckled, turned around in a stumbling circle and raised his hat in the air. "I'm a soldier, Lily! Gonna teach those Huns what an American looks like." He was before her again, breathing on her again. "Gonna make sure my face is the last thing they see before I shove the bayonet through their gut." He thrust out a wobbly arm in an exaggerated sword parry.

As much as she tried not to, as much as she knew she needed to face him, she turned her face away, and her lips curled. He grabbed her chin hard. "A man gets tired of being ignored, Lily. You hear me?" he shouted.

She glared hard at him, clenched her teeth, wouldn't turn away again.

"You're always disrespecting me an' I'm done with it! Teasin' me like you do, walking by me acting like you don't want me, makin' me think I got to beg for it!"

He grabbed the basket from her hand and threw it into the brush, grabbed her arms fiercely. "But you listen to me, Miss Lily. I'm a soldier now. Won't have you teasin' your prize at me. Gonna give it to me or I'm takin' it!"

Thought stopped. A cry left her lips as she struggled to get out of his grip.

"There a problem?" Andrew's voice approached from the road and she nearly crumpled with relief.

Dan loosened his hold on her arms but did not let go. "Who are you?"

Andrew walked up to them, his figure tall and strong and unwavering. He didn't remove his eyes from the man. "Take your hands off her."

Dan dropped his clutches and put his palms up in the air, his body swaying slightly. "Yes, sir," he said sarcastically.

Andrew turned to her, his eyes grave and stern. "You all right, Lily?"

She nodded, crossed her arms across her chest and rubbed the bruised biceps. He stepped in front of her, blocked her body from Dan's view. "I expect you'll be on your way now." It was not a question.

Recognition seemed to settle slowly in the man's mind. "You're one of 'em Kisers, ain't you?" He laughed as if at a good joke. "Heard about you."

Lily heard the chiding tone in Dan's voice and shuddered. She knew his reputation for brawling. "Come on, Andrew," she whispered, and tugged on his hand. "Let's go."

But he stood rigid, didn't even seem to know she was there.

"Oh, now I see how it is!" Dan snorted. "Lily taking pity on the cripple. Can't handle a real man, eh, girl? Afraid what I got in the pants be too much for you?"

Andrew landed a right hook square against the man's jaw and sent him sprawling into the rocks. Lily covered her mouth in shock. "Get out of here, Lily," he ordered. But she was too stunned to move.

Dan swiveled in the dirt to his belly and slowly rose to his knees, holding his jaw in his palm. "Why, you son of a—" He lunged at Andrew, throwing his full weight upon him and sending them both in the dirt. Andrew kneed him in the side, put him on his back, but the man came at him with two quick jabs to the face, leaving him blind.

Both men rose from the ground and Dan charged him like a bull, hitting him twice in the ribs and sending Andrew to his knees, knocking the wind from his lungs. Dan pulled back a fist, but Andrew shot a kick to the man's knee and Dan buckled to the ground. Andrew raised a fist but didn't need to deliver the blow. For Lily smashed a rock to Dan's skull and left him reeling in the dirt, clutching his blood-covered head.

Andrew stooped over Dan's writhing body, his chest wheezing for air. "Hold still," Andrew told him. Dan readied for another blow and crimped into his stomach.

"I'm not going to hit you," Andrew huffed irritably. He put a handkerchief to the man's cut and held it there, looked at the gash that bled badly. "You're going to need stitches. Come back to the house and we'll get it closed up." Andrew reached a hand out to the man. "Keep you from bleeding to death."

Dan smacked the hand away. He scrambled to his feet, holding the handkerchief loosely to his head. "Rather bleed to death than let a dirty Kiser touch me!"

He crawled upon the horse, the animal nervous with the smell of blood. "Frank's going to hear about this, Lily. You just wait." He pointed a shaking finger at Andrew. "Don't go hitting a soldier, cripple! They'll hang you by the neck for this. You wait!"

The horse took off at an uneven gait, the man's slouched figure stirring the animal to the left. Andrew turned to Lily. "You okay?"

She ignored the question, reached a hand to his face. "You're bleeding."

With the words, the pain awakened to the surface. His ribs hurt with each inhale and his face felt like it was growing and expanding. His left eye started to close and he tasted blood in his mouth.

"I must look pretty handsome." He tried to smile, but his swollen lip cracked.

She half-laughed and half-cried. "Come on, let's get you some ice."

Back at the house, Lily had him sit at the table while she smashed shavings from the icebox, put them in a cloth and held it to his eye. Claire came in and screamed.

"Hush, Claire!" Lily scolded. She knew Claire couldn't stand the sight of blood, but she had no patience left. "He's not hurt bad. Just go if you can't look at it."

Claire hurried out with her hand over her eyes.

"She gets on my last nerve sometimes," Lily murmured as she cleaned the cut at Andrew's mouth. As she pressed, she softened guiltily. "Not her fault, I guess. Little things set her off, you know? I shouldn't lose my patience with her like that."

"You're good to her."

She shrugged, checked the cut over his eye. She was grateful he had been there and she didn't want to remember their last argument. Here he was perfect and for a few minutes she let the memory of what he had done in Pittsburgh fade away.

"Your ribs all right?" she asked. "He hit you pretty hard."

"Not broken." He touched his side gingerly, grimaced. "Least I don't think."

Lily started to giggle, tried to keep her lips closed. "I'm sorry."

"You're laughing at me?" he chided. "Here I am bruised and bleeding and you're laughing at me?"

"I'm so sorry. Oh, God." She held her stomach. "I'm not laughing at you, I swear. Just remembering that look on Dan's face when you hit him." She erupted in titters again. "Never saw anyone look more surprised in my whole life. Thought his eyes were going to pop right out of their sockets."

He started to laugh, moaned with the jostling of his ribs. "Stop that. Don't make me laugh. It hurts."

She wiped her eyes and composed herself. "Where you learn to hit like that, anyway?"

"Back at the colliery. A boy learns to fight the same time he learns how to walk." Then, in a sudden shift, he took the ice from her hand, put it on the floor, his expression changing. "Of course," he said tersely, "I know how you feel about men standing up for themselves. But guess this is different, isn't it? Because it has to do with you."

She pulled back with the tone. "What does that mean?"

"Know it was a long winter, but I doubt you forgot our last conversation. Said you never wanted to see me again, remember? Because I defended myself."

"Defended yourself?" she questioned, aghast. "Against what?"

He cocked his head. "At the game, Lily. You heard what those men were slinging at us and you stormed out when we put a stop to it. Nice to know whose side you're on."

Her mouth dropped and her eyes beaded angrily. "You think that's why I was mad at you?" Her eyebrows drew together like magnets. "You don't think being with a prostitute had anything to do with it?" she accused hotly.

The word hung in the air and drifted, left him momentarily speechless. "A prostitute? H-h-how did—? Wh-h-ho—" he stuttered.

The hurt grabbed again, the sting renewed and as fresh as that day at the baseball field. She gathered up her skirt and turned to stand. "Just go."

"Wait." He clutched her arm. "Lily, wait." She tugged at her limb, but he held tight. "I was never with a prostitute."

"Don't lie to me, Andrew! Fritz told me how you were with her."

"Fritz." Andrew rubbed his eyes. "Fritz didn't

341

know what he was saying. I did see one of those . . . ladies, but—"

Lily jerked from his hold and he stood quickly, pressing his hand against his aching rib. "But not like that. I swear, Lily. Just listen to me for a second. Okay? Just let me explain."

Reluctant, she sat back down, her head hanging low.

"My uncle brought me to Pittsburgh, brought me to that . . . woman." He tried to make sense of the words. "I had no idea until we got there. I swear. But Lily, I didn't do anything with her. Didn't lay a hand on her, I swear."

She sneered and crossed her arms.

"Listen, Lily. You've got to believe me. I'd never be with a woman like that. Never on my life. And I told her so."

"But Fritz said—"

"Fritz didn't understand. Please believe me, Lily." He took her hand gently and stared into her eyes. "I swear on the life of my father, I was never with that woman."

Her eyes lifted and scanned his face, tried to read the depth of the blue eyes for truth. His face melted with remorse and begged for understanding, his gentle fingers gripping her limp hand. "That's not how I want to be with a woman, Lily. Not like that. Not ever like that." His lips moved, then stopped. "There's only one woman I want to share a kiss with," he whispered.

"Only one woman I want to be with in that way."

She softened. For the first time since that autumn day, she relaxed from her toes to her forehead. "Really?"

"Really."

The hope entered and brought its own brand of terror. The relief blinded and she needed to see, couldn't bear to be a fool. But Lily drifted. This man flowed into her marrow and her blood and burned along their paths.

Andrew wrapped his arm around her and she buried her face into his warm neck, the smell of his skin disintegrating any restraint. "I'm so sorry, Lily." He sighed into her hair, his breath seeping into her pores. "No wonder you hated me."

He kissed her forehead, pulled back to look at her face. "Please talk to me, Lily," he pleaded. "Tell me you believe me."

She fell into the contours of his figure. The strong, straight nose; the lean neck; the lips that belonged upon her own; the wide shoulders that had blocked Dan Simpson. Lily nodded. "I believe you." The sound of her voice scared her, the weakness of it, the pure surrender to the man who had shattered her heart without intent. A tear dropped, bloated and singular, from the corner of her eye. "I'm scared," she breathed.

Andrew's lips parted, his face sanguine and filled with compassion. "I'm not going to hurt you, Lily." He met her green eyes and held them as with arms. "Not ever."

She rolled into his neck again and he held her just as he had on the first day they had met. He held her without movement, without disruption, let her emotions settle and translate as they needed, for as long as they needed.

He smiled into her hair. "I can't believe this whole winter I could have been snuggling with you next to the fire instead of you sitting in your house cursing me. I'm such an idiot."

She grinned against the skin, tilted her chin to look up at him. He lowered his mouth to hers then, the soft lips grazing, the tips of their tongues touching lightly. He pulled her closer, kissed her top lip and then the bottom, before taking them both languidly. His hand etched the outline of her jaw, traced the curve of her ear, slid to her neck and cradled her head.

Lily pulled back in distress. "Your lip." Gingerly, she touched his swollen face. "It must hurt."

But he only grinned and bent to kiss her again.

CHAPTER 35

Lily grew feathers and stretched in the tepid wind. Freedom. A world in bloom wiped away the grime of winter and painted the earth in living color. She let down her hair, rich in golden curls from the conditioned months of French braids. She wore no sweater and her skin exhaled from the pores. Before she had left the house, she had opened every window and every door to banish the ghosts and invite the spring herald. And with the shoots of renewal, her heart opened, called out a name—a face and body— that left her warm and aching.

Lily paced in front of the doughy, black Kiser lane debating the safety of heading down the muddy slope. One wrong step and she'd tumble and roll and plop into the running water below.

Above the sound of the rushing creek, Andrew cupped his hand and hollered, "Stay there! I'm coming up for you."

His gallant order thrilled her, brought a tingle of pride to have him coming to her aid. She smiled widely, gave thanks to the blue swollen sky and the full sun and the tall, muscular body working its way to meet her.

Andrew agilely picked his way over the mud to target uncovered stones and hardened dirt mounds. A difficult task and more than once he sank to his calves before prying loose again. When he reached the raging creek, he found the narrowest stretch and leaped. Here the sludge lessened and the pine needles acted as stitching across the ground, like seed bags buried under earth to keep the weeds from coming up. At last, he climbed the ridge to Lily's side, bent and held his side as he caught his breath. The smile upon his lips was the most handsome sight she had ever seen.

With lungs full, Andrew rose to his full height. Without embarrassment, he stared intensely into her eyes. The heat of his thoughts brought her fingers to her throat. Her eyes drifted to the open collar of his shirt, the skin already tanning at the neck. Her focus slid to his chest and then to his waist and then she erupted in giggles.

Andrew raised one eyebrow as if she had gone mad. But she couldn't speak and shook with laughter, her face red.

"What?" he asked.

She couldn't form the words through her torrent and just pointed to his clothing. He was covered in mud from ankle to chest.

"Think that's funny, do you?" he accused slyly, his blue eyes twinkling.

She nodded mutely, snorted with laughter.

"And here I am trudging through the mud to give you a hand," he said with feigned indignation. "Some friend."

Tears streamed down her face.

"Well." He stepped toward her. "Owe me at least a hug for hurting my feelings."

"No!" Lily screeched, backed away. "Keep your muddy body away from me."

Andrew pounced and grabbed her, squeezed her tight against his dirt-stained clothes.

"Ugh, Andrew!" She pushed him in the chest and wiped the mud from her cheek, her smiling lips splattered. "Look at me! I'm filthy."

"Teach you to laugh at a gentleman, young lady."

"Some gentleman," Lily scoffed, her expression dancing with mirth. "Here I am trying to look pretty for you and I look like I just climbed out the pigpen."

Andrew relented. "Here," he said as he pulled out a handkerchief from his back pocket. He gently wiped the muck on her cheeks and tried to keep his face serious.

"What?"

"Just smearing a little."

"Er!" She grabbed the handkerchief and wiped her own face. "Better?"

"Not really," he teased.

She tossed the handkerchief at his chest. "Well, at least walk me down to the house." Lily stuck out her elbow for him to link. "We can look like we crawled out of the pigpen together."

With arms held tight, their hips and thighs brushed as they walked across the sloped front yard. Andrew's eyes flickered to her dress, at the pearl-colored buttons dotting the front. They glanced at each other often with shy smiles and lowered lids and between them the energy of the spring, of new growth and warmth, of young vibrancy and attraction, made the world glimmer in shimmering waves.

As they strolled, arm in arm, the sun slowly dried the mud on their clothes. Soon the dirt flaked off and drifted into the gentle wind, the unsheathing making their bodies lighter, cleaner and more lithe. Andrew steered her to the narrow opening in the creek and unhooked his arm. He jumped across and held out his hand for her to follow.

Lily's arm wasn't nearly as long and so she reached across and barely touched his fingertips. "Don't let me fall, Andrew," she begged.

"I won't let you fall, Lily girl." He clutched her fingers.

She jumped across and held his hand. He wiped a hair away from her cheek. "I won't ever let you fall. Not ever."

The fragile plant shoots uncorked, pale and feeble, finally relieved from the suffocating burden of dead maple and oak leaves. Grass and weeds birthed from the blank land, an immaculate conception. The farm animals lit up. The runts had grown into strong pigs that now rolled in the soft mud, the only ones in love with the piles of liquid dirt that beleaguered the human inhabitants. And the pigs rolled in it, grunted wet noses through it, bowled their scaly skin within its depths while filling the farm with humorous squeals of ecstatic pleasure.

The cows sniffed for fresh vegetation, batted long eyelashes under the bright sun, their soft fur slick and clean and untwitching, knowing that in a few months the flies would hound them to no end. And the chickens flapped wings and danced with bobbing necks, picked at the ground, flung small rocks while searching for seeds and ticks.

Wilhelm and Eveline decided that little Will would start school with the spring despite coming into his studies midyear. The boy's grammar was slipping to the simple tongue of Fritz Mueller and his reading fell in favor to stick whittling and sling shooting acorns. And on that first day of school, poor Will disappeared in the woods in rebellion, hiding until he was assured that Anna and Fritz Mueller would walk with him every day. Fritz didn't go to school, but he had always escorted his sibling, never letting his little sister out of his protective sight.

Over the last few weeks, Andrew split his time between the farm and Mrs. Sullivan's house. He assisted the woman's favorite mare with her birth, delivering a healthy and wobbly-legged foal. With the help of Will's hands, Andrew cleaned and trimmed all the hooves of the widow's beloved horses. The tasks were small and the pay little, but it meant more than gold. He was working with animals and beginning to save money to bring his mother home.

At the farm, Andrew helped Eveline tackle the old garden, nearly a quarter acre in size. The fence and chicken wire lay tangled amid old fallen tree limbs and the rectangular space was so thick with leaves that one had to dig half a foot down through the dry leaves to the layer of black moldy leaves until the dirt could be found. Edgar raked and sulked without his brother by his side and stuck out a puffy bottom lip as he carried the rotted leaves to the wheelbarrow. Slowly, the old wood of the raised beds was uncovered, the slats broken and the rusted nails bent, pointing to the sun or to the earth in odd angles.

Eveline Kiser's dress was soiled to the hips, and with each inch of black loam exposed the life of the earth rose rich and full to her nose. She did not wear gloves, let her nails scrape upon the dirt as she lifted the dead leaves to her chest and flung them into the pile. She exhumed the earth, enlivened it again. And they worked together, this open, dark land and her pale white hands—together—and they saw the life that would bloom in the summer and feed them through winter.

Once the leaves were cleared, Andrew set to work repairing the raised beds, tearing out the old wood and resettling the planks upright or replacing the worst of the beams with new wood cut from the broken piles of barn slats. Edgar held the corners steady while Andrew hammered in the nails.

By supper, the garden had been tidied, the beds open and ready for planting. Eveline and Andrew stood in silent reverence at the open plot. In the black soil, they saw the hope, envisioned the growth that would come, and the pride calmed them both.

Eveline turned to her nephew—her blood. The contours of his Dutch features, infused with a tired respect for the land, held a terrestrial love that mirrored her own and she hoped to her soul that he would never leave them. Andrew turned to her then and smiled peacefully. And the air caught in her lungs at the sight of this young man, the indigo eyes and handsome face that no longer carried the remnants of insecurity. Perhaps he was finally ready to leave the scars behind. She leaned her head against his shoulder gratefully and he hugged her with his right arm—the solid arm of a man.

The letter arrived late afternoon, tucked between the *Pittsburg Press*, a notice from their Germania Savings Bank stating the name change to Citizens Savings Bank of Pittsburgh and a copy of *Volksblatt und Freiheits-Freund*, the only German American newspaper left unbanned.

Eveline opened the soiled and flimsy envelope, already fondled and resealed by the censors. Inside, her sister's letter was succinct and brittle, five curt lines drafted one on top of the other instead of flowing in a paragraph. At first glance the design appeared to be poetry, but there was no rhyme, no poetic sentiment.

The grandfather clock ticked behind each word. Two birds fought at the kitchen window and charged each other in a flurry of harsh chirps and rustled feathers, a battle of love or of defense. Through the clatter, Eveline read the slanted writing, each blunt statement a small punch to the stomach. Her hand yearned to crush the paper into a ball, but there were other eyes that needed to read it first.

Outside the porch window, Andrew and her sons had the pigs, a few of the saved runts from the Muellers, in the front yard. The boys took turns hiding old potatoes in various spots and waited to see which pig could root it out first.

With the game, the pigs sniffed like hound dogs, playful with the boys, as comfortable with the children as they were with their own species. And the pigs grunted and searched while Will and Edgar chortled and Andrew stood amid them all, a solid figure around which all the laughter and squeals revolved.

The porch screen bounced as the door closed behind her. "Will, Edgar," she directed, "time to put the pigs in the pen."

"Ah, Ma!" Will's nose scrunched in complaint. "We just started."

"You heard me. Gather them up."

"But—"

Eveline's face pinched and stunted any argument.

"All right," Will said grudgingly. "Come on, Edgar."

Andrew watched the interaction, circumspect until the boys and hogs were out of earshot. Eveline handed him the envelope and folded letter. He met her eyes for a long moment before turning them to the words on the paper. The wooly clouds floated easily in the sky ahead. The apple limbs swayed in the pained pause.

"She remarried."

"Yes."

"Says I shouldn't plan to come to Holland." Andrew bit his lip. "Says it would be better if I stayed on here." He had written his mother that he was going to save money to visit her, to bring her home, and told her about the special woman he wanted her to meet.

"We have no idea what's going on overseas, son," Eveline justified. "Have no idea what she's seeing and living with every day."

He glanced at the envelope. "She didn't even write me," he added bitterly. "The letter's addressed to you."

The anger toward her sister ignited fresh, the slight to her son unforgivable. "She blames herself for what happened, Andrew," she defended weakly. "For sending you on the railroad. It's her own shame, her own guilt."

He wasn't listening. "She remarried," he repeated.

"Women have a hard time on their own." She clenched her jaw, dug for comfort. "With the war—"

"Don't defend her." He handed the letter back. "Just don't."

CHAPTER 36

Posters from the U.S. Food Administration lined the butcher shop and general store— the decrees for a rationed nation. Schools and churches sent pamphlets, drilled reminders in voice and verse:

> Save a loaf a week—help win the war.
> Eat less, save more.
> Avoid wheat on Mondays, meat on
>   Tuesdays and pork on Saturdays.
> Clean plates and avoid snacks between
>   meals.
> Eat more corn. Save wheat, red meat,
>   sugar and fats for the troops.

And the farmers ate fine on what they could raise, while those in the city found pantries shrinking and bellies rumbling in patriotic servitude.

The first load of eggs, milk and butter was ready for market, stacked and packaged in wooden crates painted with the Kiser name. Andrew and Wilhelm and the two boys piled on top of the old wagon along with their wares and left before dawn for the East Liberty open market in Pittsburgh. They followed in a trail behind the Mueller sausage wagon and the Stevens bread truck, said good-bye to the open land and headed into the hungry smog pits of the city.

The three Plum farmers parked next to a litany of other wagons, a few motorized, on the perimeter of the market square. One after the other, they opened their wagons, stacked their crates and boxes, propped up wooden, hand-drawn signs that listed their products. But there would be no worry of competition. The market was packed, drawing in patrons from all sides and angles of the great city, searching for fresh food from the farm, for butter hand churned, for milk squeezed that morning, eggs that still had tiny feathers stuck to their shells, trout from small lakes, butchered chickens, lambs, cows and pigs. The people from Pittsburgh flocked for unblighted potatoes, beans that were fresh and not woody and cabbage heads still intact without wormholes.

Trams dropped off a steady stream of customers while a motley crew of vehicles, of rusted Lizzies and new Fords and horse wagons and buggies, lined the parking field. The divide between the old and new as clear as worn serge against fur-lined cuffs.

City boys in knickerbockers and short jackets and flannel caps darted between stands of popped corn and gingerbread cookies with burnt sugar and cinnamon drops; gambled in shell games, nearly feral in their excitement. Farm boys with dirty overalls leaned against splintered wagons, posing in mirrored posture to their leathered, chapped-lipped fathers. Women with long skirts and high collars, with ostrich plumes in their hats, kept tabs on the girls near their sides in clean and pressed pinafores.

In the middle of the market, vendors set up stands. There were jams and honey. Crates of asparagus, rhubarb, lettuce and peas. The smell of funnel cakes and fried dough filled the air, competed with the scents of roasted peanuts and chestnuts. Pickles soaked in brine in enormous barrels. Salt rock ice cream dripped down the chins of children. Smoked fish and smelly triangle blocks of cheese called forth tornadoes of flies. Candles of beeswax and tallow sat in front of an obese woman who did not smile. Hard sausage, smelling woody and gruff, hung from string tied from sloppily made awnings.

And the market burst with sound that made one feel at a great event, the clatter vibrating between the ribs. Banjoes played on a makeshift stage. Boxes of puppies and kittens barked and whined; canaries chirped in metal cages. Hens and roosters clucked and crowed in wire mesh squares. Children laughed. Vendors shouted prices. Young men whistled at pretty girls.

A swarthy dark man in a satin turban promised fortune-telling and horoscopes. A J.R. Watkins salesman sold salves, ointments, liniments, soaps, shampoo, spices, cocoa, flavoring extracts, baking powder, toothbrushes and toothpaste.

The milk and butter, hand-wrapped by Eveline, sold out within the first hour of the market and Wilhelm held on to the money as if it were glued to his fingers. They were the first dollars coming forth instead of going out and his voice deepened with dignity. And with each accruing cent, his manner became more open to the customers, his expression more pleasant. He moved out of the shadows, nodded to some, began to smile at others. The money was coming in. The flow was back. And when the first crate of eggs was purchased, he proudly gave Will and Edgar a few pennies to buy candy at the taffy stand.

Andrew took a break and walked around the stalls, eyeing the goods that went on as far as the eye could see. "You there!" shouted the dark-skinned man in Indian garb. "Want to know your future, young man? Come, come! Let me see your palm."

Andrew stopped at the man's booth out of curiosity, but on closer inspection he saw the shabby stitching at the shoulders and collar of the costume. The guru's made-up face revealed he was no more Indian than Andrew was. "I think I know what the stars have in mind for me," Andrew said. He and Wilhelm would start on the fields tomorrow and for the next six months Andrew's future would keep him knee-deep in dirt and behind a plow.

Along the fake Indian's table, among ivory and rosewood boxes, silver trinkets and a crystal ball, were lines of colorful gems presented on black velvet. Andrew picked up a round green stone, held it up to the sun, the color pale green but dark when shadowed.

The man nodded wisely. "Beautiful as a woman's eyes, no?" His voice rose and fell like a rubber ball, his head jostling from side to side. Andrew squinted his eyes at the fortune-teller, wondered if he could really read minds.

"What kind of stone is this?"

"Emerald."

Andrew's laugh was quick and immediate. "And I'm guessing the glass pieces next to it are diamonds?"

"You insult the great Babija!" The man recoiled painfully, his face stretching in shock. "It's emerald! I make an oath." With that, he put his hand on his heart and bowed.

"Nice try." Andrew grinned and put the stone back in its space, began to turn away. "Thanks for your time."

"Wait! Wait!" the man beseeched, bustled

around the front of the table. "All right, maybe not an emerald, but it's pretty, no?" The accent vanished. The glue under the man's mustache glistened in the sunshine.

Andrew inspected the stone again, the color curving his lips into a smile. He rubbed the smooth edge of the gem. "Okay, I'll take it."

Pieter Mueller snaked through the crowd, plowed forward and grabbed Andrew's elbow. "Come on." The young German's face was resolute, stern. Together, they flowed into a stream of other men until the confines grew a current unto themselves and carried them all to the edge of the market square.

A young man in flannel shirt and dropped suspenders pulled up an empty produce crate and stood on top, stuck two fingers in his mouth and whistled shrilly, then waved his hands for silence. "Listen up!" he hollered. "It was just announced that the second draft registration is on June fifth. All men who turned twenty-one since last year's draft are required to sign up."

A hush settled over the previously distracted men, the words descending like a fine mist upon the crowd. Pieter stiffened. He turned twenty-one two weeks ago.

"The generous people of Pittsburgh have opened their wallets to the cause, sent the best nurses and doctors to help our brothers overseas," the man droned. "But it's not enough. We need men. And as everyone knows, the bravest, strongest men live right here in this city!" He clapped his hands and the men followed, the tenor of applause growing and competing with the speaker. "It's time we teach those Germans a lesson, eh?" he shouted. "Show the Kaiser and his baby killers you don't mess with America! You don't mess with Pittsburgh!" Men cheered; some whistled and hooted. Furtive glances shot to those who stayed silent.

"But!" The man on the crate raised a pointed finger, paused for silence. "But you don't need to wait to June fifth to show your loyalty. You can do what the rest of us just did and sign up now!" The young men roared again. And the joy of war sapped the strength, left the body dense like a scourge, played out in a way that could not be stopped.

Pieter had black in his eyes. "I'm packing up."

"Market doesn't close for another four hours," Andrew said.

Pieter drew daggers at the men handing out sheets of propaganda to the patrons, his shift in demeanor a storm cloud over the sun. "I'm packing up, and if you're smart you'll do the same."

The edge seeped into the crowd and spread. Men walked harder now, shoulders stooped forward. Children raised worried eyes to adults speaking loudly, looked to mothers who had turned away from the talk. Andrew trusted Pieter, had never heard this tone in his friend's voice before. "I'm going to find Will and Edgar."

Andrew weaved through the bodies toward the sweet stands, which meant crossing through the line of young men handing out flyers. The speaker stood on level ground again, spoke to whichever ear was close enough to blabber in.

As Andrew passed, a man tapped him on the shoulder. "Hey," he said amiably. "Joinin' us against the Germans, brother?" But then Andrew turned and the young man saw the other half of his body. "Sorry." He turned his eyes away. "Well, guess you can be there in spirit, eh?"

Andrew blocked out the reference, pushed past the papers in his face and scanned the crowd for his cousins. His neck muscles stiffened as his vision filtered over the swarm of people and the little heads could not be seen. He pushed through the flood of men to the vendors, finally finding the children huddled between stands. Will's fingers clutched Edgar's brown hair.

"Ow!" Edgar screamed.

Andrew knelt down, tried to figure out who was tangled into whom. Will pulled again and sent Edgar whining. "Will got taffy in my hair!"

Will looked desperate, held out his hands, his fingers latticed and joined together with stringy strands of pink taffy and brown hair. A wad had lodged in Edgar's hair, and the harder Will tried to pull it out the louder Edgar screamed.

"Just hold on a sec." Andrew inspected the pink-globbed hair and tried not to laugh. "Going to have to cut it out. Have to wait till we get back home, I reckon."

Will licked at his fingers, chewed the sticky remnants. "And you," Andrew directed, "don't touch anything till we get those hands washed." He plucked the boy's fingers from his mouth. "And don't eat it, either. Got more hair and grass there than taffy."

The boys nodded, forlorn and in despair with having half their candy wasted. As they followed Andrew back to the stand, Edgar snarled jealously at Will as he continued to lick the dirty candy from between his fingers.

The crowd mutated to tentacles, the lines branching off in different directions, some darker than others. Andrew slowed his steps, motioned for the boys to stay behind him. A group had formed at the Kiser stand. "Look." Will pointed. "We got a line of customers waiting."

But they weren't buying eggs. Andrew felt the tension in the crowd, taut as sinew as he approached. And they moved for his entrance, fanned and parted with downcast eyes. Directly in front, there were three young men. A burly one with soiled overalls that rose past his ankles took a handful of eggs. His steely eyes did not leave Wilhelm's face. He raised the eggs in his palm, stretched his arm to the sky and watched Wilhelm's gaze for any trace of defense. As if satisfied, he smashed the eggs to the ground, one by one.

The dull sound of each breaking shell against hard earth—one, two, three, four, five—thudded down and through the feet. Fire ripped through Andrew's veins and he pushed the young man hard in the center of the back. "What the hell are you doing?"

The man met him length to length, eye to eye, scanned him and smirked. He pointed to the crates that were stamped in black letters: *Kiser*. "These eggs are rotten," he said innocently, then leaned in and scorned, "They stink!"

And with that, the man turned, picked up the full crate of eggs and tossed it over. Andrew lunged, but Wilhelm stopped him with a steel grip, squeezed with both his eyes and his hands for Andrew to stop.

Andrew pulled his arm back, his fist so tight that his nails cut into his palm. Indignation crept up his legs and sizzled each nerve ending. The anger rose up his neck, flushed his face and raised the hairs at each pore. The eggs oozed under the crate, puddled the ground between Wilhelm's feet and colored his boot sole.

Little Will's breath came quick and he ran forward and hit the man on the back. "Don't touch our eggs!" he cried, tears rushing down his cheeks.

The man laughed, raised his brows at Wilhelm as if to say, *What you going to do about it, Pa?* But with the crying of the child the crowd lost their pleasure and turned.

The tears touched upon a few of the boys' humility. "Come on," one ordered with a tilt of his head. "Let's get outta here b'fore we step in this shit."

They turned to leave, but the burly man turned around once more, picked up a solid, wayward egg and threw it at Wilhelm's thigh, covering it with dripping yolk.

Immobile, Wilhelm stared stonily ahead, his jaw clicking in and out as the only movement or sign of life within the man.

Edgar tugged on his father's sleeve. "Why didn't you stop them?"

The boys had worked so hard to collect the eggs, spent days lining the crates with paper and cradling each egg they set in. Andrew put an arm around Edgar's shoulder to quiet him, but the little boy blurted through his tears, "Why didn't you stop them, Pa? Why did they do that to our eggs?"

Wilhelm grabbed the last crate of eggs, didn't even seem to notice that half were broken and headed to the wagon, ignoring the boys as he did the broken shells. Will and Edgar turned to Andrew with confused, tear-streaked faces. "Why didn't Pa stop them? Why didn't he do anything?"

Andrew knelt down between them, saw the taffy still stuck to their innocent faces and hair. They needed to know. The war had come and they needed to know. He couldn't fold the ugliness away like he did the newspaper. They were only children, but they needed to know now. The war wasn't going away but was coming across the Atlantic straight to their doorstep. They needed to know that their father wasn't a coward, that some hate has to be fled.

"Boys," he started, spoke to them as men, looked into their sweet eyes with the seriousness shared by men. "You heard those men talking? About the war."

They nodded in unison. "Yeah, in Germany," chimed Edgar.

"That's right." Andrew sighed deeply. "War can make people angry. Makes people not treat each other very well. People get scared and it makes them angry. Then they hear stories, some real and some not, but it makes them get angry, you see?"

The boys stared blankly. And he said the words he hoped he would never have to say out loud, words he finally had to face himself. "When they get angry they start to blame the Germans. Start to think that everyone who came from Germany is bad."

"But we're not from Germany," defended Will. "We didn't do anything wrong."

"No, but your father and grandparents were and that means about the same thing to some people. Your name, Kiser, is German. Sounds just like the name of a really bad man who started the war. There are going to be some people that don't like Germans or that name. Do you understand?"

"But Pa should have stopped them!" shouted Edgar. "Should have told them we're not the bad Germans."

"When people are angry, they close their ears," Andrew explained. "Your father did the right thing, Edgar. He did the brave thing. A coward would have reacted and fought with those men and lost. Your father showed how brave he was by not letting their anger turn him, you see? A coward would have started a fight because his feelings were hurt, but your father stayed strong and fought them in his own way. You should be very proud of him."

Will's chin crinkled. "How we gonna get money now?" he whispered over choked tears.

"We'll be fine." Andrew rubbed a tear away from the little boy. "People got to eat, Will. We'll be fine."

But things wouldn't be fine. This was just the beginning. A gray, green dawn before a twister ripped through the land.

CHAPTER 37

The last remaining apple blossoms unsheathed from stems and snowed delicate petals over the yard, carpeted the land in white and pink, stuck in Eveline's hair as she weeded the garden. Wilhelm, Andrew and the boys had left for market before dawn and the day was her own, a heavenly reprieve from catering to the men.

Eveline planted zinnias and cosmos and nasturtiums on the perimeter of the fence, a sturdy fortress of vertical sticks to keep the deer and rabbits out. In the raised beds, she planted marigolds to keep out the aphids. She started geraniums that she would grow and fill the window boxes that Andrew built for her. She would line every window of the old house. The bright flowers would be rouge to the clapboard face, its scented breath strong enough to keep mosquitos and flies from the open windows and ripped screens.

Between the flower seeds, the lettuce grew in bright green heads, the asparagus rising like long digits in the squares beyond. The cucumbers, peas, beans and zucchini were already sprouting.

Wilhelm promised to bring more seeds from the market.

On the other side of the house, the orchard readied with peach and plum and apple trees. She and Andrew had pruned the mulberry and gooseberry bushes, raspberries and blueberries that mazed around the trunks. And beneath the apple tree, the crosses of her children called to her. Otto and Harold were always there, observing the garden form, watching and sighing as the ground came to life.

A man on the high street turned into the lane. Her throat caught. *Frank.* She looked at her dirty hands and fumbled with the bun that had fallen half-undone on her head. Giving up, Eveline hurried into the house to wash her hands and inspect herself in the mirror, giving her cheeks a hard pinch for color despite the pink already there. She was being silly, she knew. But it was nice to feel like a woman. Not a mother or a wife but a woman. Then the door knocked and her heart jumped into her throat again.

Eveline stepped outside into the full sunlight. "Good afternoon, Mr. Morton." She smiled nervously before composing herself. "This is a surprise."

He went to speak but seemed to grow just as nervous. He laughed. "Well, now that I'm here, I feel a bit silly."

This calmed her and she folded her arms easily.

"Whatever for?" Then she noticed the box sitting at his feet. "Didn't bring me another crystal pitcher, I hope?"

He shook his head. "No." He lifted it up and handed it to her. "But it is a little something for you."

Eveline blinked fiercely, waved her hands and stepped back. "No. You've already been too kind. I can't accept another gift."

He put a gleaming cowboy boot on the large stone slab and stayed quiet for a long moment before gazing at her face. "I know this isn't proper, Eveline. I know it." His face twisted in real penance. "A married man shouldn't bring a married woman gifts. I know this."

The shudder of something electric, of something so wrong and so longed for, made her heart race. She was suddenly acutely aware of the feeling of her legs under her skirt and the fabric touching against her skin.

Frank rubbed the front of his shirt. "I know it's not proper to do these things. But"—he met her eyes square and did not flinch—"it's a hell of a lot more proper than what I'd like to do to you."

Her lips fell open and the rush flowed to her inner thighs in a hot flash. She couldn't think. "I can't," she mumbled. "I—"

He smiled and put up a hand. "I know. You don't have to say another word. I put you in a bad spot right now and I'm sorry." He chuckled heartily now. "Guess you have to open the present now. Make me feel less of a scoundrel for saying such things."

Eveline sat down on the step before her legs gave out, tore into the package just to keep her hands from shaking and to keep her mind focused on a task. Sensations swirled, sailed around her, the prickles growing under her clothing.

Frank sat next to her, his shoulder touching her own, and she inched her body away slightly. She couldn't breathe. She opened the box. It was filled with seed packets, each one vibrantly illustrated with a carrot, watermelon, cucumber, bean, tomato—the number of them and the variety spread endlessly in the box. Her mouth dropped.

He pointed to the seeds. "Something else in there for you."

Eveline shook her head in disbelief and dug to the bottom, pulled out a delicate straw bonnet with a coral silk ribbon.

"Figured with all this planting, you'll need to keep the sun off," he explained. He watched her profile.

"I don't know what to say." Tears laced the voice, the thoughtfulness beyond words. The gift was more precious than diamonds. And some-how, he knew this.

"Look inside the hat," he suggested.

She turned it over. A simple stitched tag read:

Gemaakt in Nederland. "It's from Holland?"

"Yeah. Had a hell of a time getting it with the war, but . . . I got it."

"I don't know what to say." She said the words again. And in her mind, they repeated. *I don't know what to say.*

"Don't need to say anything, Eveline." He winked and stood. "Made me happy to give it to you. Makes me happy to see that look on your face. So, guess you could say, it was more a gift for myself. Kind of selfish when you think about it."

She smiled. "Well, selfish or not, it's just about the nicest gift I ever got in my whole life." Her tone stroked soft as the touch she wanted to deliver to his skin.

He stuck his hands in his back pockets and tapped his foot, squinted at the sun above her head. "Can I be honest?"

She nodded, though she wasn't sure if she could handle much more from the man.

"I'm worried about you."

"About me?" She pulled back in surprise. "Whatever for?"

"There's a lot of unrest right now. I see it. Hear it. Can't get away from it. It's a hard time to be German. Now, I know you're only German by marriage, but that doesn't matter to people. Just watch out is all I'm saying."

She thought of her husband, away at market,

trying to make a living off this land—the land she wanted—and the regret blew fierce and harsh. She stepped away from Frank, closed off the feelings that had tickled and now threatened as an affliction. She was proud to be married to Wilhelm. She was proud to carry his name.

"The prejudice of others is no concern to us. We're a strong family, Mr. Morton."

Her tone and sudden formality stiffened him and he nodded, tugged at his earlobe. When he spoke again, his voice was higher, a tinge of spite tainting it. "Well, I can see that. Just could be hard times is all I'm saying. Seeing that Wilhelm came to me for a loan and all, just figured the war can't make it easy paying it back."

Eveline froze, blinked spastically. "A loan?"

"He didn't tell you?"

"No." Eveline turned away. Her ears picked up a noise from the lane, but she gave it no mind. This news from Frank blocked everything else. "When?"

"Before the blizzard hit. Figured he told you about it. Figured a husband shares that sort of decision with his wife." His features took on a sharp look. "Figured that's what a man and woman talk about when they share a bed."

She didn't feel well, nearly faint. She had always scoffed at sensitive women who took their hands to their foreheads and feigned dizziness at anything disagreeable and yet she was that woman now. She swallowed, didn't have any words to speak or feel.

Frank stepped off the granite stone, tucked in the back of his shirt that already was tucked deep into his jeans. He picked up the straw hat from the box and affixed it to Eveline's head. She watched his movements as if in a dream. He let the silk ribbon fall near her face and tucked a stray hair behind her ear. And she let him make these small advancements and gestures and she watched them as if they were happening to another.

He straightened the bonnet. "You look right pretty, Eveline."

"Get your hands off my wife."

Wilhelm appeared from the walkway, his face white and his arms shaking. Eveline pulled off the hat and stuffed it in the box, her whole body trembling.

Frank put his hands up mockingly. "Steady, boy!" he placated. "Claire got your wife a present and I was just dropping it off."

Wilhelm snorted like a beast. He stepped into Frank's space until their noses nearly touched. "You don't touch my wife."

Eveline touched his arm and it was like rock. She pulled her hand away. "He didn't mean anything by it, Wil."

Wilhelm grabbed the box and thrust it into Frank's chest. "Take your present and get off my property."

"Watch it, Kiser." Frank's eyes shone black and he pushed the box back into Wilhelm's chest, his strong arms knocking the man back a step. "The present wasn't for you. It was for her." Frank stepped upon the path and clicked his tongue against the roof of his mouth. "And as for getting off your property, I suggest you start making your loan payments. Otherwise, you might not be saying those words for much longer."

He tipped his cowboy hat and winked at Wilhelm's wife. "Always a pleasure, Eveline."

CHAPTER 38

In the farthest fields, the crabgrass stuck out in needles, the blades wide and pale, the tips browned and dead, all softness now a memory, fossilized into rigidness. Now there was grass. Now, when the Kisers had to plow and the summer heat grew, there was grass and it seemed that with every turn this land taunted them. The land teased by giving them mud that eroded fertile soil and pushed it piled against the forest line and gravel line of the lane. And the land shackled their efforts by placing deep-rooted weeds and clay-packed dirt wherever a shovel could be hoped to spade.

Andrew's boots crunched the grass, bent the straight lines into disfigured angles. The sound of cicadas vibrated and rose like a drumroll with no finale. Sun centered the sky, the white orb strong and warm, beating down on everything that lay below. The hot rays pushed atop his crown and Andrew pulled the cloth cap from his back pocket and fastened it with rebellion upon his head. He looped his thumb through one suspender, felt the cross rub across his back with the pull, the sweat pressing against the white shirt.

The field was a level one, flat with just a hump leading off into the horizon. He dug into the ground with the heel of his boot, kicked up the chestnut-colored clay. He knelt, pressed his fingertips into the material, soft enough to sculpt. No topsoil. None. Washed away from years of sheep overgrazing.

Plowing the stagnant fields was a task neither Wilhelm nor Andrew could have foreseen as being so arduous. From the distance, the fields were open expanses of promising land, an empty canvas that would soon be filled with the vibrant greens of corn and the deep yellow of hay. But upon closer inspection, the ground appeared littered with rocks, wedged between deep roots of bittersweet and poison ivy and young, whiney oaks.

The Fordson tractor handled well, the lid to its steam pipe yawning with black smoke before closing again with its next gulp. The noise of the engine drowned out any other noise, scattering the crows and the grouse in panicked waves of flight. Wilhelm and Andrew had to scream above the sound of the engine to be heard.

Wilhelm ran the tractor and the plow, the hard metal grinding against the stones. Andrew followed behind with the hoe, cutting out the wide roots that were left nicked but intact. Within the hour, Andrew's ears numbed to the engine, the hammering clutching his neck. His hand was rubbed sore and blistered. But he worked through the pain and the noise, let the sun heat his back and drip sweat down his cheeks. He ignored the bleeding in his hand and did not mourn the loss of the one but was thankful for the work of the remainder—bloody or not.

The muscle and bone and flesh pain didn't matter. He would work by Wilhelm's side silently and without complaint until his uncle gave the word to stop. For Andrew had seen a man die that day at the market. He had watched a proud, strong man who had tamed the railroad turn to ash that day. It would only take a fleeting wind to blow that ash away. So, it did not matter that his hand bled or that his shoulder was nearly disjointed or his head dizzied from dehydration. Andrew would work next to his uncle and step between him and any wind that dared to blow.

The corn seed had been delivered earlier in the week and they were already behind getting it into the ground. Andrew didn't ask where the corn came from or how it was paid for. He already knew. Saw the way Wilhelm had nearly pummeled Frank Morton, the taste of disgrace hardened and stuck to his mouth.

At the mount, after the endless rows of overturned earth, Wilhelm turned off the engine, and the sudden lack of noise was startling. It made the *ding* in Andrew's ears throb worse with the reprieve.

"Slow goin'!" Wilhelm shouted, his ears still deaf. "Corn should be in by the end of the week, though. Don't you think?"

Andrew nodded, scanned the acres of hard-won clearing.

"Let's break for supper and pick up later. Moon will be full, so we can work late."

Back at the house, Lily cooked at the stove and Andrew knew a good midday meal was coming his way. She set the roast chicken and boiled potatoes in front of the men. Andrew picked up the serving spoon and it dropped from his fingers, the ting loud upon the table. Eveline caught a glance at his swollen fingers. "My word, look at your hand!" She turned on Wilhelm. "His hand is nearly raw to the bone."

Andrew hid his hand under the table. "It's nothing."

"Nothing? Let me see you pick up your fork."

"Let it go, Eve," Wilhelm ordered. "Comes with the work. It'll heal."

"You let him drive the tractor until it does," she commanded.

Wilhelm ignored her and stabbed into his potato.

"It's too hot in here. Going to eat outside." Andrew didn't want the stares or the pity and carried the plate outdoors, sat on the granite slab.

He used his tight and bloated fingers to pop the small potatoes into his mouth, his appetite nearly gone.

The screen door opened. Lily sat down, tucked her dress around her legs. The calico cat crawled from under an azalea bush and rubbed against her shins. Lily gave her a good scratch behind the ears.

"Rather you didn't see me eat right now," Andrew said. He stared at the food, gave a half smile. "Embarrassing enough I can't hold my fork."

She smiled and took the plate from his lap and gently pulled his wrist to her lap. From her pocket she removed a small, round tin and took off the lid to reveal a yellowy paste. Gently, she held the hand and opened the curved fingers. Andrew flinched, the scabs breaking with the movement. She took the cream and with a touch of a feather rubbed it thickly into the red and broken skin. At first the pain left him squirming, but soon the oils made the tight skin pliable and his muscles relaxed. "What is it?" he asked.

"Mutton tallow." She watched her work as if she were playing a beautiful song upon the piano keys. "Found it in the root cellar. Doesn't smell so great but will keep your hand from tightening."

The pain was leaving and the feel of her fingers upon his skin came through; the rhythmic circles of her tender strokes left him mellow and sleepy.

"I heard what happened," she said softly. "At the market."

He didn't expect the pang of humiliation, but it entered, hard and swift. He didn't want her to know and yet he wanted her to know. He wanted her to look at him in that way that was at once gentle and urgent—that look that said all would be all right and if it wasn't, she would still be there.

"How'd you hear?"

"Old man Stevens."

Andrew stared into his plate, remembered the look on Will's and Edgar's faces. He remembered how Eveline had cried when she heard, remembered that white, deathly look on Wilhelm's face.

Lily's arched eyebrows narrowed and her forehead creased. "It's not right. Not right what people are doing. What they're saying."

Andrew picked up a potato, long cooled, and chewed slowly.

"Were you scared?" she asked.

"No."

"I didn't think so. You were mad, though. Weren't you?" She grinned. "Bet your blood was boiling."

"Yeah." But he didn't grin, continued to chew slowly. "I'm still mad."

"I know." Her head nodded as if she were still saying it.

Andrew watched her. He pushed the words away, pushed the day of the market away and leaned in, kissed her on the cheek.

Her eyes sprung wide and she touched the spot, glowed. "What was that for?"

He wasn't tired anymore. He wanted to lean her against the stones and kiss her neck until she squirmed and giggled underneath him.

She stared back at him. "I want to show you something."

His veins ignited just with the tone. "And what's that?"

"Finish your meal, then meet me by the woods." She pointed to the row of pines that stood as a line between the deciduous trees. "I'll be waiting there."

"I can't." He shook his head, back to reality. "Got to get back to the fields."

She laughed. "Mr. Kiser's asleep on the couch. Passed out as soon as he finished gulping his meal. Think you have a little time. Besides, won't take long."

Her face was so beautiful, smiling as if all of nature were part of her skin, and his heart leaped to her. She picked up a dandelion and placed it behind her ear.

"No." Andrew waved a finger in dissatisfaction and took the flower from her hair. "You're too pretty to wear weeds." He leaned back and plucked a yellow daylily and tucked it behind her ear. "That's better."

She touched the petals, gave him a slight wave before heading toward the woods. "Take your time and eat," she reminded him. He watched her thin yellow dress flow with the breeze, and if he hadn't been suddenly starving he would have chased her into the clouds.

"So, where are we going?" Andrew asked as they weaved through the shady pines.

"A spring."

"A what?"

"A magic spring," she insisted as if he should know it.

"Think you've been reading too many fairy tales, Lily girl."

"You'll see." She took off at a run, her long wild hair trailing. She was like a tree nymph, made of the land and all the colors of nature. He did his best to keep up as she darted through the browning needles of the forest floor. Down a slope, the air cooled considerably as if in a cloud.

Lily slowed and finally stopped. "Listen," she directed quietly.

Andrew listened. The sound of tiny trickles of water came from the distance like raindrops in a meadow. When she saw that he heard them, she beckoned him with a curved finger. Around the bend, a wide pool glistened deeply at the base of the hill. The rock wall was covered with wet moss, the individual rocks deep black and shining as they filtered each drip of mountain water into the spring.

She peered into the black water. "Don't know how deep it is, but it's so clear, like you can stare into it forever." Lily reached her hands into the water and took a long drink, wiped her lips with her sleeve.

There, among the moss and the shade and the canopy of chirping birds, she was a woman from another time, another existence. A fairy or a flower. She blended into the forest, belonged within the magic of the place. But it was the woman who made it magic, who made the world seem as if it shimmered from the heavens.

"Give me your hand." She took his injured hand and slowly placed it on the surface of the water, the cold instant and chilled throughout his body. She gently pushed the hand and fingers into the ice-cold water. "Is it all right?" she asked.

He nodded. The pain melted into the cold, disappeared, and all the while her eyes were on him, flooding him with warmth even while their hands chilled beneath the water. Their fingers intertwined, the palms pressed, skin upon skin, warmth and cold that left his senses reeling.

He tugged her hand closer, the movement causing ripples in the smooth surface, and her body followed, pressed against his chest as their hands had done. Her eyes were wide and scared, but her lips parted and he bent his head to catch them before they could speak. He melted into the delicate lips, found the tip of her tongue against his own. He withdrew their clasped hands from the icy water and let go, placed his wet fingers against her back and etched the buttons of her spine. Her hands found his hips, held on with clenched knuckles as if she might fall into the pond.

The ground held them. The birds surrounded the air and drowned out all thoughts so only senses lived, breathed. He traced the curve of her mouth with his lips, moved his hand up to her neck and kissed her fully, felt her body bend to his, grow limp in his arm.

He wanted to know her. He needed to know her just as he needed to touch her. The woman in his arm, against his chest, against his lips, was something wild, something that dies slowly in confinement—a hummingbird in a cage. And he wanted—needed—to know her. He wanted to watch her sleep, wanted to hear her heartbeat beneath her skin, to carve into his memory every word she had ever spoken.

Andrew pulled back, stunned momentarily by the beauty in his embrace. Lily's hair blew around her face, long and unbraided like that of a woodland goddess, and the sun drew to her as if she were the only figure worthy of its rays. The fingers laced in his were where they should be. Skin atop skin. Her palm against his. He saw his life in advance. Saw him aged and walking forward with this woman. He wanted to take Lily into the future—a future where their touch would never separate. The tiny green stone sat in the deepest corner of his pocket and he felt it intensely and with new significance.

He moved closer. Her body rose to meet his. His thighs pressed against the thin fabric of her dress. Her hair swayed slightly and tickled his cheek. His palm moved from her hip to the small of her back and her lips parted completely. He bent his neck, found the lips with his own, melted into the ground with their touch. Her hands inched up his back and her fingers curled into the fabric of his shirt. He leaned into her; she leaned back for support, leaned back to raise her hips to his. He turned his lips to her neck, rolled slowly into the bend, into the length of it. Her nails dug into his shoulder blades, her breathing quick in his ear.

He rocked his pelvis between her thighs. Small, futile thrusts against the clothed parts, but they both fell into the rhythm, moving into each other with pounding hearts.

A bell clanged distantly, muted the birds. Lily closed her eyes, lowered her head so that her forehead rested against Andrew's lips. She sighed, tried to ignore the noise that rose again.

Andrew grunted, dropped his forehead against her neck as if in pain. He could live in her veins and he'd still miss her.

Lily's chest rose and fell. Her eyes closed and she swallowed hard. He smiled, etched the line of her cheek with his cool fingers. "Guess you're wanted back home."

"I hate that bell," she said in anguish. "Makes me feel like a five-year-old."

"Or a wayward cow."

She dropped her head into his chest and snickered. Then turned her face again to find his lips. Playfully, he flung his arm around her shoulder. "Come on, Bessie. I'll lead you home."

CHAPTER 39

A week later, little Will's cries wafted from the road. Lily was going to Widow Sullivan's and heard him first. She put down her egg basket, then sprinted, her dress held above her knees.

The boy ran to her, hid his face in her skirt. She pried his hands from the folds and knelt upon the gravel to see his panicked face. "What's wrong, Will?"

"I have to get Andrew," he huffed, the shallow grip of air closing his throat. "My legs can't run anymore," he cried, and buckled. "He's gotta come!"

Will had seen something awful, the look of terror scratching upon her own childhood memories. A belt to her sister. Claire's pleading, silent call to her to run, to hide. And yet she had stayed, rooted, a witness to the brutality that mirrored her conception. And when it was over, the tethers broke and she found the strength to flee, to run into the woods and vomit within the curled leaves.

A prolonged flash of heat washed over her

body and congealed in her skull. Bile rose to her throat. She should have stopped it, but she hadn't known how to kill an abuse she couldn't comprehend. The sour of her stomach stung her mouth as she pushed against the dross. Will shook in her arms. *No. Not this time.* She straightened— ascended as a woman who would no longer hide. "You go to Mrs. Sullivan's," she ordered fiercely. "I'll get Andrew. You stay there until I come back. Understand?" He nodded.

Lily ran hard, the gravel spraying behind the hammering boots. But she didn't flee from the terror; she ran into the heart of it. The cows dotted along the Kiser property line and she knew Andrew wouldn't be far beyond. "Andrew!" she yelled. She pulled force to her lungs and called out again, "Andrew!"

The sun reflected off the white shirt as he started at a trot from the low field, his hat held in his hand. She bent under the fence, her legs wobbling with the exertion. "It's Will," she panted as he came into earshot. "Something's wrong. I don't know what, but something's happened."

Together, they took off over the crest of the road, down to the widow's house. Will sat on the step of the front porch, Mrs. Sullivan's bowed figure holding him against her fragile bones. He scratched at his tears, saw his cousin coming. "Andrew!" He broke from the old woman and ran to Andrew's side, clutched his thigh.

"What is it, Will? What's happened?"

"We were walking home and these boys came. Except they weren't boys. Not like me. Older ones. I don't know," he groaned. "They started cussing at us, pushing Fritz." Between gasps of air, he snorted, his nose running. "They took Anna's hair right off her head!" he screamed. "Ripped it all up, pulled it between them like tug-o'-war." His face crumpled. "Hair was floating everywhere. Flying up to the sky. They tore it all to pieces."

"Is she hurt?"

Will shook his head. "No. But she was all curled up, crying. Her head all bald and white." He started to wail then and he squeezed Andrew's hand. "Fritz tried to stop them. He tried to stop them and they hurt him bad."

The land spun, the dread sinking to Andrew's knees. "Where are they now?"

"Down by the creek past the school. Anna's hiding. She's crying so hard. Never saw somebody cry so hard. Won't come out with no hair. Just hiding so nobody sees her. The boys chased Fritz, ran into the woods and hurt him real bad. Could hear him screaming." His eyes turned up to Andrew, wide and shining with guilt. "I didn't want to leave them there. I swear it, but I didn't know what to do."

Andrew hugged him. "You did the right thing, Will."

Widow Sullivan stepped up. "Take my buggy," she directed firmly. "I'll see to it the boy gets home safe."

Lily hurried to the barn, hitched the small wagon to the draft horse, brought it to the gate, then climbed onto the seat and waited for Andrew. They rode in silence, each with their own thoughts of a world spiraling out of control, wondered how a land filled with flowers and vibrant green had soured and turned rancid.

As the schoolhouse came into view over the ridge, Lily put her hand on his arm. "Park it there." She pointed. "I know where the creek is from here."

Andrew and Lily ducked into the woods under lowered limbs, dodged spiderwebs and knobby roots. "Anna?" Andrew called. "Anna, you in here?"

A sniffle emanated from behind an old oak. Andrew curved to the tree until two small arms stretched out. He put his arm around the little girl and hoisted her to his hip, her bald head white and pale, the tiny blue veins prominent near the temples. Remnants of her wig settled in piles of ringlets along the ground, rose and floated in low bursts of wind. The tiny girl cried into his shoulder. "I've got you now, Anna," he whispered into her ear, rocking her gently. "You're safe now."

Lily hid her face, the embrace so tender, so

protective, that she leaned against a thick tree for support. "Lily." Andrew's appeal was nearly inaudible, as he did not want to startle the child in his arm. She looked up and he motioned with his head for her to come closer. "It's all over now, little one." He comforted her, repeated, "I've got you now."

Anna sobbed. "They hurt Fritz."

"Where is he, Anna?"

She pointed to the woods and Andrew could see the shadow of large shoulders and curved back as it rocked between the thorny bushes. He handed Anna to Lily, the little girl wrapping her legs around Lily's waist.

Andrew ducked deeper into the brush, the thorns catching his shirt and drawing him back. With effort, he reached the giant man who had buried himself within the nasty prickers. Fritz's shirt was ripped in lines across the back, the bloodied gashes slim and curved. The weapons, a few dripping willow saplings, lay cracked around his hips.

Andrew touched Fritz's shoulder with no response and inched around to face him. The amount of blood stopped him cold.

Andrew steadied, tried to keep his voice calm. "How bad are you hurt, Fritz?" As if out of a dream, Fritz put his head up, looked at the new face as if he couldn't put the voice and image together.

"I not hurt." He shook his head fiercely as he rocked. The body moved back and forth while his head turned from side to side in opposition. "Fritz not hurt. Anna hurt."

Andrew inspected the bloody face, sighed with relief. The blood stemming from a cut at the forehead hadn't been wiped away, just left to spread down his eyes and cheeks. Besides that, his lip swelled and a front tooth was missing. Andrew knew it could have been much worse.

"I need you to listen to me," Andrew said sternly but with compassion.

The man shook his head, rocked into his internal dream.

"Anna is all right," Andrew assured Fritz. "But she's scared for you."

He put his head up. "Fritz not hurt."

"I know." He fixed on the man's eyes so he would understand. "I know. But you have a lot of blood and it's scaring your sister. Come to the creek and wash up and then we'll show Anna and she'll feel better."

"Make Anna better?"

"Yes."

Fritz unfolded like a sleeping giant and plowed through the twisted bittersweet to the creek. He plunged his face in the water and shook it hard, reared up and then submerged his face again. He turned to Andrew with dripping face. "Better?"

Andrew nodded. Fritz looked much better,

didn't even seem pained by the lashes on his back. The cut above the brow line began to bleed again. Andrew scanned the low limbs and found one covered in tent worms. He pulled the webbing off and shook off the tiny caterpillars.

"I'm just going to stop the bleeding, Fritz. Might hurt for a second."

But the man didn't flinch as Andrew stuck the webs across the cut, clotting the crimson flow instantly. They walked up to where Lily and Anna sat.

"Fritz!" Anna fell on her brother and wrapped her arms around his thick middle.

"Fritz not hurt, Anna."

She smiled at him, struggled to touch his face, but he was too tall. He bent down low and she looked at the cut and his swollen lip. Her chin quivered. "You lost a tooth."

Fritz smiled widely. "Like a jack-o'-lantern!" The little girl hugged him harder.

"We should get home," Andrew recommended. A sudden thought rushed and chilled his cells. The people who had done this might come back. He glanced at Lily, wondered what they'd do to her if heartless enough to steal a child's wig. The very idea shot fire up his body, the commitment staunch—he'd never let anyone hurt Lily, ever.

Lily gathered Anna by the shoulders, but the girl stepped back. "I can't go out there," she cried. "My hair."

Lily took her handkerchief from her pocket, wrapped the blue square over the bald head and tied it behind Anna's ears. She held the wet cheeks in her hands. "Better?"

Anna touched the fabric, nodded in confirmation. Lily reached over and pulled Andrew's handkerchief from his back pocket and tied it around her own head. "Mine's not as pretty as yours, but I'd say we look pretty good." She flashed a smile to Andrew. "What do you think?"

He met the lovely faces, one and then the other. "Think you're about the prettiest women I've ever seen in my life."

In the buggy, Andrew and Lily acted as bookends to little Anna, keeping her still and sheltered between their steady forms. Fritz sat on the backseat, mute and scarred with a memory that his mind couldn't understand.

"There's Pieter!" Anna pointed. As they turned the right to their road, Pieter was already coming toward them, his gait severe.

"Let me talk to your brother first." Andrew stopped the horse and gave the reins to Lily, jumped off the sideboard.

Pieter hurried his pace, no different from a bull charging a red cape. Andrew blocked his way, put a firm hand against his friend's chest. "Hold on, Pieter."

He slapped the hand away. "What did those

bastards do to my sister?" he shouted as he tried to move again.

"You wait." Andrew grabbed him harshly by the arm. "They're scared enough as it is, don't need you rushing at them. Got to calm yourself first. All right?"

Pieter's face burned red, but he relented, bit his lip so hard it blanched white.

"They're going to be all right." He let go of his friend's arm and spoke dimly. "Fritz got cut, but it's not too bad."

"And Anna?" he shouted. "So help me if they hurt her!"

"They took her wig but didn't hurt her. She doesn't want anyone to see her without hair. Why she hid."

Pieter's face twisted as he forced back the angry tears. He grabbed at his own hair with two fists. Sounds sputtered from his mouth as he tried to form words. He spun in a half circle. Finally, he dropped his hands and grabbed Andrew by the collar. "Who the hell does that? Who the hell does that to a little girl?" he hissed.

Andrew pried the fingers from his shirt. "People aren't thinking straight and you know it." Andrew lowered his voice and spoke roughly. "But you need to think straight, you hear me? I know you're riled. I am, too, but you got to think straight."

"Riled?" Pieter started to yell but lowered his

voice to a growl. "If you think I'm going to stand by and let someone do that to my family, then you don't know me at all."

Andrew squared his shoulders, met the eyes level. "I'm not saying you don't do anything about it. I'm just saying we got to think this through."

"We?" The severity left his voice. "This isn't your fight, Andrew."

"Yes, it is." The weight was his own. "And you know it."

Andrew dropped them at the Muellers' home, watched as Pieter carried Anna in his arms while Fritz's large frame shed a shadow across their narrow walkway. He turned the buggy back up the lane and headed toward Lily's house.

The sound of crickets rose from the goldenrod and poison sumac that hugged the slope near the road. "What do you plan to do?" Lily finally asked.

"I don't know." He felt her gaze on his face and turned, met her eyes for only a moment. "Pieter's out for blood."

"Please don't get involved." The fear in her voice left her limp. "I couldn't take it if you got hurt."

CHAPTER 40

A ndrew climbed the small foot ladder to the lower limbs of the apple tree. The fungus that had sprouted in early spring had spread to several more limbs, the black knots as hard as wood, cracking open the bark where it emerged. Andrew leaned his weight against the tree and used the handsaw to cut off the afflicted branches.

A rustling came from below. Lily's crouched body picked up the cut limbs, then dragged them to the edge of the fence, threw them into the brush pile. Andrew stepped down the ladder and put the saw down, wiped the sawdust from his forehead with the back of his hand.

She dropped the last of the branches into the pile and waited as he approached. He stepped close and stopped, could feel the energy of her in the inches between them.

"I need to give you something." She handed him a white box with a gold seal at the top. "It's for Pieter. For Anna actually."

"Why don't you give it to her?"

"I'd rather they didn't know it came from me.

I know what they think of Frank, of me." The muscles of her throat stretched. "I don't think they'd accept it."

"What is it?"

Lily didn't answer, waited for him to open it. At first, when he lifted the lid, he thought he was looking down at a large doll's head, but as he lifted the stand out he saw what it was. A small brown wig, only large enough to fit a child.

"For Anna," Andrew said, nearly to himself.

Lily nodded. "I know the Muellers don't have the money for a new one. Not now, anyway, with their accounts being cut. They're very expensive. The good ones anyway."

"How did you afford this?"

"Had some money put away. Was saving for a trip. Seems kind of silly now." She brushed a strand of hair from her lowered eyes. "Would you give it to her?"

Lily's profile could have been chiseled from glowing quartz—the pure, white skin, the curve of her forehead to the straight line of her nose and curve of her lips. He fell lost into the still profile, unable to remove his gaze. Finally, he found the only two words brave enough to come forth. "I will." She smiled sadly and gave a short wave in thanks before walking away.

Gerda Mueller bent over a patch of spinach, her enormous backside swaying and twitching as she grabbed any weeds insolent enough to sprout in her garden. Given she didn't see him approach, Andrew cleared his throat. Gerda spun, her hands still strangling the mangled roots as she tittered. "Oh, Andrew! Some velcome, eh? With my bum wavin' hello to ya!" She threw the plants to the ground and wiped her man hands on her skirt. "Lookin' for Pieter, then?"

"Yes, ma'am." He met her at the row of vegetables, scanned the even, abundant lines. "Got the hardiest garden I've ever seen, Mrs. Mueller."

A mighty arm wrapped around his shoulder and a wet kiss landed on his cheek. "You! Charmer, Andrew Houghton!" She pinched his cheek in the spot that she had kissed. "A good man."

"Ah, Ma!" Pieter carried a harness over his shoulder while several horseshoes lined his wrist like a bracelet. "Stop bruising the neighbors."

She laughed and squeezed Andrew heartily, thumped him on the chest while he tried not to let the wind get knocked out of his lungs. "Psssh! You're a strong one, eh?"

"Yes, ma'am," he answered, and coughed, cringed in case she squeezed, kissed, thumped or broke him in half.

Pieter put down his supplies. "Ma, don't let Fritz put the shoes on the horses anymore. Idiot put them on backwards."

"Hush wiv those words, Pieter!" she scolded. "He's a good boy."

"Good boy or not, still put the shoes on back-wards. Thick as peat, that kid."

"All right." She waved him off like a horsefly. "Orf wiv you now. Git!" She pushed the boys away with a whack to their backs. "Got to get back to vork. Grass growin' in my vatermelons."

Andrew and Pieter crossed the even path to the lane, the far fields crowded with pen after pen of rolling pigs. Andrew reached behind a whiskey barrel planter and handed the box to Pieter.

"What's this?" he asked as he lifted the lid.

"It's for Anna." He stopped and peered back at the bent figure of Mrs. Mueller. "It's from Lily."

Pieter shoved the box at him. "I don't want it."

Andrew pushed it back. "It's for Anna. Not for you."

"We don't need anything from the Mortons," he spit. "Take it back or I throw it to the pigs."

"Listen, Pieter," Andrew defended Lily, "I don't know what your beef is with the Mortons, but Lily hasn't harmed anyone. Bought this for Anna with her own money. And remember Mary Paulsen? How you thought Lily had taken all her goods from auction? Well, she bought them all and shipped them to her."

"That what she told you?" he asked sarcastically.

Andrew stepped toward his friend and warned, "That's enough."

Pieter closed his eyes and sighed, dropped his

401

head low, sat down on the grass. "I know it ain't her fault. I know it," he conceded. "I'm just so damn mad, don't even know who to be mad at anymore."

His jaw hardened and he stared at the perfect farmhouse cradled on the sea of grass, surrounded by pink and red roses climbing over the stone foundation. "I'm so tired of being cursed. So sick of being a target with this damn war."

Pieter picked up a rock and dug the point into the soft earth. "Got no credit in town. Can't even show up at the market with our name on our wagon. Then they go—" His voice broke then and he shook his head savagely. "They go beatin' my poor dumb brother and hurt Anna." He squeezed the rock, hard enough to draw blood. Andrew leaned against the fence, his stomach tightening with the same memories.

"This war making people itch like they got fleas," Pieter said. "Looking for someone to blame for all that itching." His voice dropped confidentially. "Pa's been sending money back to Nuremberg. Cousins are fighting on the front lines for the Kaiser. Breaks Pa's heart knowing his brothers and sisters sending their children to war. Scrambling for food. But famine or no, I don't think he should do it and I told him so." Pieter looked aged, older than his years. "Somebody find out and there'll be hell to pay for sure. They'll say it's treason. Make what they did to Fritz look like child's play. But Pa won't hear talk against it." Pieter tilted his head. "Know my sister's married to a Mennonite?"

Andrew shook his head.

"Says if he gets drafted he'll refuse. Says it's God's commandment not to kill. Know what they're doing to Mennonites who won't serve?" He paused. "They're beating the crap out of them, that's what. Torturing them just for not fighting, sending them off to Leavenworth." Pieter pounded the rock into the ground. "So help me, that'll kill my sister. Somebody hurt him like that. It'll kill her."

Pieter glanced at the box from Lily. "I know Lily ain't got nothing to do with this, but Frank Morton's stirring the pot. He's holding meetings in town, all tied up with the American Protective League. A bunch of hotheads with cheap badges that say they got a right to keep an eye on Germans, keep them in line." A look of real terror entered Pieter's face. "They find out about Pa sending money, they'll tar and feather him. Might throw your uncle in for the fun of it."

Andrew sat on the heels of his boots. "We're not going to let that happen, Pieter." His voice was steady, resolved. "You know that."

"That's right." Pieter met the look. "Because I'm enlisting." He stood, tossed the rock into the space between the trees. "Only way I can protect my family is if I'm serving."

CHAPTER 41

Andrew and Wilhelm checked the lines of thick hay, assessed their readiness for harvest and baling. Wilhelm paused, peered over the ridge. "Looks like we got visitors." Two men, a policeman and a civilian, huffed up the hill.

"Officer," Wilhelm greeted him.

"Mr. Kiser?" the policeman asked.

"That's right."

"This your son?" He motioned at Andrew.

"My nephew." Wilhelm's tone deepened with the questioning and he folded his arms, opened his legs slightly in a stance that said, *What the hell you doing on my property?*

"This is Mr. Simpson, from the bank. Says your boy clobbered his son."

Mr. Simpson kept silent, saw Andrew's arm, his face suddenly angry—a look of failure knowing his son got beat up by a cripple.

"Heard about that," acknowledged Wilhelm. "Seems your boy was drunk, Mr. Simpson. Giving a young lady a hard time. Way I heard it, sounds like he got what was coming to him."

The officer and Mr. Simpson exchanged

404

knowing looks. "Normally, I'd agree with you, but that's not why we're here."

The sun landed hotly on their backs, the fire of the earth rising with hay pollen and the sound of katydids jumping. The officer rolled a stone under his foot. "Seems some words were thrown around during the fight." His gaze pierced Andrew. "Unpatriotic words."

"What?" Andrew stepped forward, but his uncle pressed him back.

Wilhelm said, "I'm not one for beating around the bush, Mr. . . ."

"Tipney. Sheriff Tipney."

"Well, Sheriff, I expect you come right out with what you and Mr. Simpson are accusing this young man of so we can get back to our work."

Mr. Simpson spoke up. "Your son . . . your nephew . . . said it was just a matter of time before Germany won this war. Said the Kaiser would be headed to America next and he'd be the first one to shake his hand. Said he was honored to share the name. Then he called my son a coward before hitting him on the head with a rock."

Mr. Simpson heated now and his mustache hairs blew with the thrust of air coming from his nose. Andrew squared his shoulders, his dark gaze turning his blue eyes indigo, landing first on the sheriff's and then Mr. Simpson's.

"Don't need to answer to them, Andrew." Wilhelm put on his hat and prepared to go back to the fields. "His boy got beat and looking to make up for it through lies. Any man with half a brain could see that. Good day, gentlemen."

The sheriff chewed his gum slowly. "Not that easy, I'm afraid. Using that talk is a criminal offense. Young man's coming with me to the courthouse." He waved Andrew forward. "You're under arrest, son."

"Whoa. Hold on!" The fury stretched out Wilhelm's tan neck. "It's one man's words against another."

"True, but in these times can't be too careful. We'll bring him to town until it's figured out." The sheriff shoved his hat high upon his forehead and eyed Andrew. "Look, you don't look like a bad kid, but sometimes things are said in the heat of anger and we can't have this now, not here. Not with American boys fighting and not coming home."

"I never uttered those words." Andrew seethed. "Besides, why aren't you out finding the boys that terrorized the Muellers? The ones that beat a young man to pulp and destroyed a little girl's wig."

The sheriff nodded solemnly. Motioned him forward again, ignoring the accusation. "We've done enough talking now. Let's get going." He scratched his ear. "We're at the Plum jail if you want to inquire about bail. They'll deny it, but you're welcome to apply." The men turned and walked through the blond rows of hay.

"Coffee?"

Andrew shifted in the small cot in the jail cell, rose and took the steaming mug from between the bars. "Thanks." His limbs ached from the stiff, springless bed. He hadn't slept a wink during the night, finally dozing off just before the sheriff entered.

The officer pulled up a wooden chair and sat down, propped his shoes against the bars and rocked back and forth. "You hungry?"

Andrew shook his head.

"Didn't think so. Something about being behind bars sucks away a man's appetite." The sheriff sipped his coffee easily; the reserve and seriousness from yesterday's ride to the station had disappeared and his manner was friendly.

"Look, kid," he started. "I know Danny well. He's spent more nights on that cot than any other young man around here. But he's pretty hot right now on account you taking him down. He don't like to lose, that one." He chuckled to himself. "Hothead.

"Anyway, I don't think you said those things. Despite your name, I don't believe a word of it. But Mr. Simpson's got clout and he wasn't going to shut up until there was some justice served. Arresting you is about the most humane thing I could do." He smiled. "You can thank me later."

"Thank you?" Andrew couldn't help but chortle. "You'll excuse me if I don't send flowers."

The sheriff laughed at that, lowered his feet to the floor. He rested his elbows on his knees, held his mug between his two palms. "You hear what happened in Illinois?" he asked. "To Robert Prager?"

"No."

"German American said the wrong thing to the wrong people and they came for the man. Stripped him naked and wrapped him in the American flag, paraded him around town, beat him up pretty good. Finally, a couple of level-headed citizens called the police and they took the man into protective custody. Well, the mob was still thirsty, flooded the jail and pulled out poor Prager and lynched him." He drank his coffee as easily as if he were talking about the price of corn or the hope for rain this summer.

Andrew's stomach soured, and he let the image settle, remembered Pieter's talk of tar and feathering.

"That's why I had to do something," said the sheriff. "Least now Danny can save face. Mr. Simpson can tell people you've been punished. Danny be heading to training in another week and it'll be over. Just got to sit it out until then."

"Doesn't give a man much comfort seeing I'm sitting in a jail like Prager."

"You're safe here, kid. I'm tougher than I look. Besides, police in Illinois didn't try to stop the mob. Between you and me, my wife's half-German. Hard keeping that stuff hidden. Having a name like Kiser is like a curse. Nowhere to hide."

"I'm not German." It was the first time he said it out loud and he wasn't sure why he did. "My last name is Houghton."

"Well, why on God's earth didn't you say something before?"

"Would it have mattered?"

The sheriff shook his head. "No. Not as long as you're living with the Kisers."

"They're good people. Love this country as much as the Simpsons. Except they don't have to attack people to prove it."

The sheriff took in the words and shrugged. "A strange time," he said slowly. "A strange time indeed."

The bell rang at the front door. "Speak of the devil. No pun intended." The sheriff rose and pushed in his chair. "Probably your uncle now."

The sheriff left and when he returned a few minutes later someone other than Andrew's uncle was by his side. Lily. Her hair brushed smoothed and clipped behind with a beaded barrette. Her dress was new, pressed and tailored. She wore heels and clutched a small purse in her hands. "Hello, Andrew."

He hardly recognized her, the demeanor stoic and serious, like a different version of his friend had sprouted in her place, and he was left speechless. "Was just explaining to Sheriff Tipney that I witnessed the entire exchange with you and Dan Simpson. That it was me who hit Dan over the head."

Andrew rose. "You shouldn't be here, Lily."

"Of course I should be here. Frank sent me."

The sheriff unlocked the cell door and opened it slowly. "Looks like you got a witness." He turned to Lily. "You sure Frank said he should be released?"

"Positive."

He held the door open. "Got a guardian angel after all, kid."

Andrew followed Lily to the buggy, her posture stiff as she walked with purpose and without a word. She picked up the reins with confidence and clicked the horse to move. When they reached the far edge of town, Lily's shoulders relaxed. She pulled the buggy to the side of the road. "I'm not going to be able to see you for a while," she uttered plainly.

"Frank didn't authorize my release, did he?"

She was silent for a moment and her eyes fluttered nervously. "No."

Andrew wished she had left him in the cell. "Shouldn't have done it, Lily."

She swallowed, tried to look brave. "I'm a grown woman, Andrew."

"What are you going to do when he finds out?"

She made a poor attempt at a grin. "Hide."

"You aren't going back there."

"I *am* going back there." The tone was firm. "Just leave it be."

"I can't have you disappearing out of my life again, Lily. I can't. I have to know you're all right."

"I told you to let it go. Look," she pleaded with a drawn face, "just give me some time to smooth it over. All right?"

"All right," he agreed reluctantly. "Just do one thing for me?"

"What's that?"

"Meet me at the spring in the woods on Friday. Frank heads to Pittsburgh for his meetings then, right?"

She paled. "I don't know."

"Please, Lily. Will you meet me there?" he asked again.

A long pause and then she nodded once. "Yes."

"Promise?"

"Yes." She nodded again, her expression worried but truthful. "I promise."

Andrew kissed her on the cheek and jumped from the buggy. "Where are you going?" she asked.

"Have to take care of something in town." He

gripped the smooth wood of the buggy as if he planned to keep it from moving. "If Frank bothers you, you get out of there, Lily. You hear me?"

She smiled meekly. "You just worry about yourself, Mr. Houghton." And with that she clicked and set the horse at an even, high-stepping trot out of town.

The gravel crunched under Andrew's worn boots as he headed behind the town shops, avoiding the main road and the people at its core. The hot afternoon sedated the branches of the overhanging trees.

The night spent in the jail had altered him. Messages drifted from dreams; images splashed and stayed lucid upon his awakening on the hard cot. Focused clarity brought intent, direction, and his skin pulsed. Change embedded the molecules of the air and left it living and breathing. He remembered the letter from his mother and his hair prickled. He thought of the Kisers, the family who took him in when no one else would, who defended him as one of their own.

Take care of your family. Always. Frederick Houghton's voice, the husky sound that had been absent for so long, whispered in his ear during the night. The Kisers were his family now. The old farmhouse was his home; his cousins, his brothers. A sudden pride burned. Then Lily. And the future took shape from the past, birthed new.

Andrew turned stealthily onto the main street

of town, jogged past the post office to the blacksmith's shop in the back. The open stall was stained black from wall to ceiling and the blacksmith stood over a steel drum of water. With each submerged tool, the water cried and hissed, rose in steam to the rafters. The man didn't turn. "Need something?" he asked curtly.

Andrew pulled his father's miner tags from his shirt and held them up. "Can you melt these down?"

The man touched the tags, inspected the brass in his onyx hands. "Into what?"

"A ring." Andrew pulled out the green gem in his pocket. "Set with this."

CHAPTER 42

L ily bent over the cucumbers. She should have picked them earlier. The biggest were cracked on the top, the brown-scabbed skin knitting the crevices. Absently, she placed the vegetables in the bucket, her mind distant and active while her fingers did the plucking.

The wind shifted and she hurried with the task, her heart beating fast in her chest. She reached for the last fat cucumber, saw the swift movement of a man's boot and ducked her head just as the kick landed with a shuddering smack against the metal pail, sending it flying above her stooped shoulders. Vegetables bounced and scattered across the garden. The bucket skipped and then landed, rolled slowly. Lily kept her head buried even after the noise stopped.

"Stand up, goddammit!"

Lily uncoiled, stood straight and faced Frank.

"I swear I could wring your damn neck with my bare hands!" he screamed.

She didn't move, set dead eyes upon him, surrendered to what was to come. She could almost feel his hands on her neck squeezing out the life, could feel the way she would close her eyes and drift into death under his fingertips.

Her silence rattled him. He took a step forward and raised his hand to strike her cheek, but she didn't waver.

He dropped it and turned, spit into the ground. "Goddammit!"

He cursed and kicked the dirt, turned in circles mumbling obscenities. "If they kick me out of the APL for this, so help me . . ."

"I was there," she defended. "Andrew never said those things."

Her voice only fueled Frank's rage. "I don't give a damn what he said!"

"He was helping me! Dan was coming after me. Andrew stopped him," she cried. The fire rose in her throat. "All he was trying to do was protect me."

Frank barreled upon her, his finger pointing at her face in jabs. "You . . . don't . . . ever . . . see . . . him again. You hear me?"

"But he didn't do anything wrong."

"So help me, if you ever talk to that man again, ever so much as look his way or pass him on the street, I'll have him back in that cell before you can blink."

Lily's brows inched together and she gritted her teeth.

"Think I'm bluffing, don't you?" Frank snorted. "Try me, Lilith. Just try me," he threatened.

"Next time I'll make sure the officer accidentally leaves the cell door unlocked. Never know when Dan and his buddies might want to make a visit."

"I hate you."

"Oh, Lilith," he jeered. "I hate you more."

On Friday, Lily waited next to the spring in the woods as promised. Frank would never know, and besides, she had to warn Andrew to stay away.

The air in the forest hung cool and shaded, mystical. The stones seemed to sweat water, each damp, some with trickles and drops, some just glistening in the filtered sunlight. She pressed her fingers into the spongy moss, dark and brilliant.

She touched the surface of the pool with her palm, the water frigid and so clear she could see the rocks piled at the bottom. The ripples left by her hand soon faded, the surface turned to glass, her reflection as refined as in a hand mirror.

She studied her nose and eyes, the arch of her brows, the hair that hung around her shoulders, and wondered if she was pretty. Squinting, Lily tried to see herself objectively but stared so long that her skin blended with her eyes and features. She cocked her head at the image, thought of Andrew and smiled. And she realized that she was pretty when she thought of him, as if his light shone straight through her eyes.

The cool air dropped a degree and another form

entered the glass surface; two eyes and a hat grew above her head like a serpent emerging from the lake. Lily jumped and turned, just long enough to see her smile morph into terror.

"Thought you were out milking," Frank accused. "But you were coming to meet that cripple, weren't you?"

She backed up, braced against the spring's wall, the water instantly freezing and soaking her back. Lily's fingers found a rock and she traced her fingers around the edge, thought how easy it would be to strike it against him. If she hit hard enough, it would kill him; if it didn't, the nightmare would grow worse.

Frank's anger left and he seemed suddenly lost. He looked up at the trees as if the limbs and leaves confused him. "You know I don't like this any more than you do."

Something about his tone made her skin break out in a cold sweat. A look passed over his face, the ashen contrition she had only seen once before. "You need to come back to the house and get changed," he ordered softly.

Panic swelled and she shook her head. She tried to step back, but there was no room. "No," she said fiercely.

"Now, Lilith, I don't like it any better than you do, but it got to be done."

"No." The woods became walls that twisted and warped, made her dizzy, and her chest contracted until she drowned. "I won't do it. I won't do it again." The memory of a rough hand between her legs made her whimper. She shook her head, the smell of a man's breath pungent in her nose.

Frank reached to her kindly—reached to her like he held a pillow for her head, even as he pressed it against her face. "This is the last time. I swear."

"That's what you said the last time!" she screamed, the tears streaming from her eyes now. The memory of that day poisoned her, nearly broke her to her knees.

"I know it. I know what I said." He put his hands on his hips, his patience waning. "But had some trouble again. Just need it cleaned up."

Cleaned up? Cleaned up! A mop across a dirty floor. The filth submerged everything around her. Her lungs ached for air. This couldn't be happening again. Again. She moved away from the damp wall, the back of her wet dress sticking to her skin. "I won't do it!" She inched farther away, readied her muscles to run. "You can't make me!"

He grabbed her wrist hard, jerked her to him. "So help me, you'll do what I say."

She struggled against his pull, slapped his face hard with her free hand, hardly reddening the cheek. But the cold, cruel, cruel look came over him and she instantly regretted hitting him. Terror lashed. "Andrew!" she screamed.

But he pulled her arm behind her back and covered her mouth with his big hand. She couldn't breathe between her sobs and his fingers.

"You will do this!" he seethed into her ear. "You'll do this or I'll take the belt to your sister—to your mama—so hard she won't be moving till Christmas." He jerked her arm higher and she screamed out, the sound muffled under his palm. "What? You going to sit by and let her get the crap beat outta her like when you were a kid? You going to let her take the beating for you again just because you're too proud, think you're so special?" He let go and pushed her away. "Well, you ain't special, Lilith. Not a thing special about you." He spit on the ground. "Not a damn thing."

Life fell away, disintegrated into the words and the darkness. The black closed in, the knowing of what she would have to do, what she was going to do, and it broke her in pieces, whole and standing, yet broken and splintered. She tilted forward, weakened and soft as a dying willow.

Frank gave a long sigh, took off his hat and wiped his brow. His work done. "Claire's been there for you her whole life," he pointed out calmly. "Aren't you going to do one thing for her?" He stepped away as if opening a door for her to pass through, an open gate to Hell.

"Besides, you do it and it's done. Last time. A promise is a promise."

Andrew waited for hours at the spring. He rolled the ring in his palm, played with the metal. He touched the water and replayed the words that he would say. He recited the number of ways he could tell her that he loved her.

Andrew waited. He waited for his Lily girl to keep her promise. He waited until the dark shade of twilight leadened the leaves and made it clear she wouldn't come. Yet he still waited.

Now his mind took away the sentiments of the heart. His body turned cold against the flutters of her touch and her lips. His mind told him he was a fool and that she did not love him, never had. His mind made up stories that told him he was only half a man and she knew this and could never share her life with half a man. His mind told him that she was only drawn to him because there was no one else. He was a distraction, a plaything. And with each ticking moment, the insult grew, seemed to crush the life out of him, one mortared brick at a time.

Shut up, Andrew, his father ordered but gave no more advice. Perhaps Frank had kept her home. Andrew squeezed the ring tightly, forced the insecurities at bay. Perhaps she did love him after all and he wasn't a fool. Perhaps.

But he didn't know. In the darkening forest, he

glanced at his arm. Thought again of his mother's curt letter. Thought of the jabs and insults and glances that hovered around his form. And he wasn't sure if he understood anything at all.

CHAPTER 43

T he splintered bread wagon slowed to a halt at the end of the Kiser lane. "Good morning," Eveline greeted them.

Bob nodded. Bernice kept her head low. Eveline's smile vanished, the uncustomary blandness of the couple knocking her sideways.

The old man leaned to the back and pulled out the bread bag, handed it to her. Eveline juggled the weight of it in her hands, felt the difference. "There's a double order in here, Mr. Stevens." She raised the bundle back toward the wagon.

He shook his head. "Keep it."

"Much as I'd like to, we can't afford it. Need to conserve these days." She raised the bundle again. "Better just take out the extra."

Bernice looked at her now. "You keep it, Mrs. Kiser. Ain't no charge. Ain't no charge for any of it."

Her mouth fell agape and she looked at one Stevens and then another. "That's very kind of you, but I can't . . ."

Bob let out a long, drawn sigh and rubbed his worn pant leg. "We just come from town. Hearin' things. Been hearin' things for a while. This war got everybody clawin' at each other." He met her eyes. "We know that Campbell cut off your credit. Know the butcher ain't been givin' you nothin' but the gristly meat that been hangin' on the shelf too long. Know your mail's been getting opened and read before it's delivered.

"Ain't jus' you," Bob consoled. "Doin' it to the Muellers, too. Doin' it to all the Germans. Ain't right."

Eveline squeezed the bread to her chest, the yeasty, warm smell at odds with the stench of war.

"Bernie an' me know somepin 'bout this hate. Know it good, don't we, Bernie?"

The woman nodded, grinned sadly. The gray between her ebony strands stood bold against her dark skin.

"When I was in the war, back down in Vicksburg, saw the same thing," the old man said. "Same with every war, I reckon. 'The army of the North were the saviors; the men in the South, savages.' You hear it an' ya start to believe it. An' a man gets pretty good at tellin' himself the other ones are evil, that it's okay to kill 'em just so you can sleep at night. But you know. You know inside that man ain't no different than you. Jus' got a gray coat on instead of a blue one.

"Like that with the Germans, too," he continued. "Men gotta make people hate 'em, otherwise wouldn't get nobody to go over there to fight."

Bernice patted him on the knee. "That's enough, Bob. Gettin' yourself all upset."

And he was. His lips glistened with spittle and his body shook with agitation, his pupils bobbing. "But it's not jus' the war. It's the hate. Still have people starin' at us, Bernie and me, with hate even though the war long over. Still got people throwin' our bread to the crows because a Negro woman kneaded it with her fingers."

"Bob . . ."

He straightened then. "So, we know a little 'bout the hatred that's stirrin' an' it ain't right. So, you take that bread, Mrs. Kiser. Make us feel mighty good you takin' that bread from us. Me an' Bernie ain't got much, a little shack with a leaky roof an' this old horse, but we got bread an' if we can give you a share, well, it make us sleep a little better. It ain't charity, Mrs. Kiser. Jus' givin' you somepin small to help against what's bein' taken' away."

He looked at the street. "A lot of people been cruel to my Bernie. More than been kind. But the folks on this route here always been good to us. Widow Sullivan, the Muellers." He paused. "Even those Morton girls, always been kind. People like that got to stick together. It's the only shield against the hate.

"So, you take that bread, Mrs. Kiser. Make

an old couple have somepin to smile 'bout. All right?"

Eveline's lips twitched and she nodded. She wanted to say, *Thank you,* but the twitching was too much. She squeezed the bread tighter, the crusts cracking.

Bob frowned at the look and his eyes grew wet. He took in a large gulp of air and pulled his old self to the forefront. "Besides, ya know Bernie gotta thing for that nephew of yours. She'd bring ya bread five times a day jus' to git a look at the feller!" Bernice batted his arm. "Be safe, Mrs. Kiser."

Eveline watched the old wagon limp up the road. From the hill, Frank passed on the other side, did not acknowledge the Stevenses with greeting or sight; and in return, the Stevenses kept their eyes glued ahead.

Eveline's heart was still warm from the words when Frank reached her side. But she was melancholy, the usual nerves around the man quiet.

He cocked his head, his eyes soft. "You okay, Eveline?"

She nodded. "I am. Just a nice old couple is all."

"I don't know." He shivered. "Gives me the creeps thinking about those two. Nice and all. Just something about it don't seem right."

Her lip curled. "What doesn't seem right, Mr. Morton?"

He caught the look and backtracked. "Nothing. Don't pay me no mind this morning. Tired is all. Been stuck in the city the last couple days."

"Oh." He did look burdened. "You want to come in for coffee?"

"That's kind of you," he said without answering the question.

He gazed at her with drained eyes. She knew her husband would not want him here, but she wasn't ready to let him go yet. "Made a batch of muffins this morning," she offered. "Let me give you some to give to Lily and Claire."

"That'd be nice. Thank you."

They walked down the lane together. His strong, firm body made her feel tiny and woman-like, safe. "Is that Andrew near the barn?" he asked as he pointed.

"Must be back from the fields." She hoped Wilhelm wasn't with him.

"Mind if I leave you for a bit? Like to talk to the young man."

She found the request strange. "I'll give you the muffins before you leave."

"Looks like you're going to have a good crop after all." Frank Morton's bulk was propped against the barn, the glib presence putting Andrew on guard. "Cows look good, too."

He didn't like the way the man soaked in the

fields and animals with ownership. "Sound surprised, Mr. Morton."

The man shrugged, followed Andrew into the shaded stall. He looked up into the beams, impressed. "Didn't think you had it in you."

Andrew grinned with the cut. "Don't you have some German spies you need to hunt down?" he cut back.

Frank laughed, long and slow. "Funny thing about that. Thinking you owe me a thank-you for getting you out of jail."

Now Andrew laughed. "You had nothing to do with that and you know it. If it was up to you and your protective league, I'd still be behind bars."

"Guess you're right." He shrugged. "That Lily got a soft spot for gimps. Even when she was young, she was always trying to save the critters that weren't quite right."

Andrew took the pitchfork and stabbed it into the straw. His hand burned and he held tight to the handle in restraint.

"Heard you came by the house looking for her," noted Frank. "Told Lily she should just tell you straight instead of avoiding you."

"Tell me what?" he parried, his eyes rolling.

"That she ain't interested. She's a tease, son. Always has been." Frank came closer, kicked at the straw with his shiny cowboy boot. "She felt bad not meeting you at the spring, though."

Andrew stopped and squeezed the handle until his knuckles whitened.

"But," Frank continued, "she and Dan had a date. He took her to the fair. Didn't even hear her come back home. Must of gone dancing after, I reckon."

Andrew turned to the man then and dropped the pitchfork. "It's a good story, but Lily would no sooner date Dan Simpson than I'd date a chicken."

"Thought you smelled like hen feathers."

Andrew chuckled again, then readied to leave. "I got work to do."

"Wasn't no story about Dan being Lily's beau," Frank announced loudly. "She's out with him now. He picked her up this morning, took her to town." He smiled cruelly. "Should have seen how pretty she looked in that dress and heels. Course, she and Dan always had a bit a fire between them. Her hitting him over the head and all and then kissing and making up just a bit later. Firecrackers, those two." He stretched his back. "Only bailed you outta the jail to make Dan jealous. Firecrackers."

Andrew didn't believe a word, but his body constricted. "What Lily does and with who isn't any of my concern."

Frank laughed wickedly and tapped the hood of the Ford parked by the stall. "You don't get it, do you, kid? She and Dan been on and off since he started for me years ago." He folded his arms across his chest. "Dan would make a good match for Lily, don't you think? He's been working for me so long he'd make a good partner for the business. That and his dad's work with the bank. Like it was always meant to be, don't you think?"

Frank rubbed one of his biceps, looked at his large hands and then turned them to look at his palms. "Another thing about that kid is he got strong hands, you know? Strong arms, strong hands . . . two of them."

The insult was quick, delivered with a smile. Andrew took a step back, fixed his thighs to keep from attacking. "Shame he's heading off to the war then." Andrew scowled.

"You didn't hear?" Frank's mouth opened in surprise. "He didn't pass his physical. On account of his head injury. Cut got all infected. How about that?" He knocked his fist on the car. "Ironic, isn't it? Lily cracking his skull kept him close to her, made her turn away from the crippled German for keeps."

Andrew's eyes flickered to the movement at the barn door. Frank turned. "Eveline, didn't hear you there." He pulled off his hat and scrunched it in his fingers. "Just joking with—"

The woman stood in the doorway, the plate of muffins in her immobile hands, her eyes spitting with fire. "Get the hell off my land, Mr. Morton."

CHAPTER 44

The lowing from the barn came all at once, one on top of the other. Andrew tossed in his bed, the sounds melding with dreams. It was too early for milking. But the sounds from the barn increased. He folded the pillow over his ear until he heard the horse. A high-pitched whine that stabbed the eardrum. In a moment, he shot out of bed, threw on his pants and stumbled onto the steps.

He thought the lamps had been left on, the brightness full in the parlor. Something seized him from the back of the head and tingled down his flesh. The lamps weren't on. Lights flickered outside. The yellow light bloomed from *outside.* "Fire!" Andrew shouted.

The house erupted and the Kisers fell out to the yard, the pine tree next to the barn bright orange, the limbs engulfed like a burning skeleton.

"Hook the hose to the well!" he shouted to Wilhelm.

Andrew sprinted to the barn with Eveline and the boys at his heels. The pigs squealed from within the pens, the bodies thumping against the bolted gate. "Get the pigs out!" he shouted to Will.

"The horse!" Eveline hollered.

"I'll get her!"

Andrew flew to the main door of the barn, but it was too close to the tree, the heat coming in waves, the very air burning and clogged with smoke. The animals screamed inside as the roof ignited and spread down the old barn wood. He ran to the back, saw Will had released the pigs that were now running in a frenzy in every direction.

"The main door is blocked!"

He pulled open the side door, but it was too small for the animals to fit through. "Hack out the opening! I'll grab the animals!"

The smoke and flames billowed to the far right. He'd have to start with the animals closest to the door to get the most out before the barn collapsed. The mare reared, batted the sky in panic. He threw a feed sack over her head and hurried her to the door where Wilhelm worked with the ax. Andrew pushed her through the broken opening, the sides tight and scraping, but the horse was out. He pulled the cows, the lead cow stubborn with fear, grinding her hooves into the floor. He heaved the rope, cursed not having another hand to grip, until finally he jerked her forward to Wilhelm and she was out.

Two more cows followed and then the heart-stopping cracking of timber collapsed half the barn in a sea of sparks. The hideous calls of the animals trapped below buckled Andrew's knees. He pulled himself up, pushed out one last cow, the barn cats nearly tripping him.

By the time the Muellers had called the fire department and run to the farm to help soak it down, the barn was gone. Three cows had died; the Ford was half-melted. The horse was tethered to the house and the remaining cows stood in the pasture. The pigs were yet to be rounded up, might never be found.

Piles of charred wood smoked and the smell filled the nostrils, deadened the soul. There were no words. The view, now unblocked from the barn, sketched a gray landscape, revealed hills and the pond that had not been visible before. All around, there was green and blue, a normal summer day, but all that was left here, on this farm, was the gray, like the paint mixed by Wilhelm's father to keep all practical and without waste.

And the family stared at the mass of destruction. The burnt bodies of the three cows, ones Will and Edgar had milked the day before. And it poisoned the heart, raked it to shreds.

The sheriff said there were no signs of foul play. An accident, maybe a spark from the tractor. Maybe a stack of moist hay spontaneously combusted. "Got to dry the hay in the fields, you know," he reminded them. "Damp hay heats quick, you know. Maybe a forgotten can of kerosene. An accident. Too bad." Bad luck, the sheriff said. Bad luck indeed.

CHAPTER 45

When a man breaks, the air breaks around him, the ground cracks below his footsteps. His face remains unchanged; in fact, little changes, and that is where the break is first seen. The blank expression, the even line of the mouth and the pupils that do not contract in light or dilate in darkness. For all is gray, all is blank. And so a man breaks even as his limbs still move and his voice still speaks and his lungs still respire.

Children sense the change first. Will and Edgar kept a wide berth from their father, fearful of the silence that hovered around the man. As if ghosts lingered and swirled around him and if they got too close they too might be sucked into the darkness. And so when Wilhelm entered the house from the fields, his clothes still clean and exposing the fact he had done no work, the children left for the outdoors. And when he came out to walk in the shadows of the day and stare at the charred space where the barn had been, Will and Edgar were quick to find work in the kitchen.

Andrew doubled his efforts in the fields. The tractor had been left out overnight and was their last remaining vehicle. He worked until the pain and exhaustion in his body made him fall asleep without washing, simply crashed onto the bed in his clothes. And Andrew worked to stun the mind, numb it, but he also worked because Wilhelm could not. The man no longer saw the fields or the green or the money from harvest; he saw the dead cows, the dead twins, the black curled beams of the barn and the debt.

And so they all spun in their own shapes. Spun in circles like a child practicing the number "8" upon his slate. Around and around and around. The children spinning at a distance from their father, whom they did not recognize and feared, circling wider and farther from his curve. Andrew circling from shed, to field, to animals, to bed. And Eveline to her garden, to the stove, to the table, to the counter. And in this infinity, they fled from the broken man, kept him at bay in hopes the fracture would mend in time.

Eveline's mouth was dry. She itched under the skin. And when she stood for more than a few moments, she would curl against her stomach in wretchedness. A nightmare unfolded and she was not sure what was real and what was not. Time and time again, she pinched her eyes closed, prayed and opened her gaze with hesitation. But the nightmare was still there; the guilt, the grief, was still there.

When she thought of Frank, Eveline gagged. She had been such a fool. She had drunk from his cup with relish and then, when she swallowed, realized she drank sour milk. Eveline retched. She wiped the corners of her mouth with her nightgown. She had heard every word the man had said to Andrew, the way he berated and hurt him, called him a cripple. She realized that Frank had not rescued Andrew from jail but was part of the reason he was there in the first place. She realized that it was at the insistence of the American Protective League that life in town became unbearable. And as the barn burned in that ungodly hour and the sparks flashed and pillowed into the infinite black night, she knew with bone-cracking despair that the man she had desired, the man whom she had dreamed of touching, had, in one way or another, lit that match.

Eveline rolled in bed. The bile rose and she gagged again. She had been blind and now she saw and she wished she could have dug out her eyes with spoons. It was nearly too much. The war. The betrayal. She didn't know how much she could take. But then there was her husband. And with this, her eyes welled and she cried in her mind, *I'm sorry*. And she loved him so. Loved him for what he gave her, loved him for the children they had brought into this world. Loved him for dealing bravely with a world where others were crumbling. How she had manifested feelings for another man she did not know. But there was only Wilhelm now. There had only ever been her husband, Wilhelm. She turned toward him and wrapped her arms tight around his middle, hoping not to wake him. *I'm sorry, Wilhelm,* she cried in her head, and wiped tears against his back. *I'll make it up to you. Somehow.* She buried her head between the shoulders. *I love you.*

Eveline did not know she had slept late until the sun stabbed directly in her eye from the top of the bedroom window. Wilhelm was gone from bed and she was relieved. *It means he's milking,* she thought. *It means he's working, he's walking.* He needed to work. He needed to pull himself out of the rut from where he hid. He had been drowning long before the barn burned down, had been taking steps in the murky water since the railway accident. She should have done more to help him before the water rushed to his waist. The thought poked until she shut it down, slapped at it. She would make it up to him now, make it up to them all.

She made breakfast and waited for Will and Edgar. They all had slept in save for Wilhelm. They were all bone and mind weary. Andrew ate in silence, shoveling in his eggs and bread and bacon without thought. Will and Edgar had little appetite and she didn't scold them. She didn't feel like eating, either.

After breakfast was cleared and the morning chores finished, Eveline grabbed her basket and headed to the garden. If winter came in anything like it did last year, they'd need every bean and cucumber and berry saved and jarred in the cellar.

Eveline passed the ancient apple tree, picked up a few broken sticks below it and flung them toward the fence. A step stool lay on its side at the base of the tree. "So help me, those boys don't remember to put anything away," she mumbled. She propped it back up and searched the ground for any other missing tools.

A chill drafted across her skin, raised the hairs along her arms and back of the neck. The creaking of a burdened tree limb ached from above. A shadow passed over her, passed behind her, passed over again. *No.* It was not a thought. The shadow took shape. *No!* Her hand gripped her heart and her scalp pricked, burned from all sides. Her body shook. She looked up. The boots pointed down. The body swayed from between the tree limbs. Wilhelm's figure rocked listlessly with the breeze.

Her body quivered uncontrollably. Her mouth stretched open, wide as a last breath. And Eveline's scream cut through the valley and shook the land to its very soul.

CHAPTER 46

Pieter and Fritz Mueller dug the grave next to the giant apple tree, a horizontal line above the vertical ones of the twins. Once again the Protestant cemetery closed to the Kisers. Suicide, a soul damned among the unbaptized little ones, those in limbo. But if there was one act of grace from a cruel heaven, Wilhelm would forever be united with his youngest sons.

Andrew reached the summit of the field, the corn to his waist, lost in a sea of green. He stood alone with the golden sun heating his dark hair. He stayed there for he knew not how long. He stood with only his body and that corn that he had plowed and planted with Wilhelm Kiser, a man who would never witness its harvest. And he stood without words, without comprehension, and stared upon this great ocean that waved around his body with dead hands.

The mount was the highest point of the property, a gradual incline and complete in its visual isolation. No road. No house or neighbor. No farm animal or vehicle. Only that sun and the green pinnacles and the graphed dirt directed and mapped to lines. He searched with unmoving eyes, waited with unbeating heart, for what he did not know. He knew nothing. Understood nothing. All a void. A life of slumber between the stiff stalks.

And then she was there. Across from him. Across from time. Lily.

The corn parted around her. The memory of her not being at the spring, waiting for him, was gone. The gossip of her with Dan, gone. With her apparition, all that came before wiped clean.

She was here now. All of her. The green eyes round with grief. He watched her approach, emerge fully from the green sea. Her hair flowed over her shoulders and the sun toyed with her dress, made the dull yellow shine to luminescence.

She was here now and he could have fallen into the pools of her wet eyes, into the warmth and sincerity. But everything hurt. Hurt to move, hurt to breathe. But she moved and she came near him, came closer until she was in the invisible field skimming the bodily form, that invisible skin that pulsed and had sensitivities like nerve endings.

Their eyes locked and he was too tired to pull away, leaned upon the open gaze as a dying man leans upon his bedpost. And then she was holding him. Not with her eyes, but with her arms, wrapped so tightly around his abdomen that her hands nearly clasped the opposite elbows. She leaned her warm head against his chest and he could feel the wetness of her tears through his shirt, but she didn't cry out or make a sound, just held him there in that steel embrace. He lowered his head and kissed the top of her silky hair, soft as milkweed threads, let the texture tickle his lips. It felt so good to feel something other than pain and she lifted her head, found his lips with her own, let her tears wet his cheeks and grieve for that which he couldn't feel yet.

"You can do this," she whispered. She gripped his back and kissed under his ear, said with a full and deep heart, "You can save this family."

And the weight of her words unleashed the fear, gave context to the ax that seemed to hang above his crown ever since Wilhelm died. He was in charge now. There was no more Wilhelm at the helm, and if this farm was to live it was up to him. He pressed his forehead against hers, gritted his teeth. It was too much. Too much.

"No," she said as if she had heard him. "It's you. It's always been you." The tears alighted anew. "You've given this family hope from the beginning. It's always been you. You knew what made the twins sick and saved the rest of the family. It's you who brings smiles to Will and Edgar when their life is falling apart around their feet. It's you who Eveline leans on when she's about to break. It's you who cares for the animals and plants the fields." She squeezed his sides. "Don't you see? It's always been you."

He heard the words, saw the mouth that they came from, and a passion sizzled inside that was urgent and without warning. He kissed her fervently, slid his hand in the thick hair and kissed her neck, kissed the tears from her eyes.

"I love you." She breathed the words between panting kisses. "Please know that I do." He unclasped her dress. She found his shirt buttons, nearly ripped them out from their threaded knots.

He stepped forward, leaned her against an invisible wall, moved his arm under her and lifted her to him. She wrapped her legs around his hips, wanting him, opening for him. They were bound by the depth of emerald stalks and by creasing fabrics and Andrew swiveled again, lowered her onto the soft ground between the bending corn.

Lily fell into the rhythm of his hips between her, to his soft kisses and the sureness of his touches. She pulled at his belt, plucked the last two buttons of his shirt, the heat rising quickly throughout her body as his shirt opened, showing the line of dark hair from his navel and the muscles at the stomach. She pushed him upward and straddled his thighs, his hand at the small of her back as he kissed her neck.

A man's face flashed in her mind, but she stomped it away, held tight to Andrew's lips, kissed them harder to keep the face away. She wanted to lose herself in his body, make the other memories go away, purge the old with their love-making. Replace one with the other. She pushed the shirt off his right shoulder. He tightened. His movements stopped and he looked at her, his eyes wide and waiting, scared. Slowly now, she slid the shirt off his left shoulder, saw the ragged scars that lined the tissue. Andrew closed his eyes and turned away.

The scars broke her heart, the pain he had suffered. She looked at his beautiful face and her throat closed. He was so perfect—so very perfect.

The other face came back and shot through her mind, cut at her with razors. She twitched her head to get the image out of her brain, but it was there, stuck and glued and bringing the sickness and degradation to her like the fire that had burned the barn.

A tear formed in her eye and dripped unmolested down her cheek. Andrew was so perfect, had suffered so much. And here she was, tainted and impure, made of filth. She shuddered with the memory that was beating its way to her present, to her now. She bit her lip, forced blood as she punched the past away.

She looked at the scars upon Andrew's shoulder and she covered her mouth, wished it were her arm that was gone, that both of her arms were gone, just to remove what she had to see in her mind every day, to know what she had done.

Andrew looked at her, watched the pain in her face as she cried. He glanced at his arm and the shame came quick and hot. She couldn't bear to look at it.

She watched his eyes turn cold against her. He saw through her. He was starting to really *see* her. Whatever veil he had seen her through was now gone. He could see what she had done, could see that she wasn't good enough. "I'm sorry," she wept.

He pursed his lips. *Don't pity me.* He thought Lily had come to know him, had seen beyond his scars. But she couldn't and he knew this now. She would never be able to see him as a whole man, not after seeing it with her own eyes. She would never be able to look upon him without pity, without disgust and horror.

Lily pulled back, turned from him. He was so perfect. She was all that was opposite. He had been hurt enough. She would only bring him pain and humiliation. He would grow to hate her and what she was, what she had done. She possessed only one gift she could give him—freedom.

Andrew watched her turn away. She couldn't even look at him anymore. He nodded. Felt such a fool, the hatred of his form making him angry. Bitterness settled deeply. Bitterness that she couldn't see past his deformity, bitterness that she couldn't see to his heart and his love for her that made a mere limb pale in importance.

He wiped away the memory of her kiss, of her touch. Crushed his wanting of her, buried it in the grave next to his father, the twins and Wilhelm. He pulled on his shirt roughly and jerked away, stormed through the waving corn.

CHAPTER 47

A month passed before Lily was ready, her preparations finalized. "Claire," Lily hushed, jostling the woman's shoulders. "Wake up."

Lily knelt by the bed, peeked next to Claire to make sure Frank still slept. The Veronal she had laced in his whiskey would keep him knocked out to noon the next day, but she didn't want to take any chances. This would only work once.

"Claire, wake up." She shook her sister again and she finally stirred, sat up on one elbow.

"What's wrong, Lily?" The voice was loud and magnified in the still room.

"Shhhhh!" Lily's heart pounded in her chest, loud as Frank's snoring. She took her sister's hand. "Come downstairs with me."

"Why?" She yawned and laid her head back on the pillow. "I'm tired."

"No, Claire," she hurried her, grabbing the shoulder again. "I need to talk to you."

Claire wiped her eyes. "About what?"

Lily pressed her palm to her forehead. "Listen,

446

Claire. We need to go on a little trip. Just you and me. Okay?"

"A trip?" She was awake now, but the confusion stuck.

"Yes. A little trip." Her pitch rose, broke the whisper with the tinge of panic. "It's important, Claire. I need you to do this for me."

Claire turned to her husband, turned back to Lily. "He won't want me to go, Lily. You know he doesn't like me leaving the house."

"It's okay." She tried to smile through the urgency, the anxiety poking like pins. "I left him a note." She hoped her sister didn't remember that Lily couldn't read or write.

With Claire's indecision, the clock mocked her, each second of delay twisting the hands to daylight. Frank stirred and tossed onto his back. Lily froze.

Claire followed Lily's gaze, her eyes resting on her husband. "We'll talk more downstairs," she assented. "Let me just get dressed."

Claire reached for the squeaky closet door and Lily grabbed her. "I have all your clothes downstairs. Have coffee already made." Her voice cracked with pleading.

In the kitchen, Lily went from cupboard to cupboard. Opened and closed—*click, click, click.* She shoved bread and cans in a burlap bag, her fingers frantic, the items wobbling in her shaking hands. By the door, two traveling bags limp

447

with the few clothes inside, the money divided and stuffed in the corners. She was sick to her stomach, the nausea threatening to make her retch. Adrenaline made her sweat even in the cool air.

Claire's firm, pale hand grabbed her forearm, stopped her wild movements. "What's going on, Lily?"

Lily covered her face, bent into tears. "We need to go," she croaked. "Please, Claire. Please don't ask me why. Just—" She pleaded with every cell. "Just please come with me."

Fear entered Claire as it always did, swift and with images that left her hollow. "No." She retreated, stilted in her withdraw. "No. I-I-I can't leave and you know it. He'll tell. He'll tell what I did." The terror seized Claire in a choke hold and she curled into the corner. "I-I-I can't leave! I can't—"

The clock ticked louder, beat in Lily's chest. Her stomach twisted—around and around—squeezed. She crossed her arms over her chest and swung her head low, swollen tears dropping to the floorboards. She fell to her knees in front of Claire. *Please hold me,* she wanted to weep. *For once, help me.*

Lily's mouth stretched in a silent wail. She clutched Claire's cold hands. "I need your help." The request was a rush of air with only a hint of sound attached.

Claire blinked. The stuttering mouth and limbs stopped. Lucidity entered sedately. "Did Frank hurt you?"

Her bones crumpled, her voice mute. She nodded, embraced her waist with wrapped arms, curled into the agony that ate with gnashing teeth.

"He let a man hurt me." Her throat strangled, but she forced the words. "Let a man hurt me like Papa hurt you."

Claire's eyes died. The face rigid and ghostly white, lost.

"Please come with me." Lily looked into the face of the woman who had raised her, birthed her. The curse of what she was, of her constant reminder to Claire of what had happened to her, haunted. "Please, Mama. Help me." *Mama.* She had never said the word before, the title longing and horrific for them both.

Tears dripped in solid lines down the woman's cheeks. "He'll tell them, Lily." The fight, the panic, evaporated, resignation in its place. "He'll tell them I killed Papa."

Lily drifted into the haze of that day, the picture now crisp. He had come for her. The belt lashed red fire across her shoulder, then the backs of her legs as she ran in circles around the house to escape. He was faster, snapping the leather at her heels. Claire chased him and screamed for him to stop, tugged at the belt until her hands bled. Lily had stopped then, dead in her tracks.

449

Tired of running. Weak from terror. Ill with Claire's wounds. She closed her eyes, waited for all to end. A gun fired. A high-pitched shriek. A splash. Her eyes opened. Her father gurgled in the reddening puddle. Claire dropped the gun, her body quaking. Lily held her—two shaking figures in the stillness.

Lily reached for her sister, for her mother, as she did that day, but she no longer shook. "No." A final word that left no room for debate. "He won't tell. And even if he did, we'll be too far away." She placed a gentle hand on Claire's skirt. "We can start over. You and me. In a place where nobody can hurt us. Never again."

CHAPTER 48

The pounding at the front door rattled the house. Eveline wiped the steam from her eyes and put the lid back on the soup before heading to the porch. The knock picked up, and by the time she saw who was at the door Frank had turned the handle and entered.

"Where are they?" he hollered.

Eveline stepped back, his figure looming in the open doorway.

"Where the hell are they?" He stormed past her, into the kitchen, through the dining room and back around again through the parlor. Eveline stationed herself inertly, too shocked to move, to be angry at the forced entry.

He circled again, a caged animal, went to the bottom of the steps. "Claire!" he yelled. "Lily! I know you're up there!" He ran up the stairs two at a time, yelling their names to the empty rooms.

He barreled downstairs and grabbed Eveline's arm. "Where are they?"

She looked at the large hand on her sleeve. There was a time his touch would have given her a rush, made her flush to her hairline. She met his unhitched gaze stonily. There had been a time she had found the face handsome. Strong and handsome. But now? Grotesque, the features transformed into monstrous flesh, devilish and distorted. She jerked her arm away and spit, "They aren't here."

"They're with Andrew, aren't they?" He headed to the door, shoulders first, his fists balled.

This time she grabbed him by the back of the shirt with as much force as to rip the seams. "They aren't here, I said!"

He grabbed at his face, the anger turning it bright red, but somewhere he heard the truth of her words and his fists unclenched. "Then where the hell are they?" Frank suddenly fell silent—an eerie space filled with comprehension. "She drugged me." He turned to Eveline slowly. "That little whore drugged me."

Eveline recoiled at the foul speech. "I'll not have you using that language in my house."

He laughed heartily. "It's what she is, Eveline! You didn't know that?" His face turned smug, cruel. "Your sweet Lily ain't nothing but a two-bit whore."

She slapped him hard across the face, so hard she could feel the saliva from his teeth through the sting along her palm. He recovered quickly and came at her. She ducked to miss the blow, but he had her in his arms and kissed her viciously against the mouth, grabbed at her breast until she pushed out of his grip. His hands clutched her blouse. She spit out the taste of him, then wiped her mouth against her sleeve.

"Don't act like you don't like it, Eveline," he said arrogantly. "You've been wanting me to kiss you from the first moment you met me."

The words sickened—a nightmare thrown back into her face. The old Frank could no longer be seen. There was no kindness in his eyes and she felt like such a fool, ill with guilt at what she had imagined in her loneliness. This man before her was a beast and she missed Wilhelm so much that her heart burned.

"Take no shame in it, Eve." He smiled scornfully. "I wanted you, too. Still want you. Especially seeing your fiery side. Claire never liked it rough. I tried, but she got all weepy." He winked confidentially. "But you . . ." He came closer and she backed against the wall with a thud. He wiped a hair away from her face and rubbed her cheek. "You're a spitfire, aren't you?" She turned away and he pressed closer. "I know how to handle a woman like you. Kind of woman wasted on a man like Wilhelm."

With that, she tried to punch his face, scratch off the gritty words, but he held her hands above her like a child's. But then he let go and retreated slowly, his hands still up in the air in mock surrender. "That loan still stands, Eve. Growing bigger every day. You got another way to pay up, you know. Take care of it once and for all. For this farm. For those boys of yours and that cripple. Remember that."

He left and the screen door slammed over and over again in his wake. Eveline fell to her knees and wept, missed Wilhelm with a hurt as raw as a body without flesh.

CHAPTER 49

A ndrew finished tucking in the boys and came down to the kitchen. Eveline had a cup of tea waiting for him, her own mug warm in her palm as she sat at the worn oak table. Without earlier words indicating a meeting, they both knew they would talk this evening.

Andrew took the hot, brown liquid to his lips, didn't bother to add cream or sugar. It didn't matter that it would keep him up. He wouldn't sleep. Neither of them would sleep. Maybe never again.

Eveline settled her eyes on her handsome nephew, the smooth features of the nose and forehead. Those blue eyes whose color and light she had never seen matched in another human save her sister. "You haven't said anything about Lily and Claire being gone," she finally began. Word had traveled through the town of Plum and beyond about the missing women. And theories, if there were any, were kept close to the vest. No one wanted to cross Frank Morton in his thrashing state.

Andrew watched the smooth surface of the

tea, fell into its depths. "There's nothing to say."

"Well." Eveline tapped her index finger on the rim of the mug. "Thought you might be worried. Mrs. Sullivan nearly having a fit."

He grinned morosely, a simple expression full of irony and without humor. After all, Andrew knew why Lily had left. She couldn't face him, couldn't look at him. He thought about the last time they were together, the way she couldn't flee fast enough. "Maybe she wanted a better life." He sipped his drink with the same irony, savored it as if it were sweet instead of bitter. "Maybe she found a man who made her happy."

"She found that here."

"No, she didn't." He stiffened his jaw. "It's better she's gone."

Eveline's mouth fell open. "You don't believe that, Andrew."

He glared at her without comment and she reached for his hand. "I don't know why she's done the things that she has, but I saw the way she looked at you. A person could live to a hundred and never see a look like that."

"Don't say that," he said sharply, and slid his hand from her touch. The weight of the words and the untruth of them grated his sensibilities like nails upon chalk. "I'm sorry. I don't mean to be cross, Aunt Eveline. I just don't want to talk about her. Don't want to hear her name again."

She nodded and let it go. "Are you hungry? I have some corn bread."

"No." Now it was his turn to talk. He shut Lily out of his mind, shoved her far away. "We're going to lose the farm."

"I know." Eveline thought about Frank's kiss, could still taste the saltiness of the mouth. She wiped her lips across her palm, drowned out the taste with tea.

"Thanks to Mrs. Sullivan's connections in Westmoreland County, we can sell there, make enough to feed the family, pay for the necessities. Nothing more, but it would be enough." His voice sounded like a man's voice and the sturdiness of it, the sureness, belied the crippling fear of not saving this family.

"But not enough to pay down Frank's loan."

"No."

"Just wish the boys were old enough to help more. If they were men, we'd have enough help, enough hands." Eveline chewed at her lip, the anxiety ripping.

"If they were men, they'd be sent off to war."

Eveline had never considered that. She thought of her little ones sleeping upstairs, their innocent little faces, their soft kisses and hugs. In the despair, she found the gratitude, as selfish as it was. As poor as they were, at least she wasn't losing her boys to the trenches.

The silence deepened. Eveline's pulse thumped

routinely, timed and rhythmic, like a train approaching from the east. Coming closer. Coming closer.

Andrew cleared his throat. "I've decided to go back to the coal mines."

The train slammed. "What?"

"Once the harvest is done, I'm heading back to Fayette County. I'll send back what money I make. Every penny I'll send back. It should be enough to pay off the principal every month. Maybe more."

She glanced at his arm and he noticed. "I know. But with the war, the coal mines can't get enough workers. They won't care about my arm. As long as I can pick and shovel coal, that's all they care about."

The stupor wore off and the anger rose. "It's out of the question," she said coldly.

"I thought it all over. Ran it through my head a million times and it's the only way, Aunt Eveline."

The woman met his eyes firmly, the blue irises stormy. "The answer is no."

He returned the look defiantly. "It wasn't a question."

"I said no!" She stood then, smacked her hands on the table. "You might be the oldest male in this family, but I am still the head of this household! As long as you live under this roof, you will listen to me, young man! You will not ever mention anything as ludicrous as that again."

The walls disintegrated, caved upon her shoulders. Heat burned her ears and she wanted to cry, cry in anger and desperation, cry with what her actions and inaction had forced a young man to do—volunteer his life to save *her* family. "As long as I'm living and breathing, you won't step into a coal shaft again. Do you understand?"

He opened his mouth to speak and she slammed her palms on the table. "I lost my babies, Andrew! I lost my"—her mouth trembled—"and I lost my husband. I won't lose you, too."

Andrew stood now, matched her stance. "You're not going to lose me." He pulled back his shoulders and set his jaw. "I love you, Aunt Eveline, but I'm not your son. I'm a grown man and I've made my decision. There's nothing you can do to stop me."

Her hand flew to her mouth and she started to cry. She bowed her head as her body rocked over the table. Andrew placed his arm around her. "Please, don't cry. I'm sorry I upset you," he comforted. "But it's the only way, you see? Not just for you, but for Will and Edgar, too. It's the only way."

She looked into his eyes, soft with love and duty in the blue depths. "Give me a week,

Andrew." Her chest opened, the decision made. "I'm going to make this right."

He shook his head and began to debate her, but she stopped him. "I'll make this right, Andrew. I swear it."

CHAPTER 50

A ndrew and the boys pulled the carrots from the sandy soil, the cluster of orange roots hanging like entrails, before tossing them into the wheelbarrow. And he and the boys looked to the lines of green tops still left to be harvested and looked behind at the few rows that had been completed, the contrast leaving the stooped backs aching with the promise of a full day of work.

Will and Edgar still carried the aged lines of shock and despair in their childish faces after losing their father. They spoke little and ate even less, the playfulness of youth strangled from their being. They worked hard, their small hands busy and their minds simple, unable to piece together the onslaught of emotions. But they looked to Andrew with the only hope that remained. In him, they saw the burdens that they did not need to carry. Saw the man who kept their mother from falling to pieces and the farm erect.

And Andrew knew this when the boys met him with their wide, broken hearts and it flattened him. For he would be leaving soon for the coal mines. It was the only way. He promised to give

Eveline time to make it right, but there was no right to be made. And so he waited. A week or perhaps two before he would make arrangements.

In the meantime, Andrew brought what little light he could to the boys. He hid his own pain and told the boys stories while they worked, old folktales his father had told him. Yes, they worked too hard in their grief. Seemed children always had to work so hard. But in these days of living not far from starving, all bodies were required.

"Need an extra set of hands?" Pieter rose from the hill, the sun bright behind his head, making his face invisible for a moment.

"An extra back would be more helpful." Andrew stretched and leaned his spine, cracking it from the base.

Pieter walked ahead and pulled out two fistfuls of carrots and tossed them into the wheelbarrow. "Comes out like butter," he scoffed. "You Dutch are too soft. Aren't they, boys? We Germans are hardy!"

The boys smiled and laughed dully. But it was laughter all the same, and with the spurt of levity they increased pulling with renewed vigor.

With the boys distracted, Pieter turned to Andrew, his face suddenly tense. "I need to talk to you."

The look on his friend's face brought new worries. "Pieter and I are going to work higher up the line. We'll meet in the middle," he told the boys. "We'll make it a race."

The young men headed straight along the green feathery heads until out of earshot. Pieter stopped. "I saw Lily."

The last word Andrew expected to fall from Pieter's mouth and there it was. *Lily.* Her name hanging in the fields, pumping oxygen to his heart. He set his jaw. Pushed the name away. "That's no concern of mine."

"She's pregnant."

The punch came straight and hard to his stomach, shot fire and numbness at once through his veins.

Pieter kicked at a round stone, looked to the right of Andrew into the woods beyond the fields. "Thought you should know. The baby being yours and all."

The punch landed again and he thought his lungs might collapse. "It's not mine." His voice was hard and low. Dark. His Lily had shared her body with another. She had kissed and touched another man, given herself away. He thought of Dan Simpson, the man with brutish features, enjoying her and she him. Andrew never felt so sick—the second amputation of his life.

"I figured—" Pieter blinked swiftly. "Thought you two had—"

"We were never together," he interrupted. "Not in that way." He thought back over the months to that day in the fields, the last time he saw her, the way she turned from him in disgust. Her lies fanned, waved deception over every memory. And it was this dishonesty that crippled him more than any accident.

"I'm sorry." Pieter blew air from his mouth; his head dropped. "Well, at least you know. Told you there wasn't something right over there."

Andrew lifted his boot and crushed a clump of carrots into the ground. His stomach was lead—sour and heavy. "Where did you see her?"

"In Pittsburgh." Everything about his friend suddenly changed, his gaze contracting as if in fear. "Polish Hill. Working in a restaurant."

"Was Claire with her?" He wanted to cement the betrayal into his history, to ensure any doubting of Lily's true nature would be forever quashed.

Pieter shook his head and his chin twisted to the side. He wasn't thinking about Lily or Claire any longer. Something had taken hold of his thoughts. Andrew's flesh rose.

"Why were you in Pittsburgh?" he asked. But Andrew already knew. "You enlisted."

Pieter nodded. "Head out for training next week."

A breeze played with Pieter's blond, shaggy hair. "Pa won't speak to me."

"I'll help your family, Pieter." Andrew thought about the coal mines, knew the burden of two families instead of one. A curse seemed to have settled on the houses and families along the main road, sinking each into a chasm one after the other. He wasn't going to tell Pieter he was going away until he absolutely had to. "I'll work with Fritz, hire out for extra hands if needed."

Pieter flared out his arms in desperation, the anger sudden. "Come on, Andrew! You can't manage your own farm, let alone ours! It's too much for any of us. We're all drowning. Like the whole world is drowning!" he shouted.

Andrew stopped him. "The war can't last forever, Pieter."

"Yes, it can." Pieter met his gaze straight. "It can last forever. Can last until it plucks us off one by one." The acrimony was hard to witness, the gaiety of his friend erased as if it had never existed.

Eveline shut her mind off, wrung it dry like a rag as she walked up the road and turned into the Mortons' lane. Her hands itched, the pounding of her heart so rough that it hurt.

I can't do this. She started to turn back, then thought about little Will and Edgar, thought about what they would do if they lost the farm. There was no hope. They'd be homeless. She had no choice. Something pinched her organs and she put her hand to her chest, thought she was having a heart attack. She was breaking, could feel it in every nerve, and she leaned her head against the peeling doorframe of the Morton house, opened her mouth into a silent howl. She thought about Wilhelm, missed him so much that it made everything snap, and yet she was so angry he had left her. So angry she wanted to break everything on the outside. She melted into the anger and gripped the old wood so hard that splinters entered her fingertips. She pushed the missing and the longing away, concentrated on the points of wood against her skin, anything to keep her standing.

Eveline didn't knock. She opened the door. She walked over the wide-planked floor as if she knew the grains, knew where her path led, and she did—straight to Hell. She heard footsteps on the floor above and found the carpeted steps, worn and threadbare as she walked one step up at a time. A light glowed at the end of the hallway. She stood in the doorway of the small room. A large desk centered the space; a green banker's lantern edged it. Frank sat, read a ledger, his fingers rubbing his forehead in thought. The Stetson hat hung on the chair and the imprint of the band still etched the man's forehead.

She waited until he felt her presence. Frank looked up, startled, before a half grin curled his mouth. "This is a surprise," he said languidly.

She walked into the room. Her heart was quiet now, silent, seemingly nonexistent. She closed the door, put the deed on his desk. "I'm ready to pay in full."

He leaned back and crossed his arms. "Is that so?" Slowly, his eyes drifted down her body, and she felt them across her skin like hands. And she let the eyes drift, stood steady with attention no different from that of a soldier under inspection. And she was a soldier at that moment and she needed to be brave in her war, even if it meant losing her soul.

"How do you know my offer still stands?" he asked, holding cold eyes to her blue ones. "Maybe I'm not interested anymore."

"Then I'll go."

He nodded. Tilted his head to look at her from a new angle. He stood then and came around, sat on the edge of the desk. They were only inches apart, their gazes level. "My terms have changed."

"How so?"

"I get to do whatever I want to you."

She thought about Andrew and the coal mines, swallowed, but kept her head up. "All right."

He leaned back against the desk, spread his legs slightly. "And you have to do whatever I tell you to do."

The silver letter opener gleamed near his hand. She wanted to thrust it into his heart. "All right."

"And"—he reached a hand up and grabbed her hip, squeezed roughly—"you have to like it. Have to show me how much you like it."

Bile rose to her throat. Her nostrils flared. She nodded fiercely.

He grabbed her by the waist then, pressed his lips hard against hers, his tongue hot and large in her mouth. Eveline pulled back. "Not until you mark the deed."

He laughed, breathed fast, his pants tented. He turned and grabbed a pen, scribbled on the paper. She took the moment and wiped her mouth, wished she could expel the remnants of him on his shoes.

With a final signature done with impatient flurry, he turned back and found her mouth again. "Remember, you have to show me you like it."

Eveline let her stiff lips yield against his. She pinched her eyes closed, fell into the rhythm of his kissing and panting, matched his seamlessly, concentrated on this matching so that it was not a kiss but a mechanical act that took no feeling.

She hated him and yet she was giving her body. She used the fire of hate to tear at his shirt in mock passion, ripping the buttons from their holes. She found his mouth and bit his lip hard. He pulled back for only a moment before coming at her swiftly, pulling at the buttons that reached from her chin to below her waist. She tore at his undershirt until it was above his head and then on the floor and she kissed his chest, bit the skin

468

roughly. She clawed at his back, knew she drew blood and kissed him harder for it.

He twitched between the spasms of pain and pleasure and growled into her neck. "Knew you were a fiery one."

Frank stood then and lifted her, swiveled their bodies and placed Eveline on the desk where he had been. He pushed down the dress to her undergarments, found her breasts hidden behind the fabric, tore until the strap ripped and pushed it off her shoulder.

The hardness of him told her he'd be quick and she hurried. Eveline grabbed the pearl buckle, the one that had intrigued her in another life, and pulled hard until the leather came undone and lay slack on either side of his waist. She unbuttoned the fly, shoved her hand into his underwear and grabbed with a tight grip.

He moaned heavily into her ear, fumbled with the remaining clothing until it lay in a puddle on the floor. He opened her legs with his knees. She stroked him, used her nails against the sensitive tip, watched his face contort with her fingers and pressure. She pushed his jeans off his hips and leaned back against the desk, opened her legs widely and pulled him toward her. He entered her swiftly, banged against her thighs and pelvis, their movement making echoes of *thump, thump, thump* in the tiny room. He finished in less than a minute, taking her deep and growling into her neck with the release. She was not a victim, she told herself. He was. And she took him fully and watched distantly the weak man get his little pleasure.

She lay there, Frank still lodged between her thighs as his chest quieted in her neck. The letter opener sat next to her fingers and she glanced at it from the corner of her eye, thought how easy it would be to slip the tool into her palm and thrust it into his back.

She twisted her neck away from the man's panting. "I'll get my things," she started, but he stopped her with a shake of his head.

"We're not done yet."

She met his eyes with as much blackness as she could and in response he just chuckled, his laugh slow and long with pleasure. Her stomach dropped and she closed her eyes, realized she had been a fool to think he would let her off easy.

"You a religious woman, Eveline?"

She didn't answer. Simply hated him. Turned all her hate into one glaring pinpoint of disgust.

He donned a look of priestly devotion. "There's a story about Adam and Eve that you won't find in the Bible. It's an old story from the Jews." He reached over and rubbed her breast, squeezed the nipple between his fingers. "The story says that Adam's first wife was a woman named Lilith. But Lilith was an evil woman, you see. Impure. She was not a good wife to Adam. She would not

470

obey him. She refused to be subservient. And so she abandoned him, left the Garden of Eden and hid within a cave to do her evil deeds."

Frank ran a finger down the line between Eveline's breasts and continued, "As you can imagine, Adam was very distraught and angry at his first wife. But God took mercy on him and created Eve."

"I don't need a Sunday school lesson, Mr. Morton," Eveline hissed.

He laughed at this. "Don't you find it interesting at least? Here is my sister-in-law named Lilith who refuses to obey me and runs off with my wife. Then you, dear Eve, come to me, offering your body. Doesn't that strike you as fate?"

"My name is Eveline Kiser. Not Eve."

He ignored her proclamation. "And you being tempted by my charms all along," he went on. "Eve couldn't wait to taste that apple." He touched the red bite marks that lined his chest. "Eve couldn't wait to bite that apple, eh?"

"Never believed much in the story," she growled to the devil himself. "Always believed it wasn't Eve who bit the apple. . . ." She paused and thought of Wilhelm hanging in the apple tree. "It was the apple who bit Eve."

With that, she lunged for the deed, but Frank was quick and slid it from her reach. "I told you, we ain't done yet."

He touched her face almost lovingly, stroked her chin and her cheeks, reached up and petted her hair. And there his palm stopped and he pressed the top of her head, pushed her into a grave. She knew what he wanted, something she never did to her own husband.

"Kneel down, Eve."

When Eveline Kiser left that tiny office, it was dark outside, dark inside. She was numb. Cold or heat could not have had an effect, did not exist against her skin. She had done things in that room that she didn't know humans were capable of doing to each other. He had left her sore and wounded, depleted of anything human, made her feel more animal than woman.

She stumbled through the Morton kitchen and out to the lane and up to the street. The air came hard to her lungs and she was running, didn't even know she was running until the stars blurred and the moon followed at a rapid pace above and to her right. She stopped and screamed. Screamed at the moon like a wounded wolf and she screamed until she fell to her knees in the road and melted into the rough gravel, let the tiny rocks press into her skin and she couldn't feel them, couldn't feel anything.

She pulled herself up. Her thighs shook with the stress of opening and widening. But she was not a victim. This in her soul she knew. She had done what she had not as a victim but as a soldier. What she had done was not sex but spite, a defiant dare against a man who had tried to ruin her family. And she had won. She had used him with her body, his own weakness against her strength.

But victim or not, she had nothing left now. Her substance gone. She had given it all away in battle and now lay wounded and half-dead. She had won, but she was too bloodied to know victory.

Eveline stumbled forward, the sword in her gut, taking one step at a time. Forward. She saw the lights of her farm and she ran again. She ran with legs that wobbled toward those lights and the safety and the warmth of what was real. There, in her home, she would wash and scald the remnants of that man and those memories from her mind. She would hold her children and tell them that all would be all right. She would tell her nephew that he would not have to go back to a life underground. But part of her feared that she would not be able to say any of those words, that she might collapse into what she had done. By walking into her house, she might soil it forever.

Eveline turned into the Kiser lane. Her property. *Her* home. Andrew and the boys were in the yard holding a lantern, shining the light to see the woman coming toward them. She tried to fix her hair, tried to hide the selling of her soul to the devil.

Edgar, her little boy, ran up to meet her. She smiled ruefully at her innocent child who was going to hug her. And she wanted him to embrace her more than anything else in her life. She opened her arms out to receive him.

Instead, he barreled toward her in a fury of fists. "Where have you been?" he shouted, and feebly punched her skirt. Tears streamed down his face. "We had no dinner. You didn't tell anyone where you were!"

She froze and her jaw dropped at the boy's anger. He cried out, "You only think of yourself! You don't think about us anymore since Papa died!" He shook with anger. "You don't care about any of us!"

Her blinking quickened and everything dropped away. She pulled back and with a thrust of iron backhanded her son clean across the cheek, sending him flying into the dirt.

"How dare you!" she attacked him blindly. She hit him with fists against the ground. "How dare you!" she screamed.

"That's enough!" Andrew seized her arm, met her eyes hard so she heard him through her haze. "That's enough, I said!"

She pulled her arm away, saw her child on the ground bruised and crying, and the world blurred. She ran to the house, stumbled over roots and rocks. Dying. Running. Death. Running. She went behind the log pile and grabbed the ax, the weight making her drag it rather than carry it. She pulled the ax and her broken body to the apple tree, swung hard and like a maniac at the trunk.

"How could you!" Eveline wailed, slammed the ax into the trunk again, splaying only a chip of bark. "How could you leave me!" She swung the ax, screamed at every futile hack at the ancient bark. "How could you do this to me!"

This tree had fed them with its septic apples, lured them with its bounty, then held her husband as his neck broke. This tree mocked her, shaded living limbs over her dead babies and husband. She had loved this tree and it had poisoned her. She was Eve. She was tempted and now fallen. But she would not fall alone.

Eveline screamed and cursed and pummeled the tree with no thought or sight of anything else until her body fell into exhaustion and her arm could not lift the ax for another swing. She pulled at the wooden handle, had to take down the tree, had to erase what Wilhelm had done, what his death made her do. She was falling, but Andrew caught her, kicked the ax to the ground. He held her there under the moon and next to the barely maimed apple tree, and she sobbed into his shoulder, broke limply against his chest.

Andrew walked her into the house, brought her

475

up to her room and helped her into bed, saw the scratches and tears along her dress. He smelled Frank's cologne on her skin. A crumpled, signed deed dropped from her pocket. And the truth of what she had done sank in with each of her brutalized sobs. *I'll make this right,* she had said. The words replayed, left him broken. He covered her with the blanket and left her to her grief.

He put the boys to bed, hugged them until they finally wept for their father and for their mother. He hugged them as they shook with events and a war and a terror that they did not understand. He hugged them until they cried themselves to sleep.

The old farmhouse was quiet now. Andrew sat on the edge of Will's bed. He looked at his large hand sitting on his knee. He bent the fingers, then relaxed them again. He rose and stepped with purpose down the creaking steps, went outside.

With ax in hand, Andrew stared at the enormity of the ancient apple tree. The limbs, old, had witnessed too much suffering. And they seemed to ask to be relieved, to say good-bye. A wind blew and rustled the branches, the leaves waving in surrender.

Andrew touched the space in the bark that was engraved with the word "Lily." She had cut them both. The young man patted the deep and wise bark, rested his forehead for a moment against the jagged skin before lifting the ax and swinging it hard into the tree.

The *ding* and reverberation nearly knocked him backwards. Andrew pulled the ax from the nick and hit hard again, the shudder to his good shoulder rough and painful. He took the ax to the same severed spot. Again and again and again. His arm ached and his fingers blistered against the smooth handle and he didn't stop. Again. Again. Again.

The moon arched and moved on its journey and still Andrew hacked at the tree. His hand bled now and he only stopped to rub it clean on his trouser, the sting of stopping nearly worse than the sting of movement.

Andrew weakened and he called upon the fire. He called upon the fire that filled the breathing spaces and breathing bodies of the coal mine that took his father. He called upon the pain and fire of his shattered body, the fire that reminded his skin and bone and cells of what was once whole. He called upon the fire of Eveline's sacrifice.

Andrew called upon the fire at the core of the earth. The molten lava that rose with his cry through his feet and through his veins. Up, up, up it moved and filled his muscles and made them crackle against the heat. And he glowed. And he took the ax and swung with the flames and he hit and he hit and he hit. The pain rattled across his nerves—a shattering, brittle pain like metal pans clanging, their harsh throbbing vibrating each rib and vertebra.

He found the fire, he gritted his teeth with its burn and still he swung. He swung until the burn became him. Until he became the fire and then the pain left. The fire now glowed white and strong and hot, but it did not singe, for he was the fire now and a fire does not shrink away from its own power; it lets it rise and ignite.

Lily. Andrew thought about the woman he had loved. She had moved on. She had never loved him. He hit harder and quicker. He had felt ashamed, worthless. He hit harder. But no more. No more.

Andrew thrust the ax blade deeper into the fissure of the tree. A crack, a wounded sigh from deep within sounded, and he hit again. He watched his one arm as he swung. Watched the deep lines of its muscles and he grew even as it weakened. He grew strong with each thrust. He had nothing to hide. He was complete and whole. He grunted as he worked through the fire of his hand and arm and shoulder. He would not hide or feel less than. He could take down this tree with one hand. He could do it. And he hacked harder and fiercer than before until just before dawn the tree bowed its head, cracked from its ancient depths and crashed to the ground.

Dawn broke. With the smell of smoke, the boys found the fallen apple tree in sparks. Andrew worked around the burning branches, pushing sticks to contain the fire. The boys broke off stray limbs and flung them into the centered heat of the fire. Through the haze, Eveline joined them, a gray wool sweater wrapped tightly around her shoulders. She watched the flames and the curling of wizened limbs and seemed to take power as all fell away into ash. When only the skeleton simmered with glowing red veins among a black charred body, Andrew went up to Eveline. "I need to go to Pittsburgh."

She nodded. Her eyes were calm, grateful, nearly at peace. He ignored his raw hand and numb arm, his hunger, the fatigue of being up all night, and walked to the Muellers' to borrow their car. He would do it now while he had the strength. One tree was down; now he had to put to rest another standing in his way.

CHAPTER 51

Polish Hill hovered on a rise above the city, overlooking the burping, savage steel mills. The line of row houses and squat wood houses decayed in varying degrees of rot, no different from any of the other immigrant tenements inhabited by the steel and factory workers. The soot-stained buildings sagged under concave roofs, with windows of taped over broken glass and yellowed newspaper.

The restaurant owned the corner; a bleached poster for Heinz pickles hung upon the grime-covered brick. A handwritten sign in the window said simply: *Pierogis*. The building, perfectly square, a block with flat roof and the side closest to the chimney completely black. The smell of onions and potatoes and grease emanated from the homes, from the very sewers, but came strongest near the little eatery.

Now that he was here, Andrew couldn't go in, couldn't remember what he wanted to say. In the window, he did not see Lily among the customers. He tucked his hand in his front pocket and turned the corner to the back of the building, leaned against the back wall. His fingers found the ring in his pocket and he looked forward to throwing it in the river after this ordeal ended, another scrap of useless litter clogging the Pittsburgh waterways.

For a moment, he thought about leaving but resisted. He wouldn't leave without an explanation. He wouldn't leave until he put her behind him once and for all.

A line of steam rose from the bottom of the steel back door, carrying the smell of all that was being boiled inside. The sounds of the kitchen echoed against the walls, the sounds of large pots moving, the slurred voices in Polish and English, of shouted orders.

The steel door opened. A rush of warm air spilled out, magnifying the sounds within for a split second before the door clamped like a lid to a pot. Lily hoisted a garbage bag with two hands, her shoulders struggling with the weight. Andrew pushed his back against the wall, his insides cold and frantic.

Her hair was pulled back into one braid, the short strands hanging loose around her face. Her dress was spotted and smeared with grease. A blue sweater reached past her hips and the sleeves past her wrists, must have been given to her by a very large woman and made Lily look all the more tiny and fragile.

Lily opened the metal lid of the garbage can,

releasing a torrent of flies that she did not seem to notice; then she lifted the bag and dropped it into the can with a bang. The young woman wiped her forehead with her sleeve, her eyes closed.

She looked so tired. A part of him wanted to run to her and pick her up in his arm, feel her head against his shoulder. He wanted to rub her hair and kiss her softly and tell her to rest, rest against him, he had her now. But then Lily put her hands to her lower back and stretched, the slight bulge of her pregnancy visible beneath the sweater.

The sight bruised and left him weak. Pieter had been right. Her growing abdomen plain to see left him queasy. And Andrew then realized that he had come in hopes that Pieter had been wrong. In the hopes that there had been some terrible mistake and she was still his, would still be his. He had come with hope and now there was none. There was nothing to do but say good-bye.

"Lily."

The woman jumped and spun. Andrew emerged from the shadows. Her whole face dropped and her hands pulled the large sides of her sweater to her middle, clasped them closed with a tight embrace, her eyes wide as those of a hunted rabbit.

"What are you doing here?" The question barely had muscle to give it volume.

"I had to see for myself. To make sure."

She shook her head frantically. "But how? How did you . . ."

"Pieter." He stood straight without wavering. "He saw you working here."

Lily tightened her grip upon her sweater, her eyes drawn to her feet. "I'm sorry." A tear rounded and dripped off her downturned cheek.

Andrew nodded, his stomach cramped. "You could have told me, Lily."

The outstretched sleeve flew to her mouth and she bent into it, covered her sobs, her shoulders shaking quietly. Andrew watched her, watched the woman he loved, for the last few seconds before he would never see her again. There was nothing else she could say. The lead weight of acceptance numbed. There was no anger or regret or hope, just the numbness and a readiness to go, to leave this all behind.

He turned to go. "I would have done anything for you, Lily. I'm sorry you didn't think I was good enough for you."

"Good enough?" she sputtered.

He met her tear-streaked eyes only briefly. "I just hope this man, whoever he is, treats you well. I hope he loves you even half as much as I did."

"Love?" Her mouth opened and her face twisted in repulsion. "You think the man who did this to me loved me?"

But he couldn't hear anymore. The numbness

grew up his neck and closed his ears. "Good-bye, Lily."

She came up from behind and grabbed his arm, twisted the material of his shirt in her hand. "You think I wanted this? You think I left you because you weren't good enough?" Her crying melted into shouting, her eyes stretched and wild.

He was tired. "Let go," he ordered wearily.

"How could you think that?" She beat against his arm with a weak fist. "How could you think I don't love you! I'm the one not good enough. Don't you see?"

He closed his eyes, just wanted to leave. She let go, her body shaking. "Don't you know what I am?" She pounded on her chest. "Don't you see? Look at me!"

The detachment shattered under her disgust, under the pain writhing the body in front of him. Her anger fled, left her unable to stand, and she collapsed onto her knees on the broken concrete. Her head lowered to her hands and she cried from the very depths of her small body. She turned her face upward, the way a flower leans higher to the sun. "Don't you see? I'm the one not good enough for you. I never was."

Andrew knelt in front of her, oblivious to the dirty concrete. "Why are you saying these things?"

Beneath the quivering chin were signs of exas-peration. "You don't want anything to do with me, Andrew. I'm no good." She reached for his face, touched his cheek. "But now you see. Now you know who I am."

He pulled her cold hand into his and it was without life, lay limp in his warm palm. "You're not making any sense."

The fight was gone. The tears were drying in clear lines and leaving pink edges along her soft face. Her eyes were sleepy and listless as she stared through him. "I didn't want to do it. Be with that man. I swear to God, I didn't want to do it."

Andrew remembered the smug face of Dan Simpson. "Dan made you do this?"

"Dan?" She looked disoriented. "I haven't seen Dan since I hit him with that rock. This has nothing to do with Dan."

They stared at each other for a long while until Lily shook her head, long and low. "Don't you see?"

"No."

She started to cry again like he was hurting her, pinching her skin. "I gave my body to a man, Andrew." Lily's mouth stayed open with the sound. "I'm no more than a whore. It didn't matter that I tried not to, that I fought and I cried. I did it."

Suddenly, Lily's face froze and her eyes went blank. "I didn't want to do it." The words siphoned of life, the tones muted. "Frank made

485

me. Told me I had to do it. He was in a bad way. Got in a heap a debt from his gambling. Told me I had to clean it up. Said he'd make Claire do it if I didn't. Said he'd beat her raw, if I didn't do it."

Her voice quieted and she spoke to herself. "I couldn't let Claire get hurt. I couldn't. She protected me all her life."

Her hazel eyes turned to him, glistening green pools with emerald depths. She placed her hands gently on her belly. "And now, I got a little one." Her chin dimpled. "Got this little one to take care of. It isn't her fault, being made the way she was."

The young woman smiled now, a sad, rueful smile that cracked with sorrow. "I'm no good, Andrew. Never was. I'm sorry I hurt you. But you didn't do anything wrong. You're like an angel and I had no right bringing blackness to you and your family."

She looked at him, her face so soft and tender in open despair. "Now you see. You see why I wasn't good enough for you. That day we were going to be together I wanted nothing more in the whole world, but I kept seeing what I had done, how I had no right being with you after what I did with that man. How you deserved somebody smart and beautiful like those girls that always come to church with their white dresses and pretty shoes.

"At least you know now. You can go and move

486

on and not give me a second thought. You can marry one of those pretty girls and pretend I was just a bad dream from long ago. And . . . I hope you'll be happy," she said in a soft voice. She pulled herself up, cradled her growing baby and looked toward the steel door of the restaurant. "I'm sorry I brought you pain. I—I just want you to have the very best in life. It's what you deserve."

Lily turned. The smoke from the crusted chimney swirled and blended with the poisoned sky, a mingling of grays that suffocated the forgotten blue. She stepped away from Andrew toward the clanging, filthy building, her body pulling without a fight.

The fire burned again. Not the flames that rippled through his arm to cut down the tree but a power just as strong, a white fury of knowing that flashed through the chest and under the skin.

Lily reached for the door of the kitchen.

"Lily."

She squeezed her eyes closed and turned the handle.

The knowing thrust him forward and then he was beside her. The sky was clean again, the air fresh, and the decision beamed bright enough to wash away the grime of all that came before. Andrew grabbed her arm, cupped her limp hand in his large palm. "Marry me."

She bent her neck in defeat. "Please," she

begged plaintively. "Don't be cruel. I'm sorry and maybe you got every right to be cruel, but please don't tease me like that."

"Marry me, Lily." He pulled her against his chest and smiled into her hair, held on to the thin shoulders with all his might. "My God, Lily, don't you see I love you? None of this was your doing. None of this was your fault. You didn't have any more choice in this than that baby did."

"No." She pushed at him. "You're not thinking straight—" But her words were cut short by his lips. And he kissed her between smiles because he had been wrong, because it had never been him, and then he kissed her nose and her forehead gently, worked to erase the suffering she had endured. And the hope rushed, flooded in an eddy, and he kissed her until she giggled with disbelief.

He stopped abruptly and put his palm against her cheek, his forehead against hers. He fumbled with the ring in his pocket and slid it on her finger. "Marry me, Lily. Come back to the farm with me and we'll raise this baby together. Claire can come, too. You'll be safe. I swear I'll never let anything happen to you; I'll protect you all. I swear it."

"But what about what I did? What about—"

"None of it matters. None of it."

"We can't go back. If Frank finds out, there's no telling what he'll do. He'd have you thrown into jail or worse. Make up something awful just to make you pay."

"We'll figure it out. You'll be safe. You have my word." He kissed her again. "I love you, Lily. Say you'll marry me."

She covered her mouth with her hand, wrestled between crying and laughter, fumbled for words. "I—I don't know what to say?"

"Say yes."

A choked gasp sprinted from her throat and she wrapped her arms around his neck as if she were drowning. "Yes."

CHAPTER 52

The hour was late, well past Will and Edgar's bedtime, but no one could sleep—no one would sleep. The house was wired from each body, lightning rods that summoned and waited for the electrical charge.

Andrew presided at the head of the old wooden table, Wilhelm's old seat, without intimidation. He had earned this place. His legs were strong; his arm and chest held the muscles of hard work and perseverance. No weakness bent his posture as he looked around the table at the eyes that searched for guidance. He grounded this home now, his home. Reassurance and power remained steadfast in his jaws and the lines of his strong neck. This was his family and he would protect and care for them as a warrior between battle lines. *Take care of your family. Always.*

Lily sat to his right, Claire beside her. He reached for Lily's hand, felt it quiver under his touch, the fear constant.

"It's important that no one knows Lily and Claire are here," he started quietly, firmly. "There are things that need to be settled first. So,

490

we're depending on you all to keep this within the house."

"Is it 'cause of the war?" Edgar asked. " 'Cause of our name?"

"Shhhh . . ." Will hushed.

"It's all right, Will." He smiled at the two boys, would not give them reason to doubt their security. "No, it's not because of the war. I'll explain more, but for right now we have to keep Claire and Lily safe and that means nobody can know they're here."

Eveline gazed at her boys. "You understand what Andrew is saying?"

They nodded. Eveline rose and put a hand on each small shoulder. "Claire, let's get you settled in a room upstairs. Will and Edgar can bunk up tonight until we clear a room for you tomorrow."

When the four were out of earshot, Andrew turned to Lily, her face drawn and pale. "You all right?" he asked gently.

"I'm scared."

"I know."

She shook her head and her chin crumpled. He pulled her to him, traced her spine with his fingertips. "I'm not going to let anything happen to you," he promised.

"I know." She held on to his waist, gripped his leather belt. "But it's not right bringing this to your family. Making you hide us like fugitives. Making the boys lie."

491

He held her closer, smiled into the hair. "We're family now. All of us. We take care of each other. You'd do the same for us."

He slid a finger under her jaw and kissed the soft mouth, bright pink and open. He fell into her lips. He slid his hand down her body, rested it upon the small bump of her belly, let the warmth of her closeness heat his palm and send it back through the skin to the budding life inside.

Her kiss grew longer and she did not break it as she moved from her chair to his lap. Her hand found his neck, her fingers stroking the smooth, tan skin. She unbuttoned the top of his shirt.

The smell of her hair, of all things fresh and of sun, dizzied and made the room fade. He moved his touch to her breast, swollen and round beneath the dress. She sighed, placed her hand upon his and squeezed it gently, then harder, till his fingers cupped the breast fully. She rolled her head, kissed under his chin and up to his ear. "I want to share your bed," she whispered, her words breathless.

Andrew swiveled her hips so she straddled his thighs and pressed his pelvis against the opening of her skirt. He rose, kept his arm firmly under her body, her legs gripping tightly. Even pregnant, Lily was nearly as weightless as a barn cat, and he carried her up the steps blind as she feverishly kissed his lips and neck, fumbled with his buttons.

He brought her to his room, kicked the door closed with his foot. He laid her on the bed, cradling her golden hair as it spilled across the pillow. Andrew arched above her upper body to find her lips again. She unbuttoned his shirt, one urgent pull at a time. She stared at the open chest revealed between the edges of the shirt, the strength and expanse of the muscles. He watched her, watched the way the green eyes slid across his skin and then met his and locked. Tenderly, she touched her palm to his breastbone, let the pulse beat between her fingers and align to her heart's vibration and cadence.

Lily fell into Andrew's gaze, innocent in its restraint and hesitation. She moved her hand to his beautiful face, to the soul-numbing features, the perfection of him nearly stopping her heart.

She slowly moved his shirt from his right shoulder and he tensed. His face angled away. Assuredly, she removed his arm from the sleeve, rubbed her fingertips down the balled shoulder and biceps, the hairs along the tight forearm, raising the gooseflesh in a trail. With a feathered, calm touch, she moved her fingers back up his arm, across the base of his neck along the collarbone to the other shoulder. She held his eyes, their breathing matched with uncertainty. She nudged the material tentatively from the severed shoulder.

"Don't," he murmured. He closed his eyes and grimaced.

She moved the shirt, let it fall to his hips and rest on the quilt. His nostrils flared and he turned his head farther away, his forehead creasing and his eyes squeezed shut. The scars, white and bold against the tan skin, shirked from the air, seemed to breathe like lungs, haltingly. Lily traced the scars lightly with her fingertips, found the network of lines no different from the chiseled structure of his face and figure.

With the touch, Andrew's heart sped, the veins in his neck throbbing. Lily bent forward, placed her lips upon the scars, kissed each gently, loved them as if they were individual beings, loved them as she would an injured wing on a butterfly.

Andrew's body shuddered, softened from granite, and he watched her now, bided for any sign of discomfort or pity or revulsion. But she smiled up at him—smiled as a pond shines under the sun. And Andrew kissed her—kissed her gratefully and hard—kissed her as a sentenced man kisses freedom.

He pressed against her body until her head settled back upon the downy pillow. He unclipped the clasps of her dress, urgently but with care. Her body arched to open them faster and her thighs stretched wide to fit the strong hips pushing against her pelvis. He opened the dress and kissed the breasts, slid her slip off her shoulder and kissed her hard nipple.

The sensations in her breasts tingled, hardened them to points. She reached down and slid his pants over his hips and down his legs until he kicked them to the floor. He pulled at her slip again until it was off, her cotton drawers sliding off with the flood of flowing clothes. Without the impediment of clothing, the rush to remove it, time settled slowly. She stared at his figure, chiseled out of marble yet pliable and soft and warm. Alive.

He looked at her, all of her. The small body at once fragile and strong in lithe womanhood. And the face, the curve of lips, the pink cheeks that glowed with desire. The white shoulders and silky hair that draped like that of a goddess from an ancient time.

She touched his neck and advanced him closer. She reached for his hips, pressed her nails gently into the flesh and beckoned him between her legs. His breath was warm against her cheek and agitated with self-control. "What about the baby?" He halted, the concern arching his eyebrows. "I don't want to hurt it. Or you."

"You won't hurt it." She grinned into his cheek, kissed his chin and lips. "Or me. I promise."

His body still struggled, stiffened with debate. "Please," she begged as she raised her hips. "Make this baby yours, Andrew."

He entered her then. Slowly and carefully, a small moan leaving his mouth with the warmth and the wetness that surrounded him. He pressed farther, each thrust sending his nerves to fire. She writhed beneath him, a small noise coming from her throat.

He stopped. "Did I hurt you?" he gasped.

"No." She laughed and pulled his hips to her again, arched her back to take him deeper. "God, no!"

Every cell of his body throbbed and trembled. He tried to hold out, prolong a bit longer, but the wanting, the sensations, were too much and he came, smothered his mouth into the pillow next to her ear to keep from yelling. His heart thumped straight through the mattress, loud and defined in his ears. His back glistened with a light sweat. He kissed her face, beaming and smiling. Then remembered his lesson in Pittsburgh. "I want to make you feel good, Lily."

"You already did." She smiled serenely.

"No." He glided his fingers between her legs. "I want you to do what I just did."

She gently pulled the inching hand up from her thigh and kissed the palm, laughed sheepishly into it. "I meant, I already did." She touched her belly. "Things feel different down there since I got pregnant. I had mine as soon as you entered, when you thought you had hurt me."

"Oh." He ran a hand through his hair so the

strands stood up in wisps. "Well, you could have told me. I nearly bit my lip off trying to hold out."

She giggled into his chest and he laughed. He wrapped his arm around her, held her tight, the warmth held in one combined body.

"You're the only one, Andrew," she promised into his chest. "I need you to know that. There was no one before you. This is my first time." She glanced at him. "Do you know what I mean?"

And he did. He kissed her and he knew just what she meant. Nothing ever existed before this moment.

CHAPTER 53

A ndrew waited in the empty stalls of the Morton barn. The cow, chickens and horse had disappeared the day Lily and Claire left, evaporated into the unknown while Frank dreamed in a drug-induced reverie. The man would have let the animals starve, let the cow's udder swell with unattended milk until pained and ill with mastitis. There was no sign of the animals that Lily had made arrangements for. But if one had visited old man Stevens and his wife, Bernice, in their tiny shack deep in the woods one would find the couple smearing new butter on their warm bread and with more eggs in their basket than their few teeth could eat in a week.

Andrew leaned against the rotting wood of the ramshackle barn. Mounds of blackflies loitered in the straw- and dung-filled corners. The chicken coop had lost its fence long ago and the remnants of old corn and feed sprinkled the compact dirt along its edges. Indignation seized, left him wanting to hit the old barn wood with a tight fist. This had been his Lily's life and he wanted to hack the stench and blackness away as he had the apple tree, burn her past in a rubble of ash and sweep it into the wind.

After they had made love, Lily told him everything. Told him of life with her father, of what Claire had endured, told him with quivering abasement that Claire was more than just her sister. He had held her in silence as the torrents of her suffering cracked from her slight body, left her shaking and whimpering against his chest. She told him of the babies Claire lost, of the teas Frank would make her drink whenever she was pregnant. And she told him about what she had been forced to do. The first time at fourteen. The second time leaving her pregnant. There would never be a third time.

Andrew's insides curled and he grunted with rage in the humid barn. He thought of what Frank had done to his own family, what he had done to Eveline. Pieter had warned Andrew, but even his friend hadn't known the level of Frank Morton's savagery.

The old Ford lumbered onto the lane, the exhaust spewing and the wheels bouncing over the narrow width. Andrew took one step into the shadows, watched from the open seams of the barn. The vehicle stopped.

Andrew didn't have a plan. He hadn't brought a weapon and loosely scanned the stalls for something metal. He looked at his hand. No. If he met Frank, he wouldn't hide behind a gun or a knife or an ax. He'd meet him pummel to pummel.

Frank stumbled from his car, his shirt untucked and his face thick with sharp whiskers. A gin bottle fell from the car and rolled in the gravel. Frank bent to pick it up, saw it was empty and kicked it to the side. He wobbled to the corner of the house, put one hand to the crooked gutter spout and fumbled with his pants with the other before relieving himself against the stone and mortar. He swayed, then stopped, his bottom showing above his pants.

His left hand gripped the whining gutter in a strong hold and his right hand rose and smacked flat against the clapboard. He leaned in, his head bowed. A long, low wail cried from the deepest recesses of his throat and then he retched. Vomit splashed upon the ground and his shiny cowboy boots, splattered against the house.

Andrew turned away, the hate mixing with revulsion. He could take the man easy, drunk or not. He could beat him, bloody him to pulp. But then Andrew thought of Lily and the child she carried. He was going to be a father. He had a family to care for, people who looked up to him for guidance. He thought of the war, the spilled blood that seemed to drip across the world, fed the violence that only escalated and multiplied.

He looked at Frank again. The man patted the peeling paint as if an old friend, spit to clear his mouth and wobbled to the porch, his pants slipping unnoticed down his hips. Frank stopped, put his hand to his chest, opened his mouth wide as if trying to swallow the clouds. The man's body erupted then, a hacking cough the likes of which Andrew had never heard. Frank's face turned blue. He stumbled to find the side of the house, his body convulsing.

Andrew's blood iced. They all knew about the influenza that had ravaged Europe and appeared in Kansas a few months prior, had recently leaked into the crowded streets of the Pittsburgh tenements. Slowly, the virus was spreading and breeding across the nation, crippling the army camps, closing schools, public meeting places, even the church.

Frank wasn't just drunk. He was sick.

Andrew slunk back, covered his nose with his shirt as if the germs were reaching for him. He waited until Frank skulked into the house, watched the slice of a man fade away into the shadows.

With a conscious will, Andrew loosened his body. He could go into the house and kill Frank. He could add another murder to the war's tally, to the running count of those dying from the Spanish influenza. But he would not draw more blood to already-soaked ground. Frank would pay one way or another, but not through Andrew's fist—not with the hand that would one day hold his and Lily's child.

CHAPTER 54

"T ake a break now, Lily," Eveline recommended.

Lily smashed the green tomatoes and garlic into a fine pulp for Eveline's piccalilli, wiped her hands and took the woman's advice. Over the last month, Claire and Lily had fallen into the routine of the farm and the house had never been cleaner, the boys more catered to.

The Morton women remained in the house during the day to stave off any chance of seeing Frank. But upon the inching twilight they would emerge from the kitchen like foxes, sitting in the warmth of the setting sun. Lily's belly swelled and her face flushed with health and happiness.

Lily taught Edgar and Will how to pencil sketch animals, how to roll a perfect piecrust. At night, she'd let them rest their hands upon her belly when the baby waltzed inside. In return, Will read to Lily, taught her the simple words he had learned in school, holding her fingers as she traced the lines of sentences.

Pieter Mueller left for the war. They saw the Muellers when they could, but with the top of the harvest season underway, both families were tethered to their fields and animals. Fritz came often, though. The great man-child came with Anna in tow, would help Andrew in the fields, as if a day's work on his own farm hadn't taken more effort than blowing a dandelion puff.

And in those weeks, Eveline watched her nephew with pride. Watched the way he and Lily cherished and revered each other. The young man worked hard and ate well. His blue eyes glowed as an ocean that knew and loved its expanse. Eveline ached and grieved for Wilhelm, but there were days that she was happy, too. Truly happy. There were sad days also, but the sting lessened, became somewhat bearable.

And the war against Germany went on. But the Kisers insulated themselves. They did not bury their heads to the war, but they also did not entertain it. They prayed for Pieter and they sent food and wool socks to the Red Cross when they were able.

Then there was the baby. The new life that grew inside sweet Lily. Within the confines of the old farmhouse, they all loved this child. They each took pride and protective responsibility for the unborn infant, as if they were all in silent competition to see who could love it more.

Andrew worked in the lower field cutting corn. He had nearly five acres to go. The corncrib was filled and so the rest would be sold at market. It had been a robust harvest.

The kitchen was double the degrees of outside and Lily's face flushed. She leaned against the table and drank in long gulps from the water Eveline offered.

Eveline stroked the sweated hairs from Lily's forehead. "You all right, child?"

Lily nodded. "Just hot." She rubbed her small belly absently as she always did.

"Go on and get some fresh air, Lily," Eveline directed. "Too hot in here. Not good for the little one."

"Better not." Lily shook her head. "I'll be all right."

"No, the air will help," Eveline insisted. "Besides, if Frank was anywhere close, we would have heard his spurs jingling."

Lily laughed and took her water outside. She had been cooped up for so long that the sudden onslaught of pure sun seared her pale skin. She edged around Eveline's garden, smelled the zinnias that colored in a fanned rainbow around the fence. She settled her hands under the growing belly and went to the old apple tree stump. She lowered herself, one hip at a time, and sat upon the rings of the cut trunk. She touched the sap, felt it still sticky against her fingers. She remembered when she used to climb this tree. It hadn't been so long ago she had dreamed of this farm being hers and here she was. She patted her belly. It was a new life for them all.

Lily leaned her head back, felt the full strength of the brilliant sunshine upon her face and closed eyelids. A wind drafted. Her braid jerked hard, nearly bent her neck to her shoulder blades. Another jerk and she screamed, her body suddenly yanked up from the hair roots.

Frank held her hair like a rope, wound and seized it in his fist.

"Help!" Lily screamed. Frank pulled again and she shrieked.

"I don't want to hurt you, Lilith. I don't," he wheezed, his breath shallow and moist. His skin heated as if with fever and he wiped his nose on his sleeve, pulled tightly so her head was against his chest and her ear next to his mouth. "Just want my wife back. You hear me?" He jerked her hard for a response.

His arm moved in front and Lily felt something sharp bite. Her pupils strained to see. The light reflected sharply off the knife blade held at her stomach.

Lily closed her eyes, her body limp with what was to come as if she knew it would end this way all along. But not the baby. She couldn't let him hurt her baby.

"Please, Frank." Eveline appeared. Will and Edgar were at her side and she pushed them behind her skirt. "Please," she begged. "It doesn't have to be this way. Let Lily go and we can talk. We'll figure this out."

"Figure it out?" he screeched, then stumbled to regain his footing. "Claire!" he yelled. "Claire, you get out here now!"

Frank stepped back, pulled Lily with him. She began to cry. "Please, don't hurt me. Please. The baby."

He pulled her hair hard and she cried out. He put the blade under her neck. She felt the cool metal against the lines of her throat. He was going to kill her. She thought of Andrew. Below her panic, she was thankful he was not here to see. She cried for her baby. Cried for that life more than her own.

Frank growled into her ear, "Been wanting to slice your throat for as—"

An enormous crack shattered the air, reverberated from the very ground. Frank stumbled forward, crumpled over Lily's stooped body and collapsed into a heap.

Andrew dropped the crowbar and grabbed Lily, clutched her to his chest. Frank Morton twisted on the ground, his back curling.

Andrew's arm shook at Lily's shoulder before he moved from her side, his eyes filled with the first hate she had ever seen in them. "Don't, Andrew," she called. But he was deaf to her voice, his footsteps weighted with rage.

The young man's face twisted as he landed a

506

swift kick to Frank's ribs. "Get up!" he ordered, his body rigid as he readied to deliver another blow.

Will and Edgar hid their faces behind Eveline's skirt.

Lily winced. "Please, don't—"

"I said get up!" Andrew was blind to the world, to the faces turning away, his focus singular against the man on the ground. He landed a swift, harsh kick to Frank's wrist that clutched his bruised side.

Frank coughed into the dirt, his lungs spluttering. He rolled to his back, his face purple with hacking, his face dripping with pain and sweat. His broken hand trembled and reached for the clouds.

Andrew's gaze fell to the knife thrown in the grass. The silver gleamed in the light, promised a resolution. He stepped toward it, bent to grab the handle.

"Stop, Andrew!" Eveline shouted. She broke from her sons and pulled at Andrew's sleeve. "Don't touch it."

Her nephew blinked spastically, the need for revenge driving him like a caged animal. "Look at him," Eveline directed. Disgust pitched her voice and she stepped back from the writhing body. "He's sick." She didn't need to say more.

"I ain't sick!" Frank climbed to his knees and coughed, his mouth wide and gasping for air.

He clawed his chest, the wheezing loud and suffering. He clambered backwards clumsily. "Tell Claire to get ready!" he threatened. His lungs hissed, the veins in his forehead and neck blue and bloated as he tripped over his feet. "I'll be back for her. Just wait." He coughed endlessly, spit blood to the dirt as he found his way to the lane. "Get you, too, Lily. You wait!"

The wildness left Andrew. He stepped back from the knife as if it were a cobra ready to strike. He reached for Lily and hugged her to him, his breathing desperate and protective. And they all watched the man fumble, the anger dissipating among them. Claire came out, white as a ghost. Will held her hand.

Frank was without sight now, swaying and snaking up the rutted drive. He wouldn't bother them again. He would be dead by morning.

PART 5

War is organized murder, and nothing else.

—Harry Patch,
last surviving soldier of World War I

CHAPTER 55

On November 11, 1918, the armistice was announced. The Great War had ended. In its wake, over 116,000 American fighters perished, another 200,000 wounded. Worldwide, over 37 million soldiers lost their lives on the battlefield.

But the greatest cost to lives did not come from guns or bombs but from the Spanish influenza pandemic that killed over 50 million men, women and children across the globe. In Pittsburgh alone, six thousand people died of the flu, 1 percent of the city's total population.

As the war ended, the citizens of the nation tried to recover from the carnage. They looked up and blinked at the sun again, shook off the stupor that had paralyzed and crazed a country. Posters crafted with hatred and propaganda were torn from windows and telegraph poles. The American Protective League faded into obliteration like exhaust. And those who had cursed and abused their German American neighbors, colleagues and customers now averted their eyes. Their actions distant and inexplicable to their own hearts, clouded as a nightmare.

Pieter Mueller returned from the war. He had only been stationed overseas for four months, but enough time to leave him thin and limping from shrapnel and with a pretty young bride on his arm.

Those who lived along the narrow country road on the outskirts of Plum gave Pieter a hero's welcome. Widow Sullivan gave him her favorite tan mare, refused to take her back. Bernice Stevens made a cake the size of a butcher block. Every Mueller from every inch of Pennsylvania brought beer and roasted chickens, sausage linked like garlands. Heinrich butchered two hogs. Lily and Claire brought piles of cookies and pies of every fruit. Accordions squeezed and Germans sang. Old man Stevens danced a jig with Widow Sullivan, their hunched backs twirling like dancers in antique music boxes. Chinese firecrackers lit up the night while Fritz, Anna, Edgar and Will spun under the sparks as they rained in pink and green and gold splendor. Gerda clapped with her thick hands, nearly made the earth shake with her stomping feet.

Andrew sat on the ground, leaned against a giant maple in the Mueller yard, Lily sitting between his legs, her head resting on his chest. A violin started. A voice of deep baritone sang into the night, the handsome tune reaching straight to the stars.

Pieter carried a full glass of frothy beer in one

hand, his other flung around his wife. And she held the hand of another young man who walked with a cane, his eyes blind, clamped shut and scarred.

Andrew and Lily rose to meet them. Pieter let go of his wife and gave Andrew a burly hug, the men thumping each other on the backs, grinning ear to ear. "How's it feel to be a hero?" Andrew asked.

"I'll let you know when I meet one." His old friend smirked, the harrows of the war still embedded in the tired lines around his eyes. Pieter turned to Lily then and sighed, gave her a long, easy smile that washed away any hurt of the past. "Hi, Lily."

"Hi, Pieter," she greeted him, the relief swelling her cheeks.

"I want you to meet my wife, Gwyneth. If it weren't for her, doubt I'd be standing here." He kissed the shy brunette by his side. "Something about a pretty nurse picking shell bits out of your thigh makes it almost worth getting shot." Pieter's face turned sublime, serious. "Thought you two would get along."

The women shook hands, timidly at first and then naturally, as if their paths had crossed before. "When are you due?" asked Gwyneth.

"Early spring." Lily rubbed her belly. "She's kicking already, though. Think she's hungry for some of those cakes."

"Come on," the woman urged. "Didn't want to be the first one to grab a plate. Now I have an excuse." She laughed and the ladies headed to the rows of tables piled with food.

"Andrew, there's someone I want you to meet." Pieter put his hand on the shoulder of the blind man beside him. "This is Gwyneth's brother, Robert Weiner. We served together."

The man put out a strong hand and Andrew took it in greeting. "Pieter's told me a lot about you," Robert said. "Talked about nothing else at the hospital. Almost had to tell the nurses to bandage my ears along with my eyes."

Pieter chuckled, then raised his chin at Andrew knowingly. "Robert was with the Veterinary Corps, in charge of the horses in our battalion."

Andrew's stomach dropped, the yearning for a dream sudden and unexpected.

"He ran a practice in Maryland before the war," Pieter continued. "Looking to start anew in these parts."

Robert Weiner's face waited, the blind eyes placed on Andrew as if with sight. "I was hoping you might help me." The request came humbly, a pang of grief laced with the words. "I need someone to be my eyes. Help me with surgeries."

"I'm sorry, Robert." Andrew's voice dropped away. "I never made it to college."

"Well, I've done enough schooling for us both, I think. I could train you. You'd still have enough time at the farm. We'd start out slow. Be better for us both."

"So, Houghton, what do you think?" Pieter rocked on his heels, grinned. "Ain't polite to leave the man waiting. You in?"

From the corner of his eye, Andrew saw Lily laughing with Gwyneth, her hand on her belly while the other balanced a forkful of cake. Close behind, Eveline listened with mirth as Gerda's animated figure told a story with its whole enormous form. Claire discussed baking tips with Bernice Stevens. Will and Edgar chased Fritz in the tall weeds. And in that moment, the land stilled. The movements of the season slowed and pulsed.

A slow smile crept across Andrew's face. "I'm in."

CHAPTER 56

Marilyn Claire Houghton was born with an early spring. Gerda Mueller delivered the baby with authority and grace, guiding Lily through the pain as she had when her own daughters delivered. And Andrew was there, despite the protests of everyone that his presence was not appropriate. But he would not leave and held Lily's hand through the endless hours of contractions and birth. And when he held his daughter, *his* daughter, in the crook of his arm and she looked at him with that endless stare it struck him that her first impression of him would never be of lack. His daughter would never think it strange that his arm was not there. He was simply her father, whole and complete. She would not know that she was held in only one arm. She would simply know that she was held.

And he worshipped this little being—the sunburnt-colored skin and the hazel eyes of his wife, the V between the brows as she scrunched up her face with the new sensitivities outside the womb. Andrew's eyes drifted from his baby to the small room. They rested on Eveline hugging

Mrs. Mueller and the two women doting on Lily and he looked at his wife, at her tired glow, a woman who had traveled a long journey to find her home in his embrace.

His daughter squirmed in his arm. She opened and closed her gummy mouth and struggled to open her eyelids. A tear dripped from his eye and landed on his daughter's cheek, startling her. He blinked away the rest.

Look at my child, he said silently to his father in Heaven. *Look at your granddaughter.* And he called out to his mother overseas, realized that she hadn't slighted him with her letter but protected him with her distance. *Look at my child,* he told her. And they did. And his daughter smiled in that gurgling, gassy way and he laughed. He laughed and he cried and he held his daughter while his parents held her, too.

She's perfect, they said. *Perfect.* And they held him, too. Kissed his temple.

The baby scrunched her forehead and let out a tiny, shrill cry. Eveline gently took the child from her nephew. "She needs to nurse."

Eveline handed the baby to Lily. The tiny infant rubbed her nose down her mother's breast hungrily and latched on quickly. Lily's eyes rounded in awe. She met Andrew's eyes gratefully and mouthed, *She's drinking!*

Lily fed this child from her body. She had conceived this child and birthed this child from her body. And she was no longer a being of the dark. She cried hard at this and the baby had difficulty holding on with her mother's sobbing. Andrew stepped forward, but Eveline held him back. "Let her cry."

She was not impure. Lily looked at her baby. Something that was black and tainted could not create light. Only light came from light. And her soul and her heart cracked open and she cried with forgiveness for herself. She cried for what she had never seen within herself. She cried for all that she was and for all that had been locked away.

It was a personal, sacred moment and Gerda went to tidy the kitchen. Eveline left the room, just long enough to see Andrew wrapping his wife into his arm and kissing his child between them.

Eveline Kiser wrapped her shawl around her shoulders and went out of the house. The air was cold and bit at her skin, but she relished it, the first sensations that touched alive and real against her skin in a very long time. The sky was blue and open, the sun too bright to look at, yet she tried, let the sharpness burn her pupils for a moment before closing her eyes. She wanted to look at the sun. Wanted to look at all the brightness again, the light. She felt she had been locked in a closet for eternity and now she was out and she wanted to feel the cold air and look straight into the core of the sun and walk barefoot across the cool earth.

Eveline was drawn to the place of the old apple tree, scanned the empty space still seeing the girth of the trunk, the thick lines of the rugged bark and the branches that sprawled outward from the center. She sat down on the round stump, clutched the firmness and steadiness of it under her like sitting in the earth's palm. The breeze stirred the tiny hairs around her face. *Gray hairs,* she thought to herself. *Not all, but some.* She had aged; this she knew. She had been to Hell and back and climbed by her fingernails to this place.

The sun warmed the side of her face despite the chilly spring air. She glanced at the old farmhouse, the perimeter of her dead garden and the fields that lay flat and barren as far as the eye could see. But these sights did not bring despair but all that was opposite and she smiled, felt the oddness of her lips shaped in such a way, wondered the last time she had smiled and meant it.

Soon the garden would sprout again. The fields would show the green shoots and rows upon rows of new life blooming and her sons would run to the creek to fish and ride the horses and go to town fairs.

A new breeze entered, wrapped around Eveline's shoulders and held her close. The beautiful, subtle scent of him entered. The goose bumps rose across her flesh and her hair stood on end. Her heart swelled and her mouth stretched in a pained smile. A tear dripped from her eye and trailed to her chin. "Hello, Wilhelm," she whispered.

There was silence, warm and bright and thick. The energy moved up the left side of her body, filled her through the cells. She turned to him. He was there. She could see him and yet he was unseen.

I'm sorry I left you, came the words.

"I know."

But I never left you.

Tears squeezed. "I know, Wilhelm. I know."

The screen door from the porch opened and closed. The voice silenced, but the warmth remained. Andrew escorted Lily carefully over the walkway as if she were an invalid.

"Can you tell your nephew I'm not going to break?" Lily called sweetly to Eveline. The young woman cradled the child, smiled at her bald head.

"You just delivered a human being," Andrew interjected, still in awe. "You're lucky I'm not carrying you."

Eveline stood, patted the old trunk of the apple tree. "Come sit. The fresh air will do you all some good." With that she headed back to the house, looked back only once to see Andrew sitting down and Lily perched on his lap, her head nestled in his neck, their baby tucked within their embrace.

A burst of warm air cut through the cold, strong enough to blow the leaves up and around the stump of the tree. As they settled again, a vibrant green glowed from the base. Andrew bent, tossed the rotting leaves to the side, found the new shoots growing victoriously from the bottom of the cut stump, strong and firm and pulsing with new life.

Andrew and Lily smiled deeply, exchanged swollen hope. For life began anew, grew again, beneath the apple leaves.

DISCUSSION QUESTIONS

1. By all accounts, Andrew Houghton's destiny should have followed the same route as all the other young men in the coal patches—an endless existence underground picking coal. Yet, from his earliest memories, he knew this was not the life he was to live. Did this ambition come solely from his father or were there traits in the young man that made him think differently? What would make him expect or even desire a different life? Who was more realistic about Andrew's future, his mother or father?

2. Wilhelm Kiser, a German immigrant, has a seemingly ideal life in Pittsburgh during the early 1900s. He has a beautiful home with an indoor toilet, a lucrative job with the Pennsylvania Railroad and a growing family. What does this sort of life represent for Wilhelm? What was considered success for a man of that time period? For a woman? How was Wilhelm's identity wrapped into his profession?

3. After Andrew's father is killed in a mine accident, his mother decides to send him to Pittsburgh to become an apprentice on the railroad while she moves back to the Netherlands. Did she have Andrew's best interest at heart? Were her motivations selfish? What would you have done in that situation? Given the few options women had in those times, did she make the right decision?

4. America entered World War I on April 6, 1917, bringing a global brutality that had never been experienced on such a scale. How did the war invade every fiber of society? How did the war forever change the face of industry and agriculture? How did men and women handle the savagery and bloodshed differently?

5. During World War I, Germans were the conceived enemy spawning prejudice and hate. Throughout history, wars have ignited this hate. World War II was against the Japanese; at one time Britain was our enemy. Who is the enemy now? Where is current prejudice targeted? Can we learn from history that our foes today may be our greatest allies tomorrow? How did propaganda, the media and political rhetoric spread fear during

World War I? How do those vehicles distort the truth now?

6. Eveline Kiser finally has the farm she has always yearned for, yet the reality of their existence quickly shadows the dream. Is Eveline responsible for the downfall of their family? Was she ungrateful? Does her inherent love of the land bring new life to a family who would have otherwise been shackled to the pollution and industry of Pittsburgh? If given the choice, where would you have rather lived, on the Kiser farm or in the home in the smog-filled city?

7. Over the span of a year, Andrew's life has been shattered. He lost his father, his mother left for war-torn Holland, his dreams of college were stifled, he lost his arm in a terrible accident and now he must find a new life with a family he hardly knows. How does he go on? How does he find himself after so much loss? What has the accident taught him?

8. Lily Morton and Andrew meet on the day that the twins are born. Why are so many emotions coming up for Lily? Why does Andrew feel instantly protective of this

young woman? Do you think the attraction was instant for both of them?

9. From Pieter Mueller, Andrew learns the truth about Lily's past—that Claire is her sister as well as her mother. Given the shame and secretive nature of incest, how shocking would it have been to the community to know of this truth? How did this revelation affect Andrew's view of Lily? How has Lily been made to feel dirty and cursed about her conception? What must it have been like for Lily to carry around this secret for her whole life?

10. Frank Morton, Lily's brother-in-law, has designs on Eveline Kiser and the feelings are mutual. Is it understandable to see how Eveline fell for his charms? Where did her marriage with Wilhelm fall short? Do you believe that most women of that time had to settle in marriage? How are marriages different today from those in the early 1900s? Do you think Frank had real feelings for Eveline or was she just a conquest? Do you believe Eveline had real feelings for Frank or was she simply trying to find some pleasure in the darkness?

11. Lily and Andrew have a falling-out and sever ties due to a miscommunication. Did Andrew

do anything wrong with the prostitute? If you were Lily, would you have reacted in the same way? Was it understandable that Andrew thought Lily abandoned him after the German slurs? How did past hurts and insecurities skew their individual perspectives of the situation?

12. The Kiser farm is finally beginning to produce. The animals are growing. The garden is flourishing. Eggs, milk and butter are ready for market. Yet the dross of war enters their tiny town and brings the anti-German sentiment straight to the Kisers. After the humiliation at the city market and then the burning of their barn, Wilhelm Kiser breaks and commits suicide. Did you see this end for Wilhelm? Was he a coward? What things could he have done to keep himself from taking his own life?

13. On the day that Andrew plans to propose to Lily, she is forced to give her body to another man due to Frank's threats. Did Lily have a choice? If she had said no, how could she have protected her sister? Given Lily's grim conception, did part of her think she deserved to be treated like a prostitute? How could Lily grow to love and respect herself after all she had been through?

14. Widowed and impoverished, Eveline Kiser must do the unthinkable to save her family— have sexual relations with the man who helped bring their demise. Did Eveline have any other options? Given the time period and the limited resources for women, what would you have done? When Eveline gave her body to Frank, was she a victim?

15. As Andrew's family and home crumble beneath his feet, he must dig to the depths of his being to find his power and strength again. How is cutting down the beloved apple tree symbolic? What does he learn about himself during this process? How did all of the hardships build him into a new man? Could he have fully loved and been there as a husband for Lily if he hadn't faced his demons and come out on the other side?

16. After Andrew brings Lily and Claire home, he goes to the Morton house to confront Frank. Should he have killed Frank? Would an act of revenge have healed any of their wounds? Did Frank get his due justice? Do you think Claire missed her husband at all? Did Frank have any positive characteristics? Do you think he died with any remorse?

17. The end of the novel brings a child for Andrew and Lily, a canvas for healing the entire family and a chance for Andrew to follow his dream of being a veterinarian. *And so life begins to grow again, beneath the apple leaves.* How did each character overcome his or her personal demons and what did they learn as a result? Were their struggles worth it? How did Andrew and Lily heal? Do you see a future of happiness for the characters? In your own life, how have your personal battles made you stronger?

Center Point Large Print
600 Brooks Road / PO Box 1
Thorndike, ME 04986-0001 USA

(207) 568-3717

US & Canada:
1 800 929-9108
www.centerpointlargeprint.com